D1036684

Miriam & Other Stories

M.Y. Berdichevsky

MIRIAM
& OTHER STORIES

WITH AN INTRODUCTION BY

Avner Holtzman

The Toby Press

First Edition 2004

The Toby Press LLC
POB 8531, New Milford, CT. 06676-8531, USA
& POB 2455, London W1A 5WY, England
www.tobypress.com

Introduction copyright © Avner Holtzman 2004

"The Red Heifer," translated by Richard Flint. Reproduced with permission of Brandeis University Press/University Press of New England. *Reading Hebrew Literature: Critical Discussions of Six Modern Texts*, Alan Mintz, editor.

All other translations © The Institute for the Translation of Hebrew Literature, Ramat Gan, Israel 1965, 2004.

ISBN 1 59264 066 4

A CIP catalogue record for this title is available from the British Library

Typeset in Garamond by Jerusalem Typesetting

Printed and bound in the United States by Thomson-Shore Inc., Michigan

Contents

Introduction

Avner Holtzman

M.Y. Berdichevsky's literary world

Micha Yosef Berdichevsky earned his special status as the guiding authority and central literary presence of his generation of Hebrew writers almost overnight. For the first fifteen years of his career, Berdichevsky was strictly known as a literary critic and essayist, publishing articles on the whole gamut of Hebrew literature and Jewish life. But then, in a single twelve-month period between 1899–1900, he published an astonishing *nine* books that would occupy the new writers of that generation completely: four collections of short stories, four collections of articles, and one book of stories and lyrical essays from the hasidic world.

Due to the unusual concentration of his publication, and the controversial subjects of his stories, Berdichevsky is often thought of as the father of modern Hebrew fiction, the writer who most impressively broke with the tradition of the Enlightenment period. His stories demonstrate the gaping chasm between the certainty of traditional Judaism and the divided consciousness of his generation.

The extraordinary intensity of identity crises in Berdichevsky's fiction derives from the profound synthesis of the autobiographical and the historic—both his own life experiences and those of his contemporaries at large find their way into these important early works.

"The autobiographic foundation is so strong in Berdichevsky," writes Shimon Halkin, "that his work can be perceived as a kind of very profound personal key to the understanding of the crisis in the spiritual life of the Jewish people." Indeed, as we will see, Berdichevsky's life story echoes the major spiritual processes which afflicted the Jewish people at the turn of the century, the unprecedented crises of faith that accompanied their decisions to abandon tradition in favor of assimilation and secularism in the modern age.

In an article published in 1912, in which the writer Yosef Chaim Brenner delineated trends in the history of Hebrew literature since the Enlightenment, he discerned two main schools of thought. First are the authors whose main focus is the description of the "national, public dilemma," including the writings of Mendele Mocher Sefarim (Shalom Yaakov Abromovitch), the articles of Ahad Ha'am (Asher Ginzberg) and the poetry of Chaim Nahman Bialik. In contrast to these "national" writers, Brenner points out that by the second decade of the twentieth century, individualism was taking over Hebrew literature, spearheaded by Berdichevsky's writings. These works focused on the complex psychological world of the young Jew of the time, and various national tensions were condensed in their private but intensive inner worlds. As we will see, Brenner's early instincts proved correct.

Micha Yosef Berdichevsky was born in the town of Medzibuz, a cradle of Hasidism in the Ukraine, on August 19, 1865. The first-born son of his parents and a descendant of a prominent rabbinic family, he received an outstanding hasidic Torah education, and was designated to become a rabbi himself. His childhood and youth were spent in the town of Dubova, next to the city of Uman, in an extremely Orthodox and conservative environment. He was married as a teenager and moved to Teplik, his wife's hometown.

However, the spiritual harmony between Berdichevsky and his forefathers was soon undermined by his insatiable enchantment with the ideas of the Enlightenment. So immersed was he in this "external" literature that his father-in-law pronounced him an unfit husband and insisted he divorce his young wife. He was nineteen years old. At age twenty, he left the Ukraine to study at the renowned Volozhin Yeshiva in Lithuania, far from the closed hasidic environment of his youth, and it was during this period of study, 1885-1886, that he began his literary writing.

The first fruits of his writing—descriptions of the Yeshiva life and short Halachic discussions—were published at the end of 1886, and during the next four years he frequently contributed to the Hebrew press with articles, critiques, historical reviews and reports from the cities in which he resided. During these years, he became known as an "enlightened Torah scholar" who aspired to integrate Jewish and European culture, and even published a literary-Toraic collection called *bet hamidrash* (the house of study) in 1888.

In 1890, after a short and unsuccessful second marriage, he moved to Odessa on his way toward Western Europe, where he had always dreamed of studying in university. In 1891, he enrolled first at the Breslau University in Germany, then at the universities of Berlin and of Bern, the capital of Switzerland, until he received his PhD, in 1896. During his six years of study in Germany and Switzerland, Berdichevsky almost completely disappeared from the literary world, but in those very years he gained the crucial knowledge that would form his viewpoint and his artistic style. First he leaned toward rejecting the whole of Jewish tradition in favor of Western philosophy and high European literature. Then he favored negating all culture, perhaps under the influence of Frederick Nietzsche, whose works he had been reading since 1893. Finally, toward the end of his studies, Berdichevsky began to return to the Hebrew and Jewish context of his past, and sought to synthesize Jewish tradition with modern European values such as a direct affinity for nature and love, aestheticism for its own sake, and high literature and the plastic arts.

From the end of 1896, Berdichevsky appeared at the head of a group of young Hebrew writers who penned a series of polemic articles against the concepts of the respected thinker and writer Ahad Ha'am, founder of the monthly magazine *Hashiloah*. Ahad Ha'am had argued that Hebrew literature of the time was unable to bring pure aesthetic enjoyment to its readers. He likened it to "shriveled ears of grain" in contrast to the rich, fertile fields of European literature, and suggested that readers turn directly to the European sources rather than making do with faded Hebrew substitutes. To writers themselves, Ahad Ha'am advised them not to waste their energies in useless attempts to imitate the complex artistic achievements of other nations' writers, it being more worthwhile to dedicate their efforts to "more essential and beneficial concerns." In more specific terms, he advised them to avoid writing belletristic literature that had no value beyond aesthetic beauty, and to use fiction and poetry as a means of bringing about a greater nationalistic awareness among the Jewish people.

Ahad Ha'am's arguments spawned widespread anger among the younger set of Hebrew writers in Berdichevsky's circle. In his first response, Berdichevsky criticized Ahad Ha'am's intention to limit his magazine solely to discussion of Jewish causes, arguing that this furthered the already problematic sense among young Jews that they were defined by their difference from the wider world. Berdichevsky called out for the healing of the same "torn, divided heart"—a central idea in his writing—in order to enable young Jews to remain Jewish but to be people of the world "at the same time, in one breath, nourished from the same source." For two years, a heated debate raged between the camps of Ahad Ha'am and Berdichevsky, perhaps the most significant argument in the history of modern Hebrew literature. In the process of the debate, Berdichevsky became the undisputed leader among the young generation of Hebrew writers.

However, the desire to synthesize Jewish tradition and Western culture soon waned for Berdichevsky. Gradually, he came to the unfortunate realization that the rupture dividing the heart of the young Jews of his time was not repairable, and that his generation was doomed to wander back and forth between their love for tradition and the desire to rebel against it. "In my opinion," he wrote to one of his friends in 1898, "we will be torn forever." But he also came to realize that this very painful experience of division and rupture also led to the sort of tension necessary for the creation of genuine art. By the same year, he began to argue that the greater the desperation and distress of young Jewish youth was, the stronger and more profound Hebrew literature would become. Sorrow, he claimed, both personal and national, "leads me into the hands of the hope of poetry and the expansion of Hebrew verse."

With this philosophy in mind it is easy to understand what motivated Berdichevsky to turn suddenly to writing stories in 1899, after exclusively writing essays in the previous stages of his career. The last three years of the nineteenth century were for him a period of feverish writing, the beginning of his remarkable presence in fiction. With the four books of stories and novellas published in 1900, notably *Two Camps* and *A Raven Flows*, he marked one of the most significant points of departure in all of modern Hebrew fiction. The central theme in all of the stories is the much-divided consciousness that had occupied Berdichevsky's earlier philosophical arguments. His characters are torn between competing worlds of tradition and change, the comforts of family and heritage (with their simultaneous suffocation) and the primal yearning for erotic and artistic experiences beyond that safe, enclosed world.

The forty stories that Berdichevsky published at the beginning of the twentieth century include a series of stories which follow the history of one central protagonist, whose life more or less echoes that of the author. These autobiographical stories describe the protagonist as a child in a little town when the seeds of doubt in his forefathers' faith penetrate his heart and arouse questions and regrets. They depict a premature marriage, the introduction to the forbidden fruit of knowledge and the Enlightenment, the forced divorce, the departure to study in the West and the enchantment with the world of academic learning, then the tragic discovery that knowledge alone cannot fulfill the heart's deepest yearnings, and finally arrival at a desperate position of spiritual and intellectual dead end.

These stories were especially influential for young Hebrew writers of the day, who were amazed by the extent to which Berdichevsky had captured their experience of inner turmoil and conflict. He soon had an enormous following of adoring, aspiring Hebrew writers who hoped to absorb some of his literary influence in their own works.

Another group of Berdichevsky's stories published in that same watershed year (1899–1900) is essentially a series of portraits and sketches of a little Jewish town in Russia, based largely on his childhood in the Ukraine. These stories, too, depict the author's duality vis-à-vis Jewish reality. Seemingly, the main goal of the stories is to document and thus save from oblivion typical characters and episodes that comprised the traditional way of life once known to the storyteller from firsthand experience. However, the same stories also manage to express the opposite impetus, the desire to be liberated from that world and to justify its abandonment by exposing its flaws.

But perhaps the most powerful aspect of these "little town" stories is the commentary on the hidden desires of the Jewish people living in the Diaspora, and the almost unbearable anticipation of the moment that those desires can be revealed. Not far beneath the surface of these regulated, depressing towns, whispers of sin and of social and sexual taboos are heard everywhere. Berdichevsky's tendency to uncover the life that is concealed under the traditional spiritual covering of Jewish life became more and more profound in his stories, until in his last years it took on a mythic character which led him to shape his characters as reincarnations of ancient powers or biblical super powers, battling to deviate from the limited human frame of existence and instead to deal with the mighty forces of nature, sin and their punishments. The stories are set in small towns in Russia and Western Europe in the nineteenth century, but the entire expanse of Jewish culture and its heroes reverberates through them.

Beyond their groundbreaking themes and statements on the changing nature of Jewish culture, Berdichevsky's prose was itself unconventional and inventive. His use of dense metaphoric language, unique personal symbolism, fragmented syntax, and intricate plot design together created the strange charm of Berdichevsky's work, its spiritual and aesthetic power, its modernity and its relevance.

Through his fiction and essays, Berdichevsky argued for the individual's right to remove the fetters of rabbinical Judaism, its laws and traditions, for the sake of actualizing creative and intellectual impulses. His famous, impassioned plea to cease being the "last Jews" and to become "the First Hebrews" is just one of his many calls for a change in values in Israel. These statements would gradually become accepted slogans, turning him into one of the founding fathers of secular Jewish nationalism. In this vein, Berdichevsky sought to create an alternative understanding of Jewish history, compiling legends and biblical stories that proved the existence of an anti-normative current, nationalistic and worldly, which was pushed aside by those who wrote the history of official Judaism. In this way, the strong presence of evildoers and outsiders in his stories—characters who violate convention—is consistent with his worldview.

Berdichevsky's fiction and his philosophical writings, composed in Hebrew, Yiddish and German, were largely influential in the spheres of literary, national and theological subjects, in the development of Hebrew thought, and in the development of Zionist movements in Eastern Europe. Thanks to his call for a change in values in Israel—that is to say, to liberate the powers of desire and the hidden life of the Diaspora Jews—he became one of the main guiding figures for the Second Aliyah pioneers. Personalities such as Berl Katznelson, David Ben-Gurion, Shlomo Lavi and Shlomo Zemach, the founders of the worker's movement in Israel, all expressed their various debts to Berdichevsky, who inspired their immigration to Israel even though he never belonged to an official Zionist party himself. David Ben-Gurion, for example, wrote a personal letter to the writer's son in 1968 in which he acknowledged the enormous impact Berdichevsky's writing had had on him and his friends in their Polish hometown, Plonsk. "I have to admit," he writes, "that after my *aliya* [...] I re-examined all my previous ideological concepts and withdrew from many of them, but my admiration for Berdichevsky (among very few other writers) remained the same. Indeed, I did not accept many of his ideas, but his 'otherness' captured my heart."

In 1902, when he was thirty-seven, Berdichevsky married Rachel Ramberg, who became his literary assistant until his death. A year later their only child, Emmanuel, was born. They resided in Breslau.

After his marriage, Berdichevsky turned to new areas in his literary work: writing stories and articles in Yiddish, adapting and compiling Hebrew legends and folklore, researching Hasidism and the roots of Judaism and Christianity. At the same time, he continued to write stories and articles in Hebrew and assemble them in books. In 1911, he moved with his family to Berlin, and increasingly dedicated himself to the field of legend and research. In 1913, the collection of legends he adapted appeared in German translation and he simultaneously published two volumes of *From the Treasures of Legend* in Hebrew.

During the First World War (1914–1918), Berdichevsky was safe in his house in Berlin, but as a citizen of an enemy country (Russia), various limitations were imposed on him by the German authorities. Only after the war was his request to receive German citizenship granted. During the same period, he responded to a request by the publisher, Abraham Yosef Stiebel, who took it upon himself to publish all of Berdichevsky's writings under the condition that he return to writing Hebrew fiction. Thus, in his last three years of life, Berdichevsky dedicated himself to the adaptation of his writings, perfecting and preparing them to be published in an authoritative edition, and to writing new works—notably three novellas "You Shall Build a House," "Street Inhabitants," "From a Place of Thunder," and a novel, *Miriam*.

In these last works, Berdichevsky achieved his greatest accomplishments as a storyteller, masterfully penetrating the Jewish reality with legendary-mythic foundations. His characters struggled with their imperfect, human dimensions and their helplessness in the face of destiny, their lives echoed those of their ancient Jewish counterparts and played a part in the grand cycle of history. They acknowledged the great battle waged between God and Satan. At the same time, their sins were perceived as legitimate channels for realizing their desires, as was the breaching of social norms. The stylistic language of exaltation in these stories also helps to intensify the experience of a conflicted reality, and has been greatly influential on prominent Israeli writers like Amos Oz, Yoram Kaniuk and Pinhas Sadeh.

In 1920, Berdichevsky learned that his father and brother had been murdered in the widespread pogroms which accompanied the civil war in the Ukraine, and that the towns of his youth had been destroyed. This news only deepened the already tragic sensibility which is emphasized in his later writings, as well as his desire to memorialize the disappearing Jewish world, but it also undermined his health.

Berdichevsky died in Berlin on November 18, 1921. In 1936, his literary archive and private library were brought to Israel by his widow Rachel and his son Emmanuel Ben-Gurion (1903–1987), who dedicated his life to the preservation and fostering of his father's heritage. These rich archives are today housed in the city of Holon.

The six works compiled in this collection belong to the second, more mature half of Berdichevsky's career, beginning with "The Summer and the Winter" (1904), and ending with *Miriam* (1921), whose concluding sentences he dictated to his son two days before his death. Also included here are "The Red Heifer" (1906) and "In the Valley" (1909), and two longer stories, "You Shall Build a House" (1920) and "From a Place of Thunder" (1921).

These stories mark the end of Berdichevsky's autobiographical work and the beginning of his focus on the characters and communities of the traditional Jewish world. All of the stories gathered here are set in small Ukranian towns and villages where a certain mysterious or controversial event has occurred, and in which the narrator, from but no longer of the same community, struggles to unravel the plot and make sense of it.

In these stories, the narrator, representing Berdichevsky himself, describes a world he has long since abandoned, and his telling is rife with the tension between his attachment to the people and places he describes and his desire to rebel against it, to break through its limits, deny its attributes, and to present it through a critical, satirical looking-glass. This tension begets a kind of ceaseless game of changing masks, voices and viewpoints. Sometimes the narrator uses the collective inner voice of the community; sometimes he appears as its embittered ideological adversary; sometimes he observes it from the outside with astonishment and other times he acts as a chronicler. However, despite the various perspectives of their narrations, Berdichevsky's stories elucidate and explore several consistent themes: the social, psychological, moral and nationalistic dimensions of the given town and community. There is a focus on the hierarchy of social structures and the various dynamic power games between poor and rich, weak and strong, successes and failures, privileged and plain folk—often illuminating the fact that all such hierarchies are nothing but illusory visions doomed to fail over time.

In psychological terms, the towns are teeming with repressed primal urges represented less by individual characters than by prototypes. Whole families and generations struggle with these psychological urges and the moral conflicts they pose in contrast to the rigidly defined laws and regulations of traditional Jewish life. Finally, the implied author of these stories is painfully aware of the current misery of the Jews in Eastern Europe in contrast to the supposed glory days of their ancient, biblical forefathers. In this way, the protagonists are defined by and also impossibly conflicted with their Diaspora placement.

In "The Summer and the Winter," Berdichevsky describes a group of Ukrainian peasants who live their lives in an obvious, clearly erotic, Dionysian atmosphere. Christianity, the official religion of this village, is but a thin covering over the powerful current of a pagan foundation that has never disappeared. Here we find an open conflict between the official ecclesiastical ritual to which these villages obey and the primal, pagan urges their inhabitants experience. This story was a new departure for Hebrew fiction in two important ways. First of all, it includes no Jewish characters, in contrast to the unwritten rule that Hebrew literature is meant to shape and clarify the distress, desires, and lifestyle of the "tribe" or national group by occupying itself with individual but representative Jewish characters. Secondly, the story describes unleashed sexual lust, a kind of erotic madness that attacks the men of the village as a result of the vision of Marta the Beautiful. The directness with which the story places Eros as a deciding and controlling factor in the life of human beings and challenges the overly conservative norms which prevailed in this area of

Hebrew literature at the beginning of the twentieth century caused Berdichevsky much difficulty when he attempted to publish the story in 1904. It was rejected by Bialik, the literary editor *Hashiloah*, and by others editors, and only three years later did Brenner accept it for publication in his monthly magazine, *Hame'orer* (*The Awakener*).

A similar criticism is described in "The Red Heifer," a story about a creature, the possessor of supernatural virtues, who cannot survive in the human and destructive Jewish environment. One of the most significant of Berdichevsky's works, "The Red Heifer" is about a brutal criminal act. A band of butchers join together to steal a prize cow, slaughter it, divide among themselves, and ultimately receive their punishment. In a terrifying climax, we read of a daring nocturnal vision of rape, murder, the devouring of flesh and ecstatic frolicking in gushing blood. What, we may ask, was the message Berdichevsky sought to convey through this story about the nature of Jewish communities at the beginning of the twentieth century?

In the biblical context (Num. 19), the red heifer represents impurity and purification at the same time. On one hand, the ashes of the slaughtered cow are meant to purify whoever has been contaminated by the impurity of death, but on the other hand it is said that everyone who is occupied with slaughter is himself contaminated. That is to say, the red cow purifies the impurities and yet it contaminates the purified. This paradox is akin to the other basic conflict running throughout the story—namely, that the villagers sway between normative Jewish existence and the breaking through of sensual barriers. In opposition to the ritual slaughterers, who represent the rule of the Orthodox, stand the butchers, who represent the world of flesh and blood alone, devoid of spirituality. But the line that divides these two groups is perilously thin.

The atmosphere of cosmic disaster that descends upon the city in the wake of this murder, "as if an eclipse of the sun and an eclipse of the moon had taken place over the city at the same time [...] as if the world became a valley of ghosts," suggests that something much more profound has happened here. The macabre descriptions that fill the end of the story, indeed, clarifies that the slaughter of the cow is a profoundly sick symptom nested in a Jewish society that cannot assimilate the values of beauty the cow represents, and is therefore doomed to failure. The murder of the red cow is to be understood as a symbolic, fatal act of the cutting-off of Jews from animalism and eroticism. The daring ecstasy which possessed the butchers is no more than a passing spasm, a last gasp at life before succumbing to a symbolic communal death.

In "In the Valley," the protagonist is a Jewish woman named Hulda. In contrast to Marta's active sexuality in "The Summer and the Winter," Hulda is an angelic character, child of the heavens and nature, and the aura of her virginal purity prevents her from being caught up in the turbid material world. When she is sent to obey the rituals of matchmaking and is forced to marry the young man selected for her from the neighboring town, the ceremony is described "as the hour of burning bones in the ancient world of the days of sacrificing human beings." The expression hints at the fate of the protagonist, who drowns herself in a river after her innocence has been violated.

Another character who meets a bitter destiny is Sara of the short novel "You Shall Build a House." Sara, beautiful, angelic, bewitching, is married to a dubious businessman named Reuven when she captures the heart of Naftali the Bold. The more passive, naïve and unaware she is, the more Naftali becomes obsessed with her. Although the setting for the story is clearly defined, geographically and historically, it operates not on a realistic-psychological level, but a mythic-demonic one. The story's title is taken from the *Tochacha* (admonition) portion of the Old Testament (Deut. 27–28), which lists the punishments designated for sinners and heretics. Reuven, Sara's husband, has stolen a large sum of money which he claims was lost, and to cover up his theft he vows to the local rabbi that if he has indeed sinned, he should be condemned to the punishments from this terrifying biblical chapter, which was read that same Sabbath in the synagogue. Indeed, just as Reuven succeeds in finishing his luxurious house that he has built from the money he plundered, he dies a sudden death that echoes the verse, "Thou shalt build a house, and thou shalt not dwell therein" (Deut. 28:30). The same verse begins, "Thou shalt betroth a wife, and another man shall sleep with her," and this curse, too, is fulfilled when Naftali hurriedly marries Sara soon after Reuven dies.

Yet although Naftali weds Sara according to religious law, he is also punished for the sin of lusting after another man's wife, since his obsession with her began while Reuven was still alive. His punishment comes on their wedding night, when Sara is attacked by a horrid hallucination of her first husband, and she runs out of bed and from the house the moment her new husband enters the room. Like Marta from "The Summer and the Winter" and Hulda from "In the Valley," and also like the cow from "The Red Heifer," Sara is also forced to pay a heavy price for her consummate beauty and purity.

Perhaps the most important of Berdichevsky's three novellas is "From a Place of Thunder," a story that grew out of a short sketch written in 1900 called "A Father and A Son." Though it is anchored in the concrete reality of Jewish life in Ukrainian towns of the nineteenth century, the story operates on a mythic level. The protagonist, Shlomo the Red, is portrayed with almost super-human height and weight, masculinity and awesome social standing, sensuality, self respect and restraint. The great tension here is between the powerful father and his moderate, temperate son Daniel the Silk. The stark contrast between these two prototypes is formative in Berdichevsky's writings.

Shlomo the Red's social status allows him to break through the moral limits of the society, to make new laws for himself and to cast authority over his surroundings, all in an intensified and unrealistic way, as is made apparent in the very language of the story, which characterizes him with divine expressions. As Gershon Shaked suggests, the story can be read as a metaphor for the struggle of the vital Dionysian powers within the framework of Jewish existence, for it is not only Shlomo the Red, but the entire town that is seized by the breaking asunder of sensuality which leads to nearly total sexual anarchy.

The central focus of the story is the love triangle between Shlomo, the possessor of sensual power, Daniel, the weak, refined son and his second wife, Shoshana, the beautiful woman who is a clear embodiment of the femme fatale, the carnivorous, man-eating female demon. Shoshana is certainly the most powerful feminine character in all of Berdichevsky's writings, and the climax of this story is the all-powerful destructive sexual encounter between Shlomo and his daughter-in-law. When she appears in the town, seemingly out of nowhere, Shoshana immediately represents a satanic, potentially destructive eroticism. Within moments of her arrival the town's men are paralyzed by fear and enchantment, and her sadomasochistic relationship with Daniel lays the groundwork for the sexual encounter between her and the father-in-law, which are described in terms of a cosmic storm.

The plots and parallelisms in this erotic tale are deeply rooted in Jewish sources. The story of Daniel and Shoshana, for example, is from the Apocrypha, the story of the Garden of Eden from Genesis, and the story of Judah and Tamar, also from Genesis. Woven into the story at large are additional explicit and implied analogical references to ancient stories such as the story of the House of David (specifically the tales of Adonia and Avishag, which open Kings I, and the story of Abshalom's revolt against David). Berdichevsky experiments with the disassembly and reinvention of biblical stories.

The sense of explicit tragedy lingering in all the stories comes to its clearest expression in one of the opening paragraphs of the novel *Miriam*:

> I am engaged in the birth pangs of creating a memorial for the people of my generation, to give a pen-picture of life in the towns in which I was reared. Many thoughts were mine, emotions of my youth surged up in me, my mind was thronged with different faces and events, transient personalities, shadows of the warp of life and the woof of former things. Son am I of the men of the exile and from this time-old goblet I have drunk my fill. And behold, the destroyer came to all these towns, swooping down upon that life and those books. A period of total destruction fell upon all those places where my hopes and my muse have revealed their tender buds. My native town was laid waste, the enemy's hand ruined all that was dear to me. The God of righteous-

> ness relentlessly swallowed up all the habitations of my people, He had even desolated the souls of His instructors.—My harp sounds an obsequy, my spirit moans, mourning consumes soul and flesh. Lamentation is all I know now. How shall I tell the tale of a young girl, of everyday incidents, snatches of the song of everyday life. Only a few brief pages are left to me and I shall set them before the reader in turn and they will be all that remains. (*Miriam*, Part III, Chapter II, Section I)

Apart from the sentiments of mourning and the lamentation over the sacrifice which are reflected in this paragraph, the author is also aware of his own diminishing lifetime. Perhaps because he knew he was dying, Berdichevsky felt a certain pressure to put into writing as many concise, undeveloped sketches and character portraits as possible in what time he had left.

This urgency is what inspired Berdichevsky to persevere with writing his final and ultimate work, the novel *Miriam*. As Dan Miron explains, *Miriam* (which Berdichevsky painstakingly outlined in his diary in 1905) was meant to align the two major streams of the author's work up until this point—the autobiographical stories and the social commentary. The novel was originally conceived as a story that would follow a young woman from her Ukrainian town and childhood, through her education in Switzerland, and ultimately to her death by suicide after having struggled with her unrequited love for the husband of a good friend. Fifteen years after he initially sketched the novel, however, Berdichevsky chose to limit the story to the heroine's early life and her familial history in the Ukraine. It seems that the author was unable to achieve the richness and sustainability he originally sought in the protagonist, and therefore her character slowly vanishes to the margins of the story, and her place is taken by an abundance of secondary characters and plots.

Perhaps Berdichevsky, who during the years 1905–1920 dedicated most of his time to editing anthologies of folk tales, was so influenced by the traditional poetics of the short narrative forms that he was unable to achieve the "finished novel in all its compartments and rooms," as he himself described it. The question of the novel's structural unity has indeed widely occupied its critics, who failed to discover its overall uniting principle, and often considered it an artistic failure. Nevertheless, a contemporary reader, familiar with modernist and post-modernist poetics, appreciates that it is precisely this free, dismantled, pluralistic form of *Miriam* that is indeed one of Berdichevsky's greatest accomplishments. It is my hope that this "anti-novel" may have, after all, a new life and new readers even in the twenty-first century.

The Summer and the Winter

Shoshaka, a large, sprawling village in the Ukraine, lies in a winding valley between mountain ridges, near the big forest which extends on both sides of the highway to the city of Uman, the pride of the countryside. The Yatran river divides the valley into two fields, and the grain rises on its tall stalks as soon as one leaves Lodizhin, stretching out in all directions, a feast for the eyes. From there the river makes its way, winding and twisting—at times visible from the highway, at times disappearing behind a tall hill—until it finds a haven of rest in Shoshaka before it goes on to join the Uman river, where it is swallowed up on the way down to the Bugg. Here, in Shoshaka, the river undergoes a surprising change until it finally bursts out of the ice and frost with the death of winter and the coming of spring. The river does not irrigate the fields and gardens—this task is performed faithfully by the rains from above—but it does add to the fertility and richness of the earth. The task it performs continuously is to drive the wheels of the water-mill and to grind the wheat and corn and barley that the farmers bring from far and near in bulging sacks loaded on carts and wagons. The mill was built out of hewn stone and rock by the owners of the village, and the sound of its wheels and break-waters has become the life-giving pulse of the village…

The further one goes from the mill, the fainter are its sounds, until at last even the echoes vanish and are buried in the quiet of the low houses. These houses seem to have been planted where they stand, with their thatched roofs, their fences of stone or wood, each house bearing the mark of its maker. A tranquil silence reigns there, even if from time to time it is broken by the barking of a dog or the rumbling of a passing cart. The Polish masters no longer rule here, and the villagers govern themselves. Simple peasants they are, peasants who toil to coax a living out of the land and, if there is no year of plenty, they go out to work in the nearby forest, chopping timber, or they hire themselves out to transport logs in their wagons to far-off places. For there is no railway in Uman yet, and everything must be loaded on carts which drive to Whitefield, a week's journey away, like caravans in the desert.

Each of these peasants has a plot of land and a house, a wife and children, an ox and a horse, sheep and calves; once a month he slaughters a pig, and its singed hairs glint in the fire; the flames rise around it, and the day of slaughtering becomes a minor festival for the peasants. Every market day they bring their ducks and ducklings, hens and roosters, eggs, potatoes, onions, watermelons and vegetables, seasonal fruit and the grain of the fields down to the town, where they exchange them for money. The tillers of the land do not always have enough bread: they are fond of liquor, the angel which accompanies them in years of abundance and years of drought. When they drink, they shout and quarrel and fight each other, or they pledge eternal friendship and kiss one another. And when they raise their voices in song on their way home in the dark of the night, one can hear the sound of the suffering of men who are part of the land around them. My story is of those days, when the tavern was still open to all comers, when each man sat by his table with his glass in front of him, and drank to his own health and that of the whole company. It is not so today, when spirits are sold in sealed bottles that stand dumbly in rows like drugs on a pharmacist's counter…Ah, for the good old days!

Martha, the second daughter of Vasil Kutcherenka, whose plot of land was on the slope leading down to the river, was the beauty of the village. She was tall, with an aristocratic air in her face and carriage. Her mother had been a servant in the house of the gentry for many years, and the village seemed to sense and accept something noble in her blood. The grace of her walk and the classic lines of her fair skin enchanted all who met her, young and old. Vladimir Hadovich, a strong and husky youth, almost went out of his mind when he saw her dancing with her girlfriends in the courtyard of the tavern, and when he reached out to embrace her she shoved him away bodily, felling him to the ground. He was found the same day, hanged with his own belt in his father's stable, and the whole village had something new to talk about. Maxim Dubrovich, Vladimir's friend, chased Martha when she was alone in the fields one day, but when she raised her scythe at him, he flung himself on the ground and begged her to tread on him with her foot…

With the coming of spring, when every bird, tree, and beast of the field renew their youth, the youths of Shoshaka would sing beneath Martha's window at night: "Come, let us go together to the fields, let us run!" Her name was on everyone's lips: the women all envied her, the men all adored her. It was as if her presence fluttered into every lover's embrace, and her charms were engraved on all minds and hearts. Even the dogs never snarled at her; the cows would follow her everywhere; and when she sat in her father's cart with the reins in her hand, the horses would obey her like brothers, even among the treacherous mountain tracks. Every male would tremble on hearing her peals of laughter, and every heart would turn over on hearing the sound of her horses' hooves. She knew the morning and the evening as the animals know the seasons of nature. She would sip her milk slowly, like a lady, and would cut her bread with a knife. Then she would anger the neighbors' wives, and would disappear suddenly while they looked for her. Or (as though to attract the attention of passersby) she would sit on the porch of her father's house in her gleaming white blouse. She was the one shining star of the village, the wonder of every heart…

It happened during an interregnum. The people were all rushing to the church to pledge their loyalty to the new king, and

Martha was sitting on a log outside the house, dressed in her red Sunday dress and knitted blouse. Everyone who passed crossed himself mentally on seeing her. Like a magic charm she appeared that morning in all her beauty, piercing all hearts. The church bell chimed in loud, thundering peals as for the Day of Judgment: Oh, the spells of woman! The thunder of beauty! The bell-ringer had lost his soul to her.

Osip Bushkanov had been found as a child in the marketplace, with no trace of his father and mother. He had grown up wild, and had been in turn a swineherd, a horse trainer and a blacksmith's assistant. Then he had worked in the army and had learned to write a little, and for a time had worked as a kind of clerk in the jailhouse of Phillipia, a neighboring village. He had not been a success in this work, and on being dismissed had for a long time lived the life of a gypsy, wandering from village to village, working a day here and two days there, or living off charity. Then he had become a shoemaker, but he sold the shoes he had been given to repair. That was around the time that he met the priest of Shoshaka, Father Konstantin. The priest's wife had died, and he was forbidden to marry again, so he took Osip in as a house servant. Osip did well at the priest's, and began to feel free in spirit again. He slept in the left wing of the house, where he also had a table and a crate for his meager possessions. After some time he rose in station and became the bell-ringer of the church, work which he enjoyed greatly. He drank copiously, but rarely got drunk. At times he would take a net and go fishing in the river, wading into the water up to his waist. If the fish he caught did not please him, he would tear them apart alive with his hand and throw the squirming pieces back into the water. In those days his heart was already captive to Martha and, awed by her beauty, he longed for her as a lion pants for his prey...He could have ripped up the foundations of the house whenever her image appeared before him. His flesh burned and he felt faint whenever he met her in the street or at the well, and the sound of each galloping horse passing through the village toward the city, carried him away with it. Once, in a dream, he beheld himself taking hold of the girl by the hair of her head and dragging her to the edge of a rock, and there they embraced, and the witch screamed, and he opened up his ribcage and took out his heart and gave it to her to eat...

When he climbed up to the bell tower on this day to pull the ropes that rang the bell, it was as if everything inside him was gathering together to roar out his passion. The bell chimed loudly, and in his imagination it seemed that the bell of the next village answered him, and that of a third village joined in, and all the chimes made one great voluminous peal, and he alone was pulling all the bells together. All the ropes seemed to be spliced together in his hands, into one single rope, and he was holding it, driving his teeth into it, grasping it with his feet, and the iron tongues beat fiercely on the solid copper cups, and a great peal was heard, peal upon peal, chime upon chime, peals soaring into the firmament, chimes which sang out the fear of God and the madness of love, and all the people in the church below fell on their faces in awe and kissed the earth beneath their feet. For who can halt the storm of the soul when it bursts out of its hiding place; who can hold it back?

The night stood silent and spellbound. It was the beginning of autumn. Nature, which had celebrated the festival of its creation during the spring, and had worn its festive garb in the summer fields, giving food and life to all creatures, heat and summer to every soul, was now preparing for its great Sabbath—the ox and the cow were still eating from the harvest, and the stubble of the fields remained to be gleaned. In the inner rooms of nature's house, the doors were about to be shut for the winter. The angels of the forest were already stealing away into their caves, the trees were standing silent, the beasts of the field were dreaming a dream of darkness and the dogs' tails were drooping. The serenity of the river brought a sadness to the heart, the earth seemed to be laden with a heavy burden, and the sky and the stars above kept their closed mysteries to themselves. For this was the fifth day of nature's week, before the Sabbath of winter, the fifth day for the dwellers in the wilderness...

Martha wandered about restlessly that night. She strolled around the hill that gazes down on the river. For many days now every peal of the bell had filled her with a sort of dread. She had grown like a plant of the fields for twenty years; night had been night to her, and morning, morning. But now, at the opening of her twenty-first year toward the end of the summer, a different spirit seemed to have entered her being, as if a strange secret deep inside her was sloughing its skin, and she wandered in a trance, seeking her unknown fate. A shepherd's flute would speak a wondrous message to her and the churning of the millwheels would move her blood. She began rising late in the mornings, and she stayed out late at night. She had met Osip once or twice and had turned her back on him, or had stood stock still, closing her eyes tightly. Once she dreamed that she was vomiting blood; another time she dreamed that flames were rising around her father's house, burning it to the ground, and the horses and cows shrieked and whinnied as they choked in the smoke; then she dreamed that she took a dog in her hands and threw it down from the mountaintop onto a rock where all its bones broke as it splattered over the stones. Every morning she got up and went to draw water, and every evening she went and stood behind the fence. Once she stood on a hilltop at the edge of the village, and picked up pieces of stone which she threw into the water one by one. She sat on the rock and watched the broad river rippling in the moonlight.

And Osip was drawn from his room in the church that day by an invisible hand, and he traversed the length and breadth of the forest with an axe in his hand, striking all the trees in his path, to wake them from their slumber. He had intended to go up to Uman, and to sleep there that night. In his pocket were three pieces of silver, and a few odd coppers. The money jingled in his pocket, but all his efforts to direct his feet to his destination were in vain. He seemed to be held within a magic circle, as he shoved his hands deep into his pocket and rubbed the coins together. He walked backward and forward, backward and forward, until he was near the village again and he seemed to scent the pulse of life beating from a distance. Martha's shadow fluttered in front of his eyes, and then it seemed to him as if he had leaped half a mile in one stride, and there he was, standing behind her. The witch was sitting on the hill, and Osip grasped her by the head. His heart shuddered and his strength flowed up, overwhelming him. The girl jumped up, determined to escape from him, and he too was ready to throw her into the water if she did not obey him. Nature flared up once more, the autumn awoke to a universal terror, the hilltop became a living flame, and the river sprang out of its bed. The strengths of the two opposed and obeyed each other…

But Osip never knew her again after that night, for he swore to disappear that very night, to leave the village and never to see her again. Martha returned to her father's house, and, to the ire of her parents, became pregnant, and gave birth. She suckled the child and bore him upon her shoulder, and became betrothed to a great and wealthy man from Russia who passed through Shoshaka, saw her, and took her into his house. And she went with him, as a dog follows its master.

Translated by Richard Flint

The Red Heifer

This is a story about a red heifer and something that happened not long ago in a little town near Horan, where a certain rabbi lived. I, the storyteller, was not present and did not witness these things myself, but I did hear about them from reliable people. The story is definitely unsettling, and at times I thought it best to cover it up. But when all was said and done, I decided to write it up for others to read.

Our generation, after all, is destined to die out, and the next generation will not know its ancestors and how they lived in the Diaspora. Now, if one wants to find out about how that life really was, let him know about it, its lights as well as its shadows. Let us know that although we were Jews, we were also just "flesh end blood," with all that the term suggests.

There was a ritual slaughterer in the town of Dashia who was qualified and was about to become apprentice to the ritual slaughterer in another city; but he was eventually found to be ineligible, so that he could not become a ritual slaughterer, after all. Instead of becoming a teacher or Torah reader or prayer leader or just a laborer without a particular craft, or a *luftmentsch* or a storekeeper, he chose a vocation that was close to slaughtering, even though it was, in terms of social class or religious standing in Jewish life, a long way from it. Put another way, this man had really wanted to attain the pious office of ritual slaughterer, but he had to become a simple butcher in the Jewish street and open up a simple butcher shop. He abandoned his studies and his uniform and the holy laws and prohibitions of ritual slaughter and became a butcher like any other butcher, a profane man standing all day in his shop, dressing the carcasses and the slaughtered lambs on pegs, stripping them of their skin, extracting the proper veins and selling measurement by the pound.

And not only that. He took religious matters lightly and wasn't fastidious when it came to Jewish law, in the way of most butchers who were not exactly the most observant. Not to wash our dirty laundry in public, it must be said that they sometimes inadvertently sold non-kosher meat as kosher for the simple reason that unqualified meat in towns like this, where there are more Jews than there are villagers who eat pork, was about half the price; while the kosher meat, because of tax and duty and other such things, was certainly not free and its price might be twice that of non-kosher meat. While these butchers may be punished for this in hell, any Jew with a family needs to find a way to make some profit here on earth. It is well known, moreover, that butchers love to eat and drink and provide three meals a day for their families and not restrict themselves to modest or purely spiritual sustenance, as do Torah scholars and pious people.

All butchering has an element of cruelty in the blow to an animal's throat or when its limbs are cut off, even if the animal is slaughtered properly. Just yesterday a goat may have been grazing in the pasture, the lamb hurrying along to its fold, and today their blood is drained, their breath extinguished, and they are hanging upside down on a pole. Blood, which is life, is now on the hands and fingers of the butcher. It is the butchers who assist the ritual slaughterers, preparing the cow or the bull while the slaughterer's knife is being sharpened. The ritual slaughterer remains pious, for religion and its sacred commandments protect him and his life, and the crueler aspects of this business are left to the butcher and his destiny. Butchers are plenty strong, and when, for example, a disturbance breaks out in town, they are called upon to be the roughnecks. All the spiritual folks fear these physical butchers because they are bullies, and it is best not to anger them, for they can be merciless.

But there is something good about all this. The Jewish people is a weak and timid people, fearful of the slightest provocation; and whenever there have been pogroms against Jews, a hundred might flee from one drunken peasant and passively submit to broken windows and vandalized households. But the butchers learned to fight back and to arm themselves with clubs and axes when the times called for it. Something like this happened once at Easter during a brief interregnum, a full generation before the Jews had learned how to stand up for themselves. Is it any wonder that they called themselves the vanguard of Israel's heroes?

The Torah treats the thief, or *ganav,* more stringently than the robber, or *gazlan*, because the *gazlan* treats all people equally, whereas the *ganav* does not. And to be precise about it, when you are dealing with butchers, you are dealing with two opposites. When these heroes, who are afraid of nothing, do steal a bull or a cow, they do it secretly and without the owners knowing, or they have others do it for them. One can see this as a way of making a living rather than as an act of theft. In the butcher business, when you slaughter a cow or a bull and actually pay for the animal directly, it costs five times as much as an animal for which you haven't paid. Perhaps a bull wandered off and was abducted and turned over to the butchers, or perhaps there had once been fifty cows in a pen and now only forty-nine remain, a number that is still plenty from the owner's point of view. Reckon how many things can go wrong with the slaughter of a cow: sometimes the ritual slaughterer will do damage at the moment of killing, sometimes a lung can be punctured, or damage may occur regarding any one of the eighteen prohibitions. Dashia was a poor city, and often Jews couldn't pay for their meat. Meat that isn't soaked within three days becomes unfit, and in the summer it spoils. How could a butcher survive without some little benefits on the side?

You may say that this is forbidden, that a Jew ought not to do this. Yet do not all social dealings and commercial transactions involve a bit of deception and cheating? There is no essential difference, except that when it comes to business, this is not just a manner of speaking. And it surely won't stop those who do it from wearing the garb of the pious folks who pray in the choice seats in the synagogue. The other ones, that is to say, the butchers and their ilk, don't get reckoned among the pious and have to pray at their own house of worship, the synagogue of the morning watch instead of at the main synagogue in town. The householders have holy excuses and pious terms for the drink that they have in the morning after prayers, as they do for all the gross physical things they do. The butchers down their brew without apology and don't need a death in the family or a holiday to justify having a glass. While I know that the butchers are not saints and I don't want to make too many claims on their behalf, I would not have called them scoundrels were it not for this one thing that happened. It was plain evil! Who among us can pronounce that word in all its bitter meanings? People want to live and they do have uncontrollable urges in their bellies, which do not have silken linings and which can be very insistent.

And here is how it happened: in Dashia there lived a man named Reuven, an average fellow who didn't stand out; and who knows if he would even have been known in Dashia were it not for his cows?

Most of the citizens of Dashia, if they had means at all, kept cows that gave enough milk so that they didn't have to buy it. Reuven always had the best cow in the city. In this he was successful, and this he understood. He knew how to take care of his cows, to fatten them up and to make them look like the healthy cows in Pharaoh's dream. Reuven was not above feeding his cow from his own food and drawing her water himself. The shed was always kept clean, and he watched out so that no accidents would happen. His entire life was devoted to taking care of his cow, and that is what he was known for.

The people of Dashia are city types without much knowledge of nature; but when a cow or a goat gives milk to its owner, some contact with nature occurs. In every corner of the city, people know the local cows and goats; and when the larger or the more delicate animals return from grazing, all the residents look at each cow and goat and express their opinions about what they're worth and the price of their milk. Each household loves its animals, and men walk with their cow or their goat as if they were walking with a friend. And why not? Animals, after all, are living things who get hungry and need that hunger satisfied; they have sad feelings and affections and mothers who love and long for them. If you don't know this already, just take a cow or a sheep or a goat home with you, and you will be looking at a living soul.

In those days, Reuven had a ruddy Dutch heifer, the likes of which—for its beauty and soundness and fullness of body—the inhabitants of Dashia had never seen. When she came back from feeding with the flock, her head was held high like a queen's; and the other cows paid her proper respect. She was indeed of a nobler race, as one could see from her strong body, her healthy udders, and her beautiful coat. Reuven was once offered one hundred fifty rubles for her, whereas the most any other cow had cost, even the one belonging to a nobleman, was seventy or eighty rubles. How in the world, you might ask, did Reuven even come to possess a cow like that, given that he was not rich? But the citizens weren't so amazed, since people had come to expect good fortune from Reuven when it came to cows. This fellow's cow simply had to be the most wonderful in and around Dashia, for that is what was written in the book of destiny and that is the way it always was.

And Reuven in those days was as happy as a man whose daughter was going to marry a brilliant Torah scholar; he would gain great delight whenever he heard people praising, glorifying, and exalting his cow. They told wonder stories and spoke in hyperbole as if they were speaking, excuse the comparison, about their rabbi. They even said that the cow yielded four measures of milk at a time. They also said that from the butter alone, left over after they had all the milk they needed, Reuven cleared three rubles per week, and he had thirteen children and fifteen mouths to feed. In short, Reuven's red heifer, who gave birth each spring and whose offspring cost fifteen pieces of silver, gave folks a lot to talk about when they were sitting in the synagogue.

Dashia enjoyed its good fortune over the excellent heifer who could crown even one of the great cities on God's earth. And ineffective were all the incantations of the jealous women who practiced witchcraft and schemed to stop up her milk. Neither Satan nor his minions could do anything against such a grand creature, for God had created her.

But amazingly, all that meant nothing on the day of reckoning. The time came when the heifer's destiny was scaled even though she was the source of life for an entire family and the noblest part of the city's fabric. Were she to die in the fullness of her years, or be felled by a plague or even die a simple death, we would certainly be sad, but we would be resigned. Extinction comes to human beings as well, after all. The house that a person labors to build may burn down; and who can stop a city from being destroyed when enemies attack? When tragedy happens in the course of life, who can complain? Or, if it was said that Reuven had gone crazy, or that the heifer had ceased giving birth for a period and thus had been sold for ritual slaughter, and was found kosher, and had her skin removed and her veins extracted, and was sold for rich flesh for someone's Sabbath table, sweet to the palate when fried or boiled, we might nod our heads in assent at the destiny of the milk-giving heifer. That would be in accordance with the order of things and the way of the world: things like that happen in life. But in the case of Reuven's heifer, a murder was committed, an awful murder as bad as the ambush of a human being. This happened in a way that was not in the natural order of things, or at least in a way that we expect to happen among Jews.

There was a drought, and the price of meat rose. It was very hard to make a living in Dashia, and even butchers who most always could make a go of it were struggling. Disputes broke out, and there were hostilities, as one might expect. Reuven, a peaceful man by nature, took part in those disputes, and the butchers opposed him. One can't explain all the reasons for what happened afterward, but I will tell the reader anyway, one by one. And I am not judging here, just telling the story, but others will come and judge, and they will expound and clarify the course of events.

It was the heifer's fate to be taken from her owner by a group of butchers. Many had their eyes on her when she returned from grazing, and she had no idea what was going to befall her. The group gathered to conspire in the house of the slaughterer.

It happened on a Saturday night at the end of summer. Reuven and his household were sitting at twilight and enjoying their heifer. His youngest were patting her, the older were praising her. The eldest daughter got up and took some fodder and gave her a nice ladle of water. Suddenly, the heifer let out a piercing moan, and everyone trembled because they didn't know what had happened. Winter would come and darken the hearts of Jews when they realized that there was no firewood or warm clothing for their nakedness. Their deeds must have been wanting, and that is why they had no sustenance.

It was midnight. Everyone was resting, and no light shone in any window. They were dreaming deeply in the gloomy night, because on the morrow the breadless day would begin again...Yet one butcher pierced that darkness and sneaked into Reuven's pen, where the heifer was standing. There was no lock on the door, and only a thick rope attached the heifer's leg to a tree. The prowler cut that rope with a sharp knife and took the heifer by her horns, leading her out a narrow pathway, while the heifer followed in astonishment.

And, hush! The man and the animal stood at the door of the large cellar of Shoel the Butcher, where everyone had gathered. Two of them faced the heifer and pulled her while she involuntarily wagged her tail. They abruptly pulled her into the cellar, leading the reluctant animal as she held back and forcing her to do what she feared to do.

Now the heifer stood below, agitated. Seven of the men got up to receive her, dressed in aprons and furs like peasants, with faces aflame. Each man had drunk a little glass to get his strength up, and the little candles shining in the dark made the scene seem like hell. They surrounded the calf and fondled her.

Suddenly, one of the butchers got up like a lion and tried to cast the heifer to the ground, but her legs were like iron. Some others came as reinforcements and struggled mightily with her, but she dug her hooves into the ground while her eyes raged. The heifer got up as if to gore and banged her head against the wall until the cellar shook. One of the butchers crawled under her belly and secured her hind legs with a thick rope. He did it also to her forelegs. All of them got up and girded themselves and climbed upon her back and pushed her. She fell and let out a mighty groan as she tried to sever the ropes. But her attackers grabbed her with a vengeance that no one had seen before. Outside, rain began to fall on the roof and the wind howled. Sweat the size of beans fell from the butchers' foreheads from their efforts; and they looked at one another like strangers and took off their clothes and rolled up their sleeves as if ready for a fight. What pent-up feelings sought release!

One of the butchers, himself a ritual slaughterer, stood up calmly and sharpened the old blade; he took it out and rubbed its point with his fingernails. Once again, the butchers leaned on the back of the heifer. Some took hold of her thick legs below and above, and two especially strong men twisted her head with incredible might. It was as if doom filled the air, an awful decree of the end of days, and suddenly the butcher who was a slaughterer took up his blade and ran it back and forth across her delicate neck. The heifer let out an awesome earth-shattering groan and blood poured out like a fountain, spreading in a great arc and shining in the midst of the light from the lamp that hung from the ceiling. The blood kept flowing, splattering on the roof and walls, on the ground and on the trousers of the men and on their hands and faces. The heifer struggled with her remaining strength, shuddering while the ground became a river of blood. The murderers put her off to the side, and after an hour her ruddy soul departed and she died. Man conquers beast!

Then another of the butchers took a sharp knife and plunged it into the belly of the heifer so that the innards came out, and then others tore off her skin. They did this with a pent-up power and compressed emotion they had never known.

The animal was stripped. The men began to divide her into pieces, cutting off her head and her legs. One butcher couldn't restrain himself. He took the fat liver and put it on the hot coals that had been placed in the corner. When the blood reached the flames, everyone ate it without proper salting and with ravenous hunger, licking their fingers eagerly. A large bottle of brew was ready, so they ate and drank until they satisfied their lust. They were like priests of Ba'al when the sacrifice was on the altar. But this did not happen at Beth El or at Dan; it happened in the Jewish city of Dashia, not at the time when the ten tribes were exiled from the Northern Kingdom, but in the year 1884.

The second watch passed, and the rains poured while the wind raged. They divided the heifer ten ways, each man putting his portion in a sack. Each carried his share on his shoulders and then repaired to his shop in the dark of night in order to hide the spoil. The city slept, and the people dreamed while dogs barked and the skies were gloomy with rain. No one knew what had transpired!

In their haste, the butchers forgot to close the cellar door, and so the dogs came and licked up the blood. In the morning, folks saw that Reuven's heifer had been stolen and they searched for her. Within an hour, they found her ruddy coat still wet. The matter frightened them, and everyone who heard about it was shocked. In Reuven's house, there was moaning and deep grief.

From the time of Dashia's founding, there had never been such a terrible day. Men wandered around aimlessly outside, women came together whispering and talking. It was as if there had been an eclipse of the moon in the midst of an eclipse of the sun, and everyone looked at one another as if the world had been turned into Job's Valley of the Ghosts. To slay an animal in the middle of her life is an awful thing.

And as for what happened to the butchers who took part in the murder of the animal, the various quarrels and court trials and their punishment—both by man and God—if I would tell all these in detail, they would take up much space. In brief, however, everyone who had a hand in doing in that red heifer experienced bad things in his family life, as if a curse had been cast on him and his house, without leaving any remnant. But all these things are written in the history of Dashia and its chronicles.

The reader can find out more there.

Translated by William Cutter

In the Valley

In the valley of N…, which is named after a large river that encircles a range of small hills in White Russia, there is a small settlement, more than a quarter of a mile from the nearest village, and difficult to reach because of the steep hill which leads to it. The settlement consists of seven houses (inhabited by four peasants, a blacksmith, and two workmen) which cluster around a spacious white house belonging to the flour mill and, together with its two granaries, looming over the waterfall. For many years the white house had been occupied by a Jew, Shmaryahu Avigdor the son of Nahum Shlomo, who rented the mill from its Greek landlord. He had inherited the right to rent it from his wife Malkishua's father.

Although the mill was of the old-fashioned type, it served its purpose admirably. The water supply was plentiful and the tenant operated the mill independently. His flour was sold in the market, providing him and his household with a livelihood.

The millstones turned on their axis. Peasants came and went. There were wagons outside used to transport the grain to the mill, and to carry back the full sacks of flour. Not far away, the blacksmith reshoed the horses to the regular pounding of his hammer. The miller and his workers were always busy at their tasks, and Shmaryahu would be occupied from morning to night. Since there were no Jews within miles of this settlement, all Shmaryahu's dealings were with gentiles. He spoke their language and he knew each one by name, but within him dwelt an alien god, the Lord of Israel!

Shmaryahu Avigdor was a tall man, with sunken cheeks and a short, pointed beard. He swayed slightly when he spoke, and treated everyone courteously. He never lost his temper, even when something was mishandled, nor did he punctuate his words with curses and swearing. He rose at dawn to tend to his mill, prayed regularly, and was observant in matters of foods prohibited to Jews, as well as in his business dealings. His father's teachings had provided him with learning and piety, and from his father-in-law he had learned to work with his hands a living. These different qualities had made a whole man of him. On ordinary days he did not have time to do much thinking or to read books, but a quiet air of piety hung over everything he did. When he entered the storehouse, upon seeing the neatly arranged sacks or flour, a blessing would fall from his lips—something suited to the occasion, like "May my soul bless the Lord," or a simple prayer of thanks from the heart. On the Sabbath when the millstones eased their toil, as did his workmen and his horse, the sixteenth chapter of the book of Exodus usually came to his mind—about how the Manna did not descend on the Sabbath Day and the children of Israel ate the double portion from the previous day; and how some of them nevertheless went out to gather the Manna and did not keep the Holy Sabbath.

On the first Saturday night of the month, when the time came to bless the new moon and its glory overflowed into the silent square, he would reflect on the passage from the Psalms—"Thou art clothed in honor and majesty." Nature around him did not distinguish between man and man. And it kept to the seasons. The sun rose and set, and the stars shone at night. In the summer the hills were covered with grass and clover, and the cattle and sheep grazed there. They ate and were satisfied in plenty, and without fear. In the winter the fields were buried under a mountain of snow, the rivers froze to the very entrance of the mill, and the waters hid beneath the ice, flowing silently. The birds no longer chirped their morning prayer, for they had gone to seek God in warmer lands. And amidst the flux of nature, a son of the Hebrew covenant made his home here. In days of yore, he had crossed the river with his forefathers, he has lived among the hills of Judea, in Babylon, in Persia, in Spain, in all the countries of the Disapora, and now he had built his nest here, in this spot.

His wife Malkishua, in spite of the fact that she had been born and bred in this settlement, was not happy with her environment. She was always restless. She was a beautiful woman and village life was not to her liking. She accepted her lot with pious resignation, but sometimes she felt hemmed in by her house. In the bloom of youth, in fact, she had longed to move to the city...but I shall not dwell on her early years!

The two married daughters, Sara and Leah, were, like their mother, both beautiful young women. Year after year they gave birth, nursing and rearing their children, and as the children grew, the mothers still retained their youthful looks. Their husbands, the sons of well-to-do merchants, were in the lumber trade; their business prospered, and they loved their wives. In fact, Shmaryahu and Malkishua derived great joy from these children.

They had a younger daughter who bore the ancient name, Hulda; and her beauty was different from that of her sisters. She was endowed with great charm—with something of her mother's innocent expression and her father's strength of character. But more than anything else, she reminded one of a character out of a fairy tale. Flowers such as these occasionally grow in these hidden corners.

Hulda was of a capricious nature. Sometimes she helped willingly with all the chores, milking the cows, and even mixing fodder for the horse before the servant came; but sometimes she did nothing. She would spend the day sitting on the threshold of the mill, listening to the hum of the millstones, or she would cross the narrow bridge and wander barefoot through the hill. She could neither read nor write because she had not been taught. She had never learned to sing either, and she expressed the music in her soul only by skipping and dancing, or by rolling down the hillside. When she picked herself up after rolling down the hill, gracefully shaking off the dust, the air seemed to be filled with an echo of paradise before the fall.

Her long braids gleamed like gold, her eyes reflected the purity of a noon sky in the springtime; and when she turned her head, revealing her slender neck, she looked like a year-old doe, full of wonder at the joy of the forest.

Once, finding a snake crawling on the ground, she picked it up and wound it around her neck like a necklace, and there was no fear in her heart. Whenever a passing stranger saw her, he would stop and gaze at her in wonder. On fair nights she would sleep out of doors under the dome of the sky, as no Jewish girl would ever do; yet no one dared to touch her. Once, two of the village urchins planned to molest her in an isolated spot. But when the time came and they saw her from afar, lying on the grass like a wandering star—their courage failed them.

Thus lived this wondrous creature far from the din of civilization and from the contact of man, until one day the shadows began to fall…

Follow me, dear reader, and I will lead you to another world.

Let us leave the valley and ascend to the nearby village. We pass through the village to its gates, and here we find ourselves at a crossroads: one road leads to the right and the other continues diagonally to the left. We take the latter road and walk for about three quarters of an hour until we come to another small village, whose houses are like small tents. Beyond the village stretches a large forest, which takes about an hour and a half to cross. The trees stand close together, their branches entwined—man with his ax has not yet ventured here. Our heart grows heavy as we walk here alone, with no man in sight. But when we come to the end of the forest, the world opens up before us once again. A weight is lifted from us. The fields stretch out on all sides and the road is straight and paved. Every hundred paces there is a stone fixed at the side of the road with a number written on it. Here we walk refreshed. Man finds peace from his toils and tribulations in the open air! In about an hour we stand at the entrance to a large city of Jews, a well-known open city, though not the district capital.

We are in B…a city of long streets and large houses, full of doors and windows on all sides. The city is cramped because of its large population, and therefore the houses stand close together, side by side. Each father builds a small apartment for his sons and his sons-in-law in his yard, and they all live crowded together, sharing the burden of the taxes, whether to the central government or to the local Polish gentry, who own the city and all the land under the feet of its inhabitants. At the same time, they worship the God of Israel and obey the commandments of the Torah. No man ever says: "My work is heavy—I will seek compensation in this world."

The people of B… were ordinary Jews, and the wheels of their life moved smoothly. There was no dissension, no political parties, and very little gap between social classes. In small synagogues scattered throughout the city, everyone found a niche for himself among friends. There was nothing to drive people on, and instead of the usual Jewish ambition, what reigned here was a sort of coolness, a lack of imagination. What is man compared with the King who created heaven and earth, and what shall he gain if he probes and questions!

Two families lived in the town, near one another; they differed completely from the rest of the inhabitants. They were the sons of Reuven and the sons of Yehuda, and it is of them that we shall speak.

Reuven and Yehuda were brothers, and they had made their mark before the power of the Polish government was broken. They traded on a large scale with the pleasure-loving Polish gentry, and became very wealthy and well-known. The scales never tipped in the favor of either, and the wealth of one never exceeded that of the other. But after their death when their inheritance was divided among their sons—Reuven had nine sons and sons-in-law and Yehuda had eleven—their luck also changed. The sons of Reuven continued to prosper and to increase their wealth, becoming the rich men of the town as they are today, while the sons of Yehuda, even if they held their ground, were simply considered well-to-do townsmen. A hidden rivalry existed between the two families, but toward the outside world they were united, always meeting for holidays and weddings in one of their houses, the sound of their merriment filling the air.

Shmaryahu Avigdor sometimes came to the town to negotiate a deal, or to raise a much-needed loan (on the High Holy Days he prayed in a large village where the brewery was situated and the Jews made up a *minyan*), and when he come to town, he was besieged by matchmakers with offers to marry his daughter to a member of the Yehuda family. Engagement at sixteen years and marriage at eighteen! Such was the Jewish custom. A dowry is promised from both sides. The groom's family is a notable one, as you know, and the bride is well spoken of. Shmaryahu had already talked the matter over with his wife, and she had agreed. Plates were broken, and the traditional engagement formula recited.

Hulda has become engaged to a lad from B…Come, oh bride, I will bow to you and the riddle of your beauty, and you will cover your face with a veil!

Naftali, son of Yehuda, the seventh son of the family, had sometime ago broken away from the family trade at which he was unsuccessful, and instead, he ran a shop where he sold wools and silks for Sabbaths and festivals. The family of Yehuda, though they patronized him because he was a relative, did not always find in his shop the sort of materials they were looking for, and when they had a chance to go to the nearest town or city, they preferred to shop there. But there were plenty of Jews in B…, there were many market days, and near the town there was also a bakery which employed many people. In short, Naftali had a position in life, and he was dependable and trustworthy as well. He found a helpmate in his wife Bracha. Bracha was thin and pinched-looking, but she was a great talker and she knew how to get along with the customers whether Jews or gentiles.

The bridegroom, Moshe Avraham by name, was their eldest son, He was sixteen but looked twenty. He had no inclination to study, and he was no stranger at the shop, but he spent much of his time attending the yeshiva, gradually turning into one of those well-known types who is bored most of the time for the lack of anything to do.

I must mention here that the houses of Reuven and Yehuda had the tradition of keeping marriages within the family. When a beautiful girl or a clever son grew up in one of the houses, the brother or brother-in-law of the father would come to his relative and say:

"Give your daughter to my son (or your son to my daughter). Why should they seek someone outside, and thus diminish our inheritance?" Only if the opposite were true, if the girl was not beautiful when ready for marriage, or if the appointed son was not very talented, did they try to make a match outside the family. In this way they kept the best within the family and they rid themselves of the worst or the mediocre. Moshe Avraham, the bridegroom, was not one of the worst but neither was he one of the best, and so he became betrothed to the lovely Hulda. Thus it was stated in the betrothal contract.

It must be said that Bracha, the mother of the groom, had not yet seen the bride. During the month of Elul she departed from her daily routine, left the house and the shop in her husband's care, and journeyed to another city to visit her ancestral graves as she was wont to do every three years. Thus one afternoon she made her way to the home of her in-laws.

To tell the truth, she was not really satisfied with the match, despite her belief that matches are made in heaven. She did not regard the dowry as sufficient for her eldest son, and felt that it was a pity he would have to move to a village in order to become a member of his father-in-law's household, as had been agreed. This is what her face expressed as she stepped over the threshold of her in-laws' house. But her heart softened at the sight of the cleanliness and orderliness in the house.

Hulda had not yet entered the room. Her mother had asked her to dress in her best Sabbath clothes. When the door opened, and her beauty flooded the room, her future mother-in-law was rooted to the spot in astonishment and awe, for never on this earth had she seen such loveliness. But she pulled herself together, went over to the girl, stroked her cheek, and kissed her. Later, when they were sitting down at the table for sweets and fruit, and Hulda remained leaning against the couch opposite her, her heart remained heavy. If only the bridegroom had been one tenth as good as the bride, she would have been happy…

On the same day she gave her gifts to the bride, a gold bracelet and chain, and, in spite of their pleading that she remain, took her leave. The next day she arrived in the town where both her parents were buried. She hurried to the cemetery, opened her prayer book, and poured out her heart, first on the grave of her father, and then on the grave of her mother. She wept profusely, more than on any previous visit, and she did not know what had come over her. The humble cantor who lagged behind the mourners, recited the *El Male Rahamim* prayer, as was his custom. Neither the dead nor the living shall answer you. Your prayers are in vain!

The summer came to an end, and the winter also passed. The spring, which had brought restfulness, was soon over and, once more, it was summertime. Gone was the season of mourning and lamentation, and the questioning of God's ways had already passed. Now came the season of weddings and other joys for the pious. There was no congregation in Israel which was not celebrating a wedding, and so it was in our town B…On one street a bridegroom is being called up to the Torah, on another everything is being prepared for the appearance of the groom. The town is full of vitality and movement. Those who are not marrying off their sons, are invited to the weddings of their neighbors and relatives. One young girl asks her father for a new dress and he has nothing left in the till…Gifts have to be given on all sides. There is no counting pennies now, no miserliness. The sons of Israel are giving their children in marriage. There is rejoicing everywhere.

During one of these weeks the families of Reuven and Yehuda prepared to journey together to the valley of N…, to the wedding of Moshe Avraham, the son of Naftali, and the bride Hulda, the daughter of Shmaryahu. All members of the family were present. They set out in a long line of carriages with their wives, sons and daughters. A band also went along with them, and a rabbi, a *shochet,* and three *shamashim*. To show their joy, some of the young men went on horseback. Whenever they passed a village, all the villagers came out to wave to them and they were astonished at the splendor which met their eyes.

When the party began the climb uphill, emissaries were sent ahead to announce their arrival. The bride's family came out joyously to greet them, and all the members of the two families were introduced. What joy there was! Cries of jubilation and flag-waving, and the groom led like a king among his people. The village square, which had never welcomed so many new faces, was full of tumult.

Room had been made for many of the guests in the homes of the peasants, some of whom had to sleep in the barn. The merry young men arranged the carriages and the wagons, and spread tents over them. A fire was kindled outdoors, and they cooked and roasted under the stars. They looked like desert dwellers.

Afterward, when the travelers had rested, washed and changed their clothes, the bridegroom was received by the bride's family; and the groom's family also came to see the bride. When the first visitors came to the threshold of the house, and saw the bride sitting in all her glory, they were awed, and could not believe their eyes, for they had never seen perfection such as this.

Night fell. It was a night of dancing intended for the women. Only afterward at the feast and banquet did the men appear. Shmaryahu Avigdor was full of joy. The trumpets were silent, and the flute player began to play *Kol Nidrei.* Everyone listened in silence. It was already midnight. Through the openings in the tent, the stars twinkled brightly.

When the feast was over, a great weariness descended on the guests, and they all went to sleep. I will not tell you of their dreams. The bridegroom slept on a bed and his sleep was sweet.

Dawn rose, and none of the guests saw the vision, some distance from the settlement, of a late star which rose from the water, while two old women stood by and watched…

It was a day of fasting for the bridegroom and his bride. The jester chanted lamentations, as was the custom, and he was accompanied by the musicians. At noon they covered the face of the bride with a veil; she sat like a statue on the chair in the middle of the hall and the women stood around her and chanted.

Twilight! The sky reddened, the sun began to set and the earth was reflected in the river. The bridal canopy was set up. Men and women came, bearing torches, in the light of which their black garments gleamed. Trumpets blew. The peasants and their wives also came to see the spectacle, and the shepherds from across the river were late in bringing home their flocks, camping with their animals at the foot of the hills. People stood closely packed, the veiled bride standing in the center like an Indian goddess. They began to walk around her as is the custom. The rabbi read the contract of marriage and broke the glass. Shouts of *Mazal tov*! The drums beat, the cymbals clanged. A crackling fire rises from a distance, reddening the air. It is the friends of Shmaryahu Avigdor, the peasants, desiring to gladden his heart. They have made a huge pile of dry twigs and built a bonfire. The fire seems almost like the burning of bones in ancient times in the days of human sacrifice…

The bridegroom, Moshe Avraham, arose on the following morning and wrapped himself in his new prayer shawl, as if it were his protection and refuge…He stood next to the wall praying. The guests began to wake from sleep and came to the room after the drinking and celebration of the previous night. The women also came to take part in the customs of the day following the wedding, but the bride had not yet arrived.

All morning her mother sat in her room in the house belonging to the seventh peasant, coaxing her to get up, but the poor girl's face remained turned to the wall.

It was only in the afternoon, when one of the wealthy relations was about to leave, and the turmoil was at its height, that the bride arose from her bed, for her head ached. She left her chamber, and went again to the waters of the river—but this time she did not come back.

That same evening they retrieved her body from the river. Everyone was grief-stricken and silent. Each kept to himself, for the pain was too great for speech.

Slowly they left the valley. They came together but they left separately, for they were ashamed. The *shamashim* watched over the dead body. The groom was stricken with consternation.

The next morning they tied two oxen to the wagon and in it they laid the girl who had been taken out of the water. Shmaryahu and his wife journeyed to the city to bury their dead, the oxen lowing on the way. The people of B...gave the lovely girl a burial plot, and said nothing more.

It became the custom for everyone to visit her grave each year and mourn for the dead girl who had gone, never to return.

Translated by Tirza Zandbank

You Shall Build a House

Chapter one

For a long time I have kept pent up within me the burden of this tale, knowing that I would find no peace until I had set it down on record in a book. Those forces which motivate us in life and weave the web of our existence, compel the heart to actualize events by giving them a lasting form.

One of the four heroes of my story was the second in line of the sons born to Simon Raphaeli, by his first wife whom he had married in his youth. In the home there was also a number of stepsons brought to him by way of dowry by his second wife, the present mistress of the household. Simon was a respectable burgher, well thought of in his city, a man who went unassumingly about his business, was faithful to the God of Jeshurun and cared for the education of his sons. Dan, the first born, was to some extent involved in the "Enlightenment" movement and was its protagonist in the town. His second born, Reuven, was quite different. He was tall and handsome, never pursuing any argument to excess. He was balanced in mind and body. Dan loved his books and sought to find in them a way of life; Reuven, on the other hand, naturally inclined to the spirit of the times—he was sociable, he loved conversation, his voice was always to be heard in the synagogue, which served also as the venue for public gatherings. Simon's sons were always very well-dressed. They had a well-to-do uncle in the nearby county town, and the bond with the county seat shed a kind of reflected splendor upon them. This was the time when Jewish periodicals began to make their appearance enabling all their readers to keep up with the news of what was happening in the world.

Dan was betrothed to the daughter of a leaseholder, but the girl's health was precarious and deteriorated from day to day. He waited for her several years. During this time he composed immature poetry, wrote love letters in the Hebrew tongue, mostly for his friends to read. His brother Reuven's aim was to find some goal in life. He knew a little Russian and arithmetic. He had heard in his uncle's house that officials enjoyed a good life. Meanwhile he, too, had become betrothed, having entered into an engagement with a young lady from a nearby city. She was a girl of remarkable beauty.

Various incidents at that time caused me to travel away from my father's house, but when I retraced my steps in this familiar ground, I passed by way of that city. I had heard that Reuven had already married and was living at his father-in-law's and I turned aside to pay him a visit at his home. Before me was a long house near the hub of the city. The plaster was crumbling off the walls, the window shutters were broken and the roof tiles were loose. When I opened the door a man of about fifty, haggard of face, with a straggly beard, greeted me. He wandered back and forth in the room with the restlessness of a man who had come down in the world. A few moments passed and Reuven entered from the adjoining room. He wore a black beard which enhanced his good looks. He was glad to see me. We talked of this and that as friends are wont to do. In the middle of the conversation, I looked up—and saw a girl of about twenty standing in the doorway, clad in a dressing gown, her head bound in a kerchief such as married woman wear. What should I say and what comment should I make? I have seen many lovely girls in my time—but I had never seen anybody as wonderfully beautiful as she was. There was magic in her figure, magic in the full flow of the hair visible beneath her kerchief. Her eyes were as mysterious as the moon peeping through the clouds on a festival. She was the epitome of health and bodily perfection. Nature had made everything about her just right, even to the little toe of her foot which was not crooked or intertwined with the next one, as every man who met her noticed. What this vision did to me, and to my muse in those first days, I shall not reveal here. I myself have no part in the actual story.

After a few months, Reuven left the dilapidated house of his father-in-law and returned home to the town of his birth. He managed to extricate a hundred rubles from his impoverished father-in-law. Even at that time, this was not a large sum among Jews. Reuven rented a clean room in a large town house inhabited by other tenants. He borrowed a few hundred more rubles on interest and began to engage in petty trade. Sometimes he dealt in wheat, sometimes in flour, sometimes in honey and sugar. He made a living and lived a pleasant life with his beautiful wife. He always spent more than he earned and behaved as if he were a man of means.

His wife bore him a son and after that a daughter, giving birth on both occasions without the aid of a midwife and without any impairment of her beauty. The disarray in her dress, which is natural with nursing women, only added new dimension to her loveliness. When she laid her breast bare to suckle and her husband chanced to come into the room, he would close his eyes as though dazzled by the sight; but she was unaware of this. She had a certain lack of warmth in the inner recesses of her soul. Strong desire and passion were wanting in her. She was rooted in the garden of the world, but only her husband knew it and no other.

It took only a few years for Reuven to consume the whole of his small capital, after which he did business with other people's money or with what he could borrow. One miserly creditor once called at his house to go over some accounts with him. Whenever he did so, he looked lasciviously at the mistress of the house so that, apart from the interest he was receiving, he had a bonus by feasting his eyes upon her. Once when he came to see Reuven and found the wife alone, he had the impertinence to touch her neck, the neck of marble, and she asked him what he wanted of her.

In vain did Reuven make every possible effort to earn a little more so that he should be able to rent two rooms for himself. One room was far too cramped to house four people. In the small town where he was born, people do not make spectacular progress, or achieve sudden wealth.

In connection with his business, Reuven occasionally called at the home of his rich uncle in the county town. There he often came into contact with an entirely different world. Money was made hand over fist and people lived lavishly. Men of his class would own a number of rooms, and even keep a servant in the house, but his own position was unfortunately far from lofty. When he looked in the mirror, he found his appearance gave him satisfaction, his clothes were clean and not inordinately long, his collar was glossy and shining in its whiteness, his fingernails were grown to a fashionable length. He washed himself properly every morning with soap and duly toweled and rubbed himself dry. In other words, he was a man suitably groomed and fit to mingle among modern people and enjoy a respectable life. Why did these others have all the comfort while he lived in straitened circumstances?

Something new happened in the county town. For the first time a theatrical touring company visited and stayed there a week. The people who came thronging to see the performances consisted of all the attorneys in the city, the apothecaries, the doctors and everyone who was attracted by the new spirit of the times. One of the men, who had wed one of Reuven's uncle's daughters, came from Vinytza. He also decided to go to one performance. He persuaded Reuven, who was staying in the county town at that time, to come with him. A world within a world! Live people appear on the stage, performing in front of the audience and singing as well. It seemed like a waking dream. Your senses of seeing and hearing are indulged. That night sleep departed from Reuven's eyes.

He woke in the morning and returned to his small town feeling depressed. He had come to a clear conviction that it was shameful for a man like him, who had visited a real theater, to be fated to live in one room in a shared house. He was certainly worthy of a different kind of life. He made up his mind firmly that from that time onward he would get rid of his shackles come what may.

Chapter two

At this point I must interrupt the flow of my narrative and make a digression.

In the town of Ladyno, which is about twenty miles from the place where Reuven dwelt, lived a young man called Naftali the Bold. I want to focus attention on him.

Naftali was an orphan, fatherless and motherless, and was reared by one of his relations. He persistently absented himself from *heder* and threw off the yoke of his teachers. While still a lad, he was already as strong as a young bull, and spoke arrogantly and roughly. He had blue eyes, blond hair, a broad forehead, the wide mouth of a glutton, powerful arms and thick, stubby fingers. His feet were planted solidly on the ground like two posts. He was corpulent and hairy. When he sat down to a meal he would roll his bread in salt covering all sides, swallow it with relish while quaffing a quart of water at a draught. Though he knew little Bible or rabbinic lore, he had a smattering of Hebrew words, and could trot out apothegms from the Talmud which he had picked up by ear. He sang snatches of the liturgy with satisfaction and pride, and chatted continually with his friends about topics of the day.

Once he heard a secularist mention the words "Max Nordau"—I am talking of him not as the Zionist but as the free-thinker. From that time on Naftali kept dropping the name with a peculiar pronunciation and in this way Max Nordau was a constant peg for his conversation.

Twice in his young days he had been a "bridegroom." The first time they returned the marriage agreement to him, and the second time he sent the betrothal deed back to the bride without giving any reason. His first wife died of an infectious disease during the first year of their marriage. The second was very sensitive by nature, and during the hot summer season in the month of Tammuz, became insane and was pronounced incurable. He went the rounds of numerous rabbis in many towns seeking permission to marry again. This traveling widened his horizons. Eventually he wed a girl of a family of injured reputation. Her two older sisters had apostatized. Three months after the wedding, she went bathing alone in the river and drowned; the waves swept her away and there was no one to help her. For her he mourned sincerely. During the seven days of mourning, a quorum of men came to his room to pray with him. He talked to them constantly uttering a verse personally compounded from the books of Job and Ecclesiastes. While doing so, he would stroke his moustache and beard, and turn as though removing the veil from the mirror to see his reflection. 'Mighty God! Man is born to live, and such is the custom through all the generations!'

It was at this time that Naftali began to make friends with the city's marriage brokers. He talked secretly with each individually, and promised each one faithfully that he would consult him alone in preference to other brokers. He stipulated a dowry of three hundred rubles, and subsequently raised it to five hundred. The bride he desired to marry must be a virgin among her people; no widows or divorcees for him. When he went for a stroll on the Sabbath and saw the young girls of the town coming out in their best attire, he would inwardly ponder; which of these gets the preference? Jacob married two sisters, so did David. In those far-off days the interdict of Rabbenu Gershom against polygamy was not in force. At the lobby in the hotel, the woman innkeeper, who had been deserted by her husband, would speak flatteringly to him. Every time he came there, she would make his bed for him herself. He was quite attractive to the other sex. That he knew for certain.

The Reuven of our story had another uncle in the town where Naftali the Roughneck dwelt. This uncle was making a wedding for his only daughter; and as is the wont of relatives, Reuven and his wife came to the nuptials. It was the night of the bridegroom's celebration, when the maidens from all parts of the city donned their best finery and assembled to dance. A galaxy of chandeliers blazed in the tent given over to dancing and celebration. One heard the sound of drum and violin, while the young belles tripped gaily in the dance, each joining in the merry round with her companions. There is a time for sitting at home house-bound and a time to dance. Several hours passed in this manner, then the place emptied of the uninvited guests. The two "sides"—the bridegroom's guests and the bride's—who had been invited to the wedding arrived for the feast. Fried fish and rich, fatty soup appeared on the tables; closely followed by roast chicken and stewed fruit; not the local variety, but imported figs and raisins. What more was there to wish for in this world completely given over to joy and pleasure?

Reuven's wife was the queen of the ball, and her beauty even outshone that of the bride, attired though she was in all her glory. A full dress of the softest silk undulated to her proud figure, and a graceful joyousness increased her charm sevenfold. This woman had never in her life provoked a man, never rebuked one; charisma was innate in her, and around her was an aura of laughter and radiance. Happy the man who possessed her.

This thought occupied the mind of Naftali the Roughneck, who was one of those invited to the feast. He was placed at a table directly opposite the lovely guest and his face turned toward her. Every time she laughed unaffectedly, an inward trembling shook him. His eyes blazed, his mouth widened, and a terrible urge arose in him to get up and wander about like one possessed. He twisted his leg around the leg of his seat so as to curb his will and desires and avoid a calamity. Throughout the proceedings he did not utter a word to a soul; he drank nothing and did not touch the rich viands on which he would normally have feasted. His eyes stared straight ahead. To Reuven, who sat complacently on the right of his wife, the man who sat staring opposite him was a monster. He did not know who he was, or what he was. He felt a continuous urge rising in him to get up and spit at him or punch him in the face. He had never felt this sort of emotion before. Never previously had he felt such jealousy for his wife or her beauty.

Now the reader is surely eagerly awaiting a description of the clash between these two persons. That is how narrators usually go about things. Well, I do not operate that way.

Chapter three

Emptiness! The wedding days had passed, the music was no longer heard, the beautiful woman and her husband had returned whence they came. Naftali the Roughneck woke up from his sleep rather late in the day. He rubbed his eyes, washed his face, put on his clothes and his boots. He looked through the window into the wide world outside and found it empty…He was not a man given to daydreaming and his heart was not inclined to poetic fantasy. However, man does seek some warmth. You cannot look into the heart of this our hero, without finding that even there depression finds a niche and that his periods between wife and wife were not just a time of careless hunting.

Nature has two mouths. It is not the same thing if with the sandal which is on your foot you knock against a log of wood or a hard stone, or when walking barefoot your foot encounters a soft goatskin spread on the ground. Naftali suddenly felt a strong desire to push the walls of the house outward. He was urged at one fell swoop, to lift up the roof and overturn it. He bit his lips, clawed at his yellow beard with both hands and suddenly he saw a vision like a rainbow in the clouds…

He is sitting beside the beautiful woman and staring constantly at the majestic beauty of her face. If she is a princess then he is her faithful servant, if she is a lioness he follows closely after her going around and around her den through the dark tunnels of the night. He tears her dress from her and is maddened by the sight of her white petticoat. The day does not pass, the brain does not conceive thoughts, a kind of strange ringing is in his ears, a ringing which comes from far and near.

He will get up and journey to the town where this couple dwells. He will enter into business relationships with the woman's husband and ensnare him from all sides. He is neither a robber nor a murderer, but nevertheless he will hire a man to smite the keeper of the garden and take possession of his inheritance. It is the eyes which take possession, it is not the marriage act which gives one ownership, but strength of hand, the taking hold of body by body with passion and tumult.

I am omitting what took place in the life of Naftali from here onward. He got married and divorced, married again and became widowed. The world goes on as usual. In every instance, he never achieved closeness with those he married. His mind was fully occupied with the wonderful woman whom his soul envisaged. He hardly recalled the names of his wives, but what he never forgot, in summer or in winter, was the movement of the body of the woman in the black silk dress which he had seen at the time of the wedding I have described.

I am now returning to the city where Reuven dwelt.

Chapter four

Many days after Reuven visited the theater in his county town, a guest came to the city and wrought a complete change in Reuven's fortunes. He was no stranger, but a friend. Actually it was his stepbrother who had gone away many years previously to seek work in distant places, and now returned like a lord with a watch in his fob, and spectacles upon his nose. He had a position in a large forest from which timber and boards were exported to many districts in the Ukraine. As the young Reuven had been born to the first wife, his stepbrother occupied a lesser status. Now Reuven honored his brother and invited him for the Sabbath meal. All that day of Jewish rest, the guest spoke about the business affairs in the forest, which was enormous in size and value. Although it did not belong to its owners who had leased it for ninety-nine years yet the lessees dealt with it as if it were entirely their own possession. Trees grew there which were as thick as large barrels and long enough to bridge a river. The felled trees were rolled to the saw mill and there cut into baulks and planks. Many merchants came and bought all kinds of timber, some for cash and some on credit. People who deal in timber make ten times the profit that ordinary traders in flour and wheat obtain.

However, it is a business which requires a thorough knowledge. There are many kinds of trees; this tree is good only for building and that only for making furniture. One must be able to estimate the thickness of a plank. One must know when a tree is dry or wet and whether it, in the course of time, will split or harden; whether it has knots or defects or is all clean.

Reuven paid great attention to all such talk and derived great satisfaction from this visitor to his home. His wife too was very cordial to the guest.

When the Sabbath was over they both sat down to talk things over by lamplight. When the glasses of tea were placed on the table, Reuven was suddenly struck with an idea and spoke about it immediately. He would definitely accompany his brother to the forest and reach an agreement with his employers and try to establish a warehouse for selling planks and timber, something which hitherto was lacking throughout the district. The other man was very favorably inclined to the proposition; indeed this was what he had wanted to achieve by his conversation. He would now be the eyes for his older brother, something which he never imagined could have come to pass.

The next morning Reuven borrowed a fair sum of money from his friends and in the middle of the week accompanied his brother to that place where so many people derived wealth from their labors. They journeyed together in a small, fast, two-wheeled carriage. It was summer and warm; the horse trotted spiritedly along the highway in a cloud of dust. The world was entirely free from care.

If I were to continue to describe the impression which the great forest made upon the protagonist of my story when he reached his destination, I would only distract the reader. Of course, Reuven knew from the descriptions he had perused in his brother's secular books that there is such a thing as nature and that poets grew excited about it. He knew all about the "crimson sky," about the "shades of evening," about "whispering trees," etc. However, Reuven had not come to the forest to write poems about trees, but to do business, to get to know the prices of every kind of timber and to learn what use man could make of them. Reuven made a good impression on the superintendents of the forest and his brother recommended him strongly. He spent five days there and bought wood and planks for ten times the amount of ready money he had with him. The owners of the forest found him worthy of trust.

I shall not dilate. Reuven returned to his town in an exalted mood and immediately hired a plot of ground from the local nobleman and fenced it round. Every evening the urchins of the town gathered together to stare at what was going on. Even older people used to come out when the day was done and chat with Reuven, who was efficiently supervising the work. They wanted to know explicitly what the whole thing was about. In the synagogue, the main topic of conversation was this occurrence which was something quite unprecedented in that city.

A few weeks later, a large procession of wagons delivered the timber and heavy boards from the forest. There was no railway in the county at that time, but horses and oxen hauled the transport as they had done from time immemorial. They would load a consignment of logs or beams on two wheels; place two more wheels at the other end and two draught horses would pull the burden over long distances. The city was stunned. Men, women and children gathered from all sides to watch them unloading the timber, beams and planks and to see how they stacked them on top of each other in rows. Children jumped on the timber. The know-alls came closer, felt the great beams with their hands and pretended to estimate their exact value. In short, it was a great day for the town where Reuven dwelt.

There was Reuven selling his goods, making his profits, and recording his transactions in the ledger, day by day. Many people now began to turn their attention to repairing their houses. They looked into the matter and came to the conclusion that it was better to cover their roofs with boards rather than thatch, which in the course of time deteriorated through the action of the rains. A number of wealthy people, thinking that it was not suitable for them to live in rooms whose floors were made of clay, conceived the notion of flooring them with thin boards. Carpenters found ready to hand the necessary material for cupboards, beds, tables and chairs. They no longer had to go to the trouble of looking for it in other towns as they had done hitherto.

After six months, Reuven had paid back in full to the owners of the forest the money which they had advanced him. He now tripled his previous order and began to enlarge his warehouse. Farmers came from numerous villages to buy timber and boards for their pens and for fencing. A certain noble lord of a great estate rebuilt the bridge which stood on his lands. Reuven supplied the timber for the piles, the large beams and the wide planks and made a very considerable profit in this single transaction. It is true that Reuven was still sharing a house, but now he was living very comfortably and was on much more genial terms with his neighbors. He could now be truly reckoned as one of the magnates of the town; a fact which nobody would deny.

Chapter five

The big market day arrived. Every Thursday Reuven's hometown put all its efforts into this important day, took a deep breath and let itself go. The Sabbath day is a day of rest for God and the people of the Covenant. The market day is just the reverse; it is a day of tumult when man breaks out of the narrow confines of his house and the life which is circumscribed by mere kopecks and half kopecks and swims about freely in the ocean of commerce. On the one day he can earn enough for the whole week. Every corner has a place to do business, to cheat to one's content. If on the other hand, you want to spend money, all the wares of the whole wide world are spread out on the ground in front of you. However, what are these regular and stereotyped market days compared with the great fairs which come three times a year; before Christmas, before Easter and before the Ingathering Festival. This latter is the time when all the people from a very large area roundabout bring in the produce of their fields. The earth had yielded up her produce unstintingly; it was a year of blessing.

The farmers brought the fruit of their land, sack-full by sack-full, which they had ploughed and hoed and reaped with the sweat of their brow, to the city. They exchanged the bounty of the Lord for minted silver and the czar's bank notes. Horses, oxen, cows and calves, year-old sheep and goats had only yesterday been working or yielding milk or grazing in the pasture. Now they stand crowded together gazing in dumb wonderment amid a mighty throng. In all the streets of the city, row after row of venders assemble in front of their stalls, or temporary shops made of tarpaulin, spread over makeshift roofs. Such a market does not merely spread out over the whole city; it invades the fields round about it. Normally Reuven's timber warehouse and yard stood a little isolated. This time new fences and palisades sprouted up next to him. Just beyond his place, the sack merchants put up their marquees and Naftali the Bold was among them. He had done very well in that prosperous year; thousands of sacks new, old, whole, white and patched constituted his stock for the market day. He was not only an expert at this trade, but he actually loved the business. It might seem that a sack is only a form of outer packaging. But you can fold it, you can carry it on your arm, you can sit on it, you can cover your feet with it. If you only stop to think a while, you have to recognize immediately the important service the sack performs in the world. Skin only protects the flesh, but without the invention of the sack, which can contain all the fruits of man's and nature's work, which can carry eleven thousands of grains which would otherwise scatter all over the place in one moment, business and commerce would dwindle away and all substantial labor cease.

The timber business and the sack business confront one another. In the timber and plank compound that day, Reuven's wife came to help her husband a little. Reuven was very busy; men surrounded him on every side. He was talking, rushing from one row of planks to another; counting, measuring, making notations with a lead pencil in his ledger. His wife was standing taking care of things from the side. She was clad in a short white woolen coat and her linen dress was not long enough to conceal her pretty shoes. She wore a red kerchief loosely tied on her head. She gave the impression of a beautiful young maiden who had only come to maturity that summer.

Naftali the Bold left his marquee for a moment, leaving his young helper behind and stood at the entrance of the timber compound. That day he had already taken in more than a thousand rubles and he felt in an expansive mood. He would have thrown away most of his capital for the sake of the woman who was standing there inside. In ancient days, women taken captive in battle would be sold in the market place. He did not have the courage to approach her and stretch out his hand in greeting. How happy is the man who drinks from the well of beauty. A heavy beam splits the brain of the woman standing there and he licks her blood. His assistant ran from the marquee and called his master, and Naftali went back reluctantly to his bundles of sacks. The sun was still high in the sky, and the strident noise of the people in the market place continued.

Once again Naftali emerged quickly from his marquee to the gate of the timber warehouse and once again feasted his eyes on the woman's beauty. His heart was in a ferment of passion and longing. He too was surrounded by merchants and buyers, but he was away in a world of his own.... Were he not embarrassed, he would have fallen down on his face and wept. Suddenly he roused himself. He ordered his assistant to go to the timber storehouse but did not know what to write down as the nature of his errand. He spread out his arms. Let his soul be torn out by its roots if but once in his life he did not uncover this woman's breast; he would embrace her dead or alive....

Chapter six

Two years passed. For a long time a large capital had accumulated with Reuven. He had taken in ten thousand rubles in notes and coin for timber and planks, beams and baulks. Such a sum neither he nor his fathers had ever seen at one time. He had to take the money to the owners of the forest. Reuven put the money he had counted and recounted again that day in a leather purse and tied it up very securely. In the middle of the week, he hired a carriage, again a two-wheeler. His wife prepared him food for the journey. He parted from her affectionately and went on his way proudly, but fearful.

It was a very hot day; the sun was burning and dried up the grass in the fields. Reuven held the reins of the galloping horse and his gentile boy held the whip and flourished it. Reuven, as the reader knows, was not an imaginative man, but as he closed his eyes against the rays of the sun and the enveloping dust, and from time to time felt the purse which was tied to him, strange thoughts came into his mind. A man goes naked out of his mother's womb, but nevertheless he covers himself with garments, puts shoes on his feet and a hat on his head. One man's pocket is almost empty, another's pocket is always full and he wants for nothing. A hundred rubles is quite a sum; ten bank notes of a hundred mount up to a thousand; a thousand—that is like a benediction announcing prayer...What would you say about a man who is carrying ten thousand rubles all in one package? Ten thousand is made up of a hundred times a hundred. What would happen if the cord which tied the sides of the purse together should be torn and a hidden hand should dip into it? Or his belt should slip open accidentally by itself and the pouch fall onto the ground without its owner noticing and when he went back to look for it, it would not be there because some passerby had picked it up and hurried away with his find. What would happen if a highwayman suddenly appeared at the crossroads and said, "Your money or your life!" Reuven began to reckon up his debts insofar as he could do so by memory. He counted out the details of the sum which he had expended that year and which he would have to pay out in the near future. He made a discovery; the bigger the turnover, the bigger the expenses. He conjured up a picture of his wife. She was dressed in a fine light woolen robe which he would soon buy her. He thought, too, of his older brother who had already married his ailing bride and who had never established himself. The gentile lad was sweating because of the heat. He wiped his face, took out a flute from his pocket and blew on it once or twice. A great bird was flying in the remote spaces of the sky above the traveler.

Why should I weary the reader? I am not writing a chapter on psychology, but telling a story. This I know; Reuven stole the ten thousand.

Toward evening he turned into an inn not far from the city. Gay in spirit, he leaped down from the light carriage. The boy who accompanied him unbridled the horse and gave him some fodder. The sun was shining brightly and the whole valley was peaceful. They brought the guest milk, cheese and white bread and he ate and drank to satiety. What else did he need in the world? The owner of the inn had died three years previously and only his widow, a servant and a maid were in the house.

Suddenly Reuven began to cry out aloud, "My money, where is my money?" He ran outside like one demented, searched everywhere under the carriage. He seized the terrified boy by the hair of his head. "Idiot, have you seen anything? Have you heard anything?"

The woman and the maid servant hurried out and they too searched for the lost purse all over the field.

"Woe is me, my capital," wailed Reuven. "All that I worked for and all that others worked for has been taken from me—only a few hours ago I had it all with me and now there is nothing..."

He went to retrace the road by which he had come, perhaps he would find what he had lost. As he searched, his eyes looked as though they might start out of their sockets. At almost every step, he lifted stones which he found, he turned to every side as he went along searching. He managed to get about half a mile from the inn. There he sat down on the ground, opened the money bag, took out all the money, tied it in a handkerchief and put it in his pocket. He took the open purse with him and returned to the inn wailing and crying as he went.

"In this very purse was the money which I brought with me," he complained to the unhappy innkeeper. "Now I have found it empty with nothing inside...There were ten thousand rubles there. Fifty bank notes of a hundred, thirty fifties, forty twenties, one hundred and fifty tens, one hundred fives, two hundred threes and one hundred one-ruble notes. I counted it all up very carefully and I was taking this money to a certain place to hand it over to its owners. Now I am as bare as the day I was born."

Just imagine for yourself, a man of about thirty-five and father of two children weeping his heart out. He sat at the table where he had eaten, leaning on his elbows ashamed of himself and weeping in real truth. What could the innkeeper say to comfort him, what advice could she give him? She was powerless.

That night Reuven again was deserted by sleep. He got up in the morning, gave orders to harness the horse and to get the carriage ready for the journey. He paid the innkeeper for his food and lodging, and said to her, "I am going home now, the most miserable of creatures. Should the matter come up for investigation, will you please give evidence that the whole thing happened in front of you."

The woman said, "Perhaps God will still help you."

He had already begun to get into the carriage when he returned to the inn and asked for ink and paper. He wrote a hasty letter to the owners of the forest telling them of the terrible thing which had happened to him. He liked to be brief in his letters, but this time he wrote at length, describing the incident in full detail. He put the sheets in an envelope, gave it to the woman together with money for the postage. He then left the inn and journeyed on his way, almost out of his mind. The money rested in his pocket but to all appearances had been lost on the way...

Grieving and completely dejected, Reuven returned to his town. His wife was startled to see how downcast he was. The story of what had happened was immediately revealed to the whole community. Such and such had happened to Reuven, the son of Simon. Many people came to commiserate with him. I say many, because a section of the inhabitants of the town, and specifically not the stupid or simple ones, had their doubts about the whole matter and did not believe in that loss. I and the readers know that they did not suspect him without cause.

Chapter seven

A flurry of correspondence began between the owners of the forest and Reuven. The letters of the claimants were sometimes written in the form of requests, and sometimes as threats. These sorts of "losses" were not unknown, and it was usually surely up to the loser to pay back. Reuven kept up the refrain—an accident; who could blame a man to whom an accident happened? Reuven not only regarded himself as not liable in the matter, he was even somewhat displeased at the obduracy of these owners. All right, he had caused them a loss of ten thousand rubles. Didn't they have millions? Did not these great capitalists understand that he was as upset as they were and that the whole matter distressed him greatly…! He found himself compelled to tell the whole story again from beginning to end to everybody whom he met. The important people in the synagogue advised him, each man in his own way, how and by what means it might be possible to find that which had been lost to him. One of the secularists in the city knocked on his door early one morning and told him he should advertise the matter in the newspaper. On the other hand people all over the place were making imputations about him behind his back. The scandalizing of a small town, where all the community are on intimate speaking terms. How bitter and painful it can be!

Night after night while his wife slept quietly in her bed, Reuven would sit and reckon up his accounts…expenses had gone up tremendously in the past year, but he had also made a very satisfactory profit. In actual fact, even the "loss" was a profit. Are you surprised?

His wife breathed heavily and with each breath the cover rose above her chest. Her hair, which had not been cut short, was spread over her face. One foot, beautifully shaped like alabaster, was uncovered and protruded from the bed. Reuven got up from his chair, smoothed the hair of the sleeping woman and stood looking at her fabulous beauty. Reuven did not know passionate love, but he did know gentle affection. Such gentle affection filled him as cannot be expressed in words. He passed his hand over the naked foot, raised it and returned it to its place. The room was still, the house was quiet. Outside it was quiet. The whole world was still. On the table lay a large sheet of paper full of accounts of the money going out and coming in…

The next day the stepbrother came from his home to Reuven's town. This time he was certainly an unwelcome guest. He explained what Reuven would bring upon him if he did not make up, by every means in his power, the deficiency caused by the loss. His employers would drive him out of his job and he would be left without bread. Wasn't he a security for him and had he not recommended him? Reuven just stood without uttering a word during all this talk, only shaking his head from time to time as a sign of disagreement. He just did not know how he could put things right, there was nothing that could be done. Ten thousand rubles had been lost on the way. A man of modest means like he could not possibly return them out of his own resources. Any man of common sense would know this. Certainly he was upset about his relative's trouble and that he had been made to suffer on his account, but was he God?

His wife, in a dressing gown which increased her charm, brought tea and biscuits for the visitor and pressed him to eat and drink. She had not understood the full nature of the talk, although she did have some idea about the tragedy. But how could you really continue to worry when the samovar is boiling and sparkling on the table. The charcoal underneath it hisses and Reuven her husband is at home with her. She also felt the fullness of affection. There was no man to compare with her Reuven in the whole city. He would certainly not make her angry and he would not quarrel with her, even if, by accident, she did something he did not like. The poets talk about divine unions, about how fate brings people together, how people who are far from one another become close, and the profound nature of the cleaving of soul to soul. Innocent nature does not operate that way. Without any calculation, it brings together two healthy people of two sexes and joins them together. They live together in amity and tranquility and bring forth sons and daughters to populate the earth.

Chapter eight

The next day the stepbrother went to the town rabbi, to pour out his heart to him. His complaint caused that good-hearted man some distress. This rabbi was a sincerely God-fearing man, one who had never run after money. He could not understand that a man could hurt his neighbor, although he had actually seen and heard of such things being done every day. There are the Torah and laws, there are evil impulses and lusts in the world. In heaven they know all that is done here below. It is true that the side of merit has become lighter in the scale, but nevertheless the side of guilt is not completely filled. This is how the matter has been going on throughout the whole of the exile and the end is hidden...Here is a man sitting before him and complaining about his kinsman. He wants to help both of them, this one materially and the other one spiritually. It is obvious that the claimant is speaking the truth; but on the other hand—how can he call the other person and say to him, you have lied and put into your own pocket that which is not yours. Can he, a mortal man whose end is worms and maggots and who is full of iniquities and transgressions, put a Jewish man to shame?

"Rabbi," cried the visitor, "I have three children and a wife, I shall not be able to face my employers who sent me here, with empty hands. Moreover I stood security for my brother. Just imagine, Rabbi, if you were in my place what would you do?"

The rabbi stroked his blonde beard and mumbled vaguely, "Yes, yes, but...."

The busy rebbitzen came and sat down at the end of the table some distance from them. He began his story from the beginning and said: "You are a wise woman, you tell met what solution I can find? I was very fortunate to obtain a decent job in these hard times and now once again the earth has opened up under my feet."

"Judah," said the rebbitzen to her husband, "you have got to do something to put this right. Try and talk to Reuven, maybe he himself will find some way out."

The rabbi opened a large folio—one of the sections of the *Shulchan Aruch*—and lowered his eyes to its paragraphs. He did not glance at the laws of theft, but at those of "forbidden foods." It says in the Scriptures, "You shall meditate on them day and night." The guest wanted to get up and leave, but the rebbitzen pressed him to drink a glass of hot tea in order to calm his distress. Between each sip, the woman talked to him. She wanted to know if in his area, too, they suffered from the czar's decrees—at the same time she asked him about his wife and children. Suddenly the rabbi raised his head and wrinkles appeared on his forehead. "Well, we shall see," he said to the guest and gave a little cough.

That evening, when Rabbi Judah was on his way to the synagogue for the afternoon and evening prayers, he went around in the direction of Reuven's house and saw him standing and leaning his head out of the window. He beckoned to him to come out and said, "Come with me to prayers!" Reuven understood the rabbi's purpose. As they went along he spoke at length about the tragedy which had occurred and his grief for his stepbrother.

"Rabbi," he cried in a firm voice, "believe me, if it were within my power to dig out this money from the depths of the abyss, I would wear myself to death trying to do so. Rabbi," Reuven added, "Rabbi, may I suffer the curses of the *Tochaha** which are read in synagogue this Sabbath fall upon me if I am guilty in this matter."

The rabbi was shocked and said, "These days we do not raise up our right hand to take an oath, even about the truth…"

* Deut. 28: 15–63.

Chapter nine

That Sabbath they read the section from Deuteronomy containing laws and commandments about the first fruits and the tithes, descriptions of the entry into the land of Canaan, and at the end the message of the prophet of Israel. In the middle were blessings for those who obey God's voice and after that rebukes and curses, terrible curses. Readers belonging to the older generation will know we did not call up men of the congregation for the reading of these middle chapters, but the beadle of the synagogue or a poor wandering Jew. Who would willingly stand before the clear lettering of the open parchment, for a passage which the Torah reader in fact dares not pronounce audibly and clearly but murmurs hastily, "Cursed be you in the city, cursed be you in the field, God will send anathema against you. God will turn the rain of your land into dust. You will build a house and not dwell in it." It once happened in a certain congregation as they opened the scroll of the Law on that Sabbath on which the "Rebuke" was due to be read that the people became terrified of the curses written down in those days and got up and fled precipitately from the house of God. The Book of the Covenant remained open on the table for more than an hour. God saw the insult put upon his

Torah and in anger sent fire against that city so that it all went up in flames. This matter is recorded in an ancient chronicle.

Were I living at the time of the Giving of the Torah, I would have said to the chief of the prophets, "Moses, Moses! How can you set down curses and imprecations in the Book of Testimony, seeing that in the second Torah, the Oral Law, it states that a curse of a sage comes true even if uttered to be fulfilled only upon certain conditions?" But let us stop reflecting on past generations and return to the context of our story.

They say that some kind of compromise was reached between Reuven and the owners of the forest who were claiming from him. They did not want to close down this new outlet for their goods, and devised a plan for continuing the timber business in that place. They renounced half the loss completely, whereas the second half would be made good in gradual payments over a number of years. From that time onward purchases would be two-thirds cash and only one-third in credit. I don't know the exact details.

Immediately after the settlement, Reuven began to build himself a residence. At first he thought of buying a courtyard not far from his parent's place. However, he thought the matter over, and rented from the town ruler a large plot near the gate which had up till then been unclaimed. They began to level the site. They laid down a foundation of hewn stones and erected a wooden building on it. "Uncircumcised" experts and builders worked energetically at the task and Reuven supervised the labor. Toward evening, the pupils of the religious schools used to gather there to spend their free time playing about on the materials piled up for the building. On the Sabbath, their parents too would stroll out to see the portion of the structure which had already been completed and to offer their criticism. They would reckon out how much the completed building would cost Reuven.

Eventually the project approached completion. They covered the room with red tiles and constructed chimneys of burnt brick. They worked for half a year erecting the house. Stone steps led up to a broad entrance in the middle on each side of which were three windows. The lintel of the door and the windows were painted white while the shutters of the windows and the door were green. The foundations of the house were black, but the lines between each row of stones could still be discerned. The whole building gave the impression of having been carefully planned from the beginning. Inside the house they set up square stoves. The floors in all the rooms were made of boards planed by carpenters, while the walls and ceilings were white-washed. Reuven supervised every detail and took great trouble to beautify the house. Something he had longed for over so many years was now becoming a reality before his very eyes. He could already envisage setting up the furniture, with the cupboards, the beds, the tables and the chairs all occupying their proper places. He had also decided to buy an open bookcase for the drawing room like the one he had seen at his uncle's place in the county town. He would no longer share an apartment, but would live in his own residence on his own estate and inheritance. God should only be kind to him. He did not know that on High there are two authorities...

Reuven fenced his estate around and at one corner he built a cowshed and a wood store. He dug out a pit for a cellar. It is said that he even thought about digging his own well in his yard. Anybody who knows the difficult life in the small hamlets, where no water is laid on at all and how every house and family is dependent on the grace of the water carrier who sells this gift of nature bucket by bucket, will understand the desire of this new householder.

Chapter ten

One day Reuven left in the morning for a village not far from his town to arrange his business with a certain nobleman and intended to return home toward evening. When the night was already fairly well advanced and he had not arrived, his wife Sara began to worry. She kept looking out of the window and pricking up her ears at the sound of every vehicle that passed by. Why is he so late? The children were already sound asleep in their beds. The lamp had been broken and only a dim light emanated from a tallow candle flickering on the table. Her heart throbbed. Would Reuven stay overnight with the village squire? He would not defile himself with their delicacies…The matter Reuven had to discuss was neither complicated nor difficult. It should have been settled in a few hours. She arose, opened the front door of the house and went down the few steps. The streets were quiet, most of the inhabitants of the town were already asleep. The night was still, the sky bewitched. If one were to split the universe in twain, tongues of fire would come up from the abyss and consume the whole of creation. Sara had now returned to her room. The clock hanging on the wall chimed the hour of eleven; Reuven was still not back. What could have happened to him this time to make him stay over in the village when in the morning he had not intended to do so? She sat in an armchair, waiting a further hour for her husband, then she undressed and went to bed. The tallow candle burned itself out.

In the depth of the night, the Angel of Dreams came and took the sleeping woman by the locks of her hair to a certain great forest on the King's Highway which leads from that town to the county seat. It left her there alone. She did not try to go very far on foot; she was tired for an invisible heavy stone weighed down on her heart. She heard horses neighing and suddenly the sound was stilled…A great coal fell down from the sky. It had eyes and a tongue and consumed all the grass and vegetation round about. In the timberyard, stacks came apart and board began to quarrel with board and beam with beam. Her husband Reuven was riding on a long plank, dressed in the skin of a wolf with its fur outward. She approached him and called but behold darkness hid him. She was standing in the cemetery; she saw row upon row of dumb tombstones and an inner trembling cut into her flesh as though with a knife. She had never thought about the Angels of Wrath and this time she saw their striking weapons thrust right down into the earth…She began to sweat, cried aloud in her great terror and awoke. There was a long tear the whole length of her nightgown, from top to bottom. It was a new garment and had been whole earlier that evening. Who had stretched out his hand against her, who had touched her? This puzzles me and I do not know the answer even today…

Chapter eleven

It was a hot midsummer's day, the sun blazed high in the sky, sending its beams in all directions. Drought and a terrible shortage of water afflicted everyone. Ants came out of their holes, running madly hither and thither, grasshoppers were flying about a yard high. In the pastures, the cattle lay sprawling and rubbing themselves while the lambs were skipping about, seeking cool grass and moisture. Mosquitoes were zooming about in mad intoxication. Tiny insects were buzzing in the air by their thousands and tens of thousands, soaring up and circling round without any purpose or object recognizable to human beings.

The blacksmith and ironworker stood sweating, fixing locks onto the doors of the rooms. Reuven, clad in a thin jacket, was standing next to him and explaining something to him, while he was rattling and fidgeting with a bunch of keys he held in his hand. Suddenly he felt a peculiar itching in his neck. He touched it with his hand a few times. Had a hornet bitten him? He felt a kind of pain. He took his handkerchief out of his pocket, moistened its corner with his mouth and placed it over the place where it itched. When he was a youngster at the religious school, during the early part of the month of Av, they used to learn legends from the tractate *Gittin* in the section of torts. The Talmud had spoken about a certain kind of mosquito which entered into the nostrils of the destroyer of the Temple for his heart had grown haughty.

He went back to his dwelling to drink tea and between each cup, he felt at his neck which was now starting to swell. His wife got up from her seat, looked at the place of the sting and said to her husband, "I can see a kind of inflammation there."

She took the yolk of an egg, mixed it with salt and secured it with a piece of cloth to the inflamed spot. It flared up even more. Reuven tore the bandage off violently and cried, "The remedy is doing more harm than good."

In the town there was neither a doctor nor an apothecary. A certain neighbor who had some skill came into the room and examined the place where it hurt. A kind of swollen black spot could be seen. He advised an immediate visit to the county town. They hired a post carriage and that day Reuven and his wife traveled to the city. All the way he felt a severe pain in his neck which had become very swollen. When they reached their destination they went to their uncle's house. They called a doctor at once and he only shook his head at what he saw. He jotted down on a pad some kind of prescription to calm the patient. When he left the room he said to the uncle who asked him what was the matter, "He must have an operation on his neck without delay."

The next morning Reuven's uncle traveled with him to Odessa in order to have specialists operate there on his sick kinsman. Reuven's wife returned home to look after the children. The whole affair took place very quickly and hastily, and when he parted from his wife he said to her, "Don't worry, silly. Get everything ready for the dedication of our home. In a week's time I shall be back and well."

She felt a choking sensation in her throat. Who could tell her then that she would never see him alive again?

There in the great bustling metropolis, Reuven, the timber merchant, died quietly three days after the operation. In the prime of life he was laid to rest in the Jewish cemetery. There was not even time to tell the astonished, amazed man to make his will. Mourning and broken-hearted, the uncle returned to his city. He could not believe that the Angel of Death would take the sickle in his hand and violently cut off this living tree. The beautiful Sara was left a widow without any inner preparation. Only a few days previously she had a husband who ate and drank with her and cherished her. Now she was sitting at the table with her orphan children while he who had begotten them and won a livelihood for them was laid away in a distant place in six feet of earth. When they erected his tombstone who would read it? They only said *kaddish* for twelve months and after that just once a year. The son was quarreling with his cheeky sister and there was no father to control them. Tears streamed down from her eyes and fell into the bowl before her. Faithful guardian! Come down from Your throne of glory and see how You deal with Your creatures.

My story is not yet ended.

Chapter twelve

One bright morning a heavily laden wagon drew up at the only inn in the city. A rather bizarre and powerfully built man, very well dressed, descended. His intention was to stay over for a few days and to find a room in which to lodge. When he entered the chamber which they prepared for him, he decided to rest from the fatigue of the journey and he closed the door firmly. The innkeeper knocked twice without avail. He had wanted to talk to his guest and to find out what sort of man he was, as was his custom. No one opened up. Later on the guest called one of the servants and asked him for soap, water, and towel. The door again closed fast. The guest removed his clothes, took off his shirt, washed and dried himself. He combed his hair and beard, changed his clothes and put on new shoes. It was clear from his actions that he had come on an important mission. He took a mirror out of its case and looked at himself in it with approval. He smoothed his beard again, stroked his moustache and changed his hat. What was his purpose, and what was he about?

He said his prayers very perfunctorily in order to be quit of his obligations. He did not even rise from his seat for the Eighteen Benedictions which are to be recited while standing. They then brought him hot tea, white bread and sugar and he sat down at the table to eat his breakfast. He had traveled quite a number of miles to get there and had got up in the middle of the night to begin his journey. If the innkeeper came into the room, should he ask him about the woman or should he refrain? He took a lead pencil from his pocket and began to jot down various figures concerned with his capital and resources. He was once more a widower and had a child of five years. His head dropped down on his hand and he fell into a doze. No! he just closed his eyes. Beams of blue, mixed with red flecks and pinpointed with shining lights swam before his mind's eye. When he raised his head a man with a bent body and a straggly beard was standing opposite the table and saying, "I am the keeper of this inn. You must be tired. You have journeyed a long way. Are you coming here to look for a suitable match for your son or to buy timber?..."

"Leave me alone, now," said the guest, "and come back later."

"But what is your name, sir, and where are you from?"

"They call me Naftali and I come from the town of Shichor."

"Good," said the innkeeper, "but I want to give you one strong piece of advice. Don't take anyone else's advice except mine...people here are swindlers...You can rely on me, do you understand?"

The guest got up after the innkeeper had left the room, put on an overcoat which in his own city he only wore on the Sabbath. He took a handsome walkingstick in his hand and went out. Hens were pecking at the garbage. He almost trod on some horse manure. A barefoot lad picked up a stone from the ground and threw it at a barking dog. He passed through the market place where a number of shops were open. From all sides people called him to buy something. He ignored them and walked straight on. In one street he met a girl of about twelve carrying a jug of milk and asked her where Sara, the wife of Reuven lived.

"She is already living in the new house."

"Where is the new house?"

"By the city gate."

The guest wended his way there, his heart pounding within him. He was already nearing forty, but his inner emotions were those of a young man. In a fury of thought he stood for a few moments by the steps which led up to the entrance. He would go up and quietly open the door. In small villages there is no bell or anything like it, and it is not the custom to knock at the entrance. The door from the small corridor to the first room was open. There by the window sat the young widow, dressed in a house gown and a three cornered white kerchief on her head. Her hair shone; she was sitting occupied with a long piece of knitting. She raised her head and asked him what he wanted. The moon shone in the room though it was broad daylight. The eyes of the stranger stared straight at her.

"If you will allow me, Sara, I shall sit down and talk."

He sat down on a chair at a distance from the mistress of the house. Sara was startled at the entrance of this guest. With one hand she adjusted the kerchief on her head, and the action enhanced her charm. Outside somebody could be heard calling and she thought it was her daughter. She got up and opened the window. This was the first time that he had seen the nobility of her stature at such close quarters. She closed the window again, sat down in her place and resumed her knitting. Her fingers moved gracefully.

"Sara," he began the conversation, leaning on his stick and making a desperate effort to overcome his excitement and speak calmly. "Sara, I wanted to send you a matchmaker. Why are you so shocked and gaze at me so strangely? It's the way of the world. It is a sin that a young woman like you should sit in loneliness for the whole of her life. Your husband, Reuven, was a very industrious man. So I have heard, but he is no longer alive and life has to go on."

"No, no," cried the startled woman. "Don't talk to me like this, go away from here. Please, go away!"

"Sara," added the stranger, moving his stick from his right hand to his left, "I am telling you this would be stupidity on your part. Your children need a father to take care of them, and what about you yourself? Just imagine if you were to fall ill, who would sit beside your bed? A woman without someone near her is like a summer without the sun. You look at me. Do you know who I am or what is in my heart? I am—let me tell you…" He brought his chair a little nearer to her. "I am as innocent as a child. The woman who will enter into marriage with me will be a lucky woman. I can pull a tree out by its roots to satisfy my wife's whim. I will carry you around on my arms and I will fulfill your every fancy without giving it a second thought."

Sara put down the wool and the needles in her lap and looked in astonishment at the speaker. She had never heard talk like this in all her life. What brought the footsteps of this man to the house of a woman who had never heard of him until that moment. Wretchedness of heart! What if Reuven were to enter the room suddenly now and see this man sitting next to her. Her lips moved, a shadow of grief came over her face, but he could not turn his eyes away from this picture of beauty.

Suddenly he jumped up from his chair and cried out, "Sara, I love you. I have loved you for many years now; since I saw you for the first time I have loved you with all my heart. Your eyes are doves, your neck is like a tower, you are wholly beautiful, my heart is all yours, Sara!"

These expressions had come to him from the Song of Songs, but only now did he really understand what they meant. He took hold of her two trembling hands and said, "Look straight at me and see what is in my burning heart. Without you life is not life, I will go down to my grave if you drive me away. Have pity, Sara, on a man who loves you and stands before you like a child, seeking the nearness of his mother. Be my wife, be my sister, be my daughter."

She tried to free her hands from the speaker, "Leave me alone," she cried, "leave me alone."

"No," he exclaimed loudly, "I shall never leave you alone. I'll lift you up in my arms and fly away with you for two miles. You just don't know how strong I am and what I am capable of doing. You don't know what you mean to me. No," he added and stamped his foot—his stick had already fallen out his hand and lay on the floor—"If you drive me away, I shall crawl under the bed, I shall sleep in the kitchen and be your servant and lick bones."

He took hold of his stick and said, "See this stick? If you refuse and send me away from you, I shall smash it on my own head and beat out my brains. No, I will drown myself in the river; but that is not all I shall do, I will seize you by sheer force."

In the flood of his words, he sometimes addressed her by the formal "you" and sometimes by the more intimate "thou."

"I'll drown with you in the depths of the ocean. Not even death shall divide us one from the other."

Perspiration streamed down from his forehead. He took his handkerchief from his pocket, wiped off the sweat and kept his eyes unblinkingly on her changing features. He saw that his words were making an impression. He started counting, one two, one two three, three four, four five. The ball of wool fell off Sara's lap and rolled away. Naftali bent down, picked it up and placed it back on her knees. Were he not afraid that she would cry out then…His whole body trembled. He would fall on her neck and kiss her even if she repulsed him and sent him away. She got up and said, "Leave me today, I'll think about the matter further."

Tears of joy rolled down from the eyes of this forty-year-old man.

"You know my name, I am Naftali from the town of Shichor. I am a sack merchant…I am well off…"

Chapter thirteen

An hour after this man of strange speech left, Sara's two children, her eldest child a boy of nine and a girl of seven, who had been playing outside, came in from the street. They were handsome children and anybody would have known that they were brother and sister. The boy started telling his mother about a bridge which he and his friends had made out of sand and how the stupid Yerahmiel had trampled on it and broken it down. The little girl put her hand over her mouth and laughed. Sweet innocent; she did not know what was shortly about to happen.

"Are you hungry my little ones?"

The mother got up, straightened one of the window curtains, went to the kitchen, brought the children white cheese, bread, and two glasses of milk and put it all down on the table. The boy snatched a piece of bread and began to eat, greedily, walking about the room as he did so. The sister sat down and sipped. Suddenly she jumped from her place and ran out of the room. Her brother took his cup and stood it on hers; it slipped out of his hand and the milk spilt on the table and over the floor.

"Hooligan!" called his mother, "If your father were alive, he would punish you for your naughtiness."

A shadow passed over her face as she mentioned her husband's name...

The sun was setting, the rumble of cartwheels passing in the street was heard, a neighbor knocked on the window and said, "Sara, is my boy Yerahmiel with your children?"

"No!" answered Sara.

A black cat, which had been sleeping till then on the couch, woke up and jumped from his place. Sara took a cloth and wiped the table and the floor. She opened the window and squeezed it out. She trimmed the nightlight. A sigh welled up from the depths of her heart.

With great difficulty and with much persuasion, she got the children into the bedroom to sleep. She removed their shoes and their clothes and arranged everything on the chairs, one on this side and one on that. The boy recited his night prayers, nor was the girl free of this duty. Who can measure a mother's love when she sees her children whom she has carried in her bosom, has nurtured and reared, lying on their beds. She kissed the little girl and then her eldest child, who raised his head and asked, "Mummy, are the stars in the sky also angels?"

Sara returned to the room where she had been before, sat down on the couch and closed her eyes. The cat climbed up and sat in its corner. There is no more than a span between one living thing and another. The three-cornered kerchief had slipped from her head. She put her hand on her naked arm, under the broad sleeve and pressed her breasts. She was a lonely Jewish widow. During the week there was plenty to do, taking care of the house and shopping, but on holidays and Sabbaths, a kind of emptiness is felt in the whole wide world, although they sometimes go for a walk or the children sit at the table and talk. Her mother used to pray every morning, she still had her prayer book, but she could not understand the letters. God sits up above beyond the planets and no man can understand His ways.

She rose and lit the lamp. When her husband Reuven was alive, she had got into the secret habit of not covering her head at night when no strange man was in the room. She felt a certain accession of strength in her uncovered hair. She walked back and forth in the room like someone seeking the answer to a riddle...She sat down by the table and rested her head on her hands. Her sleeves were rolled back, her white arms looking like two rays of light...

After three days the match was arranged between her and Naftali the Bold, although the matter still seemed rather strange to her. Some of her neighbors tried to warn her, but without avail. It was arranged that the bridegroom would settle in the town, would give up his sack business and take over the trade in timber and boards. He would bring his son there, so that there would be three children in the house.

Chapter fourteen

There is a story of ancient times. The wife of a prince who had been killed was married to his brother although she had born a child to the dead man. The second husband also died without leaving any children. The third brother, the king, sent and took her to wife and brought his sister-in-law to his palace in Jerusalem. The woman dreamed that her first husband was standing in front of her. She wanted to embrace him, but he repulsed her saying, "Leave me alone."

This happened in the days of the Second Temple, when tyrannical kings ruled in Israel. The same sort of thing happened in an entirely different period. A certain famous rabbi in the Diaspora, one of the great Hasidim, died as a young man. A certain rabbi sent to pay court to his widow. The son of the dead man dreamed that he saw a great palace where his father was standing swathed in his shroud, holding on by both hands to the roof of the citadel and crying aloud, "Who is this and what sort of person is this who has presumed to enter my palace?"

If the reader is not inclined to believe the conclusion of this story of mine, let him take these two visions to heart....

The modest preparation for the wedding began. The marriage of a widower to a widow is not an event which concerns the whole congregation. They do not set up the bridal canopy under the open sky, but in a room. The bridegroom makes the marriage declaration to the bride, they read the marriage deed and after that a few people sit down for the feast. The whole matter may take two or three hours at the most. Then the few guests leave the house and the two parties, who up till now had been strangers to one another—this one from here and that one came from there—are thenceforward bound together in contract and in union which they cannot dissolve, except by means of a bill of divorcement or the death of one of them.

This was the sort of wedding which Naftali the Bold, from the town of Shichor, and the young widow, Sara, celebrated in her new house. For a few days they sent the children away to the uncle in the county town. The orphan child of Naftali the Bold was left behind in Shichor, with an aunt. Their intention was to bring them back after a fortnight. The bridegroom, needless to say, was quite satisfied with all these arrangements, but the bride in her silk dress, which gave her beauty a kind of solemnity, was like one in a state of shock. That day she had fasted to afflict her soul and until an hour before the ceremony had closeted herself in her room and wept quietly. Only a poet can look into the heart of a woman!

Ten men and seven women sat at the meal set out on two tables, the men and women sitting separately. The food was good and bottles of wine were provided. The ritual slaughterer drank a glass more than he needed and began to sing in a croaking voice. The rabbi of the town pronounced the wedding benedictions. Reuven's stepmother, who had already been twice widowed, stayed with the bride that night and the next as a kind of chaperone.

Chapter fifteen

The night of the ritual immersion arrived. Sara observed the Jewish custom and toward evening she went secretly by a roundabout way to the bath house to purify herself. She carried a bundle of fresh white linen under her arm and wore a Turkish kerchief bound round her head. The bath attendant received her with great courtesy—does not a bride pay three times as much as other women?—and the superintendent stood beside her, to supervise the carrying out of the religious laws. This time she stemmed her usual flow of words. The square bath house was built of stones like a fortress. Inside, the floor was covered with boards which had turned black from age and from perspiration. It had square windows which were broad on the inside and narrow on the outside. It was hot enough in the bath house even when the great stoves were not burning. A small oil lamp hanging from the roof gave a dim light only in its own corner. Right next to the ritual bath which one approached by steps, was another small dripping candle. The woman who was to be immersed removed her garments one by one and spread them on a wooden stand. On a chair nearby was the clean linen which she had brought. She sat on one of the shelves where the Sabbath observers have their steam bath in the evening and washed all her body in a small bath full of water. Deep in thought she combed her hair. The official cut her nails and removed anything from her person, making sure that nothing would be left to form any impediment to total immersion...

Sara got down from the shelf and took off her undergarment; a light like moonlight filled the whole bath house. Even the attendant, who stood beside her and was used to such things, was amazed at this symbol of beauty and at the perfection of her body. Primeval Eve had stood thus naked in the days before sin when she had not yet sewn a fig leaf for herself. Her two breasts had an aura of solemn beauty. It is not surprising that at that time the serpent looked into the far reaches of Paradise and envied Adam.

She walked down the steps and entered the water. She praised God, the King of the Universe, and immersed herself in the ritual bath three times, then dried herself. He who dwells in eternity gave the daughters of Israel three commandments; the ritual bath, the separation of the loaf and the kindling of the lights. It was the night of the new moon, a holy festival for the tribes of Jeshurun, which long before the gift of the Sabbath day, and even today, is still the portion of woman. She put on her new white undergarments, her dress and her shoes, paid the woman handsomely, veiled herself and, carrying her bundle, left the bath house. The stars shone brightly overhead, the world was resting from the toil of the day.

She walked like one in a dream, no dog snarled at her, she encountered nothing, she went along a gentile street which separates the Jewish quarter from the bath house and found herself in a broad field which was strange to her. She had the feeling that she had lost her way, she turned her face round like one who seeks something. Suddenly a strong hand seized her from behind, her kerchief slipped off her head and she was floating on air. She was standing on a small hillock in quaking fear. A man was confronting her; he was nine inches taller than Reuven. His hands were long and thin. Reuven, her husband, had come up from the dead and wanted to rebuke her for becoming another man's...Every bone in her body turned to water. Her tongue clung to her palate and she could not manage to utter the slightest sound....

Chapter sixteen

There are others who maintain that it was not on the way from the bath house to her home that the accident befell Sara and drove her out of her mind. They claim that it was only after she had got into bed that the vision came to terrify her. She had gone home from the ritual bath, had removed her kerchief from her head and placed her bundle next to the linen set aside for the wash. She had got up and prepared supper for herself and her new husband. He sat at the head of the table and looked at his shy beloved. He chewed the roast meat and found its taste pleasant while she ate sparingly. He stretched out his left hand and rested it on her neck. He put down the piece of meat he had in his hand and tried to raise Sara's head and look into her eyes. She hurriedly got up from the table, escaped from him to her room and did not come out from it again. The loving husband was afraid that she would lock her door from inside. After a few moments he got up and quietly tested the lock to the bedroom. The door opened and he saw his bride already lying on her bed. He went back to the dining room, walking around twirling his moustache and quietly singing snatches of music to himself. He undressed and put his clothes on a chair, blew out the candle and went in his shirt to his beloved's room. The window shutter was darkening the room. He lifted the latch which held it alongside the wall and pushed the shutter outward. By the light of the moon, he feasted his eyes on the beauty of his princess.

The thoughts of the woman on the bed were somber. The whole affair was a dark riddle to her. It was as though she were knowing a man for the first time. She lay on her back covered with a white sheet, gazing at the ceiling like one searching for something far off. There was no one she could call and no one who could help. A man burning with fire was standing only a foot or so away from her. Suddenly a shadow began to move in the middle of the ceiling and it looked like a bowl from which the head of a man gradually protruded. The head of her husband Reuven appeared, his eyes disseminating terror...She jumped off the bed with a shriek, sprang to the window, thrusting against it with such force that the glass broke and the pieces fell with a light tinkling onto the floor. She leaped outside. The whole thing took a few minutes. Naftali remained standing in the middle of the room, terrified and stunned by what he had seen.

The bed was really empty, only a certain warmth of her body remained there. Naftali ran to the window, stuck his head out and shouted, "Sara, Sara."

There was no answer. He dressed himself hastily and ran outside. He went around the house; came back and felt in the bed; nobody, no hands and feet, no head! Had she not just lain here shining with the radiance of her flesh and breathing? He had been deceived, how he had been deceived at the height of the fulfillment of his passion! He had hoped to reach the peaks of ecstasy and now sudden tragedy tore at his body as though with a pincers. He left the house again and went outside to search for his beloved and beautiful wife. There was absolutely no trace of her. Where had the fawn fled when she jumped out of the room? He thought about rousing the neighbors from their sleep and alarming them by his shout. He darted this way and that in the street. He searched round the whole house again. He looked in the yard; he looked in the kitchen, again he searched Sara's bed. Perhaps he had been deceived by a dream. He lit a candle and placed it on the floor. Only an hour ago his beloved had lain in this room and now she had disappeared from his side. She was his now, his possession, the property of his body. From the time he had married her, he had not kissed her, had not placed his mouth upon hers, had not held her in his arms. He had hoped to celebrate a feast of passion. He would put both his hands upon her, he was going to hold her with both his hands and almost squeeze the life out of her until body had consummated its union with body. All of his past until that moment, the women he had possessed, one after the other, were nothing but empty and transient shadows. You wind a kerchief around your hand and afterward take it off and put it down and it was as though you had never held a kerchief. He had craved and longed for Sara a long time, for this lovely body even when he was embracing another woman. She and only she was the one thing he wanted in life. Let them bring back his beautiful wife to her home, let him only hold her in the silence of this one night and tomorrow he was prepared to die. Let him embrace her just once; after that they could chop off his head and the dogs could lick his blood.

Naftali the Bold quenched the light, left the house again and sought for the lost one in every street and in every corner of the city. He was exhausted in every limb. He sat down on the steps of the synagogue which was also silent and forsaken, put his face in both his hands and wept like a child.

It was very early the next morning that the report spread through the city that Sara had disappeared the previous night. She had left her room and was not to be found. It was a mystery. A number of men, even gentiles from the nearby village and two of the government policemen spread far and wide to look for her. All in vain. All day long groups of men stood in the streets and talked about the completely unprecedented incident. They could not even remotely guess why and for what reason this young woman could have fled and what had happened to her the night before. Reuven's stepmother went around to the bathhouse to ask about her. The wife of the bath keeper could not solve the riddle.

"The bride came and immersed herself like all women do, there seemed to be nothing wrong, except that she kept quiet and did not talk."

After two days and two nights, they found the unhappy woman sitting on a stump of a tree in the forest some miles away from the city. She was clad only in her petticoat. Her face was burnt by the sun. She had gone out of her mind....

Translated by A.S. Super

From a Place of Thunder

A long time has elapsed since I first attempted to record the life story of the man who serves as the protagonist of this tale. His life fascinated me, but I never managed to recreate the characters nor connect the events as I saw them in my mind's eye and conceived them in my imagination. I would write two or three sheets and then stop short. The town of Loton, the locale of these events, was not my birth place. When I was very young, I came there with my parents from a far-off region—I scarcely knew the stories of Genesis in those days—and I left Loton when I was no longer a lad. I, too, had my struggles in life and was bitten by the serpent of poetry and of sin. It is the story of an ancient sin that I am about to relate.

The Owner of the Mill

Shlomo the Red was the richest man in Loton and lorded it over the city. He lived near the main gate in a palatial dwelling with a dozen or more windows opening onto the street and shady trees in front. He used to travel about in a carriage, harnessed to prancing stallions, and a footman always accompanied him to do his bidding. Shlomo was a tall man with a red neck and ruddy complexion. His beard was red also and although it had now become flecked with gray, the original color was still visible. He was a taciturn man, controlled and deliberate in his actions. He wore his trousers tucked into high boots, a fur hat during winter and a coat of medium length. In synagogue, he stood beside the holy ark facing the wall because he had no love for the common herd.

It was he who was really the emissary for the congregation, rather than the man wrapped in a prayer shawl who stood contorting himself in front of the lectern.

The tribe of Israel possess a Torah and there are those among them who observe its commandments. In heaven, God takes note of the bad deeds as well as the good, but here upon earth only wealth holds sway. If you own ten thousand rubles in ready cash, you are a man of importance. If there are thirty thousand rubles in your treasury, you are a commanding officer of high rank. If your capital should be valued at one hundred thousand rubles, then you are semi-divine, possessing power, strength, dignity, honor and renown. To change the metaphor, there is a pair of scales, on one side of which is placed learning, rabbinical expertise, wisdom, understanding, observance of the commandments and good deeds. Standing there crowded together on the same side are the local rabbi, the ritual slaughterer, the religious teachers of the city and its cantors, all the householders, the wardens and even the passably wealthy men. On the other scale stands the rich man of the town. His eyes sometimes express anger and sometimes kindliness. Is not he the omnipotent one? Are not the keys of all the coffers of the world placed in his hands? If he wishes, he can be extravagant; if he prefers, he can be miserly. At a whim he signals to one of the congregation to approach and inclines his head to talk to him for a few minutes. If the spirit takes him he can terrorize or insult a man to the very depths of his being.

Shlomo the Red owned the large mill built beside the waterfall in Loton. In it flour was milled not merely for local needs, but also for distribution to distant places. Around the mill rose great barns, built of wood and stone in which sacks full of corn and wheat were stored in order, row upon row. Others contained the flour. From morning to evening, wagon upon wagon came to the compound from all the villages in a wide area round about Loton. Some would unload the produce of the fields and others would load up sacks of flour. Peasants and roustabouts always filled the entire area. Horses ate their fill from what was set before them, their coats speckled white from the flour. The mill wheels turned on their axles and the noise of their grinding could be heard above the roar of the water. The river was wide and flowed with a strong and powerful current, affording a source of power for human use. In the beginning was the earth and upon it were spread out the waters and afterward the sky's horizon became visible.

A large bridge spanned the stream from one side to the other, with rounded arches along its breadth in order to allow the water to flow freely between them. Shlomo was continually engaged in strengthening, shoring up and keeping the bridge in good order, and there were workmen specially assigned to this task of maintenance. It is said that once at the time of a great flood, when the river overflowed its banks and threatened to tear down by force the bridge planted in its midst, Shlomo himself took part in the battle with the surging waters, and inspired the crowds who had gathered from all sides with the courage to throw up a breastwork and prevent a breach.

Shlomo the Red also owned a faithful dog which was secured by a chain near the wide door leading to his courtyard. To keep a dog was certainly not a Jewish custom, and in fact he was not over-fond of religious observances. Nevertheless, once he bought a full case of ritual citrons still packed in wool. The reason for this is that one can never tell if they are whole and perfect or if a few have blemishes. His idea was that he would secure at least one perfect one. Even on weekdays he drank wine with his meals, ate fish in the evening and it was his custom to lean with his forehead on his hand between each course and think. He was living on earth, sometimes the world was full, sometimes it was just empty. Trees and men may aspire to lofty heights but around them there is, nevertheless, level ground and even a downward slope. His small wife was a sickly woman. When he married her (he was then working for the owner of an estate) she was healthy and he found her quite attractive. Now she would wander around the numerous large rooms of the house, her wealth only a burden to her. You lift up your eyes and you see a young maid coming into the room in the raw lusty vigor of her youth. She clears away dishes from the table, her strong arms shining like flashing metal. The planets whirl around in the firmament and everything is full of life. You have an urge to tear down the walls of the house which constrict you; to whistle to every living thing to come and join you.

This man owned more than a hundred and fifty thousand rubles. He had property and possessions, debts and promissory notes. He was unique in the town. The rest of the people crawled about like worms, earning a meager livelihood, adding one kopek to another kopek, one coin to another. After that they would spend what they had scraped together and they seemed to squeeze out blood from their fingers with every little item of expenditure. The genius is very lonely in his time, the poet is lonely in his muse and so is even the rich man in his wealth.

On summer nights when the life force rises up in the flesh at a time when every animal crouches in its den and every person has his bed, existence dreams its dream and even the Creator labors heavily to move the wheels of the cosmos. At that time, Shlomo the Red would get up, leave his palace, saddle his horse and go riding anywhere his fancy took him. The horse would gallop along like the wind, carrying the man who controlled it. He would tug at the reins, flick his leather whip in the air with a sharp crack. If he had known how to fire a rifle, he would have pressed the trigger. Pent up strength, forcibly repressed, hews out its own path.

Two Opposites

Shlomo the Red had two married sons: Chaim Yona and Daniel Silk. They were brothers born from the same father and mother, but how different they were from each other! Chaim Yona, the favorite son, lived in the right wing of his father's mansion. He had a tall, intelligent wife who took care of all household matters. She brought up her six daughters but also found leisure time to talk with her father-in-law when he visited her each evening. In her apartment there was a light, warm glow of friendliness and youth. Chaim Yona found himself almost superfluous there. He was a man of simple character and had practically no needs. His jacket always hung open and he changed his hat neither in summer nor winter. There was not the slightest trace of Sabbath in his soul. He sired his daughters, and dealt with inconsequential matters at the mill. When somebody met him, he had absolutely nothing to say. He had no desire to hear about anything that was going on, and his world was restricted to the limits of the town. If the sun rose in the morning and set in the evening, that was how it surely had to be. His fortune was reckoned to be about thirty thousand rubles. At Passover time, he used to contribute ten rubles to the fund for providing the poor with flour and he paid the rabbi one ruble for the legal fiction of selling his leaven. At festivals, he purchased the right to be called to the Reading of the Law because his father told him to do so. He, too, prayed on the eastern side of the synagogue. He himself, however, knew no spiritual life. His wife, Yocheved, had no affection in her heart for him at all. Why should she? He was a man of middle height and weak physique who ate his midday meal at the same table with her and her daughters. They all addressed him as "father." He answered every question and fulfilled whatever demands they made on him. But nothing seemed to touch him personally. There is hot, cold and lukewarm in the world. Such a large proportion of human souls are created out of mire and have no spiritual content nor enlargement of soul.

It was not difficult to understand why Chaim was the son closest to the heart of his father, the magnate. Shlomo loved his daughter-in-law, Yocheved, and found a kind of refuge in her company. Six girls all growing up together, some full of restlessness, some of a quiet disposition, were very much like the fruit of a tree, which warms the heart of the onlooker. However, there was another reason which was plain to all. Shlomo the Red did not love his second son, Daniel, and felt a certain antipathy to him throughout his life.

Two years after his wedding, Daniel left his father's house and selected an old mansion which a Polish nobleman, the previous owner of the mill, had erected not far from the river bank. There were no Jewish dwellings in the vicinity of this mansion, only some stone houses for the workers with a few peasants dwelling there. Between these small properties and the town itself there was a wide open stretch, one side of which was set apart for the mayor's residence. It was next door to the magnate. He was the "second" ruler in Loton and the sole administrator of the great estates belonging to the royal city. The second side of the open space was set aside for the residence of the local priest. The Jews have an ancestral religion and so have the Christian serfs. The former have a rabbi and the latter have a priest. The rabbi is a righteous teacher and the priest a worshipper of "idolatry." The rabbi observes the commandments, teaches the Torah and lives frugally. The priest eats and drinks voraciously and is never far from the evil inclination, although his wide coat and his long hair may make him appear a dignitary among his own people. In the time of Anav and Elijah, the priests of Baal must have presented a similar picture.

Shlomo's son, Daniel, was a man of middle height, with handsome features and with a clear complexion. When he walked, his movements suggested a certain nobility. He was a man of restraint although he was capable at times of inner turmoil. He was responsible for the record books and ledgers of the mill and its warehouses, but although he recorded and totaled daily all the expenses and the many receipts, noting them down in their various categories, he paid very little attention to normal outside happenings. On the contrary, his spirit longed for other things. Daniel was the one man in the city who wore spotless white shirts over his undergarments, the shining whiteness affording him a certain spiritual satisfaction. The Polish mansion contained a great salon floored with smooth boards painted black. Along the length and breadth of the room white curtains hung on the walls and the table which stood in the middle of the room was made of dark wood left in its natural state.

In this salon there was a glass-fronted bookcase in which could be seen folios of the Babylonian Talmud, bound in red leather. In his youth, Daniel had studied with a great rabbinic scholar and he retained a reverence for the *tannaim* and *amoraim* who lived at the time of the earlier generations. These had transmitted to the children of Israel a heritage of wisdom deep as the ocean and a knowledge of great breadth. Numerous indeed were the interpreters and commentators of these sages' words, and they themselves were men of profound wisdom and understanding, saintly and ascetic.

Every day Daniel immersed himself in the ritual bath, after which he went home, drank a flask of milk and engaged in private prayer in the room adjoining the salon which I have mentioned. God dwelt in His heaven, riding upon the heights. He had speech only with the angels of destruction and with high and transcendent souls. Those who dwelt below could do no more than look at the prayer book and recite with humble hearts the morning prayer, the hymns and praises and all those passages concerning the sacrifices which the sages had ordained. Even the latter had an outer and inner meaning, the letter and the spirit dictated by the mystic unity. Some words had to be recited aloud, some very loudly indeed, while there were others which were heard only in the echoes of the heart. Here you stand wrapped in your prayer shawl, with the silver shawl-band over your head, your face toward the wall, while you hold discourse with the Creator. You proclaim His Unity and sanctify His holiness. You acknowledge His sovereignty each time you pray—although He is eternally the King of Kings.

Daniel's wife, Batya, was really well-born, coming from an honorable and wealthy family, well known even in Austria. Daniel himself had once journeyed to the city of Brody at the time when the *tzaddik** of Talna had gone into exile there. From that time onward, he had continued to discipline himself according to the teacher's rule. In Austria there were many Jewish families engaged in commerce, but also working, praying and studying. They rested on the Sabbath day and had their rabbis, their ritual slaughterers and other religious officials. However, their outlook was quite different from that of the Jews under Russian rule...From Brody to Lemberg was only one day's journey and from Lemberg to Vienna one more day. It was reckoned that the number of Jews in these two cities alone was more than half that of the Hebrews in the exodus from Egypt. The sons of Abraham had been in exile from the day that it had been decreed "and they shall serve them and they shall afflict them." The Messiah sits and waits at the gates of Rome, according to a talmudic legend to be found in one of the leather-bound folios which stood in a row in Daniel's bookcase.

Batya gave charity secretly despite the fact that her residence was far from the city and its poverty-stricken streets. She may not have needed to reckon the value of money, but she did understand what poverty meant, when members of a household were in need of food and clothing. She was a devoted mother to her children—she had one boy and two girls. She bathed them on the eve of Sabbath and was very meticulous about the cleanliness of the rooms in her

* A hasidic leader of saintly qualities. Hasidism is a popular religious Jewish movement founded in the eighteenth century.

house. She did not scold her maid servants and they were devoted to her. She honored her husband, but did not talk to him very much. Toward evening she would sit by the window and gaze steadily at the broad sweep of the river. On the altar of her heart there were no offerings of total devotion, but she did have the gift of evoking a constant, quiet love. Not for her the experience of being forcibly carried off on the steed of a royal knight to gallop far away over hill and mountain. She had never read any folktales. She knew the prayers which were current in the woman's prayer book, *Korban Mincha*. Nevertheless, she herself was spiritually akin to one of the heroines in the stories of her people...

In quiet beauty Batya looked to the ways of her household. Daniel, her husband, cherished her and felt a certain outpouring of love and nearness to her, but in the deep recesses of his soul he did not idealize her image. His father, Shlomo the Red, visited them only once or twice a year, stayed only a brief while like a guest, never establishing close ties with his grandchildren. Two worlds meet together; one a relic of ancient tyranny, the other the beginning of spiritual journeyings.

The Armor Bearers

I must now mention Shlomo the Red's "armor bearers," Abba Yeruham, the rich man's neighbor on the one hand, and Shmuel Menahem, his secretary on the other.

Abba Yeruham was a portly man with small eyes, a burgher who had lost his property some years back. He no longer dabbled in business, but concerned himself with both sacred and secular matters, although only casually, as it were. He no longer really desired to acquire wealth, nor secure a substantial status in the town nor consolidate his position there. He had married off his sons and obtained husbands for his two daughters. His wife had died at about the age of fifty, and he had married again—a relative who was a spinster some thirty years old. A sturdy, unfeeling woman with no small measure of energy, who built defenses against the intrusion of poverty into her domain…

Shlomo, the magnate, would on occasion make loans to his neighbor. He often gave him sums of money, and would instruct his servants to offload sacks of flour next door without presenting an account. If the Lord has bountifully blessed you and your household, the house of your neighbor should not be empty. Your son, descended from your loins, must obviously be your first heir; next come your relations, then your neighbors—they also have some place in the orbit of your life. Shlomo found it necessary now and then to open the small gate in the fence which separated his yard from that of his neighbor, and sit awhile on a felled tree trunk chatting with Abba. He would enquire about his horse, his cow, converse on the weather, the timeliness of the rains, the sowing of the soil. Abba had a feeling for the ways of nature. He was a townsman with something of the spirit of a rustic. Indeed, his house was practically the last one in the street beyond which the wings of the wide world spread out. Inside the town, houses crowded together, their windows overlooking each other. It was different at the edge of the village. There everything opened out freely. On weekdays one did not leave the confines of the city unless starting on a journey. But on leisure days and festivals, one really sensed the fragrance of leisure. One would stroll with a friend or neighbor, leaving human habitation far behind, and roam companionably between broad meadows of wheat or corn. The Ukraine is a mighty land, blessed by the ruler of the universe with a generous and bountiful hand.

Shmuel Menahem also lived at the end of a street that ran parallel to that of the magnate. Ten houses beyond that of Shmuel rose up the new prayer house of the town's Hasidim. It was a storey and a half high, roofed with sheets of metal, painted green. You could skirt Shmuel's house, turn left, and would come upon a windmill with broken vanes standing desolate in the distance. Go past the piece of ground where the windmill stands, turn right, and a small peasant's village begins where dogs can be heard barking night and day. Shmuel, with his brown, handsome beard, was an important man in the town. He was interested in everyday affairs, but was also knowledgeable in the world at large. He had a relative in the county town who was rumored to delve into Mendelssohn's commentary on the Pentateuch, but he himself refrained from reaping in forbidden fields, and was known to pray not only in obedience to conventional rule, but even with some devotion and exaltation. Man stands up and smoothes his beard, and the God of prayer dwells in starry heights, while bestowing sustenance and life on the dwellers below.

Shmuel was an excellent penman who could draw up deeds

and quittances. He was meticulous in the straightness of his lines and the shaping of his letters. He wrote the Russian addresses on the envelopes without error. He was indeed an all-round man. He had a clear comprehension of commercial legal matters. If there was a dispute between two parties which was to come up for adjudication before the civil courts, or for arbitration, or in front of the rabbi of the town according to the law of the Torah, Shmuel could foretell the decision, whether a clear verdict, or the terms of a compromise. He was the aide of the magnate in his consultations and talks. He was not only Shlomo's right-hand man, but also his complement. For, if you cannot single-handedly plumb the depths of a matter, because it is foreign to your thinking and experience, you need someone to sit across the table from you, sipping the cup of hot tea you pour out for him. He is to some extent financially dependent on you, although he is not your salaried creature. More often than not, he will think along with you and clarify the matter without effort on your part. Even the wealthiest of magnates comes up against obstacles; one has to know the psychology of this count or that nobleman. One has dealings occasionally with government officials and the authorities. In Russia there are anti-Jewish decrees and rules and regulations with which it is difficult to comply.

One has two sons, two daughters-in-law, and naturally, grandchildren; not to mention relatives and cousins. One has to find a dowry for an indigent female relative of marriageable age. One has to endow a distinguished *tzaddik* with a respectable living; to participate in congregational affairs, appointing or dismissing synagogue officials. All these matters require a certain judiciousness. So you talk them over with Shmuel and consult him on each occasion. You do not set him above yourself, and not for a moment do you regard him as your superior. On the contrary, he is there to serve you—and with deference. When you stand up, he follows suit; when you leave the room you precede him. For all his clarity of mind and the manner in which he complements you, he still draws sustenance from you. He is always in need of a hundred rubles or two, and sometimes even more. Most wagons have four wheels, some have two. The horse pulls the cart, but it is the man who sits in it that matters…

Shmuel's wife, Esther by name, had borne him no children for eighteen successive years. She was considered to be barren, and went from rabbi to rabbi and from doctor to doctor. Then God opened her womb, and she bore a beautiful daughter who was deaf and dumb. The joy of the parents was turned to heartache. The magnate loved the child, and would often come visiting his secretary's house and take the lovely child on his knee and play with her. A descendant of the conquerors of the land of Canaan, perhaps from the stock of the sons of Gad and Asher or the half tribe of Manasseh, would be sitting on a bench in the clean room, which sparkled everywhere with bright cleanliness, stroking the red hair of a child growing up like a flower in one of the broad fields of the Diaspora.

The First Breach

Chaim Yona, the first born son of Shlomo the Red, had six daughters whose names were as follows: Malka, Leah, Deborah, Pessie, Beila and Rachel. The first three might be considered young ladies and the latter still children tied to the house.

Malka was a pleasant pale-faced young woman, with a certain seriousness in her deportment so that talk and conversation ceased in her presence. She herself chose to be taciturn and was not very companionable with her sisters. She had no aptitude for studying languages or books, but she was so skilled in the art of sewing that the needle held in her fingers moved as though it had a separate life of its own. From noon onward she would sit by the window and work at her craft while the trees outside whispered together. There was a touch of heaviness in her heart. White specks in the blue sky fill the spirit with a kind of cloud.

Her sister Leah was distinguished by her height and the litheness of her body. She had a pleasant voice and went about singing from morn to evening. Her spirit was not like a candle burning in one corner, but shone everywhere.

Deborah had bright red hair and eyes of blue. Her mouth was

full of spontaneous laughter and she ran from room to room hiding her face so as to stem the flood of her emotions. The dawn would come and the world began to wake. She would jump out of bed and leap around in the bedroom clad only in her nightgown.

Pessie, the fourth daughter, was very tall and had the strength of a man. When she wrestled with her friends she would always win. She helped with the housework and spent most of her time sitting in the kitchen. When one of the menservants came close to her and caught her by the neck, she stuck out her tongue and closed her eyes for the moment, but after that she slipped out of his grasp and with both hands thrust off the impertinent fellow who had dared to touch her and pushed him against the wall.

Beila and Rachel were twins, with blonde hair and light skin, their faces and arms covered with freckles. Shlomo, their grandfather, respected Malka, rather liked Leah and had an affection for Pessie, but he adored the twins. Near the flock of sheep, goats and calves, leans the shepherd on a pinnacle of rock, his staff in his hands and his eyes nourished by the sight of those grazing in the meadow and basking in the light of the day…

An act of violence shattered the tranquility in which Shlomo the Red was living. A teacher of the gentile language had been exiled from the nearby county town to the provincial hamlet of Loton and had come to teach in Chaim Yona's house. He secretly cared for Pessie. Once when he was teaching her addition in arithmetic, he placed his hand on hers. Looking around and seeing that her sisters had left the room, he took hold of her and kissed her. What did she do? She kissed him on his mouth, after which she darted into the yard and began stroking the coat of a dog that was crouching there. In the east, the corners of the sky reddened.

The details of how things developed afterward are not known to me. The young teacher had not only betrayed his trust, but as a practical joke he actually performed a marriage ceremony with the granddaughter of the magnate in front of two urchins of the city, after which he moved away and left Loton.

The small town was in an uproar; this time the hornet had stung the forehead of Shlomo. They shut the "married" girl in her room and did not allow her grandfather to come near her. On the fourth day he summoned the town rabbi and ordered him to release his granddaughter from her betrothal and annul the marriage retrospectively. This particular rabbi was a Levite, sincerely religious and one who revered the regulations of the Torah, but this time he found a way out…

Shadows

When I mentioned Abba Yeruham, the rich man's neighbor, I said that he had married off his two sons and had already given two of his daughters in wedlock. Now I shall try to recount the details.

Zalman, the first-born son, was an arrogant fellow, irreligious, fond of company and of fooling around with his fellow men. His brother, Obadiah, was not like this, but was a taciturn man given to knavery. His whole ambition seemed to be to undermine his neighbor's household, to fill his pockets for the time being, or even just to engage in fraud for the sake of fraud. Zalman was meticulous about the clean lines of his garments, polished his shoes every day until they shone even at a distance. Obadiah paid no attention to these things. Even if a few buttons came off his coat he did not bother to sew them back again. He seemed a shiftless fellow and was completely ignorant of the Torah. But here's the point—the wife of Zalman was a skinny woman, not at all good-looking, while Obadiah had a handsome wife who found favor in the sight of all who saw her. This world is topsy-turvy and its ways are tortuous.

Abba Yeruham's daughters were also different in character. Chaya, the older, was a little like her stepmother. She was strong and reliable, while her sister Nechama was fair-skinned and went about her work in a lazy manner. Yaakov, the husband of Chaya, was an agent for a timber business. In his youth, he had been an invalid but afterward recovered his health. On the other hand Nechama's husband, Nahshon Getzel, was a sturdy man, hasty tempered, and quite incompatible by nature to his wife. It is God above who makes matches, but when the sons of man below take on His art, how strange are the results.

Yaakov had a fondness in his heart for Nechama and she, whenever her husband acted nastily toward her, would pour her heart out to her brother-in-law. Was he not her own flesh and blood and how gentle were his hands. A woman has many thoughts. Were she only married to him how much more pleasant life would be for her and she would have nothing of which to complain. Even more conspicuous was the feeling of Zalman for his brother's wife. What can one do about it? The woman whom he had married years ago, and with whom he had stood under the bridal canopy, was no longer desirable to him, while this one who was not permitted to him according to religious law had captivated his heart. Men have roving eyes and covetous hearts.

Night always follows in the footsteps of day, and day turns round and is joined to the night; there is tumult and labor—everything is done openly in the light of the sun and yet a veil covers all. Things are at rest and are not at rest...In the circle of society and in daily work, the heart is like a grave; but when night comes, it rises up in all its force and then we can understand its language. I am only speaking to the reader by means of a parable. He can learn its application from the sort of scandal commonly circulated by the inhabitants of a town. So I shall relate two incidents in turn.

Nechama was sitting in her kitchen peeling potatoes, cutting them into little pieces and putting them in the pot. It was evening; the world was hiding its face; but the woman's heart was in a tumult. There are no dykes to the soul; dig a little bit and water pours in from every side. Your husband is your husband, you obey him and at times you despise him. It is forbidden for a daughter of Israel to think such thoughts, but the left hand repels and the right hand does not bring near. Inadvertently the point of the knife pricked her finger and a drop of blood appeared which she sucked dry. Her brother-in-law stood at the door and said, "Nechama, are you alone in the house?"

The woman was startled by this sudden visit, rose from her seat and said, "What did you want, Yaakov?"

Their eyes locked, the walls seemed to spin, he held her and drew her into the inner room, embraced her and cried, "Be quiet!"

The astonished woman was pleading, begging and crying, "Leave me alone!"

Once Zalman came to his brother Obadiah's house at the time when he was making the rounds of the villages. He drew near to his sister-in-law who had greeted him and placed his hands over her eyes as though in a game.

"Zalman, who brought you here?"

He did not answer her, he took hold of her glamorous beauty and the woman trembled from head to foot. She wanted to cry out.

Loton, Loton, hide your face.

A Misleading Star

The festive days of the end of summer arrived. Side by side with the book of the statutes, the calendar of the seasons still holds sway. In this month and in that the fast days automatically take their places. In other months the festivals begin. In tabernacles constructed of boards with roofs covered with foliage dwelt the people of each city observing the ritual of the festival. A certain man, prominent in his own town, invited his young son with his young wife to come to him from the nearby town, to participate in the festival and rejoice with his family. After the eighth Day of Solemn Assembly in which the most High God comes together in company with his people, another great festive day for the Jews is celebrated!—The Rejoicing of the Law. On this day there is no distinction between rich and poor. It is a congregational day. The women leave their separate partitioned section in the synagogue and enter the men's courtyard. They are dressed in their finest attire, pendants on their necks and earrings in place. Boys and girls of the children of the family of Jacob come together and stand close to the dais watching those called to the Torah going round in procession with the scrolls, which are also crowned with jewels and decked in ornaments and scarlet. Our father Abraham and his chosen children are rejoicing with us. Even Moses, the trustworthy shepherd, is rejoicing with us! They kiss the mantles of the parchment scrolls. Joy and fellowship overflow in every heart.

Suddenly in the Loton synagogue every neck craned upward. Everybody stretched forward eagerly. A young woman of incomparable beauty and splendor was standing in the first row of the women's section. Her dress, fashioned of shimmering blue silk was in keeping with her vivid face. She was not a witch, but the niece of Shmuel Menahem, Shlomo the Red's secretary. She had come from the capital, Harson, to take up residence in her uncle's house.

A light was burning in the holy ark which had been emptied of the scrolls of the covenant, but every eye was fixed on the splendor of this daughter of Israel. There are many beautiful women in the world, but the inhabitants of Loton had never in their lives seen anyone like the woman standing before them. I shall not talk about the irreligious ones, but even the God-fearing people in the congregation inwardly agreed that the beauty of this woman must be similar to that of Cozbi, the daughter of Tzur, who caused a prince of the chief clan of the Simeonites to go a-whoring after her.

The name of the guest was Shoshana and she was not yet thirty. She was familiar with men and their ways, but no man had yet known her. She had been betrothed into the household of a rich father-in-law, a silver merchant and one who loaned money to the nobility. Her husband, one of the younger Hasidim, was deeply attached to her. She rejected him and broke his heart. She was divorced and when she received her bill of divorcement in the rabbinic court, a poisonous smile could be seen upon her lips. The rabbi who judged the case, himself young in years, was disturbed by the look in her eyes for the whole of that day and the next…

She once was invited to the dance of the maidens of a kinswoman. The bridegroom was also invited to the party as is customary among the wealthy. The youth saw her standing with her friends and, captivated by her witchery, subsequently refused to enter the bridal canopy, crying to those standing by; "Oh, my head, oh, my head!"

Every heart was captivated by her, but she was lonely, solitary in mind and in body. When she leaned on her bare arms, with her eyes wandering about her, the room seamed to hold a suspenseful echo, like the stillness before a thunder storm. Her two breasts cried out for victims. The whole of creation dissolved in agony.

The Destroyer

The autumn was already preceded by the footfalls of winter. The storehouse of snow opened and the cold crystal flakes descended to cover the broad face of the earth. The land was swathed in a white mantle which shimmered in the rays of the sun. The world was resting. There were no dreams and no interpretations of dreams. All creatures were short of food, men were seeking warmth for their houses, clothes and covering for their little ones and some ready cash for their pockets.

Batya, wife of Daniel Silk, the second son of Shlomo the Red, woke up one morning. It was a Friday. She stood at the door of the salon and saw her young maidservant polishing the floor with a woolen cloth tied to her feet. She said to her, "Leave what you are doing, go to the kitchen and take a look at the bread which is baking in the oven."

The girl did what she was told. She untied the strings of the floor cloth and went off to the back of the house humming quietly. She had scarcely reached the next room when the legs of her mistress began to give way. She fell on the floor and a stream of blood gushed from her mouth. The terrified maid rushed back to her mistress. Her screaming was heard throughout the house. The other maidservants ran into the salon and began wailing and wringing their hands. Daniel had left for the mill early that morning and they quickly called him home. A servant was sent speeding on horseback to the apothecary. They lifted the fallen woman from the ground and laid her down on the couch. Her eyes were closed and she was not moving at all. She had a sudden stroke and had fallen dead. An outcry of grief burst from all those standing by. Daniel pressed the hands of the dead woman and cried out like a madman, "Wake up, wake up, my darling Batya; why are you silent, my sweet one, my lovely one?"

Officials of the mill hurried one by one to the house, their wives weeping. Even the neighbors, the peasant women, stood by, looking on with grief-stricken faces. Daniel was wringing his hands and wailing. The children were restrained from entering the house of the dead woman. A terrible tragedy had occurred. Men began running backward and forward; the whole courtyard was full of tumult. The city was agog with the news. Batya, that sweet lovely woman, had died! She was no more! Death had taken her!

And Batya, the noble Batya, who only an hour before was alive and walking about her house like a veritable queen, now lay upon the ground covered with a black pall, with candles burning with eerie illumination at her head. Members of the burial society arrived to perform the ritual purification on the body lying on the ground, as religious law required. Women began sewing the shrouds. The local ritual slaughterers, who headed the religious functionaries, held copies of the book *Crossing the Jabbok* in their hands and hastened on the work. Nothing could slow down the swift passage of the day, and it was important that the deceased woman should come to rest in the cemetery before the Queen Sabbath arrived.

Popular custom is a powerful force. Every man hurried from his house to participate in the large funeral. Loton had been bereaved of a lofty soul. For the body they dug a grave in the place where the dead meet and from which there is no return.

The Closing of the Gates

The winter grew more bitter and the world was abandoned to bereavement. Just a few days previously you dwelt with your gentle wife in harmony. The touch of hand on hand expressed the closeness of love and eyes could gaze. But now both soul and body had fled and were gone far away, passed into the irrevocable distance. You walk from room to room and are quite alone. You want to speak and raise your voice but the stillness presses heavily upon you, crushing your mind and body.

God judges man according to his works and enters into a reckoning with him on everything. Up till now no one has been great enough to investigate the justice of heaven and say to the Mighty One of Nature: "Your hands, too, are befouled with blood. You may have created, but You also have done murder."

The task of the narrator is not only to depict happenings and events. Permit him also to interpret them and pour out his heart.

Daniel prayed with even more concentrated devotion after the death of his wife Batya. He struggled to combat the iniquity which abides everywhere and to find redemption and a basis in which his soul could believe. A man communes with his Maker according to accepted written formulations and it eases his pain. The consolation of the prophets had relevance only for the children of a past generation. The children of the exile need the treasures of the prayer book. The phylacteries with the four biblical quotations hidden inside them are on your head and on your arm, the fringed praying shawl enwraps your figure; but you are still standing in front of a blank wall. Nevertheless, a hidden door leads from it to Him who dwells in eternity. Now you dissolve in tears, accept the judgment as righteous, and are assured that there is One who hears and takes note. Happy is the man who is smitten, but yet believes.

But sometimes all the promises and the accepted assurances lose their validity and pangs of loneliness consume flesh and soul alike. No one can explain the riddle of death. You get up at night when sleep eludes your eyes. You light a candle and listen attentively to the bed next to you on which the white silent sheets are spread. Perhaps there is still some kind of soul hidden there? Has not your beloved wife lain there for more than ten years? You embraced her and gazed upon her beauty by marital right and not as a transgression! The body has a soul and a spirit. Suddenly only darkness surrounds it. All the threads which bind a human being with the world are irrevocably sundered; and he is almost cut off from the Creator of that world. The dead do not praise God. Those who dwell in silence are only a prey to the moth. The grief is greater than can be borne. You are the father of orphan children. You have stumbled in your iniquity; your soul had gone astray and retribution has overtaken you in this world, according to an inevitable decree with its fixed punishment. The prince of the congregation is responsible for his tribe, the head of the family for his household; a man does *not* die for his own sins.

I have heard such things but do not understand.

Intoxication

The spring came. The days of the counting of the Omer began. Nature goes about her task. Many of the creatures which crawl in the dust return to life. Earth once again has a green shroud. The grass grows, the trees bud, plowing and sowing yield pasture for the sheep and the cattle. The family of Israel are no longer the sons of kings as they were during the Passover. They rise up early, every man running to work in order to find his bread and his sustenance. The sun not only brings healing to those who are smitten; it also ignites sparks of hope in the hearts of mortal beings. Blessed be the God of the sun.

Many people thought that when the days of mourning were over, Daniel would marry his niece, Malka. There was some kind of warrant for this in holy writ, "A world is rebuilt by loving kindness." Certainly in some corner of the heart of the Father of Orphans there may have lurked some inclination toward this match. On two occasions Daniel had talked about this matter with the town rabbi who was his friend and often his confidant. Malka, too, had a secret fondness in her heart for her relative and said to herself, "It is better for me to belong to a man whom I know and honor than to be the wife of a stranger."

The girl never imagined that another would take her place. During that summer, Daniel married the ravishingly beautiful niece of Shmuel Menahem. Shoshana left her uncle's abode and went to dwell in the abode of her lover. Malka was spurned.

In the place of clear light which had burned in purity a strange flame now flared up. Daniel was obsessed day night with his beloved wife; day after day, he neglected his work. Sometimes he even forgot the God of the Torah and His commandments and yielded himself up completely to joys of the flesh. A woman incomparable in beauty, the brightness of whose body obsesses the soul with trembling and terror was actually permitted to him. He could touch her, enfold her in his arms and rest his mouth upon hers. His eyes never left her for a moment, he even kissed the hem of her garments. He luxuriated in her and thought of no one else. The father of children was transformed into a man of lust.

Shoshana neither refused him nor bade him refrain. The heart is closed with seven seals. Here was a man of thirty acting with her like a youth. All she wanted was that her new husband should stretch himself out to his full length on the ground and that his body should be the footstool for her naked feet. She would rule completely over this man who yearned after her. She would trample upon him and dig her toes into the hair of his head. There is no greater joy than this, to make a soul lie crushed within a body.

It came to pass after three months that Shoshana became revolted even with this. She lay on her bed in abandonment of spirit and found her very beauty a burden to her. Her husband came to her wishing to embrace her and she turned to the wall. Daniel was stunned and did not know what had happened to her…

At that time Daniel turned back again to the God of prayer, but saw that He had cast him off completely.

The Shining Sword Blade

Sabbath eve. God brings the world of weekday bustle to a close and work ceases. Anxieties are given pause and every soul is cleansed and quaffs the cup of blessing. The candles glow with a mystical radiance. Now the moment has arrived when the Sabbath bride is joined to her beloved in passionate consummation and heart's embrace. On high, too, praises are sung, as she is crowned sevenfold and the Ancient of Days, exalted and uplifted, bends an attentive ear to the union of all living beings.

Daniel Silk is clad in shining satin. He has strengthened and renewed his spirit by reciting the Song of Songs with deep concentration and in a pleasing voice to arouse the Rose of Sharon…"The King has brought me into his chambers…we will remember your love." He seeks no merit for having recited the verses, the words, the letters, the vowel points, the idioms and the mystical allusions. What he does feel is that this is the time for attention, hearing and entreaty…His dove, his perfect one is unique; the fragrance of her robes is like the perfume of Lebanon. His Shoshana is sevenfold more beautiful than before; in her are united creation, formation, and molding. Her Sabbath attire becomes her crown.

Daniel drew close to his passionately loved one and spoke to her in exaltation of spirit, in this wise. "Hearken to me, my sweet Shoshana, attend to the outpouring of my soul. My mouth utters words but my heart soars. You are my delight, my own sacred possession, the crown of my head. To me your eyes are like the illumination of the tabernacle; your mouth turns aside all wrath. Every limb of your body is desirable. Open your heart to me and be as you were to me on the day of our wedding."

He embraces her wildly and she does not protest, being stricken dumb by the torrent of words. Then abruptly she rises from her chair and says, "It is a sin for you even to touch me. The law forbids it..."

She was deceiving him but Daniel was deeply distressed. Only one step had intervened between him and the pit. But a moment more and he would have sinned mortally against the omnipresent.

Shoshana slipped out of his grasp and left the room. The Sabbath tranquility died away into silence. One cannot arrest impurity but it can be contained. The soul is pursued, it sobs like a dove. In his distress the humbled human being calls upon his God, but He is invisible and shut away...

There was an ancient priestly code in force within the habitations of Jacob. It has been made continually more rigid by proliferating elaborations. There are seven days of absolute separation, followed by seven of the period of becoming clean. One has to count both of these, and as long as they last there is complete withdrawal and separation of husband and wife. Even on high there is an unclean spirit which rules and there is a dividing fence between the impure and the holy. This is maintained until the day of purification after which the shadows flee away—and its validity ceases.

Day follows day. Husband and wife dwell together. On the doorposts of the house is inscribed the symbol of the covenant and within the walls a rigid separation prevails. The heart is frigid, the soul awakes and sleeps again, awakes and sleeps. It gazes to the right and the world is open, it gazes leftward and it is shut up. Shoshana is the ruler and who dares rebel against her dictates? Who will not submit to her? Daniel refrains from touching her, but he thinks of her all the time…

Daniel could quite easily burn the house down around her, drown her in the river or go up a height with her and push her down. When he takes the whetted knife in his hand to cut the loaf of bread, he imagines it slipping and plunging into her breasts so that the blood spurts onto the white tablecloth. Daniel springs terrified from his place screaming, "In your blood shall you live! In your blood shall you die!"

When first created, Eve dwelt alone. Then she raised her eyes and saw a man standing in front of her. She said, "I shall not yield up my fruit to you until you conquer me."

Just look. He is a spineless slave. She wept…

House by House

Princes rule the world and all that is therein. The Prince of Water rules in his province. The Prince of Wind is appointed over the tornados and the Prince of Fire has dominion in his realm. In days of old, sacrifices would be brought and prayers offered to them. Even now they take and exact their tribute. Who can understand their deeds?

It is the termination of a certain Sabbath. The division has been made when the gates of the day of rest are closed and the gates of the week are open. Esther, the wife of Shmuel Menahem, prepared the glass lamp, primed it with oil and lit it. The lamp fell from her hands to the ground and broke into fragments. The flame flared up and caught her clothes. It happened in the kitchen when she was alone in the house, her husband having already gone to the rich man's residence. She cried out in a heart-rending voice but there was no one to help her. The blaze illuminated the windows and a passerby in the street saw it, cried out and sounded the alarm. The neighbors, men and women, gathered together and threw rugs and bolsters on the unfortunate woman. By the time Shmuel came back from his employer's house and forced his way through the crowds, he found himself standing before a burnt and lifeless corpse. He burst into bitter tears and tore at the hair of his head. Esther was a pure woman in everything she did, there was no vice in her; but who can say to the Angel of Destruction, "Desist?"

Life is cruel; the dead are taken to the grave, the earth closes its mouth but the sun above shines on as though nothing had happened. It rises and sets. There comes a day when the man who has been bereaved of the wife of his youth seeks another and proceeds to build his house anew. After some months had passed, all kinds of eligible women were proposed for the forty-five year-old Shmuel. Certainly he refused to pay any attention to the suggestion, looking upon himself as a mortal sinner. However, important people kept up the pressure upon him and it was difficult for him to refuse when one of them came out with the idea that he should wed Malka, the granddaughter of the magnate. It was difficult to believe that Shlomo the Red would agree to this proposal.

The union eventually came about to the surprise of all the people of Loton. Malka's mother was opposed to the idea and Shlomo himself was divided in his mind, but eventually acceptance overcame the feeling that he should refuse. No man is quite consistent in his decision. What he might choose to do today he would not have agreed to do yesterday.

The wedding was not celebrated in the city with a great assembly of guests, but in a village nearby to Loton. The bride herself was stunned by the swiftness with which it all happened. At midday, they set up the bridal canopy in the open space in front of the inn. The local peasants had never seen a sight like this before. The clash of the cymbals of the local band of musicians was heard far and wide. The rabbi blessed the couple and performed the wedding ceremony.

That same evening the whole company returned to Loton. The girl now parted from her mother and her father and went to live in her husband's house. The in-laws each went to their own particular place of residence. The stars above revolved in their orbits and the moon showed intermittently through the clouds. Who can soar up on high to hear the converse of the children of the night? On the morning of the next day, Malka's mother wrapped herself in a long kerchief, for the idea had taken hold of her to visit her daughter. She entered the bedroom and found her child sitting weeping on the bed. Her honor was profaned and she hid her face....

She Made her Killing

It was the middle of the month of Av. All traces of the fast and the days of remembrance for ancient mourning had now been obliterated. Summer poured out its glory on the whole wide world, granting one portion of the blessed land of the Ukraine. It was a year of plenty. The storehouses of all the peasants overflowed with the harvest of the fields. Fruits of the trees and vegetables were stacked up in great heaps. The sheep were fat, the udders of the cows were full of milk. The calves and young of the herds, the flocks of the goats and the lambs were lying in the broad meadows. Black and white pigs rolled and grunted in the dusty furrows. Draft horses and colts were nuzzling one another. By every bank and brook, flock upon flock of geese and poultry were pecking on the dung heaps. Had they been in the habit of offering sacrifices in that district, and giving tithes from the flocks, herds and poultry, then the gods indeed would have been feasting in satiety and the fire of sweet savors would have permeated all the face of creation.

It was a beautiful day and sunset was approaching. Daniel had gone out to the nearby county town and Shoshana was sitting alone in the entrance hall of her mansion beside a round table on which a bubbling samovar stood with burning coals glowing between the crevices below. She was dressed in a thin woolen dress over which was a broad blue gown with open sleeves. Strings of pearls glittered on her bare neck. Sunset, the quiet tranquility in the courtyard and the magic wonder of her beauty mingled together into one harmony, which could only be expressed on a piano, a violin or a lute.

That particular day was full of business activity for her father-in-law, Shlomo the Red. From early dawn he had been astride his horse; had gone to see the brick kilns which were built on the slope of the rocky hill, not far from Loton. From there he had turned aside to call in at the house of a certain nobleman of his acquaintance who owned a large estate. He returned to the mill, went into the upper rooms and the lower chambers. He had talked with his officials and his functionaries, had rebuked the servants who took care of the water sluices. In all this he was not a man of sixty, but more like a forty-year-old full of vigor and strength. He had the idea of building extra stories on the mill and enlarging its storehouse. He was full of drive and ambition. He felt the urge to dominate and his field for doing so was not too broad. Suddenly he conceived the idea of visiting his son, Daniel's, house. He had not seen him since the day of his marriage. He tethered the horse to a wooden post and went there on foot. As he stepped into the gate of the courtyard he saw his daughter-in-law standing at the door of the entrance hall. An arrow pierced his heart. In a voice bereft of strength he asked after her health from the distance and then went into the hall with her. Shoshana said to him, "Sit down, sir."

He could not take his eyes off her glowing beauty.

His whole being was constricted and his heart in a tumult. Not only the touch of hand, but even the touch of a shoe against the garment of that woman ignited the flame and made the world glow red again. The dogs belonging to the peasants nearby began to bark. Shlomo the Red rose from the seat, muttered a few phrases and turned and went outside. Shoshana did not stop him. She had already made her kill, and had poured out her libation of wine.

The night spread its wings over the inhabitants of the earth; pulsating nature had woven its web. The world hung in suspense, the inner and outer ear listening as one.

The beasts of the forest were moving about, seeking their prey and their food. Domestic animals stood in their cribs. Man was returning from his toil, but as he forsook his work, love and sin were combining to dig a pit for him. God had sworn to lay firm the foundations of the earth and replenish it. Flesh was to draw near to flesh, the sexes were to come together, the world was to perish and renew itself.

Shlomo the Red saddled his horse and rode slowly until he came to his son's mansion. He dismounted, opened the gate, led the horse into the courtyard and set a sack of barley in front of it. He walked on a few paces and with heart quaking knocked on the window of his daughter-in-law's bedroom. Ten minutes passed and the woman, clothed in a white nightgown, opened the door of the entrance hall and brought her guest furtively into her house. The watch dog was tardy in rousing himself and then began to bark furiously. The noise of falling water was heard and the moon disappeared behind the clouds…

Suddenly the world trembled, two mountains were torn up from their roots, met and fused together. Life cried out in the womb of the earth, a sound of passion and thunder. Deep called to deep, the order of creation was overturned. Night flashes of lightning danced and zigzagged; Pleiades and Orion whirled in mad confusion of orbits.

Deeply disturbed in mind, the chief man of the city left the house of the woman in the small hours of the night. He led his horse back to his dwelling and the earth quaked under him. This was a night of riot for the family of Satan. The convocation of God was not heard. One man's action had rejected society.

For what was left of the night, Shlomo the Red tossed upon his bed. The couch seemed to move and roll under him like a ship at sea. The sinner was remorseful and deeply grieved in his soul. He made a firm determination and took a vow not to repeat the sin. His mind churned over his conduct. Morning came. The cherubim were hidden from it. Strong as death are the toils of passion; those who enter into them will not go free again…

Adonijah and Absalom

When I was young, I studied the historical books of the kings of Israel and read that Adonijah, the son of Haggit, asked the Queen Mother to give him Avishag, the concubine of David, for a wife. When Solomon heard of it, he swore that Adonijah was conspiring against his life. As I studied this, another interpretation entered my mind and reversed the whole of that situation completely. The son of Haggit met Avishag, a Shunamite, in the field of Salem. She was the most beautiful girl in the whole territory of Israel and no man had known her. His heart was inflamed with love for her and he went to speak to his father, saying, "One of the daughters of your servants has found favor in my eyes. Take her for a wife for me and bless me."

David saw that Avishag was very comely, far more so than his other wives, and he too lusted after her and said, "She shall become my possession and my portion."

The son went out from his father aghast. Retribution followed, the crown was removed and the decree sealed against the sovereignty of the house of Jesse.

This interpretation became part of my thinking from that point onward and it again put a different complexion on what is written down in the holy books. Adonijah also organized a conspiracy against his father, inflamed as he was with jealousy over the girl. His spirit knew no rest. The number of people who supported the son of the king grew steadily and the conspiracy became powerful. Here was a son intriguing against the life of his father because the latter had betrayed his trust.

Daniel was completely exiled from his Eden. His soul melted and cried out in grief and pain from morning to evening. Iniquity crouched at the door of the universe and even to you, the unhappy one, sin clings. You look at the changed face of your lawful wedded wife. Is she not a human being who has struggled with God and prevailed and is not afraid of the pangs of hell? The sinner wore a pure gold bracelet on her arm, fashioned like a serpent, holding its tail in its mouth. In its eyes precious stones glittered and burst through to your innermost depths. Every day you sit down to eat with this woman who is remote from you and has gone very far astray. You speak to her as a man talks to his wife and suddenly a terrible and dreadful thought comes into your mind. This woman has profaned every convention, she has overthrown all institutions. The walls of the house seem to tremble on account of your sorrow and bitterness of heart, yet you lack the courage to cry out to the one who sits with you, "You have been utterly treacherous, you have sinned and transgressed!"

You talk to God morning and evening. Three times a day, you go to the synagogue of Him who sees all and is Omniscient. You mention His great name, and you—you are a man of sin, you are the one who is imperfect and unfit and unworthy of coming before the King. How can you lift up your eyes when evil dwells in your own courtyard…?

The Judgment

Anger was let loose. The rumor current in the city about what went on in the house of Abba Yeruham, the magnate's neighbor, had been confirmed. His oldest son, Zalman, had broken down the fence of the law and he too had committed an evil deed. The ministering angels saw and, incensed with anger and wrath, decided to punish the inhabitants of Loton. Plague entered the gates and choked great and small. Many perished in the town because of the iniquity. They proclaimed a fast, they opened the ark and made supplication before the parchment scrolls. No one listened or gave heed. Both twins, Beila and Rachel, died in these days of wrath and there was bitter mourning and lamentation in the house of Chaim Yona.

On the third day of the mourning, Shlomo the Red removed the white cloth which had shrouded the mirror in his son's salon. He was alone in the room. In it he saw a serpent walking upright at the height of a man. It had long horns sticking out of its head and a naked sword hanging from its waist. His heart burst within him; he wanted to cry out aloud, but his tongue remained dumb. Meanwhile, the serpent was continuing to uncoil. The mirror was full of many flecks, like scales. The ceiling was sinking. Suddenly the whole vision disappeared, but his head spun like a wheel. He hurried out of the salon into the open. It was a cloudy day and a scepter of fire shone in the sky.

Shlomo rose in the morning and fixed his leather belt round his waist. He went out of the gate and wended his way by narrow field paths so as to avoid the town. With hurried steps he strode across the bridge, passed the mill and very soon found himself standing before his son's mansion. That day Daniel had left for a not too distant village to hire workers and laborers. The maid, a girl of about nineteen, came out to meet him, saying, "Come in sir, my mistress is waiting for you."

The angry man entered the house through the corridor. Shoshana was still clad in her dressing gown and had made up her face. Her father-in-law drew near and pushed at her with his arm. Terrified, she started up from her place and said, "What's happened to you?"

The "Red" loosened his belt from round his waist and began beating the whoring woman's back and all her body with a great pelting of blows. She did not cry out with the pain and made no entreaty nor any attempt to evade her chastisement. The anger of the man as he smote her exceeded all bounds. He stamped his feet, fire snorted from his nostrils; all he wanted to do was smash her body and cover it with bruises; to drag her backward and forward by her hair and to throw her through the window like Jezebel; like the queen who also was cast down in her day. A soul for souls! Again he drew near her in the rising tide of his anger and again began to beat her. She then said, "Stop, I am your slave!"

The man trembled, left her alone and hurried out of the room. The sun was high in the sky, gazing down on the dwellers below and the erring people of earth.

On the morning of the next day, Shoshana departed from her husband's house and left the town.

Repentance

The plague ceased. The breaches were repaired again, but in many houses in Loton the number of living beings had decreased. Here the head of a household had died and his family was left behind him to mourn. There a woman succumbed in her youth; children of school age, infants who had only peeped through a thin crack of life, left for the last meeting place of all living creatures. There were many who were saying *kaddish*, the mourners' prayer, justifying God's judgment and exalting His blessed name, in the Congregation of Jacob.

It was in those days that a rebbe came to the city. A wonder man of the holy people. He was one who had experienced much illness, his spirit had been purified and his eyes looked into the distance. By day many men thronged to him with offerings and requests. At evening he would visit the houses of the important people of the city to vouchsafe his blessing to them. When he stepped over the threshold of Daniel's house, he saw judgments brooding over the dwelling. He was terrified and turned back…

Next day Daniel found himself urged to go to the abode of the seer, pour out his plaint before him and weep scalding tears. The rabbi closed his eyes, made strange movements in the air with his hands and afterward answered in a mysterious manner, saying three times, "The way is long…long is the way…the way is long…"

But there was no way and no path open in front of Daniel. Days came and went, came and went without change. Even a man who observes the commandments during the week and on holy days, who obeys the law and is deeply religious, can be desolate even in his environment. This kind of "half-man" is different from a man who has been widowed. You sit in your room, you come into the salon, you enter the hall or even go out of doors, but some part of you remains behind and does not go along with you. The soul has certain extensions and a certain heaviness. You cannot pray aloud or sing to your God. The world seems to possess some kind of torture and hidden element. You are rejected. You have married a woman according to religion; everything had been sealed with the seal of union. Day by day you sit with her at the dining table and your eyes look at the coolness of her beauty. You talk with others who are close and those who are far from you, but beyond the superficialities of the talk something stirs in you. You wake up in the morning and an idea presses heavily on your mind; that day drags on interminably. In arithmetic there are addition and subtraction, multiplication and division, but who can measure and demarcate the soul? "The way is long, long is the way…"

Once Daniel set out early for the synagogue, which was not far from the house of Shmuel Menahem, to attend afternoon service. He had gone a short distance along the length of the street. Malka, his niece, was sitting in front of the door of her house with a baby held to her bosom. Her face expressed a kind of quiet charm. He turned toward her and chatted with her a little, as relatives do. When he parted from her he continued to think about her…God directs the steps of man, but here was he, her next of kin, who had not dealt kindly with her. Strange thoughts began to penetrate into his innermost being. That night he could not sleep…

From the World of Truth

I shall also mention the orphans of Batya, Daniel's first wife.

As has been mentioned, Batya left her husband with one boy and two girls. The only son was born last and he was called Levi. The elder daughter was Yocheved and her small sister was Miriam.

Levi was a spoiled child and slightly retarded. He managed to grasp only with difficulty what he was taught by his teacher and he attended *heder* every day most unwillingly. Daniel made an effort to help and influence the child. Every Friday night, he would read with him a part of the Torah portion for the week. But the boy had no imagination and could not grasp what had happened and taken place in olden days. The girls were entirely different.

Yocheved and Miriam were dreamy girls and, by nature, like the branches of one tree. They were dark and comely, with their hair wound in plaits around their heads, and with questioning eyes. The change-over from one mother to another, the bewilderment in which the house found itself, incessantly wove a web which enmeshed these tender souls. They understood only the language of the river. They loved the time of morning. On Sabbaths and festivals their spirits were exalted and in their hearts they felt the wonders of ancient times grasp what had happened and taken place in olden days.

It happened one night that Daniel was sitting alone in the great salon with, this time, a Jerusalem Talmud opened out in front of him. We are a long way off today from Tiberias where once they counted and reckoned up all the jots, tittles and vowel points of holy writ. In our present era we still carry on the rules based on them, observing them and meditating on them. But no man should be proud at a time when all he can do is study these things and there are no longer sacrifices and an altar. We set up memorials for the departed, but the tombstones are dumb. On that day Yocheved, the first-born, came in quietly, stood before her father like a young palm tree, opened her mouth and said to him, "Daddy darling, where is the mother who bore me…"

Passover eve arrived. In the land of the sons of Ham, the realm of impurity, the pure, sons of the pure, toiled with rigor. The God of Hosts was jealous for His people. In the middle of the night He revealed Himself to smite the first-born of the Egyptians. He manacled the sons of Satan and sent them to a land of retribution. The children of Israel have remembered in every generation the signs of their God and His strong hand; each and every man celebrates the festival of freedom and redemption in his own home, ridding his soul of leaven and eating the bread of heroes.

Clad in white, Daniel sat half-reclining at the head of his long table and conducted the Seder for his orphans. A seven-branched candelabrum made of pure silver illumined the dining-room. Long white curtains stretching down to the ground were drawn over the windows. A world within a world. Exalted visions and great lights filled heaven and earth.

The uncrowned king rose up from his divan before saying the hallelujahs prescribed for that night in order to open the door as was the accepted custom. He beheld the wife of his youth, swathed in white from head to foot, standing by the door…He was overcome with terror and fainted…

Sun and Moon

In those days yet another youth became interwoven into the web of these events. He had a biblical name: Amnon.

Amnon was the only son of one of the religious and most respectable families in the city. His father was a profound scholar and a man of fine family. In his library were gathered together many antiquities. He faithfully observed the religious laws and customs. The young man himself pastured on the ancient mountains, from morning to evening meditating on the hidden secrets of the traditions.

Amnon had an older sister who had made friends with Leah, the granddaughter of the magnate. Leah often visited the house of this religious man, bringing with her brightness and vivacity. Amnon was completely captivated by her and she found his companionship very pleasant. Amnon was by nature very shy, but Leah drew him out by her high spirits and treated him with the playful familiarity of brother and sister. She forced him to look straight into her eyes and often, as though inadvertently, put her hand on his shoulder. For him the world no longer spoke out of a book. A window had opened for him and its secrets were shining brightly in front of him.

Daniel's loneliness became unendurable and he asked Amnon's

father to let his son become his companion in study. He agreed; and once again a new era opened in Amnon's life. Three afternoons a week, the lad made his way from the center of the city to the compound of the mill house. The road sloped down, the Jewish houses disappeared and mingled feelings of relaxation and tension entered his heart. You are standing in front of a large mansion whose walls speak silent poetry. The owner of the estate would receive the guest very hospitably. They would sit at the table, drink hot tea and afterward go for a stroll within the courtyard. Occasionally, Amnon and Daniel even chopped wood to improve their strength and in the evening sat together before two open volumes of the Talmud, expounding to each other the words of the sages. Whenever Yocheved passed by them, going from room to room, it seemed as if a star twinkled into sight and slowly faded away again. Invariably, Amnon trembled at the sight of her. When he left Daniel's house, after the afternoon service, he took away with him a new image within his heart.

It would happen that on the next day, the sun of Leah would be in the ascendant, and he would have a feeling of inward release. There was a secret within him which would brook no denial. His feelings soared, broadened and spread out. You are dreaming; a shout of triumph is heard. The dry bones come together and behold there is a living body. You have two eyes but the world is one.

Daniel was perplexed and at times utterly broken. His heart palpitated and was beating violently and irregularly. He had had enough and his soul longed for death.

In the Courtyard of Eternity

Amnon had become orphaned by the death of his mother and his father had not married again; a circumstance which caused universal comment. Every year, on the anniversary of the day on which God had taken away this departed soul and restored it to its eternal abode, they would light a candle which burned from evening to evening. They learned chapters of the Oral Law, compiled by Rabbi Judah, and recited the *kaddish* three times. This was a bond between those who dwell below on earth and those who dwell on high. The spirits are purified and the living are reminded that for them, too, must come a day of reckoning—

The fast day of the Ninth of Av arrived. People were in mourning and felt cut off from the Omnipresent. God had destroyed His sanctuary and the City of David was burned with fire. The sons of Jacob went outside the city and plucked up grass in the cemetery. Row upon row of wooden and stone tombstones filled the field. The burial ground of the people of Loton was situated on a slope at the edge of the green, swampy river.

Daniel, too, went out that day with his orphans to visit the grave of his wife. He and his only son were standing and gazing on the inscription, "Here lies buried a gentle and pious woman, blessed be she above all women in the tent"...Miriam was standing behind them while Yocheved, clad in a light, fluttering dress, stood at their right hand. Homes of those in heaven here below. In the row in front of them Amnon leaned on the tombstone of his mother. All the people were silent, meditating inwardly.

One evening in autumn, Yocheved put on her overcoat and left the courtyard of her father's house, determined to visit the field of those who sleep in the dust. Hidden longings had taken hold of her and lifted up her soul. Amnon, too, stole out of his father's house and accompanied the child on the way to the meeting place of all living. Two beings bound together eternally with a single purpose. Thus both of them disappeared from their parents' homes and nobody knew where they had gone. They sought for them a full week, night and day, before they gave up their efforts in despair. Heavy rains fell at that time and filled the rivers and the streams. The stream which ran beside the cemetery filled up and overflowed its banks. The caretaker of the graveyard came to repair the breaches in the fence and beheld two clothed bodies floating on the water.

Next morning "the beloved and pleasant ones" were buried. There was mourning and excitement in Loton. To this very day, the manner of their death is a completely unsolved mystery to the congregation.

From that time onward Leah's happiness ended and she sang no more.

Meeting and Disaster

Shlomo the Red had in his time leased the mill for a period of twenty years from its owner, a nobleman who possessed numerous properties. This immovable property had been handed over by deed and by contracted bond and he had controlled it for a whole generation as though it had been his very own: "From the depth of the earth to the height of the sky." Now the time was running out and other wealthy men were coming along and greedily turning their sharp gaze on this unfailing source of wealth. They were competing with the lessee, offering a much greater rental, increasing the scale sevenfold. Their purpose was to force the present tenant out of his property. By this time the regulations of the "Council of the Four Lands" no longer possessed much force in the district of Ukraine. It was not merely two parties continually grabbing at every possession. There might be nine or ten after them. The palm went to the strongest, but even he too might fail at times.

This particular nobleman died and left two sons to succeed him, who divided the vast estate between them. The mill fell to the share of the elder who was irresponsible and addicted to gambling. In Odessa, the merchant city on the shores of the Black Sea, he spent a great deal of time and immersed himself in a sea of pleasure. Once, when hard pressed, he sold Loton and its environs to a strange person who had not previously known the "Red." Shlomo now began to have troubled thoughts. He could see a cloud coming up in the distance and felt very insecure.

It was not an easy situation. A man of over sixty, who during his whole life had never gone further afield than the large county town, now had to pick himself up and journey away on business to the bustling metropolis of Odessa. His secretary, Shmuel Menahem, the son-in-law of his son, accompanied him on the journey. The people of Loton busily discussed the matter. In Odessa, Prince Orloff, who had acquired an infamous reputation as a persecutor of the Jews, held sway and governed with completely unrestrained despotism.

It was an anniversary. The magnate and his second in command had already been busy more than a month in the teeming metropolis. They visited the home of the new owner who now possessed the mill property. He spoke to them fairly favorably and seemed to adopt a satisfactory attitude. They were content with the situation. As they walked past the great emporiums, they went in them to buy presents for their households. They saw wonders everywhere they went. The broad river of Loton was like a little puddle compared to this vast ocean.

Shlomo and Shmuel sat down on a long white painted bench on the promenade which surrounded the city. Trees were planted on both its sides, red sand was spread over the narrow paths in the middle. A constant procession of people passed and re-passed walking to and fro. They were not hurrying along, but strolled at leisure. One held a fancy walking stick in his hand, another was smoking. Men and women paraded along arm-in-arm, speaking every language. The sun was shining.

A high official, clad in official uniform, was seen approaching from the distance with a very beautiful woman dressed in the fashion of ladies of the nobility. Shlomo the Red jumped up from his seat. Surely it was Shoshana who was walking there. He pressed both his hands to his temples, fire flared from his eyes, his body trembled like one having a nightmare in broad daylight. Shmuel, too, saw the same thing and his heart was shaken. Here was his relative clinging to a man of an alien religion, completely oblivious of her husband and her birthplace. For a moment he was tempted to run after her, but he could not summon up the courage. In any case what would he say to this estranged woman, what would he tell her?...

With unsteady steps they both returned to the hotel. Neither of them talked about it or discussed the matter. Each sat in his own corner deeply immersed in his thoughts. After a short interval they pulled themselves together, packed up their luggage and prepared themselves for the journey.

At the time when the magnate and the husband of his grandchild were staying in the distant city of Odessa, Satan came and took for himself a lamb from the flock in the house of Chaim Yona.

The redheaded Deborah, one of the daughters, had grown up and her spirit had awakened. Every day she would gaze at the new servant who groomed the horses. He was a powerful young man with a face like cast iron and when he walked the earth seemed to split beneath his feet. She aroused him and he found rest in her soul. One evening, when she visited the stables, her beloved was standing by the horses and grooming their sleek hides. Barefoot, wearing only a short shirt and trousers, he was of handsome appearance. She came up close to him and caressed his shoulder. He turned toward her, seized her in his two hands and pressed her to his breast. Mouth clung to mouth and life engulfed both of them together, so that they could not be parted.

Deborah was completely infatuated. She wanted to lift every door off its hinges. She wanted to jump out of one window and leap in through another. The birds of heaven were flying in the air. From the chimneys in the houses on her street, clouds of smoke were swirling upward, soaring higher and higher, rising to ever greater heights until the eye could no longer follow them.

After some time the servant left his master's house and returned to his parent's house in a village ten miles away. At the same time Deborah, the granddaughter of the magnate, also disappeared with a bundle of her possessions in her hand. She had gone after her beloved, saying, "Your people are my people and your God my God."

The city was in an uproar. On the streets and in the market places, groups of men and women were standing and talking together. There was not a house or a family which was not upset over the incident. The whole congregation was in sackcloth and ashes.

To describe this second disaster which broke the magnate's heart when he returned home in deep distress, would lay a heavy burden upon my pen.

Coals of Juniper

A preacher of the moralistic school came to Loton, which was a hasidic city. Their method of serving God was through concentration in prayer and a full yielding up of the heart. God wants His creatures to cleave to Him and walk in His ways. Every day the gates are opened for the righteous of each generation and they stand and intercede between the sons of man and the Lord of the Universe. Beside them also ministering angels and seraphim, the *arielim* and the holy emissaries. The creator joins Himself in a unity with the created things and every being longs to return to the supernal source. In this way the influence from those who dwell above is extended to those who dwell below and continues to progress until the great day when the eternal Sabbath will come upon all things.

Those who literally fear the judgment of God and work in the way which the authorities of *Beginning of Wisdom* have made secure, have a different concept of the conduct of the world, that is as follows: There are all kinds of fire in hell. There is a fire which consumes, burning up coals as great as mountains. There are also rivers of pitch and brimstone. When a man is sent here below because his inclination has led him astray, then the destroying angels cast him down into the fire which burns in the pit and it opens up its mouth and swallows him. That is not all: coals of juniper consume this person who has corrupted his way. They cut off his flesh, limb by limb, and break his bones. The sinner sits there with no part of his body left whole and sees how swarms of worms come and surround him from all sides. He screams because of the terrible pain but there is no one to listen to him. The cruel angels come back again, smiting him with whips and chastising him with scorpions. His blood seethes but no one pities him. God, who gave the Torah, the statutes and the judgment, is a jealous God. Woe unto him who walked in the wicked arrogance of his heart. Woe unto the man who lifted up his eyes to a woman and brought upon himself and on those who come after him a sin which can never be expiated.

In a thunderous voice the preacher showered down his warnings on the heads of the people in the Loton synagogue and the whip of his tongue lashed the head of the magnate who was present. He plucked at the sinner's soul as though with tongs; he stripped him naked. It was as though he were proclaiming in the very ears of everybody who was assembled there, "Look at the wickedness you have performed and wrought! Behold, how you have sinned, erred and transgressed. Your latter end will be perdition. God will refuse to forgive you!"

Shlomo the Red fasted for three days and three nights and afflicted his soul. They had cast him down from the mountain peak to hell below and had closed up the way round about him. On the fourth day, at evening, he came to the rabbi of the town, entered his inner sanctum, and confessed to his terrible sin. The rabbi trembled and was horrified, his eyes darkened in their sockets…

On the Slope of the Hill

Something happened in Loton, the like of which had not been heard of, except in ancient days. On Sabbath morning, when the people had already gathered for the morning prayer and the cantor was standing before his rostrum reciting the psalms, the magnate of the city appeared on the threshold. But he did not go to his regular seat on the eastern wall, beside the holy ark. Instead he sat down beside the stove in a place specially set aside for the poor and the indigent. He wrapped himself in his prayer shawl and began to recite from his prayer book. The whole flock of Jacob was aghast at this phenomenon: it was like an eclipse of the sun in broad daylight…

The tranquility of the Sabbath was destroyed: every face reddened. If the cedars bow their tops, what chance has the hyssop by the wall?

Shlomo the Red began to relinquish the conduct of his business and empowered Daniel, his son, to take charge of the whole administration of the industry at the mill. Chaim Yona was unfit for anything and his assistant would be Shmuel Menahem. Daniel had long hated Shmuel Menahem. The scope of his activity was enlarged by this step, but he knew even less peace of mind than before. The jealousy between relatives, and non-relatives, greatly increased.

At that time a schemer came to the magnate and suggested that for the payment of a large sum of money he could rescue his granddaughter who had gone astray and bring her back from across the border. He refused to listen to him and was not aware of the fact that Satan was plotting further designs against him.

It happened to be the time of the Christian Pentecost. The weather was beautiful and the land was bathed in the brightness of the sun like Eden. Everyone felt uplifted, all hearts surged with happiness and in the mind of the "betrothed" Pessie awakened a strong desire to see her sister. She arose and made her way to her village without telling anyone of her intention or what she wished to do. Thus she, too, went away and did not return. She threw off the trappings of her own religion and married into a strange faith.

Chaim Yona was in mourning and deep disgrace and would ask everybody he met, "Where are my daughters who have gone away?"

At that time too his old mother died and it was more than his mind could bear.

The Legend of the Oak

In ancient days, at the top of the road which leads from Loton to the county town, stood a tall, sturdy oak whose branches spread out so far that it could be seen from a great distance. Every wayfarer found shelter in its shade and all who traveled to and fro rested there from their journey. The whole of that area was level ground without any hills or valleys or even any stretch of water. From the very womb of the earth this mighty tall tree sprang up, growing and spreading from year to year, appearing as a symbol of power and majesty to everybody who dwelt in the neighborhood. In the ancient land of the Hebrews, the pagans would have accorded it divine honor and women would have been sacrificing and offering incense beneath it.

One summer the leaves of the treetop ceased to flourish and they began to wither. Many branches were cut down and some lopped off by vandals. Rot attacked it from the roots up, and where it did so it crumbled away into powder. A man could thrust his hand right through to the middle of the trunk. The roots split, the grass round about it dried up, a raging storm tore at its top and broke it. The oak was despoiled and now became a by-word and a proverb.

The local peasants gathered together on one occasion and

agreed to fell the tree and destroy it. Like angels of destruction, they assembled from every side. One had an ax in his hand, another a hammer. They began to strike it with cruel and violent rage. A horrifying scream was heard and the earth trembled. It was as though a hidden hand had touched their necks and when they looked again the whole tree had sunk down in its place and the earth had closed up over it.

After the death of the powerful magnate, who by his own wish, was not buried in the first row of the cemetery, they opened his last will and testament. He had willed that both sons were to share equally, the firstborn not being given a double portion. He gave a tenth of all his wealth for holy purposes and various charities. They were to kindle a perpetual light for his soul and that of his granddaughter, Yocheved, who had drowned.

Shmuel Menahem, the husband of his grandchild, would receive a fixed sum every month and would continue to help in the administration of his affairs. Surprisingly, he set aside a dowry for the deaf girl, Shmuel Menahem's daughter by his first wife. It was a sum of twenty thousand rubles. Such a thing was obviously unprecedented.

The town of Loton was bereaved and desolate.

Tendrils

The seven and then the thirty days of mourning elapsed. The dividing up of the estate began and each of the two sides exerted itself to turn matters to its own advantage. In support of the simple Chaim Yona stood his intelligent wife with her son-in-law, the secretary. Even Daniel, who until then had served the God of the spirit, now felt a possessiveness ten times as strong as hitherto. Loton, having been deprived of her royalty and sovereignty, seized hold of the garment of the second heir saying, let there be a ruler and a strong leader over us! Let him not forsake us. Those who had previously turned their backs on him now tried to ingratiate themselves. Even his opponents flattered him and against his will he became a father and a patron. He was busy from morning till night. No longer could he set aside periods to study the Torah, nor could he find the leisure to pray with devotion as had been his custom. He held communal prayers in his house in order to recite the mourner's *kaddish* but, in his heart of hearts, he was no longer absorbed in heavenly affairs. There were too many subjects requiring attention and too many matters in which he was involved. One person comes to you talking smoothly but with underlying deceit. Another is a hard bargainer, being nothing more than a plain thief. A house without a wife is like a ship without a pilot, every maidservant was a mistress in her own right. There were quarrels between the servant girls and nobody looked after the children. Now and again he would go to his brother's house and settle certain necessary affairs with his sister-in-law. Talking to this educated woman worked upon his mind to some extent. When you talk with a person of this type you are likely to be disarmed. However, he never stepped across the threshold of Shmuel's house, for his heart filled with pain when he was reminded of Malka.

It occurred to some people that it would be proper for the son of the magnate to request a dispensation from a hundred rabbis to marry another wife, since his wife had left him and could not be found. At that time Daniel journeyed to the town where the rebbe had his residence, to spend a Sabbath. The *tzaddik* fortified his heart and strengthened his spirit. It is in God's hand to turn either to chastisement or to loving-kindness and happy are they who trust in Him.

A close friendship had grown up between the two lonely girls—Leah, Chaim Yona's daughter, and Miriam, Daniel's daughter. They loved each other. One day Leah would walk down to Miriam who would come to meet her, embrace her and kiss her; the next day Miriam would come up to the town to visit her friend. Sometimes they went out for a walk together. Everyone who saw these lovely girls would nod approvingly.

In an isolated part of the county town lived a certain widow who had two sons; talented and distinguished students of the Torah. The older one gave his time to talmudic studies while the younger immersed himself in rabbinical case law and the codes of Maimonides. They always sat together in a special room. One would be traversing law and legend and continually studying the stories of the early sages and various difficult legal topics. The other would be investigating decisions relating to the commandments and details of the statutes. When one of them grew tired and dozed off, the second would muster his strength and study more intensively; when the second fell asleep, his brother would get up and study standing up. Thus they fulfilled the precept, "Thou shalt meditate on the Torah day and night." Many envied the mother of these sons.

It happened once upon a time that a strange bookseller came to the city and went around with his satchel from house to house selling small volumes of the complete Bible. Were they not the holy writings? Nevertheless, they were suspect in the tents of Jacob. The young men had deep searchings of conscience. They finally succumbed to the temptation.

The Torah was known to them from the books of the Pentateuch and the portions of the week. Up to that time they had not paid much attention to the weekly readings from the Prophets. Now they had the Pentateuch, the Prophets and the Writings set before them all in order. In the chapters of the Former Prophets, there were stories and tales which exercised a powerful attraction upon their minds. Lofty were the writings of the Prophets and wise indeed the sayings of the Scriptures. Here were no arid laws and regulations, no hermeneutical problems and solutions. The vigor of the Writings enchanted their ears and moved their spirits.

Thus these fine young men gradually became diverted from the Torah of the Sages and became immersed in the Writings of God and in the utterances of the ancient Prophets. The change in the hearts of her sons did not escape the notice of their mother and she grieved inwardly. The hopes of the rest of the city for these two tender shoots came to naught.

When the two brothers reached manhood, a marriage broker had the idea of arranging matches for them with the two granddaughters of Shlomo the Red in Loton. The mother refused and said, "I shall not befoul my inheritance and give my sons to daughters of a disgraceful family and so cut myself off from salvation."

She was not to know that on High this union had been sealed and signed. That night the Master of Dreams came to the mother of the youths and said to her, "Make your will."

She woke in the morning deeply troubled in mind and called that Matchmaker and said, "The matter has been determined by God, I shall no longer rebel against His word."

The Heir to the Throne

I bid the reader accompany me a little further on my way.

In a town in the region of Volhynia, a certain rabbi of great fame and repute ministered with dignity to his congregation. He took care of his flock in faithfulness and integrity and drew many hearts after him. When he died, a split occurred among the inhabitants through a strong divergence of opinion. Half the people, among them sages and pious workers, followed his only son and wanted to appoint him in his father's place. He was a distinguished scholar of the Torah, a deeply religious man and the father of sons. The other half, among them many of the more common people, favored the rabbi's son-in-law who knew how to preach before a congregation and was very popular. The rabbi's son did not wish to quarrel with his own flesh and blood, and the preacher became enthroned as the appointed rabbi. In the course of time the other side accepted him, for he knew how to arrange his affairs. His wife, the daughter of the rabbi, was a great help to him; she was an educated woman of whom it was said that she had the brain and understanding of a man. In character and in diligence she was even superior to her own mother, the little rebbitzen.

The new rabbi had ministered nobly for ten years when a sickness struck him down in the midst of his days and he, too, died. The important people of the city thought of issuing a call to the son of the former rabbi, who had in the meantime gone away. They would appoint him to his late father's position. However this was not the intention of the young rebbitzen. Her husband had left her an only son, a spoiled gentle child, beloved of his teachers and his instructors. She intended to educate him for the rabbinate. The wise way in which she went about it gained her a successful hearing and she even persuaded those who originally opposed her to her way of thinking. One of the learned men of the city was persuaded to adjudicate rabbinical questions in the congregation while the grandson of the rabbi was growing up. The conduct of the congregational affairs, the young rebbitzen took upon her own shoulders. She became a matriarch and a judge among her people.

When the young man drew near his eighteenth birthday and it was time for him to marry, many important matches with the daughters of rabbis and of wealthy citizens were proposed. But the heavenly planner arranged a union for him with the wonderful dumb girl of Loton, with all her wealth. Who would have thought that this daughter of Shmuel Menahem would become a rebbitzen in Israel! Great are the loving-kindnesses of God.

Weeping

Chaim Yona went completely out of his mind and lost his reason. His wife caught a chill during that autumn, took to her bed and died in midwinter. Shmuel Menahem was now the heir. In the spring he leased his house and came to live in his father-in-law's residence; that is the house of the magnate. He was now second-in-command of the town. Daniel Silk had not succeeded in rallying the support of all the people behind him. Only a portion of the community gathered under his banner, the rest beginning to conspire with his brother's son-in-law. Moreover, a number of people in Loton, seeing the reins of control loose, took advantage of the situation to look after themselves. Daniel was envious of Shmuel Menahem and Shmuel Menahem in turn was an enemy of Daniel. Both were engrossed in their work in connection with the administration of the mill and its branches. Both pulled in different directions. What one man built up, the other pulled down; what one agreed to, the other rejected. At times they determined to divide the inheritance between them, but they realized that if one should lose his footing, the other too would be unable to maintain his position. The people of Loton were addicted to scandal. The prestige and discipline of the magnate no longer rested on them and now they had two houses about which to gossip. Leah, the young sister-in-law of Shmuel Menahem, and Miriam, the only daughter of Daniel, had already married the two brothers we have spoken about. Their close relationship had been based on a firm foundation and had developed strongly—but now a barrier was set up between them.

It happened that when Daniel came to examine the accounts pertaining to the last days of his father, he found a considerable sum of money missing. He began to make close enquiries and discovered that although a number of promissory notes had been collected one after the other, he could not discover for what purpose his father had expended this large sum of money. One day the idea suddenly occurred to him. Shmuel, it could only be Shmuel, must have forged his father's name on the promissory notes and put the money into his own pocket.

Now he had the opportunity to pay off old scores on his enemy and his kinsman. He sent for him and threatened that he would bring the matter before the courts and have him put in prison. The accused man tried vainly to justify himself and to cover up his misdeeds with all sorts of pretexts. He even begged and crawled to Daniel, but without avail. Shmuel Menahem went away from Daniel utterly bereft and in deep disgrace and came to his home depressed and profoundly disturbed. When she saw how miserable he was, Malka pressed him to tell her what had happened and he opened his heart to her. The young wife was horrified when she heard the story. She sat in a corner and wept.

The next morning Malka dressed herself in her best, veiled herself and went secretly to the place where the mill house stood. She went into her uncle's residence and found him sitting at his table in front of the accounts. Daniel was very upset when he saw his niece coming. He jumped up and offered her a seat, saying "What is it you want, Malka, tell me?"

Malka answered him, "Surely you know the purpose of my visit. I shall not leave here until you give me your answer, namely that you have forgiven my husband and will not hold what he has done against him."

Daniel looked at her and said, "He who robs his brother must bear the guilt."

Malka seized his hand and said, "Be kind to me uncle, have pity on me."

Large tears formed in her eyes. Daniel was moved by the touch of her soft hand. Was she not his relative and was she not very dear to his heart? If it were permitted, he would at that moment have held her strongly to him. Once he had had the opportunity to marry her and say to her: what is mine is yours, and what is yours is mine. Now the Torah had forbidden her to him and he himself was the one who had sent her away. He could no longer restrain himself and said, "All is forgiven just as you ask..." He too wept aloud.

In the Village

It was wintertime. Heavy snow fell, covering the roads, and a piercing cold prevailed everywhere. Leah and her husband were traveling by sleigh harnessed to two fast horses, toward a certain city far away from Loton to celebrate the engagement of a member of their family. They were dressed in fur coats and goat skin rugs were spread over their legs. The bells of the horses jingled and the sleigh flew over the smooth snow. However, after three hours, they lost their way. The driver turned the horses to the right and they came to an impenetrable forest. He went back on his tracks and became even more lost. They traveled to and fro in this way all day. Night fell, illuminated only by the white blanket. The travelers began to feel a sense of mortal danger. They had begun to wonder how would they reach habitation, how they could find a path, when they heard the noise of a dog barking in the distance. The horses began prancing, galloping and straining toward the direction from whence the sounds came. An hour later they stood in front of the entrance to a village where pale lights gleamed in the windows of some of the houses.

The wagon driver got down from the sleigh and knocked on the door of one house but they were unwilling to open for him. He went to the house opposite and again knocked on the door. A peasant came out and, having asked what he wanted, said, "Come in to us, take shelter with us, and let me also give fodder to your horses."

Leah and her husband got down and entered the lonely house, took off their coats and warmed themselves in front of the winter stove, into which had been thrown some logs of wood. A small light was burning on a box which did service for a table. Holy pictures in gold frames before which candles were burning hung between the windows.

A quarter of an hour later, the farmer's wife came and set before the guests a bowl of potatoes and also offered them butter and milk, saying, "Eat and you will feel better."

Gazing at the young sweet-faced woman with pitying eyes, she sat down opposite her to talk. A rising wind began to howl outside. Happy were they who had found refuge from the storm.

When they had finished eating and even the wagon driver had gorged his fill and put the horses into the stable, they spread pallets of straw for the guests on the ground, put pillows under their heads, lay the two of them down and covered them with a blanket. This is how they rested from the fatigue of the journey and they slept soundly until morning.

The travelers arose at dawn and washed their faces. The farmer's wife took the pallets off the ground, swept the room with a broom and lit the fire. Leah's husband had gone outside to talk to the wagon driver when the sound of a child's crying was heard from the other side of the wall. A few moments passed and suddenly a young red-faced peasant woman appeared on the threshold with a baby in her arms. Their eyes met. There was wonder and trembling in the room. Deborah and Leah embraced one another, almost choking the child. A flood of tears poured from their eyes and they were unable to utter a single word through their excitement and emotion.

The Question

In the garden suburb of Harson, the capital, in the quarter inhabited by the officials and the rich citizens who have retired from business and are taking life easy, a very beautiful woman was standing one morning on the stone steps of a summer residence. She was clothed in a light check dress with wide sleeves, and was reading a letter held open in her hand. Then she folded it up, opened it out again, and again put it in her bosom. A shadow passed over her clear face, and her pale lips moved slightly, showing her gleaming white teeth. There was a glow of majesty about her. In the whole street no one could be seen going to work. A gentle tranquility prevailed on every side. Here there was no toil for daily bread, no struggle for existence, just a life of ease which flowed gently like grass moving in a light breeze.

The woman descended the steps, walked around the house and entered a little garden. There she sat down on a green bench, rose again and approached a fountain. She moistened her face and wiped it with a white handkerchief. Attached to one tree was a dovecot. She raised her eyes to look at it. Inwardly her thoughts were sad. Since she was a girl the sun had risen and set, risen and set. She had been an object of adoration and now the priests who had worshipped her were utterly discredited and all her fond hopes had vanished in a whirlwind. There is no freedom for the body. After the throes of passion have been dissipated the palate is parched and empty. She plucked a few berries which were growing near the fence and rolled them about in her fingers. She went to the end of the garden and came back again. She was without purpose or desire. Those who worshipped her and her body had deceived her. Man is without content and without knowledge. You have been brought up sharply against the nakedness of reality. You have awakened and the dream is over.

She sat down once again on the bench and dug the tip of her shoe into the ground. The sound of a child's crying was heard. A pretty little girl, about eleven years of age, hurried to her mother in a storm of emotion, threw herself upon her and kissed her. Then she buried her head in her bosom and pleaded, "Mother darling, I have so many uncles, but I do not know my father."

The face of the woman reddened and she answered, "We'll be going to see him very soon, my darling."

The little girl leaped up and danced in a transport of joy. Two birds were pecking not far from them, a cock was crowing.

The Slain

Harvest time was approaching. The woman sold off her house furniture, piece by piece, and packed her belongings and clothes for the journey. Her aim was to go to the town of Loton where her husband dwelt. The summer villa where she had been staying belonged to the heirs of a friend who had fallen in a duel with one of the nobles. The day of the journey came. The woman and her little daughter climbed into a handsome carriage while their trunks and parcels were loaded onto an ordinary wagon which followed behind them. It is a long journey from Harson to Loton, taking more than a full week.

Halfway they turned aside to stay overnight in a certain inn which stood in the poorer quarters of a village. It was a hot day and the sky was overcast, the air heavy. The world was ominously quiet before the thunderstorm, and oppressive thoughts stole inescapably into the heart. The inn possessed only one low-ceilinged guest room, and it was cleared for the beautiful woman and her daughter. The inn-keeper's wife served food and hot tea and tried to start up a conversation with the guests. Outside the wind was howling and rattling the shaky roof. A sudden flash of lightning illuminated the window and the little girl clutched on to her mother.

They both lay down in one bed, mother and daughter, because the girl was frightened and nervous. The lightning flashed in forked tongues of fire. Peal after peal of thunder shook the earth. Suddenly a lightning flash like an arrow pierced a hole in the wall, passed through the sleepers twined together in the bed and struck them with its searing flame. The people in the house, terrified at the clap of thunder, got up and lit a candle, fearing the inn was surely going to fall in or become a bonfire. The wagon driver, too, got up to quiet the horse. He was worried about the people he had brought there in the carriage. The wagon with the luggage had gone much slower and had only just arrived. A pouring rain flooded down into the ground. They decided to wake the sleepers and knocked on the door of the guest room; but no one opened it. They forced an entrance and there were the strange woman and her daughter lying motionless in bed. There was a hubbub in the house. They tried to resuscitate the smitten pair, poured water on them, massaged their bodies, and worked their limbs vigorously but their efforts were in vain; not a sign of life appeared, no breath was left in them.

The next morning the wagon driver saddled one of the two horses and rode to Loton, arriving while it was still day. He stopped in front of the mansion in the mill house compound. Daniel was looking through the window, his heart heavy with anxiety at their tardiness. He saw the messenger arrive and ran down to meet him in the courtyard. The servant dismounted from his horse, removed his hat and said, "I have bad news for my master."

He described what had happened on the way.

"Your wife and daughter are lying dead in a certain village. They were killed by lightning."

Daniel began to weep as he heard these words, knocking his head against the wooden post before him.

To Her People

Two months had elapsed. It was the season between the New Year and the Day of Atonement, a day of concern and reckoning for those who dwell below and those who dwell above. The books of memorial had already been unrolled, the fortunes of the sons of man had been sealed as were the events for the coming year. This one would be raised and that one cast down. One would continue to live and prosper and another would perish in his iniquity.

In the Pentateuchal portion Judges, the section which is read toward the end of summer, Daniel concentrated on the passage which deals with the broken-necked heifer and tried to find an explanation for it. If one be found slain in a field, the elders shall come out and measure. And they shall take a young heifer of the herd and break its neck in the valley. Innocent blood may not remain unavenged in the midst of the people. Who had accompanied the wayfarers on their journey? For him there was no forgiveness or clemency. His mind was disturbed and knew no rest. Although this was the powerful season of forgiveness or prayer, it brought him no surcease.

At night Daniel sat alone in his room. Before him lay a book of moral teaching and his thoughts took wing. It was the time of judgment for all the human flock and no man knows what is right for him. He heard a voice calling, a knocking on the window. He turned his face toward the wall and noticed what looked like a human shadow moving in front of the window. He summoned up his courage, rose and approaching asked, "Who is there?"

He heard a woman's voice pleading, "Please open for me, do not be afraid."

He took a candle in his hand, opened the door and a peasant woman wearing a kerchief stood before him. He gazed at her face and cried aloud, "Are you Deborah? Tell me."

"Indeed I am," she answered. "Please bring me into your house, and do not drive me away!"

He stood dumbfounded for a moment and then said, "Enter; find shelter under my roof."

The newcomer kissed his hands and flooded them with her tears. Her child had died that summer. The meeting with her sister that morning had broken her heart.

I shall be brief. They hid the penitent woman in her uncle's house for a few days and the matter was kept secret even from the house servants and maids. At the close of the Day of Atonement, a day on which the hidden woman also fasted, Daniel and two other men, who shared the secret with him, journeyed away from Loton in a covered cart so that no curious eye could see them. They traveled day and night, until they crossed the border and came to Brody in Austria. There they spent the Festival of Tabernacles with the rabbi of the city. The lost lamp had returned and was re-admitted to Judaism according to the law governing penitents.

But the sturdy Pessie, she and her descendants have remained a gift to Edom until this day.

Translated by A.S. Super

Miriam

Part I

Chapter one

Many years ago I jotted down on a sheet of paper all the details of this affair, which had within it the makings of a novel, complete in all its parts. I envisaged everything clearly, observing the cycle of events and the interweaving of incident. However, the blows fate dealt me were harsh and, until recently, I have refrained from putting my vision into effect. Now I am advanced in years; the daytime allotted for mortals to perform their tasks is drawing to its close and from afar the shades of evening are approaching. It is only a step away to that long night in which all shall rest until the end of all creation. I now have only the light of a candle by which to write, and time presses. So I shall be brief.

Nathan-Neta of Belz, the maternal grandfather of Miriam, the heroine of this tale, had risen from the lowest ranks to attain to the eminence of being reckoned among the seven most wealthy and powerful citizens of Ladyna. It does happen occasionally that an ingot of iron is extracted from hills of copper, and tin is mined from the depths of the earth.

His father was one of the poorest people in Belz; a scavenger of rags and bones which he sold to dealers. All week, he went his rounds through hamlet and village, toting a large sack on his shoulders, in which he stowed indiscriminately anything he found on garbage heaps or waste ground. His food consisted of dry, pitted bread crusts; his feet were swollen and his clothes in tatters. He carried on his rounds for thirty years. His skinny wife was in a state of almost continuous pregnancy, always giving birth with dreadful difficulty. Nature listlessly fulfilled its promise. Who would find shoes for the offspring in such lean times? Who would clothe them? Who feed them? He who dwells on high is merciful; He is called compassionate; but His light does not shine through to the homes of the poor and downtrodden. Such has been His way since time began…

Nathan-Neta's father did not ponder about the ways of God. In his view, the whole universe was nothing more than a heap of scrap. If the bundles were left where they lay, they were of no value. But if one picked them off the ground and sorted them into their different kinds—then they were worth something. Summer and winter were like two bowls, one inverted and one not. Even Sabbaths and festivals were not days of rest for this poor man, for that was the time his wife complained about all they lacked in the house, and he was powerless to give her what she wanted. In spite of all this, he was not envious of others. With the exception of the eldest, his sons grew up wild. They did not even know the prayers. His own prayer book was in tatters, and pages kept dropping from it…He who dwells on high is not far away, but neither is He near.

In the heart of the city dwelt the well-to-do householders, some of whom were observant. Belz had a rabbi, *shochets**, and some charitable men. But he, the poorest of the poor, had no share in the affairs of the congregation.

Something happened in the city. One summer, the rag and bone man's eldest son, whom I have mentioned already, disappeared from the slums of Belz leaving no trace. His mother wept bitterly over him; his father took his sack and hoisted it onto his shoulder as he had always done. True, in the synagogue they talked about it. Wasn't it something? One arrogant warden was upset that the boy had not

* Ritual slaughterers

stayed in the city until he grew up. Then they could have conscripted him into the army as part of their quota. One woman, given to good works, dreamed that she saw the missing lad riding on a billy goat.

In the course of time all was forgotten. Other things happened in Belz and became the topic of conversation. Belz would endure until the redeemer came; and who cared about this child of the poor?

Who would have imagined that this youth would in later years become a substantial merchant in the city of Ladyna, a highly respected personage indeed? There are many paths to fortune, and the reader must not expect me to lead him gently all along the way which this boy went to secure a firm foothold in life for himself. If I were to attempt that, I would have to write a novel within a novel. As it is, I might not even manage to finish the job I started out to do.

2.

The sole inheritance which fell to Nathan-Neta was that he was called not by a single name, but by two. Had he roamed the earth with but a single name, he would have been handicapped in life...He slipped out of his native city, Belz, with no clear goal in mind. Some wind lifted him up one bright morning at sunrise, bore him along, and set him down in a very broad valley. In front of him there was no highway and no clear direction. He just went on wandering aimlessly. He worked at one thing after another, while all the time the earth rose up under his feet. Now he really faced the mountain of life. He began climbing upward, stumbling repeatedly. But he girded himself and continued his ascent. Not only did his body grow, but vitality increased with it. He climbed higher and higher. Not only were the heavens wide open; the earth, too, spread out before him. As he grew, so did his possessions multiply. A man's hands and arms may become as strong as the power of thought. If at first Nathan-Neta worked in a shop, in no time at all he was a shopkeeper himself, selling linen and flax, woolens and silks. Nathan-Neta built himself a house and took a wife. He was nearly thirty years of age when he did so, which was rare in those days. By that time he was already a reputable merchant. His yea was yea, and his nay was even more immutable. In his dealings he was neither rapacious nor a trespasser on other people's preserves. He ploughed, hoed and planted. Every yard he measured in his shop, every length he sold was to him a kind of creativity. He was sparing of his words and did not try to inveigle his customers. He neither fawned on important customers, nor did he spurn the small purchaser.

Nathan-Neta was an observant Jew, and had a big say in the affairs of the synagogue. He also became accustomed—heaven knows what brought him to it—to pay tribute to traditional Judaism and understand the needs of Jewry. As a private person he always labored and produced exclusively for the consolidation of his household; but he was also a member of the community. He did not hurry through his prayers; he ate his meals in moderation. When a customer entered his shop while he was in the back room, he went out to him like a master, not a servant. His past had faded completely from his memory. No longer was each day a random part of the week, but each day followed a set plan.

Nathan-Neta's shop expanded steadily year by year. He was not only a retailer. Medium-size shopkeepers began to turn to him, and he supplied them with the goods they required. An able assistant was soon helping Nathan-Neta. Nathan no longer bought his merchandise in the district capital as he had done formerly. He traveled personally to the Volhynian capital and to the second largest metropolis of the Russian empire.

His horizons widened. For two years he was treasurer of the synagogue. He granted a generous annuity to a certain *tzaddik* although he himself was not a Hasid by conviction. Every Sabbath a needy guest ate at his table. He contributed regularly to the soup kitchen and the communal charities. His wife, Dvorele, also dispensed alms anonymously. She came from a very respected family, and the silk kerchief she always wore on her head made her look more like a rabbi's wife. At the conclusion of the Sabbath, or when Nathan-Neta returned from his journey to the larger townships, the rabbi of the congregation would come to his house to drink a glass of hot tea and talk of worldly matters with the people who happened to drop in.

Men would make deposits with Nathan-Neta without interest and without trust deeds. Small traders would turn to him for interest-free loans to tide them over. Shopkeepers starting up in business would solicit his advice. Sar'l, his oldest daughter—one of the heroines of my story—had learned to read and write Yiddish. In the house there was a Jewish servant girl, assisted by two gentile housemaids. A gentile came in every day to fetch water from the well, which was some distance from the city gate. He also chopped wood. In the yard were milk cows, coops for geese and chickens. One descended by a stairway to a large cellar divided into compartments. This served as a winter storehouse. It was, in fact, a Jewish household firmly established and lacking nothing. If the rag and bone man were to rise from his grave and step across its threshold, he would think he was dreaming...But wrapped in pauper's shrouds he had long been laid to rest in a distant corner of the cemetery at Belz, while his son sold thousands of yards of cloth every day. Two different worlds!

3.

When I said that Nathan-Neta was one of the seven most wealthy and powerful men of Ladyna, it was not a number I picked out of the air. In addition to him there were six others who were well-known men of substance, held in respect by the populace. They were Jonathan, the miller; Simon, the moneylender; Menashe, the leaseholder; Gad, the skinner; Naftali-Menahem, proprietor of the general store; and Mordecai, the ironmonger. Simon, the moneylender, was a tough customer who always pitted himself against his fellows. Jonathan, the miller, was a man without sons, very shrewd but a little miserly and not very much liked by people. By contrast Gad, the skinner, was extravagant. He had in the past gone bankrupt and had recovered his position on each occasion. Menashe, the leaseholder, was the one man in Ladyna who understood Polish and had contact with the local nobility. Mordecai, the ironmonger, possessed the most beautiful house in the city. It was double-storied and its tin roof was painted green. From afar it resembled a public building. Naftali Menahem was always in a state of alarm, living without reckoning. But he was very affluent and his resources seemed limitless. If the reader should wonder why I describe all these characters in such detail, he should realize that the wealthy people of a city are the windows which illuminate the whole house. Shut them and you sit in darkness. These were the seven only noteworthy windows Ladyna had. The rest of the city's population was comprised of ordinary people, those employed by the religious establishment, the established merchants and those who kept changing their métier, speculators, brokers, matchmakers and the rest. Then came a whole range of artisans: leather workers, tailors, carpenters, smiths, a few wagon drivers, porters, men of no consequence and outright paupers. All these lived their own lives and basked in the light of those rich men whose names I have mentioned. Take these luminaries, magnates and prominent personalities away from the city and what would be left? One of their wives was also a warden. There was a strong jealousy toward her among the other six. But Dvorele was really different from them all. In contrast to her husband she was descended, as we have said, from a worthy family and she had a tenderness and dreamlike quality in her nature.

Her father was the last scion of a wealthy family which had once flourished but had subsequently completely withered away. He sat alone in the poorer quarter of Honyrad, a county seat, and God alone knew how he made a living. From time to time he sold off some valuable object or disposed of a piece of furniture and when his property was eaten up he would occasionally dig up some odds and ends in his house...To be obliged to receive some benefit from others was for him like jumping into a fiery furnace. When he went out and saw people busily engaged in worldly affairs, and profiting by them, he hid his face in shame. When the well is stopped up of what use is the bucket? His wife, Dvorele's mother, became sick with sorrow, while she, the eldest daughter, passed the whole of her youth in despair. Then Nathan-Neta came along and took her for his wife at the time when she had scarcely one garment to cover her body. Of course she was willing. She remained a riddle to the last.

They talk of marriages made in heaven, of justice and righteousness in the scheme of the world, of divine providence and an ordained path in the world. Questions are asked and answers given. But when we lift the veil, no hidden hand is seen writing. A stone weighs heavily upon us, though the poet bears his burden sevenfold. I tell you of Dvorele for the sake of her daughter Sar'l, who is the mother of Miriam, the heroine of this story. Who shall tell Dvorele's story? But I run ahead of myself.

4.

Let us pass from here to Linitz.

The town of Linitz was larger than the neighboring townships of medium size. It had huge sugar mills. Forests, many square miles in extent, were cut down as fuel for the large factory furnaces. What God had planted was being consumed for man's needs. Not many wealthy men had settled in Linitz. The town had no wealthy class. The leaseholder of the sugar mills was the sole luminary, casting his life-giving radiance over the inhabitants of the district. The factories worked even on the Sabbath. Their activity never ceased. For appearances' sake the factories were "sold" to a poor gentile for a token sum, in order to deceive God. Jewish law forbade Sabbath work, so the children of Israel devised a legal fiction to permit it. Apart from that the leaseholder was an observant Jew and prided himself on his piety. In the main the town was composed of shopkeepers, modest merchants, and, in addition, many artisans and common folk. There was also another category of persons essential for the smooth functioning of the economy: bookkeepers. In conducting the business of the factories everything had to be noted down and calculated. So much raw material was consumed in refining the sugar; so much of this and so much of that. Such and such a quantity of wood had been brought for fuel and so much timber and bricks to repair the houses and the storerooms. The amounts paid to the workers and laborers by the day, week and month were all noted down. They entered the salary paid to each and every clerk, steward and cashier. The processed sugar weighed such and such. This number of sacks was fetched from here and another from there. Such and such quantities of finished sugar were shipped to the coast and so much was consigned to provincial towns. There were debtors and creditors, borrowers and lenders. Payments in cash or bills of exchange, and against bills and checks deposited with the counting house. Particular accounts amounted to general accounts; there were fixed assets, surpluses and balances. All the ramifications of the figures and the columns of the accounts meshed together like small individual cogs into the functioning of a mighty machine. For quick reference each item was entered in a special ledger which referred to others. But if you wanted to locate a particular entry, there was an index which would instantly find the information you required. If an error was made in one small figure, a large deficit appeared in the total sum. Anyone who was not an expert in these matters would have been driven out of his wits at the mere sight of the multitude of figures; but the initiated grasped it easily; they worked it at once with no need for a second or third look. It is not only for talmudic argument that one needs quick grasp and ability; accounts too require a special type of mind.

Isaac-Nahman was one of these bookkeepers; and it was his eldest son, Israel, who was betrothed to Sar'l, Nathan-Neta's daughter.

5.

Isaac-Nahman was quite competent in his work. He was in the habit of doing his job standing and not seated. He counted up his columns of figures from the bottom upward and not from the top downward. He chewed on a spill of paper which he habitually held between his teeth with a lead pencil stuck behind his ear. In the heat of the day, when the sun scorched down, he would take off his hat, but would smooth his hand over his head so as not to offend against the prohibition of going bare-headed. He was punctilious. The inner significance of a matter never concerned him, only its arrangement and its outer form. Every few years he climbed up one rung on the ladder of promotion. He had been widowed for four years—an unusual situation—and subsequently married his deceased wife's sister whose husband had died. He never spent more than he earned, was meticulous about the cleanliness of his clothes, polished his shoes every morning and combed his hair every day when he went off to work. He ate moderately. He drank a little beer with his meals and never used to dip his bread in salt after saying grace before meals. Were I to enter into a description of his character, his early life, how he wooed and wed the wife of his youth and then the one that followed, I would again be committed to a whole chapter.

His son Israel, Sar'l's fiancée, was the exact opposite. He was of average height with rather long hands. One could perceive a slovenliness in his dress. His physical movements lacked co-ordination and he was inclined to daydream. His father was fair-haired but he was dark, with a fine moustache. His teeth were bad, and he had a habit of putting his hand over his mouth when he spoke. He was adept at his work. He quickly grasped what he was told but just as quickly forgot what he intended to do. When he was a pupil at the *heder** he used to doodle words with a lead pencil in the margins of his books. At sixteen he developed a tendency for the Enlightenment movement. He read Shulman's *World History* and his father raised no objection. He spent a whole year studying Russian, but the language had no particular appeal for him. He knew some portions of the historical books of the Bible—those sections which are erroneously called the Former Prophets. Of grammar he knew some rules concerning Hebrew nouns and verbs.

There were two other young men in Linitz who had strayed away into worldliness and culture. They, too, were betrothed and actually met their fiancées before the marriage. But Israel never met his bride face to face before his wedding day. Nathan-Neta did not hold with these things, just as he did not understand Sar'l.

Sar'l was tall and fairly good-looking, but blotches of red always blazed at the points of her cheeks. She was lazy about domestic matters. She loved to preen herself and was not disposed to making conversation. Usually she sat at the window of her upstairs room—the shop was on the ground floor—and looked down at the street. By

* Traditional Jewish school where the Jewish child first learned to read and was taught the Pentateuch and Talmud.

some chance, for which I cannot account, she had got hold of two Yiddish novels and reading them transported her far away. Her native town Ladyna was only a corner of the great world. There were many great cities, seaports and different lands. There were heroes and brave men, lucky people and those who had their tribulations. One man pursued a successful career, another encountered one obstacle after another. A person might be looked upon generally as God-fearing when in fact he was a common thief. There was no integrity in society. People had their ups and downs in the world, and the hypocrites waged constant war with decent folk. A young fellow might appear suddenly, speak tender nothings to a young girl and inveigle her into love, when all the while his ultimate intention was to sell her into a life of shame.—She wept and bemoaned her lot and he terrorized her. The girl stole away from him and sought refuge with a friend—but he too had evil designs upon her. She was poised on the brink of perdition. There was no escape or way out for her. Suddenly a rescuer and deliverer appeared…Another heroine lived with her beloved in poverty and destitution. Her parents had banished her because she had plighted her troth to the man she loved and not to the one they had chosen. In utter despair the love-stricken pair had determined to drown themselves in the river. Then out of the blue her sweetheart inherited a fortune from a rich uncle who dwelt in a distant land. Overnight he awoke to vast riches and affluence. He built himself a ducal palace and lived with his beloved in princely magnificence.

Just decide for yourself whether or not they knew all about life in Ladyna.

6.

At that time Dan, the assistant in Nathan-Neta's emporium, rose up in the world. He was diligent in his work, he was well-groomed, his cheeks were full and his mouth was always agape. Sar'l cast her eyes upon him and forgot that she was engaged to be married. She came into the shop at every possible opportunity and watched fondly how the assistant made his sales, measuring off the lengths of wool and linen with expert ease and then folding them neatly. Dan, while not exactly captivated by her, nevertheless felt an inward pride that he had made such an impression on his employer's daughter. As though inadvertently, he once put his hand on her shoulder, and she did not lower her eyes. On the contrary she gave him a radiant look. Once he took her hand and squeezed it, and she felt a strange new emotion pass through her whole body. One morning, when there was no one about in the shop, he kissed her full on the mouth. She fled in a daze to her room upstairs. The love she felt for him was exactly that described in her romantic novels. She would fly with him across the seas. He would clothe her in silk. They would walk hand in hand together on the sea shore. If only a fire would break out in the city and the conflagration engulf her father's house and everything perish in the flames. They would lose their all and become impoverished. She would become a seamstress, sew clothes for others and toil arduously to support her father's household. Then would the engagement with her fiancé in Linitz be broken off and Dan would come along and ask her hand in marriage.—Or perhaps her father would die suddenly and Dan become the manager of the whole business. He would expand the estate left by the deceased and increase its value. He would want to marry her out of love but her fiancé would refuse to renounce his rights. They would then conspire, she and Dan, to poison him. An accessory reveals the plan, they are both arrested and thrown into prison, together. Disaster has brought their soaring hopes crashing.

Sar'l sat herself down at her table and began to write love letters to Dan the shop assistant. She scribbled and crossed out, continually raising her eyes to the door. Suddenly her energies flagged, she did not know what to write. She got up, opened one of her novels and copied out a love letter from it exactly as it stood. Its sentiments expressed her feelings perfectly. She betook herself to the shop with the letter and thrust it softly into her beloved's hands.

No need to dilate. Sar'l was like a dreamer. Dan obsessed her the livelong day. She reread her two novels and absorbed every thought and vision. She could no longer discern where her real life ended and where the fiction depicted in the novel began. The times when her father went off on his travels to buy goods were days of longing and deliverance. On one such occasion, at twilight, she met her beloved in the cellar of the house, put her arms round his neck and kissed him like one demented. She would place sugar buns or sweet biscuits on his plate. She bought apples and other fruit for him. When her fiancé in Linitz sent her a gold chain for a gift she longed to place it around Dan's neck. She sent him a *billet-doux* every day and by this time knew how to find words and phrases to express her feelings. Dan was her crown and diadem, her sun and her light. To her he was a constant shining star. He was so elegant and handsome. He was handsomer than all the other young Jews; indeed there was no one in the whole world to compare with him. Her soul was bound up in his. Her whole being longed for him. She could kiss the ground beneath his feet. She was his slave. She belonged to him; and he, he alone was all she wanted in life. Thus she told, retold and repeated again all the burning clichés she found in her novels and was truly convinced of her tremendous love for him.

Her guileless mother neither knew nor even suspected anything.

7.

A fierce controversy broke out in Ladyna.

There was a *shochet* and inspector named Nathaniel. He was learned in the Torah, not just in its laws, and was reckoned among the God-fearing and scholarly. He was active in the community and regularly led the service during weekdays. A certain jealousy prevailed between him and the local rabbi. The other *shochets* hated him; naturally! Nathaniel had one trait which did not seem to fit his extremely pious character. He was stubborn and hated to admit a mistake even if he knew quite well that he was at fault. He was inclined to parsimony. The income of a *shochet* in Ladyna was never very large. Nathaniel had married a second time, and his eldest son by his first wife was apprenticed to him as a slaughterer. This son, whose name, I think, was Nahman, had a nagging complaining wife called Batya.

She was ugly by any standard, but despite this she domineered over her sluggish husband, making his life miserable with her grumbling. A few neighbors with whom she quarreled regularly, advised him to divorce her. Old Nathaniel was inclined to this view. Batya and Nahman had a deaf mute child who made both parents' lives a burden. Batya bore no more children. She herself often toyed with the idea of asking for a divorce in order to be quit of her ne'er-do-well if only he would take the child with him to his father's house! But this Nahman steadfastly refused to do. Once a violent argument broke out between Batya and her husband. She threw a shoe at his head and raised a bruise. What did the injured spouse do? He fled and lived in his father's house and showed no wish to return to his own home. Batya said; "So my husband has left me here holding the baby." What then did she do? She took the dumb creature, wrapped him in a bolster, crept furtively into the yard of her father-in-law's house and laid him down on the doorstep. When the people in the house peeped out and saw her coming with the child, they locked the door against her. It was autumn. The swaddled infant lay there uncovered for several hours. When at last they had pity upon him and took him into the house, he did not long survive. He had caught a chill out in the open and died two days later. Ladyna was shocked by what had happened.

There were some who took the affair up hotly and said that plain murder had been committed at the *shochet's* house. Others out of sheer contrariness claimed just the opposite. He had not known and could not be held to blame and it was useless to try to represent him as guilty. Some said one thing and some another. A quarrel in a Jewish community! The common people and the poorer elements who had little love for religious functionaries condemned him as a priest who sanctimoniously blessed the sacrifice but had no pity over a weak infant. This motivated many burghers and well-to-do to take the side of the *shochet* and refuse to remove him from office. Even the leaders of the city, who, despite their jealousies and inner rivalries, had always been looked upon as a strongly knit family, now split into two factions. A lust for victory consumed every section of the city. In the synagogues, in the market place and the streets, wherever people gathered, the incident was made the sole topic of conversation and discussion. It occupied everyone's attention exclusively. The rabbi of the town had no desire to fan the conflagration and pretended that he was holding aloof from the matter. What concern was it of his? A scholar and the incumbent of a public office must indeed be meticulous about any spot of grease on his clothes! On the other hand a learned man who had transgressed must surely be thinking about repentance and God would forgive him his iniquity. Nathan-Neta, our hero, had hitherto held back from complete involvement in communal affairs. He had never insisted that they accept his opinion. But now, when this dispute flared up, he too was infected. He made up his mind, no one knows for what reason, to stand up for Nathaniel, who had already been condemned by the opposition now refusing to eat meat slaughtered by him. In addition they prevented him from leading them in prayer. What did Nathan-Neta and his followers do? They established a *minyan* in their own homes, where the rejected *shochet* honored God with his voice. One Sabbath when the group met to pray in the large room adjoining Nathan-Neta's shop, Dan, the shop assistant, was called up to the Torah. The next room had been reserved for women congregants and Sar'l saw her beloved standing wrapped in his prayer shawl pronouncing a benediction before the open scroll of the Torah. Her heart was filled with elation.

8.

The controversy, gaining momentum, grew fiercer and fiercer. Normally vapid and weak characters summoned up strength and rhetorical powers to subdue their antagonists. Men who had hitherto modestly effaced themselves now raised their voices loud in the battle between the two factions. These were days reminiscent of the rebellion of Datan and Abiram in the time of Moses and Aaron, when Israel journeyed in the wilderness: There were Sabbaths when blows were exchanged in the street—a disgrace to Judaism. Each faction wanted to prevail and bring the other to its knees. The constant desire of the men of the town to make money and add to their wealth was almost pushed into the background in favor of triumphing in the controversy. Communal affairs in Ladyna were reduced to one single issue, namely, of having Nathaniel removed from office or alternatively of having him fully reinstated. A deep enmity split the city. It severed the bonds of kinship between relatives, and divided households. Nathan-Neta did not just champion Nathaniel with all the power at his command, but, unprecedented for him, he actually headed his faction. But his wife, Dvorele, grieved secretly over the stone-heartedness of the *shochet.* He had done something that no man should do.

It happened while all this was taking place that Dan, the shop assistant, took his suit to a tailor to be pressed. The tailor found a sheet of paper in one of the pockets. The paper was passed around and came into the hands of Mordecai, the ironmonger. He belonged to the faction opposing Nathan-Neta and was one of the enemies of Nathaniel, the *shochet.* The paper was read and found to be a love letter from Nathan-Neta's daughter. Apart from this unpleasant circumstance walls have ears and men have eyes. The affair between the shop assistant and his master's daughter could not long remain concealed from others. Everybody who heard about it for the first time promptly told his neighbor about it in confidence. A woman would pass it on to her friend and very soon every mouth had taken it up.

I shall not weary the reader. Sar'l's letter was handed to Nathan-Neta her father. His heart fell and he at once withdrew from the controversy. He did not know which way to turn. It was true that Dan was the moving spirit in running his business and he relied on him in everything. But Nathan-Neta was a man of principle. Within the week he settled his accounts with his assistant and dismissed him. He bought back from Dan all his daughter's letters; he did so on condition that the assistant leave town at once. So Dan made his departure from Ladyna.

The next day Nathan-Neta went upstairs and entered his daughter's room. She sat there sewing the trousseau which had been prepared for her marriage. She was closely absorbed in her work. Her father came up and put the bundle of letters down in front of her. A smack on the face was heard. The young girl sat miserable and all alone in her room.

Three months later Sar'l's wedding was celebrated. In the meantime the controversy had subsided. Nathaniel, the *shochet,* had departed this life.

9.

A man once planted a garden. He prepared the soil, removed the stones and built a fence around it. He gathered up the rocks and weeded out the thorns from the crevices in the ground. He dug and smoothed out the ground. He sowed seeds under the clods and watered them every morning when rain did not fall. Every seed took root, thrusting powerfully into the soil below and producing buds above. Leaves grew and covered the roots and the young plant had begun its life. When the heat of the sun is temperate it nourishes the plant and promotes quick growth, but when it blazes forth excessively it scorches and withers it. Similarly, should the windows of heaven open wide in flood, the seed might well be drowned. Someone may walk on the grass and with clumsy brutal foot trample down every living plant and seed. One sees a garden, delightful in its green foliage, the roses blooming, the fruit smelling fragrantly, and is unaware as he strolls through it, how often the lovely vision he sees before him has almost been destroyed. He cannot reckon the nights of anguish, the sparks, the pestilence which tend to destroy what the Lord of Being continually creates anew.

The reader should not suspect me of over-fondness for Sar'l. She was never my favorite and I never bowed before her; nevertheless my heart cannot be still when I visualize the bride lying on her bed with only a night-gown covering her body. The room is dark, the shutters fastened from outside, so that even the night should be unable to see what was happening within. The young man climbs out of the other bed. The hair of his beard has scarcely begun to sprout. Trembling and fearful he approaches the other bed placed a few feet away and touches the awakened, trembling plant. A quiet moan. No sexual love, no passion of the flesh, just a formal taking possession of property. The marriage deed has been duly written in Aramaic, blessings have been recited over the wine cup. The fruit, nurtured with so much toil, has been despoiled, the fence broken down, thorns and brambles grow up in the lives of two people confined to each other from now on…

I have been speaking in parable. Its application will become apparent in the pages which follow.

10.

A comet appeared in broad daylight. It had horns on both sides of its head and its long tail flared out about a mile in length. Men saw it and were terrified.

War on earth. The Bulgarian tribes decided to emancipate themselves from the Turkish yoke which had lasted many generations. The small nation battled with its powerful antagonist. A Christian people was trying to break free from its harsh Moslem masters, but could not stand up alone against their superiority in strength and numbers. Alexander II then passed through Rumania with his forces en route to assist his fellow Christians. Rumania gladly opened its gates to the soldiers and the Russians paid money for their food and water. It was true to say that a few Jews served in the Russian ranks, even more were busy with trade resulting from the war. Something new and entirely different was added to the usual run of petty trading and business. A few Jews in Ladyna too were inspired with the notion of getting rich. They traveled to Bucharest the capital and there they grabbed money with both hands.

The Turks held fast. Continuous reinforcements poured out of the confines of mighty Russia and fought with sword and spear. They were armed with brand new rifles and fire belched from heavy cannon. There seemed no end to the casualties which fell on the battlefields. Death took no note of age. Young men and old, only sons and brothers were engulfed in their own blood. The wounded cried out, and the horses whose bellies had been torn open by explosives screamed as they threw their riders from them. Those still on their four legs trampled down those who a moment previously had been lusty warriors. Dumb animals and articulate men perished without distinction. Biting teeth torn out by the row, armor flying in the air; the earth shook. The true commander of both armies was the Angel of Death. With him were his seven ministers: blood, fire, pillars of smoke, anger, wrath, whirlwind and perdition.

In all the houses of learning and of prayer in the Jewish townships of Russia the question on the tip of everyone's tongue was: Which of the two contending hosts would triumph? Some said one and some the other; once again folk were split into two camps. Every man strove and quarreled with his neighbor. Who would be victorious and who go down to defeat? Learning, prayer and even worldly business were neglected. There was only discussion about the progress of the war. A man sits down to his midday or evening meal and his attentive wife asks: "Berl!" or "Shmaya! Tell me, how will the conflict end? Will the Russians advance further or will they be forced to retreat?" Military and strategic experts were not lacking among the descendants of Jacob. And each and every one of them was wiser than his neighbor. This one would jump up and say, "The Russians are as strong as iron," and the other would retort, "These Ishmaelite hordes are a fabulous people." All domestic anxieties and all private needs were completely forgotten. Everyone was calculating and reckoning, how many months and days will it take Russia to subdue this or that fortress? Mostly the disputations were about the campaign against Plevna which dragged on without success. Joshua had conquered Jericho with trumpets and rams' horns. Obviously the Russians had no Joshua. Israel, Nathan-Neta's son-in-law, was one of the few who also had some knowledge of world affairs. When he came to the synagogue they turned to listen to him. But he was inwardly deeply worried by his own marital affairs. He could feel that his wife Sar'l was not properly affectionate to him. Yet he knew that he loved her. When he sought to kiss her she evaded him; when he took her hand she snatched it out of his grasp. When he spoke freely to her out of his full heart, she answered him abruptly. He yearned for her all the time, but she did not care for him at all. Nevertheless, she became pregnant, only to miscarry in her fifth month.

He went to Linitz to visit his parents but his young wife was unwilling to accompany him. From his native city he wrote her two letters in quick succession full of love and longing, but she was still preoccupied with thoughts of Dan. Shall I reveal some gossip? She did not look inimically on the new assistant who had succeeded Dan. Her mother, Dvorele, tried to turn her daughter's affections to her husband.—In these matters a woman's eyes see much more than a man's. But her efforts were fruitless.

Sar'l again became pregnant and bore a son, who died after three months. After two years she again bore a child, a daughter who also died in early infancy. Israel now began to acquaint himself with the affairs of the shop, at first without much enthusiasm. He had a friend who had managed to publish an article for a Hebrew periodical about some contemporary event. He envied him, saying that it was better to be a contributor to periodicals than a shopkeeper. But his father-in-law held sway over him. The first essentials for a man were to establish a foothold in business and commerce. When there were no customers in the shop, his father-in-law would talk to him about other things. Israel also began to do the bookkeeping.

That was the year in which Miriam, to whose name and memory this tale is dedicated, was born. Sar'l had no more children after her.

II.

It was an autumn day. For the Jews the solemn season of prayer and supplication had passed, as had also the days of the Harvest Festival which followed them. Out of the twelve months of the year a third of one month was given over to beseeching forgiveness from the awesome and merciful God and seven more days to dwelling in tabernacles as in the days of Ezra or Moses. The divine mystery demands affliction of the soul and confession of deeds from men; and God—they feast Him with willow and myrtle leaves and palm branches and other species. Jews in all the cities of the exile and the remnants of settlements in Israel worship these two gods.—Summer is defeated and his wide dominion has passed away. The world covers its face like a son who has lost his fortune.

It was then that Nathan-Neta journeyed to a large city in

Volhynia to buy his winter stocks. There was no railroad yet at that time. Men would travel by carriage or by cart for as much as a week or even a whole month. The Russian roads were very rough. You could go for miles without seeing a house or a living person. When you journeyed through a nondescript village the cart would tremble over a rickety bridge before passing among the small houses which resembled tumble-down tents. A moment or two later you were back again on an endless highway, with only an occasional hayrick or a solitary tree far back from the road. The countryside here was as yet unfenced and the title to land had not yet been settled. The people still had no national or ethnic consciousness. Day was only a corridor leading to evening.

The horses plodded on slowly. The cart creaked heavily and Nathan-Neta climbed down and trudged along on foot. He decided to say his afternoon prayers and turned aside from the road. He took one step, and then another few paces. He turned right and then left. The cart and the other vehicles were lost to sight and he wandered about in the field. He looked up and around and saw a distant shadow, like a fiery scepter glittering in the sky. The sky was like iron. A man of about sixty was walking along bent down, a white shroud visible from beneath his black overcoat. A twisted snake was entwined round his stomach like a belt. On his shoulder, the wanderer carried a swaddled infant. The fiery scepter gleamed again and a voice, terrifying and thunderous cried out, "Go and do not stop, Nathaniel, you man of blood!"

Nathan-Neta's hair stood on end and his eyes bulged out of their sockets. Certainly he had heard that this sort of thing could be read about in books. Now he was alone in a field and there was no one with him. He was seeing with his own senses a vision from the world of wonders. He stood rooted there like a tent peg, an overwhelming terror keeping him transfixed to the spot. A stone rolled to his feet. It seemed to move of its own accord, repeatedly rising and falling. Nathan-Neta tightly seized the fringes on the corner of his prayer-shawl and proclaimed "Hear O Israel!" At once the vision evaporated. He was a quarter of a mile from the cart. The cart driver cried out; "Reb Nathan-Neta, what's holding you up there? Why don't you get back onto the cart?"

Let not the reader think I am imagining things. I am only relating what actually took place; and not inventing fairy tales.

Reluctantly Nathan-Neta continued on his journey. He reached his destination, purchased the necessary stock for the coming season and made his way home with a cartload of fine merchandise. But a change could be discerned in his way of life from that time onward. Thenceforward he rose betimes in the morning to pray, not by himself, but with the congregation. He even did so on market days. On the eve of the Sabbath he closed his shop promptly at midday, no longer lingering as had been his wont. In talking with Israel his son-in-law he told him that he no longer believed in "the spirit of the times."...Sar'l's lazy habits became even more deeply ingrained. The sun was already high in the sky by the time she got out of bed. She never entered the kitchen and took no interest in running the household. Most of the time she moped around in her dressing gown with the belt unfastened. She ate without appetite. When Israel her husband was in the room with her, she kept going out and coming in, hardly staying with him at all. If he came to her at night, then she was a dutiful Jewish wife. By day she paid no attention to him.

12.

Miriam was a lovely child, delighting everyone who saw her. Fair hair crowned a beautiful head. Her eyes were as gentle as doves, her voice soft and her neck graceful. Her movements and figure displayed a perfect charm. When one took her in one's arms one felt a strong upsurge of happiness and all depression and sadness faded away. There are some natures which are self-enclosed and others which are lively and yet at the same time seem consciously to inspire a feeling of vitality in others, just as an inspired artist fashions his creation, gets every line right and produces beauty. There are flowers which bloom just for a day, roses which bloom in season, and some whose glory is never quenched, like the light of a soul growing from day to day, never knowing night nor winter.

Israel was distracted with the joy of seeing this shining effulgence of joyous light in his household. He would take his little daughter in his arms, lift her above his head and swing her in the air. Then he would kiss her and caress her with his tongue. Tender hands would embrace the father's neck and even Sar'l derived joy from looking at this bright creature that had emanated from her womb. She herself nursed and fed her.

Nathan-Neta had at that time already turned from business to divine affairs and in him was fulfilled the verse "and the living will lay it to his heart." Nevertheless he found, in the granddaughter growing up before his eyes, a kind of morning song. A man communes with his God and sings when his spirit is uplifted. Dvorele also offered thankful prayers for the glow in the house. The family life blossomed brightly once again and filled the emptiness which had previously existed. But she was still well aware of the character of her daughter and her attitude toward her husband. The Torah requires the wife to perform her husband's bidding and submit herself to his discipline. God has many affairs to regulate in His world. One goes this way and another that. He who finds the right way is really happy. Your heart pauses for a moment and then the innocent child comes up and tugs at your apron. There has always been the community of Israel, and individual households within it, where angels and devils abide as numerous as there are people.

There is much to say on this topic.

13.

The new army conscription laws bore heavily upon the people. Though an only son was exempt and a younger son was permitted to substitute for an older brother so that the latter could help his father in his business, to be drafted into the army was in itself akin to a decree of banishment to a land of exile. They would take a young Jewish bachelor or a newly wed husband from a house of learning or from his father-in-law's table, cut off his side locks, perhaps shave his beard, and force him to dress in clothes alien to Jews. He had to work among the other soldiers on Sabbaths and sacred festivals, and he was fed forbidden food. If a man is compelled to forgo congregational prayer, cannot recite the "Hear O Israel!", does not put on his phylacteries, and even profanes the Holy Day, all these are outward sins, and the Merciful One will acquit him who transgresses under compulsion. But the forbidden foods! They mull the brain and harden the heart. God distinguished between Israel and the other nations, and gave his chosen ones laws concerning milk and meat, warning them not to defile and pollute their souls with any unclean thing. Then comes a decree under the seal of the czar, for whom they offer regular prayers in the synagogue, forcing them to transgress the laws ordained by God. Is it any wonder then that they endeavored to evade the czar's decree, either deliberately or through some accident? One might amputate a toe, another would take medicine to produce jaundice and yet another would change his name and that of his father. One man might have three sons who had reached military age while in the same neighborhood lived a widow without sons. One bright day a son would suddenly appear in the pages of the congregational register of births as having been born to that widow. Did the communal leader or his assistants lack ideas? One family would suddenly become two. As no one asked the Angel of Death or the Angel of Birth who was to die or who be born, so did the pen of the scribe bring about events and occurrences. Ladyna suffered the same fate in these matters as other Jewish communities both near and afar.

It came about that a poisonous thorn grew up and began to torment the community. Ephraim, the son of Moses, a coarse, evil-minded person, began to solicit from every candidate "unfit" for conscription, and from everyone else who was evading the law of military service, an interest-free loan which was not subject to repayment. He insisted by threat of force and intimidation. Had this informer lived in the days when the Council of Four Lands regulated internal Jewish affairs, he would have been brought before a Jewish court despite the fact that they lacked the power to impose the death penalty. One Friday afternoon, the enemies of Ephraim cornered him in the bathhouse and wanted to throw him naked into the flaming furnace that heated the building. They were restrained from so doing, but they beat him mercilessly with whips, so much so that he had to take to his bed where he expired after lingering three months. And it was a sin-offering for the entire community.

14.

The bells in the Christian churches were tolling loudly. The communal houses of God were filled to overflowing. The streets were in a tumult, the school children free from lessons for the day. Everyone who met a friend in the street exclaimed, "Have you heard the news? The czar is dead; he has been assassinated." Alexander II, the man who had emancipated the serfs throughout Russia, had fallen a victim to the nihilists, like a wrongdoer. A bomb had exploded and killed him while he was riding in his carriage in the royal capital. The mighty Russian empire, which had subjugated so many different peoples and tribes, and whose area was greater than any other realm, suddenly lost its czar and its sovereign. His son succeeded him. If the tyrannical governors of Alexander had beaten dissident elements with whips, now would his son do so with scorpions…

Only a short while after the new czar had been enthroned, people suddenly began beating up Jews and looting their houses. In Yelisavetgrad, Balta and Belaya Tserkov the fury flared up and spread everywhere. It was the cruel lot of scores of Jewish towns to become the prey of drunken peasants, hooligans, and thieves. No week passed without some community having to drain the cup of tribulation. It brought to mind the medieval pogroms described in the classic chronicles like *The Rod of Judah* and *The Valley of Tears.* The next step was the proliferation of decrees cruelly oppressive to Jews. They were expelled from towns and villages elsewhere beyond the Pale of Settlement.* In the Middle Ages, according to the chroniclers, there were mass expulsions. Jews died in their hundreds and their thousands

* The area in Russia where Jews were allowed to live.

as religious martyrs sanctifying God's name. But now, they began to persecute Jews differently. There was no overt compulsion to make Jews abandon their faith. They did not even force them to close the Jewish religious schools and send the children to secular schools. They did not pay a fine because they wore a skull-cap beneath their ordinary headgear. Instead it was a matter of brutal viciousness and causeless hatred by which one group deprived another of its means of livelihood. And if a public fast was proclaimed to afflict the soul, was not this the custom? If they cried; "Answer us O God, answer us!"*—was it not written in the prayer book?

At that time Nathan-Neta suffered a stroke. He took to his bed and remained bedridden for several years. One day he was hopelessly depressed and turned his face to the wall. The next day he sat propped up with a bolster and played with his beloved grandchild. Although she was only four years old she could already attend the sick man and hand him the things he needed. When he prayed in his bed and wound his phylacteries around his arm and on his head she stared at him in astonishment not understanding these symbols. By the time she was five years old she was as understanding and intelligent as a girl of seven or eight. She had great charm and her voice possessed a strange sweetness. Her eyes were dark blue and her blonde hair was cut short round her head. So she was even when she grew up.

Miriam was fully nine years old when her grandfather died, plunging Ladyna into mourning. A man respected among his people had been gathered unto his fathers. The purification rites were performed by the leaders of the *hevra kadisha*† themselves, and almost the entire community, young and old, turned out for the funeral. They interred him in a prominent place in the cemetery. He left no will. No sooner were the thirty days of mourning over than discussions arose to clear up the question of the estate. Nathan-Neta had two sons and three daughters and someone had to arrange for them to be married. The notables of the congregation intervened, so that the rights of the orphans should not be prejudiced. They decided

* The Hebrew word Anenu has a double meaning: "answer us" and "afflict us."
† The Jewish burial society.

that Israel should manage the shop and should put aside every year a specified sum for every son and daughter, which would constitute their dowry. Their trousseaux would be taken from the shop itself when they were married, in accordance with the dignity of the deceased. Dvorele was to enjoy the same rights and powers as she had while her husband was alive. But her heart had already become devoted to prayer during her husband's long illness. God in His highest heaven is surrounded by angels. These angels are surrounded by ministering spirits and these in turn have ministers surrounding them. The eyes of the Supreme King behold everything. From every side, supplications, prayers, and entreaties are poured out to Him. People weep and entreat and He hears the utterance of every mouth. He gives ear and hearkens to all His creatures below, but governs His world as He wills. In the land of our fathers things used to be different. In those days the holy temple still stood and God abided among the cherubim, and both men and women came to make sacrifices. The priest would offer their sacrifices upon the altar and they would be consumed by the perpetual, un-extinguished fire. Dvorele often thought that she would ask her son-in-law, that instead of her share in the estate he should pay her a monthly pension of four or five rubles, and she would go up to Jerusalem, the holy city.

Chapter two

When a Jewish boy goes to the *heder* he learns to read, and to understand the meaning of the blessings and of the Book of Leviticus. Only thereafter do they bring him to the chapters of Genesis, arousing his interest by telling him stories of the Patriarchs and Moses and bringing to his attention the main laws and statutes. He goes along with his father to the synagogue and the cantor chants in a loud, pleasant voice all the songs and thanksgivings. He sings for the child to hear the psalms which David and the ten elders wrote. Thus the seed of devotion to God and to the Chosen People is sown in the tender soul. The lad grows up and continually absorbs into himself the lessons suited to his age. He studies the commentaries of Rashi and easier sayings of the sages. The festivals celebrated through the cycle of the year lead him back to the ancient times when the tribes of Israel lived in their own land each man under his own vine and under his own fig tree, worshipping the gods of Canaan in innocence and with tumultuous festivity. The various fasts, following the order of the calendar, tell the child of the suffering of his people, the destruction of the Temple, and the burning of the Torah scrolls. This Torah contains the Ten Commandments inscribed by Moses, the father of all the prophets. He was the prophet who spoke to God face to face and the likes of whom is not to be found in all subsequent generations. Every chapter in the Torah is holy. Every verse has its literal meaning and allusion. It was all told only to Israel, to the Chosen People who God bore out of the land of Egypt on eagles' wings.

Of Shem, Ham and Japhet, the three sons of Noah who left the ark after the earth had dried following the waters of the Flood, God loved Shem most. Out of the family of Shem he chose the sons of Abraham, the Hebrew, to be the guardians of his commandments. Among the tribes of Jeshurun, Judah was the prince among his brothers. The God of Israel is a great God, terrible and exalted, a God slow to anger, but he holds his loving kindness for those who fear Him. Not so the gentile gods, for they are the work of man's hand. The right hand of the Lord is exalted, the right hand of the Lord does valiantly, but the idols of the heathens have no spirit in them; they have eyes but cannot see. The God of Jeshurun—his existence had no beginning. He is the Lord of all and unending is His unity. He rules for all time, influencing and guarding His creatures. Angels stand to the right and left of Him, the just and the righteous surround Him. The time will come when there will be an end to the kingdom of the gentiles, wars will cease on earth and God will gather in the dispersed and scattered from the four corners of the earth. The radiance of his servant the Messiah will shine forth, to whom God said, "You are my son, I have born thee this day." Thus the myriad traditions and laws are continuously woven together in the mind of the child. He grows, gathers strength, develops, and expands his knowledge. On the Sabbath a portion is read from the Prophets, in a language which is far above him and remote.—On weekdays the pages of the Talmud open for him where there are legal principles and debates, sayings, apothegms and complex processes of reasoning. His intellect is wearied in trying to grasp these difficult subjects. It is not progress at all but circumlocution. It is all immaterial and incidental. You concentrate on a matter and you seem to grasp it, but it slips away…The tutor sits at the top of his table wearing his ragged fringed garment, perspiring and guiding with plodding determination the flock which sits around the table. Sometimes he chants and sometimes he too is weary. The whole scene is one of poverty. The lads are ravenously hungry for they came to the schoolroom at break of day. If the door should be opened they say in their hearts: Behold redemption is at hand. And suddenly according to the word of the folio book open before them, two tears from the eyes of the Holy One Blessed Be He roll down and drop into the great sea and it rages even more. God has taken cognizance of the sorrow of Israel and the suffering toil of the children who have been expelled from His table. He groans in sorrow and the grief is too profound to endure.

But for the daughters of Israel, all the activity of this life is like a closed book. They are denied these echoes of the past and they have no spiritual soil in which to be nourished. Sabbaths and festivals are the only crumbs of learning they have. They are free from the obligation to study, from the bulk of the commandments, and from prayer. The little vouchsafed to them is like wine that has lost its flavor.

2.

At first Miriam's heart was more inclined toward her mother, just as every little girl is wrapped up in her mother. However, her pure nature soon drew her closer to her father. Israel grieved that he had not been granted a son whom he could endow with all the ambitions he had cherished before his marriage. In his spare time he taught her a little Hebrew. Once he even tried to explain to her the vision of Isaiah. In fact, he himself was a little sluggish in this area. But at least he was fascinated by the magic of the prophet's language; but for the child it was a world much too remote.

Miriam had inclined her ear more to her maternal grandfather when he was alive. He frequently spoke to her when he lay on his sick bed. In the shadow of his mortal illness she observed something she did not understand. A man has a pair of legs and no longer walks on them. At first he was the sole master of the house. Now he lies for days, weeks and months, without telling the members of his household what to do at all. He had been bed-ridden many days and that was his home; then they took him away and he was no more…

Meanwhile Israel used to sit night after night reckoning up his accounts and supervising the shop by day. He labored relentlessly to preserve what had been handed over to him. The household expenses were not small and now a competitor appeared on the scene, Yossi the Hasid, a smart man who knew how to chat up the customers and win them over. This competitor also had a wife who was a great help to him. She was an able and honest woman. In contrast, Sar'l's only concern was to titivate and adorn herself all the time—but not for Israel. He felt rejected in his own home. Communal affairs no longer interested him as before. He was not reckoned among the ultra-orthodox and had cut himself off from the "moderns." He was like a tree that is dried up and in Ladyna there were no springs or fountains.

There was a *maskil** in the city, the son of a widow. He subscribed to a Hebrew periodical which he would give to others to read for a fee. For some time Israel was one of them. This modern intellectual committed suicide through utter despair. The community in Ladyna could not understand the affair at all...Some people began to emigrate to the United States. In Ladyna they had got nowhere, while there they could become wealthy. But in America people did not observe the Sabbath as they ought and the traditional ways were breaking up.

Miriam was now ten years old and her beauty possessed a tender, gentle quality. A thoughtful expression touched her features. She had also heard about the widow's son and felt sad for him. She wanted to ask her father about the matter, but when she saw him busy making notations with his lead pencil on the margin of his ledger, she refrained.

The shop of Yossi the Hasid expanded. It was a hive of activity. Yossi hired himself an assistant to help him in his work. He was very adept at his task. He was a tall man. Sar'l looked through the window into the street as was her wont and beheld the living image of her beloved standing in the competitor's doorway. She was thrilled. The

* A Jew espousing haskalah (enlightenment), an intellectual movement which arose in Central Europe about the middle of the eighteenth century in favor of cultural modernization.

passage of time had not changed his appearance. He was in fact her Dan's younger brother and resembled him closely.

3.

Ladyna was in a ferment. Something startling happened in the affairs of the world which riveted everyone's attention.

The district commissioner of Heysin in those days was a blood relation of the provincial governor. He was a man who ruled the district harshly. He took bribes and tribute from the rich Jews and the Polish aristocrats, and terrorized all the officials of the towns. They stood up before him as before royalty. He made rules and regulations which were unknown even in the provincial or imperial capitals. Widespread and mighty is Russia, greater than the empire of Ahasuerus. Each administrator does what he likes in his own jurisdiction and who can say him nay? Who is there to restrain such a man of authority?

Three times every year the district commissioner would visit the towns under his rule. Prancing horses would await him in every town and village. Lavish banquets were prepared in every place he stayed overnight, and if a woman caught his fancy—the husband just had to forgo his rights. If a man had a beautiful wife he would contrive to leave his home early by pure chance for he knew the district commissioner would visit him and he would be forced to pay this kind of homage abjectly.

In Ladyna at that time the town mayor had a beautiful wife of strong personality. They had only recently come to take up residence in the walled building which had been vacated by the local officials. They lived there comfortably and in high esteem. But when the district commissioner announced that he would be paying a visit, the town mayor was overcome with distress. His loving wife said to him, "By the living God, the hand of this tyrant shall not touch me. Have no fear or apprehension."

Nevertheless on the day of the visit she sent her husband to the next village while she received the district commissioner very hospitably. She made him supper and plied him over-generously with rich, old wine into which she had introduced a sleeping draught. He planned to embrace his hostess and to touch her majestic beauty. But he fell into a deep sleep right there in his chair in front of the burning lamp. He did not wake up in the morning. His heart had died within him. When the members of his retinue came to wake him, there was no answer and no sign of life. They were aghast. Their master was lying dead in a strange room. Only the day before he had been ranting at them, kicking them, flourishing his knout threateningly about their heads, and now—he was as still as a stone.

To be brief, the news spread throughout the whole town. The physician came, then the priest. They hurriedly communicated the news to the district capital and the district commissioner's deputy with a team of officials, came to investigate the affair. The Russian Yael was arrested. The mayor was removed from office, creating a furor throughout the whole area. In Ladyna the people once again took sides. Many supported the accused woman and said that she would ultimately be acquitted by the law. But there were contrary views. Sar'l felt a secret sorrow for the departed commissioner. She had other strange thoughts. The female sex thinks differently from us.

4.

While I am talking about the mayor of Ladyna I ought to make some remarks about the district physician and the leaseholder of the adjoining forest. They were Vassily Ivanovitch and Ivan Vassilevitch. Vassily Ivanovitch was a man with a large moustache, bald, with long ears. He had a pug nose and protruding green eyes. He had the reputation of being able to diagnose any disease quickly. When he took your pulse, he would incline his ear and count just like a specialist. The fact was that he did not know his right hand from his left. He was very meticulous about emptying the bowels of his patients, making them perspire and have lots of sleep. He would lick every wound with his tongue and bind up the bruise with rags. In his dispensary he had some assorted bandages and bottles of bitter herbal extracts mixed with honey. He would just prescribe them in monthly cycles one after the other. He always procrastinated when he was summoned to a patient. His fee was a whole ruble; he would not accept a half. The medicines were extra. He was easy with the Jews and rough with the peasants. He would pat the girls' hair and gaze covetously at their white teeth. He was unmarried but had a liaison with his housekeeper which had gone on for many years. He used to share her bed by night but during the day he treated her like a slave. This housekeeper had previously been the lover of his friend Ivan, the leaseholder of the forest, who still had the habit of patting her cheek whenever he stepped over Vassily's threshold. Ivan was a corpulent man, not unhandsome and better-mannered than his friend. He increased his self-importance by a well-bred dog which always accompanied him, and by a leather whip which he carried in his hand. He used to smoke out of doors and treated Jews with contempt. This did not deter him from taking loans from them when he was hard-pressed, nor from asking their advice in cases of necessity. He was married to a nobleman's mistress and had built up his position with the money of her protector.

The physician and the leaseholder at times went hunting together. They played dice with Arcady Gavrilov, who had at one time been a court secretary and was now a scrivener in the prison. The latter was attired in a faded blue uniform. He tippled to excess and attached himself to anyone who was prepared to offer him friendship. He was entirely without arrogance or pride and would maudlinly confess his sins when he was well in his cups. If he saw a silver fork or spoon in front of him and no one was watching he would slip it into his pocket to pawn it at the tavern. When anyone reproached him for that sort of thing he would clap him heartily on the shoulder as a sign of affection. One should not rail at people nor accuse them. Drink up your glass in good fellowship and relax happily in conversation with good companions.

5.

Sar'l began to go into the shop, a thing previously unprecedented for her. She even began to assist in selling the goods. It was a pleasant sensation to roll up a bundle of silk, and wool and dyed linen gave her a good feeling.

When an official came to buy she would beam at him. She chatted effusively with the estate holders. Had she not been a Jewess she could have married one of the landed gentry. How different these men were from her husband Israel.

She was especially popular with the district physician and the leaseholder. They would take the opportunity of seeing her from time to time either by dropping into the shop by chance or by coming with the intention of actually buying something. Each vied with his friend and spoke about the not unattractive Jewess. Sometimes Arcady Gavrilov also dropped into the shop for no reason at all. He would squeeze Sar'l's hand as he entered, whisper sweet nothings in her ear and be highly delighted at her full, gay laughter. Israel was jealous of his wife, and because of this he would deliberately leave the shop when one of her favorite customers entered. He kept picturing to himself how he might arrive late one night from the district capital and hear a man's voice in the room whispering furtively with his wife. This sort of thing happened at times in books, and he knew from the Bible about the woman who was unfaithful to the husband of her youth.

He came from the hall of the house and there was Gavrilov sitting by the counter bending his head over to the side where his wife was seated. He lost his temper and, taking up his yardstick, hit Gavrilov over the head and was going to hit his wife as well. The assaulted man stopped him by grappling with him. Sar'l jumped up and fled to her room. Her mother came in and sobbed with vexation. Nevertheless that evening she tried to calm down her son-in-law's rage.

All this took place on Thursday. The next day the Sabbath preparations began, for in the evening they celebrated the day of rest. The Angels of Peace did not turn aside to visit Israel's house that night. The table was laid, the candles were kindled and the master of the house came back from synagogue with his brow still clouded. The old lady sat wrapped in her kerchief reading her devotional prayer book, *Korban Minha.** Miriam's light was also shining. But the mis-

* A prayer book with a Yiddish translation, prevalent particularly among women.

tress of the house kept to her room. Her mother went to persuade her to come downstairs, then her daughter, but the answer was the same. Her head ached. The honor of the Sabbath was in abeyance. No one spoke a single word during the meal. Emotions of grief and loneliness constricted Miriam's heart as never before.

6.

Chaya, Sar'l's younger sister, was married to a prosperous widower who lived in the next town. This widower had two children from his first wife. Chaya was very young and inexperienced in the ways of a woman, so her mother accompanied her to her husband's house to take care of the children to which she herself had not given birth. When Dvorele left the house for a short while its protecting angel also departed.

Sar'l now began visiting nearby Heysin, the district capital, from time to time; sometimes to buy something she needed, sometimes to visit doctors. She imagined, as women are wont to do, that she was ill. In that town there was a certain quack doctor, who had a roving eye. He philandered not just to satisfy his lusts but to have some new conquest to boast of to his friends. Sar'l decided to visit this doctor, having convinced herself that no other doctor could do anything for her. Thus, of her own volition, she walked into a trap. The doctor, wearing a dark suit, was leaning back casually in a chair with his legs crossed. He greeted her warmly as she entered, and told her to sit down opposite him and tell him her symptoms. She spoke at length, while he, his arms folded, did not take his eyes off her. He began to feel her pulse; and the touch of hand on hand aroused her. He told her to uncover her breast while he bent his ear to her flesh. He could hear her heart beating.

It was afternoon. No other patients were expected at the doctor's house that day. Sar'l remained seated on the bench, although she had begun to be a little afraid. She sat there like a ewe before the shearer and did not object when the doctor placed his hand on her shoulder. He removed the kerchief from her head and ran his fingers through her soft hair. A settee stood by the wall, covered with a rug of woven wool. The doctor suggested that his guest should sit on it. An inward trembling seized her.

He got up and drew the curtain over the window, and then approached the settee like a priest drawing near the altar. A pleasant shadow filled the room. The woman tried to get out of his clutches. He strove with her powerfully and chided her, "Hush!"...

Evening was falling as a very disturbed Sar'l returned to her hotel. She refused to eat or drink and went up to her room. She sat down on her bed and thought of what she had done. She had tasted the fruits of sin. On the morrow she would have to return to her daughter and her husband. She buried her face in the pillow.

A few days later the faint inklings of the thought began to insinuate itself into Sar'l's mind that she might be pregnant. It turned out to be so. At first she concealed the fact from her husband. But after a while she revealed her condition to him. He was silent and did not answer. He was doubtful and did not believe her. It was so long since he had known her as his wife.—Israel was so busy at that time with the business of the shop. He had the impression that sums of money were being stolen from time to time according to his reckoning; and now this additional trouble!

In the seventh month of her pregnancy Sar'l was seized with violent pains such as she had never experienced before. The whole house trembled at the sound of her shrieking. That night she gave birth to a male child. The storm died away into stillness. The child lived for seven days with his mother and on the eighth day he was circumcised into the covenant of Abraham and was called Nathan.

The kabbalists say that when God in heaven is full of anger with His people Israel and wants to destroy them as a nation, then two of the seven angels of the Divine Presence descend to earth and enter the house of a Jew where a male child is being circumcised. They gather the blood of the infant. They go back on high, enter the shrine and show the blood of the circumcision to their Master and immediately He is appeased. But in the house of Israel, the son-in-law of Nathan-Neta, "the seal of the Lord had been falsified."

On the third day after the circumcision, the child died. Yet he lived on awhile in his father's imagination. From that time onward Israel's character changed. When he sat down to his meal he never spoke. Even in the shop he was often so immersed in his thoughts that he did not hear what the customers were saying. His wife was torn out of his heart; yet she was married to him.

It happened once when he was sitting at the table with members of his household that a glass bottle slipped out of Sar'l's hand and was smashed. Never in his life had Israel made a fuss over breakages in the house or rebuked his wife for them. On the contrary, he was as submissive to her as a bound slave. This time he was in a fury. His anger suddenly blazed up and he began to curse and swear at her. Sar'l kept her mouth closed and did not reply. She had no experience of these things. Miriam sat there thunderstruck, as Israel went on uttering foul curses at his wife. He stamped his feet, and her silence fed his anger. Everything that had been pent up for years within this ineffectual fellow's tortured soul now burst forth and found utterance.

Fixing his eyes on Sar'l he cried, "You gave birth to a bastard. Your breasts suckled a bastard!" He himself was terrified at his own words. His rage suddenly evaporated, like air out of a pricked balloon. Subdued and broken he sat there on his chair, his head supported on his hands, uttering, "Almighty God! What have I done? What have I said now?"

Meanwhile Sar'l had risen from her seat and left the room.

7.

Days of gloom descended on the house. Sar'l left to visit her sister and stayed there several weeks. She began sleeping alone in the bedroom and they made up a bed for Israel in the dining room. At that time Miriam began to learn Russian and found that the study helped her bear up.

Her tutor in the vernacular was a man with an angry, pock-marked face. But he taught his subject with great dedication. He bent his lanky frame, and sat with hands folded, inclining his head to those who listened to his instruction. In Ladyna they nicknamed him "Sheventy" because he could not pronounce the letter "S" properly. He had no sense of the value of time. When he was engaged in a lesson with his pupils he would never stop of his own accord if they did not remind him that their time had run out. He had never in his life eaten his meals at regular times nor kept regular hours of sleep. When he was pondering an idiomatic sentence he would close his eyes, pick up the textbook from the table, think over the difficult passage for a few minutes, then read a word aloud. Sometimes he would suddenly burst out laughing for no apparent reason. He derived special pleasure from walking about alone in his room, from one wall to the other with his hands clasped behind his head. He was a man of integrity who cared nothing about money and could scarcely tell the difference between taking and giving. Judaism was of little concern to him, it gave little and lacked little. He recited the Psalms without comprehending the meaning of the words. But in Russian he knew the semantics, structure and composition of every word. When he was dictating the fables of Krilov he did so with a kind of excited enthusiasm, emphasizing every separate line. When the moral had been taught he felt a certain pang in his heart, like a man who has had his plate taken from the table while his hunger was still unappeased. It was said of him that he never took a bath. His neck was as swarthy as a gypsy's. He wore the same clothes on Sabbath as on weekdays and only changed his garments once in a blue moon. The dust was never brushed from his shoes, let alone the clay and mud.

Was he a widower or a bachelor? I did not know his past. A rather deaf aunt over sixty years old lived with him and took care of his domestic needs. She also earned a little by knitting stockings. Sometimes she scolded him, but days could pass without a word passing between them. Some fragments of recollection still lingered in her mind. She had been married in her youth, but her husband had deserted her. Mordecai was his name. Yes surely it was Mordecai.—After a post office had been opened in Ladyna, her brother's son, he whom they called "Sheventy," used to compose letters for people. At this he was marvelous. At times he would write petitions for people to the authorities. This he did for nothing or next to nothing. He attended synagogue on Sabbaths only. His soul was nourished on some torn volumes of an almost obsolete Russian monthly periodical which had made its way into his orbit by a kind of miracle. He knew almost the whole of their contents by heart. It was all the same to him: stories, general articles, conversation pieces and memoirs. Only critiques were a closed book to him. He would read something and not finish it, and read the same page over two or three times. The Russians are a formidably brave people; and some of its finest sons knew how to write such compositions…

The bright sparks of light which emanated from his pupil, Miriam, enlightened the dark chaos of this teacher. This was the first time that he perceived a new dimension in the fables of Krilov and the articles in the monthly. He used to teach all his pupils (there were not many of them) most willingly. But with Miriam he could sit and teach a whole day long without stopping. He did not actually teach her but passed on to her as a kind of inheritance something lofty and inspired. When the lesson was over and he went home he could still feel her radiance. She created a sort of afterglow in him. A new thread entered the fabric of his inner life, something he had not previously possessed.

Miriam had already passed her twelfth birthday. She was beginning to grow up and develop her own personality. The sweetness of her face was incomparable. In the integrity of her heart she realized the innate suffering in that man, and the ugliness of his body did not revolt her. This teacher's unusual name was actually Gedaliah and in his pupil's heart an inexplicable desire sprang up to raise him from his lowly status and to cherish him.

She could not fathom why nature so distinguished one human being from another and did not distribute its talents with equal measure. She had seen an ox face to face. Lions, leopards and bears she knew only from books. The eagle soars in the highest heavens and the frog croaks in the swampy water. In the world there are lords and slaves. Old people wander, begging in the streets, and men die before their time.

8.

It was the Sabbath before the Ninth of *Av*, which commemorates the destruction of the Temple. Miriam's father brought home with him a guest from the synagogue, a poor blind man. The stranger's clothes were not in tatters. On the contrary, he gave the impression of being a person of some dignity whom God had afflicted so that he no longer saw the world. Miriam looked at the stranger with wondering eyes. This was the first time she had met a sightless person.

Her father, Israel, pronounced the benediction over the wine and let the guest partake of it as well. They washed their hands for the meal and the Sabbath fare was brought to the table: fish, soup, meat and stewed fruit. The Sabbath candles glowed at the end of the table and the white loaf gleamed. The blind man ate and drank with refinement. No one spoke. Every one had his plate in front of him. Miriam, who sat next to her weary mother, kept looking at the guest. Israel had for some time abandoned the practice of singing the Sabbath table hymns, but he duly recited grace after meals.

The meal was over. The maid took away the dishes from the table, Sar'l was no longer in the room; she had got up and left. Israel took a book of the Prophets, opened it, studied it awhile and closed it again. He was exhausted from the week's labors. He rubbed and blinked his eyes. He had been sleeping in the bedroom again for some time now. He also got up and went. Miriam was left alone in the room with the guest. The maid entered, spread a white sheet over the settee, placed a pillow and eiderdown on it and went out. The guest was to sleep there overnight. He got up from his seat and sat down again. Miriam sat opposite him. The lights were not shining for him, but he could feel that the room was not empty.—The girl tried to make conversation and he asked her her name. The conversation stopped again. Tremors of fear and pity seized Miriam. The darkness was only a curtain between living creatures. Were she his daughter, then she would lead the afflicted man on his way and always help him. The heaven and the stars were not for him to see, but earth there was and it was strewn with obstacles and in broad daylight his path was hidden. The memory of the downtrodden teacher, who only yesterday had taught her something new, was gone.—Weighed down with her thoughts she left the room. She undressed and lay down in her bed. A dreadful thought crossed the room and touched the fringe of her tender mind. The God who created the universe was blind, and that was why things were so crooked in the world He made.

She tossed in her bed from side to side. She sought some explanation, even partial. She could not understand why the Jews kept the Sabbath day and why they prayed to an invisible and incomprehensible God. At midnight the girl fell into a deep sleep and dreamed that she was wandering on a lonely path. She lifted up her eyes and saw an old man walking slowly toward her. He was carrying a heavy burden and leaning on a staff. At first, fear shook her very soul and she could not move. But she summoned up her courage, and went up to him and asked who he was. The ancient answered her saying, "I am a Hebrew and we are walking in exile!" The man was her maternal great-grandfather.

Chapter three

Miriam was now thirteen. She was full of charm; no one she met could take his eyes off her. When a person asked her a question, her answer seemed to lift a burden from him. She did not let her imagination run away with her as most girls do, but grasped things by insight. Even when she was silent, a shadow hovered over her. Some traces of the sadness of the world touched her tender soul, not with a shattering impact but with the kind of feeling which is transmuted and buds into poetry. Clouds carry the rain which brings fruitfulness to the earth.

She began to read the Russian novelists and a new spirit awoke in her. First she absorbed the sketches of Garshin and she heard only a lyric note. There was no freedom, but continuous seeking, summer and autumn intermingled. Then a much greater novelist vouchsafed his gifts to her, namely Ivan Turgenev.

The world took on the appearance of a cultivated garden where the dews of morning moisten every plant. One beholds a radiance that does not dazzle. Everything takes on size and shape. Nothing is lacking in all existence. The road is paved, paved all the way, and you know no obstacles. The eye sees and absorbs the beauty inherent in everything; the ear hears echoes of a song. There is no strife nor division despite the chasm between classes. Even poverty does not reveal the rod of its wrath. Gladness and compassion have together filled the heart of the Creator as He sits on the birthstool of His universe. Like a gardener He embellishes His works and perfects His plants every day. There is nothing novel in creation; there are no upheavals from the depths of utter chaos into the orbit of the world. All things perform and fulfill their function and everything that exists serves its fellow. How good and pleasant are the fields, the broad plains and valleys of the earth. There is no tumult in the cities, nor gloomy silence in the villages. Gaze alike on prince and peasant, intellectual and ignoramus, souls endowed with natural gifts and those born deficient! There is a fence between them, but it is not an iron wall. Tranquility prevails over discord. There is no desolation in the world, only some portions of the earth remain to be cultivated.

Now you sleep and are aroused, slumber yet are awake. Living things have double senses. Man, beast—each has his own inheritance, and every creature both receives and gives. There is not just borrowing and repaying but also fertilization and understanding. Have you totally despaired of your life? Very soon you will forsake sorrow. We behold wickedness, tribulation, inequality and loss of liberty—but all are only one step removed from the threshold of redemption. If you have fallen, you shall rise. There is no imperative requiring self-sacrifice. There is no harsh demand for the yielding up of heart and actions, only a feeling of a duty which comes by itself, the stretching out of hand to hand.

When a lad loves a lass and gives her all he has, behold there is Sabbath in the world. Nature celebrates its major festival, but it also has the minor festivals and ordinary days. The table is set and when the family sits down to eat, then is the bread blessed. Even if the poor man receives only the crumbs, even if he lets fall a tear, the sun still shines for him. Murky waters become clear and the clouded sky brightens again.

Miriam was gradually absorbing these dew-drops into her soul. Perhaps even without the tales of this great artist, something would have found its way into a corner of her heart, and would have forced its way out one stormy day. But the descriptions of Turgenev caused a stream of light to suffuse body and mind. Warmth and growth were infusing her from all sides. She, who was reading the words of the novelist, was only one rose of that rose-garden. The poet had kissed her on the mouth…

2.

Let me tell you something.

In the furthest street of Ladyna lived a fairly well-to-do widow named Serel. Her husband had been taken from her before he reached his thirtieth year, leaving her an only son. He was slightly hunch-backed, his head sat on his shoulders. The youth was named Micah. He had studied the Bible and had read the new Hebrew novels *Love of Zion* and *Guilt of Samaria.* These had made such an impact on his imagination that he continually sat and sketched with a lead pencil upon paper. It was a perpetual puzzle to the town, how such a strange tendency had come to this lad. Even his mother at times rebuked him for it although she cherished him and highly esteemed everything he did. Serel had no relatives or acquaintances in the city. Almost no one entered her house. She sat at home and sewed linen for her own needs and those of her son, or knitted stockings, and behold—her grace pervaded the whole house. Her husband had certainly forgotten all the concerns of this world and dwelt somewhere in some corner in the upper regions. But she had not forgotten him at all. Had they not lived as one couple for a number of years, during which she had looked on his face daily! They had eaten and conversed together and he praised everything she did.

Micah had seen Miriam several times and whenever he did so he dwelt upon her beauty and charm. A daughter of Zion straight out of Mapu's poetry passed before him in the street; and he was able to look at her and sate his soul on her radiance.—Love is not just something in books. It also occupies a place in the heart. From the seed grows the flower; you kindle one candle and light fills the whole house.

So Micah began to draw the likeness of Miriam on a sheet of paper, and a new spirit entered him. Every line and every mark was a part of her; her image was his inspiration. From morning to evening he sat and drew, and even at night he neither slumbered nor slept. He saw in the air a likeness of a rainbow. Does a daughter of Israel know what is hidden in him? Can her heart also awaken? Were he not embarrassed, he would have revealed his secret to his mother. Sometimes he thought of composing words of adoration in Hebrew and sending them secretly to Miriam. He haunted Israel's house waiting for the moment when the object of his heart's desire should go out so that he could follow her at a distance. If only he could, just for a moment, touch her hand. If only someone would steal her three-cornered kerchief and make it his own so that he could put it to his lips. Not even the hand of a poet can adequately describe the trembling of the soul when it comes into contact with another soul and drinks with its companion from one cup.

One Sabbath, Micah rose early in the morning and began to chew the likeness of Miriam which he had drawn, and swallowed the sheet of paper completely. He had gone out of his mind.

3.

You go out of a door and enter by a door.

Outside everything is wide open. The soul is a prisoner to the body and the body also is bound in fetters.

Nothing happens in isolation. One stone is placed on another, and a whirlwind comes and carries them away…

A rebbe* came to Ladyna, a type of guest not seen within her gates for many years. At that time the government forbade the members of saintly families to pay their believers pastoral visits. Every *tzaddik* was confined to his city of residence. Because of illness, this particular one managed with difficulty to obtain permission to travel to a clinic, traveling by way of Ladyna. The rebbe was called Nathan,

* A title accorded to a hasidic rabbi.

the Faster. He was of the House of Menahem Mendel, one of the disciples of the *Maggid*.* He had three brothers who shared their father's inheritance. The eldest was humble and innocent. His following consisted of all the Hasidim who truly believed and adhered to the faith out of sincerity. The next brother was alert and much more worldly. He had contact with the richer and well-to-do Hasidim, timber merchants and brandy distillers. The youngest was a brilliant scholar. He was associated with the rabbis, the *shochets* and inspectors and others learned in the Torah. All that was left over for Nathan was asceticism. He was illustrious for his fasting and became known as one who only partook of a small flask of water in the morning and tasted a drop of milk in the evening. On Sabbath eve he ate a small piece of bread and on Sabbath afternoon a portion of salt herring served at the third meal. This rebbe was a handsome man, of distinguished personality. His speech was solemn and deliberate, his gaze clear and candid.

When he arrived at Ladyna, some Hasidim came out to meet him. He descended from his carriage and paced a few steps to the right and a few to the left, continuing to do so for half an hour. This was a strangely wonderful phenomenon. He spent the Sabbath at Ladyna. The people prayed with him at his lodgings and they crowded round his table and harkened to his teaching. On Sunday they began to encompass him with petitions and consultations. Every evening he visited the homes of the generous and the wealthy of the city to give them his blessing in return for money. This procedure brought him to the home of our Israel, despite the fact that he was not a Hasid at all. They had cleared the dining room in his honor. The mistress of the house and her mother also stood next to the rebbe's chair. The mother had changed her ways by that time. Miriam was also invited to enter. She came in and stood at a distance. The dignitary rose up from his chair and sought to place his hand on her head and bless her. As he left he reminded himself of a maiden who lived in

* A title accorded to Ber of Mezeritz, a chosen pupil and successor of the Baal Shem Tov, founder of Hasidism.

the days of Shemhazai* and thought, "May they place my nest also among the stars..."

The next morning he left the town and ceased to glean among the sheaves.

4.

I heard the sequel to the tale of that rebbe, and so it went: While he was still a youth he felt an inclination in his heart toward the feminine universe and was more strongly drawn to the *Shechina*, the Merciful Mother, than to the Father in heaven who dwells in *Arabot*, the highest heaven. The world was certainly hermaphroditic, half male and half female. The small luminary had once been greater than her mother the sun. Eve took precedence over primeval Adam. His imagination prompted him to write a third book of the *Zohar* and in the hidden recesses of his heart he prayed to the "faithful shepherd."† The heathens and even the tribes of Israel originally bowed down to the sun, but as for himself—he offered incense to the moon...The god of the month was superior to the god of the Sabbath. Whoever was found worthy to sanctify the face of the moon uncovered by cloud would have eternity as his portion.

This rebbe's worship of the moon grew in intensity from the time that he left Ladyna with the vision of the maiden in his heart. On the eve of the new moon he fasted as was his wont, confessed his sins, immersed himself and kindled a candle in his room. Did not women on that day purify themselves of their menstrual impurity and lust, to be loved by their husbands just as this moon renews herself. The day of the new moon was made completely holy to the Lord by praises and laudations. When the moon came out and revealed her face, he wanted to unite himself with her as at a moment of consummation. Would that he had blessed Miriam and his hand had touched her hair, then the sun which dispossessed his consort would

* Name of a fallen angel in Hebrew legend, based on Gen. 6:4.

† One of the later parts of the Zohar. Moses is often called the "faithful shepherd."

have been confounded and this would have been the beginning of the redemption.

For the twelve months after this, Nathan the Faster sat shut away in his room worshipping God in solitude, devoting himself to an ancient goddess. The beadles allowed no one to come to him…

5.

The soul of Michal, daughter of Saul, transmigrated into a Hebrew maiden of the daughters of the city of Dashya whose father had taught her the speech of her ancestor and who read the chronicles of the Judges and the ancient kings of Israel. She was betrothed to a youth from a neighboring town, called David. He was a red-haired young man, handsome and also a Hebraist. He took possession of her heart and she loved him. Her ambition was that he should compose songs and psalms and polish them verse by verse so that he could become famous. She wrote him love letters in Hebrew and concluded her words always with a rhyming couplet. His soul clave unto her and this is not meant just metaphorically. What did the Ruler of the universe do? He simply cut off the life of this young man in the heyday of his young manhood, for no reason. The maiden was shocked. She would not release her betrothed from her grasp, even though he were dead. She slipped out of her father's house by night and walked several miles to the town of her betrothed to visit his grave. She cried aloud to the God of all souls that He should restore the soul of her beloved to him. At that moment the soul of Michal entered her. When morning came two souls dwelt in her. She went about the streets of the town crying out, "I am the daughter of a king."

A *dybbuk** had possessed her. Remedy and healing were sought for her, but none could be found.

Her father was quite an educated man and had ceased to believe in superstition, but in his trouble he responded to his wife who wanted him to take the afflicted girl to a "redeemer of souls" and so

* A dead soul.

he journeyed with her to the fasting rebbe.—It was the period between Passover and Pentecost. The beadles tried to shut out these seekers of salvation too. A voice was heard knocking on the door from within the room saying, "Tomorrow is the new moon. Let the daughter of Saul wait among my assembly till the renewal of the moon."

The incident came to be regarded as a miracle.

The night of the sanctification of the new moon arrived; heralding its return to its position of former glory…a faithful worker whose labor was true. A power of the obstructive supernatural forces was discerned. The children of Israel were dancing with threefold leaps according to the three attributes: foundation, glory and eternity.

The rebbe, swathed in his robe, stood with his acolytes and gave praise to the moon. The "enlightened" father and his afflicted daughter stood nearby. The maiden was clad in white, her face like the face of the moon.

"Blessed be He who formed you!
Blessed be He who made you!
Blessed be He who possesses you!"

The hand of the *tzaddik* grasped the hand of Michal and he danced with her as though a spirit had been fused with another spirit. The small group of worshippers were stricken as silent as stones when they beheld this sight.

6.

Now to return from the holy to the profane.

The son of a Polish nobleman used, from time to time, to visit the shop of our Israel. The name of this aristocrat was Vladislav Dombrowsky. He belonged to the conquerors of the fair land of the Ukraine, the people who had reduced masses of peasants to serfdom. God had made one percent of the inhabitants of these provinces lords and ninety-nine percent serfs. In poverty they served the overlords and great landowners on the very soil they had taken from them. They enjoyed the good things of the world, every luxury that man could desire, while the serfs had only a linen smock to cover their flesh, hard crusts of bread to eat earned by the sweat of their brows. You toil from dawn to dusk, the only voice you hear is that of the taskmaster, your children are servants from the day of their youth, your daughters are despised scullions. When a virgin is married the lord of the manor has the *jus primae noctis*. The finest portion goes to these genteel hands; the priests get the fat while the dogs and the herdsmen and shepherds gnaw the bones.

Vladislav was rotten with vice. Between the age of twenty and thirty he gave himself over to raging lusts. Even when he slept in drunken stupor he dug his toes between the breasts of a whore who acquiesced to every perversion. He was completely intemperate. He gormandized until he vomited. In the heat of the day, he galloped like a madman over the broad acres of his estate on his black stallion, and as he returned to his palace he hit out savagely with his stick and whipped everyone he encountered. His favorite dog ate and drank with him. He set him on to everyone who passed by; and when he rested he taught him to play dice with him. He would dance with his maidservants by moonlight and bite them till blood flowed from their necks. He paid no attention to the value of money. If he borrowed twenty thousand rubles he might give a promissory note which could amount to two or three times the sum. He never reckoned up his debts and had no idea of his income. He might over-pay a hundred-fold for a trifling article. He had no respect for Jews. The sons of the covenant had but one purpose in life as far as he was concerned. That was to serve his purpose and fulfill his every will and command.

After his thirtieth year his strength ebbed. When he was filled with energy he might tie the tails of two horses together. Or he would pile chair on chair; two, three, four or five until the pyramid reached the ceiling. Then he would topple the column with a thundering crash. He was married to the daughter of one of the greatest families in the land, a woman as beautiful as Tirza. He ill-treated her and never ate his meals with her. But the description of the tribulations suffered by the prisoners of these lofty halls I shall leave to the novelists of their own people.

7.

It was Friday morning, Ladyna shook itself out of the slough of commerce and her sons and daughters began to prepare themselves for the day of rest. The God of the earth was calling his children below to the feast in an alien land. He still had on high His ministers and angels with their spreading wings, but there are also the sons of Satan who crouch in ambush. The fashioners of darkness continually rise up before the Creator of light and each one shakes the trees of creation until their leaves fall and their boughs are broken. The universal day of rest struggles with the holy day for worker and laborer. This Jew here, this Israelite there, the survivors of those who escaped from Babylon and Spain, wake in the morning in a land drenched with the blood of the days of Bogdan, the arch-persecutor of the Jews and Poles. On the day of the commandment and the covenant, they are remembered, as is written in the Book. They clean the walls of the rooms, they clean the floors and plaster them anew. There is not a utensil which is not washed, not a spoon nor fork nor knife from which the rust is not removed until it shines. The stove burns and cooks for two days. The air is redolent with the odors of fish and roast meat. The white Sabbath loaves are laid neatly in rows as in the days when the showbread was laid before the altar. Jews run about the streets buying fruit and cherries. Boys carry bottles of wine in their hands. A galloping horse enters through one gate and leaves through another raising a cloud of dust. He has not been given understanding, knowledge and discernment like the sons of men who obey their gods. Tomorrow they shall surely proclaim:

"Thou art Holy and Thy Name is Holy,
Thou art One and Thy Name is One."

Who should not have enjoyment and who should not rest?

Vladislav stands at the entrance of Israel's shop with a parcel of white linen wrapped in green paper under his arm. He turns round to say something to the Jewish shopkeeper when, behold, his daughter is seen in the doorway in all her splendid beauty. Without thinking, the nobleman reenters the shop. A mighty stream flows out, the materials, the varieties of wool and the silks spread out and become a sea of colors billowing like waves. A subdued melody is heard, perceived only by the sixth sense. The nobleman is rapt in a waking dream. If the daughter of Jerusalem were given to him in her bridal radiance, he would then proclaim, "Thy people will be my people"—and would proceed to deny the son of God.

That night Dombrowsky knocked on the door of his wife's room and found her sitting in her chair like a silent queen. He bent down and fell before her and kissed the soles of her feet.

8.

The county seat of the nobleman was in the village of Zarkov. There glittered his luxurious palace in which preparations were in hand for a festive day to be held, for reasons unknown. Dombrowsky gave orders to repair the bridge, to fix the roads, clean the courtyards, plaster the houses, cover the roofs and mend the broken fences. The church was repainted blue and its pillars transformed to a marble white. Even the graveyard at the end of the village was cleared of the brambles and thorns which had proliferated there. The tombstones which had fallen were set straight, and the broken crosses were repaired. The villagers, their wives and children were ordered to wash the dirt off their feet and to sew up and fix every tear in their clothes. The girls combed their hair, braided it into plaits into which they wove flowers and green leaves. It was harvest time. The Lord of Nature was not ungenerous and He too said to the tillers of the soil, "Live on what you have. I shall take from you neither tithe nor offering. I am sharing with you and in your festivals."

The gentry of the entire district were invited to dine with Dombrowsky. The carriages harnessed to double teams of horses galloped along. On the flagstaffs at the gate of the palace flew the flags of Poland and Russia. Here were no restrictive laws. Priests of the Church dined side by side with local officials. On the great stone-paved courtyard in front of the broad steps of the palace sat the lords and ladies engaged in conversation. Servants and waiters, clad in uniforms with glittering buttons, ran back and forth to every corner. Foods and delicacies, royal canapés. Get ready! Tonight wine will flow like water.

Dombrowsky's wife was seated on a beautiful chair, like a bride on her wedding day with her maids about her. On her face was an expression of mystified wonder. The palace had a high tower up which the lord of the manor climbed stealthily. He stood on the parapet and looked down on the world spread out below. He threw himself down. Panic and terror! Fear congealed the hearts of all assembled there. I shall not delay the reader with an explanation of the incident…

9.

It was a cloudy day. The bowl of the firmament over Ladyna was like a dish with its edge broken. Drops of rain fell and stopped. A breeze blew and rattled the window shutters. The goats were too lazy to go out to pasture and nibbled at the eaves of the thatched roofs. Dogs were sniffing after bones, hens pecking on refuse heaps. God was not feeding and sustaining all his creatures. His prophets spoke falsely of Him.

Miriam rose and went upstairs to her mother's room. It was now hers. She sat on a low seat by the window and touched the sill with her brow. Her heart was troubled, she did not know why. She thought of her grandmother, of her father, and of her mother who was due to return home shortly from her travels and she just could not summon up the strength to meet her. Even human innocence needs to seek a path. Were her mother's father alive this was one of the times when she would know how to talk things over with him. The people to whom she belonged prayed evening and morning, they observed the ordinances of their religion, but yet in another language. Her own father praised the Prophets, Isaiah, Hosea. Her grandmother read the Psalms and murmured prayers of supplication; while her own mother had no desire for such exercises and she herself had no contact at all with them. The Jews were shopkeepers; they bought and sold, sold and bought, but had no courage, as the Russians had. Here you are drinking water out of a cask while just outside the town natural water flows...There are forests and streams, hills rearing their lofty peaks over the land and broad steppes, fishes inhabiting the depths of the lake and birds flying in the air. But her people knew only the confines of their houses, they understood no measure except that of the market place and the shop. She rose from her seat and sat on the corner of her bed. She had no real companion; Ladyna was so empty. Tear-drops fell from her eyes...The cloud enshrouded her also...

10.

A demon began to stalk abroad the places of Ladyna and its presence was clearly sensed. Sleek cows ceased to yield milk though their udders were full of it. The goat which belonged to the local rabbi got his horns stuck in the wall and could not extricate them. Every morning the doors of the ark* were found open, as though they had been opened by themselves. The congregation assembled in the synagogue for the beginning of the Sabbath. They turned around to welcome the Sabbath bride and a kind of sledge-hammer began to knock on the door. The cantor wanted to cry "God rebuke thee Satan" but his voice stuck in his throat. And behold yet another miracle, on the doors of our hero Israel's shop, people distinctly saw with their own eyes a cross scratched out with burning coal. When they rubbed it out on one day, it appeared again on the morrow. Three pregnant women in Ladyna miscarried one after the other. The wife of the beadle gave birth to a male child who had six toes on his right foot. No one dared go out of the house at night alone. People checked the *mezuzzot*† on their doorposts and their ritual fringes. Immediately after the morning ablution on waking, the slops were poured out. No black hens were ritually slaughtered; the gizzard was not slit open with a knife, but by hand. No man spat on the ground; only in a

* The ark in the synagogue in which the Torah scrolls are kept.

† Tiny scrolls containing prayers fastened to the doorposts of every Jewish house.

handkerchief. In brief every precaution was taken against the Sword of Satan and all his minions…

Even in the nearby village of Zarkov, the demon thundered. Though the wind was not blowing the trees were swaying and bending their tops. Now and again the church bell came off the rope and fell down. The oxen gored and the cows mooed for no reason. A dog and goat copulated. Lambs rolled in the dirt; horses stood transfixed. A rainbow appeared in the clouds and the ghost of the dead nobleman began to dance in the air.

Miriam dreamed once that a man was knocking on her window and crying, "Open for me, daughter of the Hebrews. You are beautiful in appearance and my soul desires you." Next morning there was a sign of the cross on the window of her room: a mysterious, horrifying thing.

Chapter four

A replenishment meal for the dead. Once a year the peasants used to hold a night feast in their cemetery. Man and wife would take dishes full of potatoes cooked in oil in one hand, and loaves of bread and bottles of spirits in the other and go up to the meeting place to feast with the congregation. When the sun had set and the world had covered its face and dreamed restful dreams—the believers in Jesus sat in the grass with their legs crossed before the rows of graves, making the sign of the cross according to the manner of the dominant Orthodox faith. They dipped their bread in salt and chewed the delicacies set before them according to the ancient custom. To begin with they ate soberly, inclining their heads as though listening to a voice calling them from afar. Then they began eating solidly and ingested with complete bodily devotion. There was no link here to connect them to the toil in the field or the house. The cows were not mooing, the horse was not neighing, the dogs were not barking, nor were the hens scratching in the garbage heap. Their master had gone down below clothed in the flesh and had gone up to the Father and become one with the Spirit and they the true believers were his inheritance all over the land...

They raised their eyes and beheld a caravan of pilgrims going by on the highway which passed close by the cemetery. Every man carried his bundle and a pair of shoes on his shoulder. Their hair, uncovered, blew in the wind. Their faces were burnt by the sun and their eyes protruded from spiritual and bodily exhaustion. These true brethren had been on their way from distant villages for weeks and months en route to the dwelling place of their Savior in the land of the Hebrews, to pass one night close by where he had lived and to kiss his grave. Happy is the man who has this privilege once in a lifetime and does not die on the way.

2.

When a Jew is at his last gasp and is clearly dying, the men of the *hevra kadisha* hasten to stand by him as his soul departs. When he breathes his last they place a feather on the nose of the departed. If it does not move, then they know that the soul has gone back whence it came and the body is ready for burial. They remove his garments, wash and purify him according to the religious rites, wrap him in the shrouds which have been hastily sewn together, lay him on the ground, cover him with a blanket and light two candles at his head. They recite selections from *Ma'avar Jabbok*. The bereaved make rents in their clothing to fulfill the requirements of Jewish law while the women of the neighborhood weep and wail.

In the meantime they dig a grave for the deceased, fix the bier with ropes and carry the corpse off to the last meeting place of all creatures. The distinction between rich and poor is the number of those participating in the funeral procession. A man of wealth and power and even a house-holder receives certain honor. This is not the lot of the masses. Those who are called to recite the blessings over the Torah maybe only once in a whole year, are buried with a small funeral procession.—But what happens to the peasants is quite different. When one of the Christian community dies, even if he were of the lower class, he is buried in splendor before a large crowd. They place the corpse in a coffin, which is borne on a black hearse harnessed to horses with black trappings. Before and behind go processions carrying flags and crosses, row after row of them. Acolytes of the priesthood follow slowly, carrying bowls; after them comes the local priest, clad in his golden sacerdotal robes and flanked by his two assistants on his right and left. They chant and a large crowd follows behind the hearse, men walking beside the women, boys with girls. A member of the community has died, the whole village from the highest to the lowest participates in the burial.

Sar'l looked through the window as one of the peasants was borne to the grave with all this pomp. The church bells were ringing, the procession wound on its way, the robes of the priest glittered in the sunlight as he walked with quiet dignity. Of the Bible Sar'l was totally ignorant, nor did she know of the priesthood and their functions in the Temple. Nevertheless, at this spectacle something stirred vitally within her. She was just a shopkeeper's wife and her heart was moved. There is a gate to the city, a window to the house, the sun shines and bursts through the clouds...

3.

The Christian priest of the Ladyna congregation and its peasants was a tall man, readily recognizable at a distance by his long robe, his wide sleeves, his round miter and his hair that flowed down behind it. A gold cross hung from his neck. His hands were clean and very white. He was said to be the son of one of the dukes of Poland by a simple maidservant. He was an agreeable personality and ministered in his church and sang the hymns in a melodious voice. Outside he enjoyed life to the full. He had a rich field, a fine orange grove and benefited from many gifts brought to him by his flock. Every peasant's daughter who came to visit him kissed his hand. The wife he had married as a young man had died of tuberculosis some time ago and by the law of the Church he was forbidden to remarry. But the women who worked on his estate were his concubines during the course of the year. Flesh does not sin with flesh.

When the bell is heard from the tower of a Christian church

at the end of the village, all the peasants know they are being called to the service of their Savior, who is God. The Jewish people have another God, the Lord of Hosts is His name who dwells in heaven. The women of Israel go month by month to the ritual baths and return home robed modestly like captives of the sword. Every day of the week and on festivals the farmers' daughters dance barefoot and with flowers in their hair in the field facing the tavern until the heart swoons at the sight of them.

Once the priest was sitting at the edge of his field toward evening when he saw a Jewess emerging from a pond of water—the ritual baths had been temporarily declared unfit at that time. His heart trembled within him. He had never given much thought to the actual nature of the two religions. He had only heard from his teacher in the seminary that the people of Israel were children of an accursed tribe. He was acquainted with only a few verses from the Gospels in the Old Slavic language. And he had almost forgotten these.

The next day he came to Israel's shop, Israel being an old acquaintance, to buy a length of cloth for his servant woman to make a smock. He also intended to ask Israel something about the laws of the Jews. Israel had gone off to the district capital and only Sar'l was sitting there with a red kerchief on her head. Her cheeks were red. She invited the priest to sit down. He leaned on his elbows staring at her. Their eyes met…

4.

Dvorele was not yet sixty years of age, but she had already settled her accounts. The world is dumb as well as deaf, but God is great and His attributes are unfathomable. Generation tells generation, the fathers dwell in eternity and you too will very soon be taken away from the prayer book. A woman's lot is miserable in the world, who knows her fate in heaven?

When meeting her husband again she would not tell him what had taken place here on earth. Things were not as one would wish between Sar'l and her husband…She cherished her granddaughter

Miriam like the apple of her eye, but was fearful for her...The soul had wings. She knew nothing of the holy tongue and the Russian books contained no knowledge of the Lord. Her very flesh pained her because our father Abraham was the son of Terah, and Isaac his son had sired Edom. She would make no deals with Satan, but would confess her sins and transgressions and would not plead with the Angel of Death by saying, "Hold your hand!"...

She became ill and took to the bed from which no person descends again to have and to hold. With a quiet mind she prayed to the Father of All. When they brought her a bowl of hot soup, she sipped a little, making a secret blessing. He daughter sat beside her and looked after her. The curtain over the window shut out the outside world. Dvorele took Sar'l's hand and the hands spoke to each other, "Be faithful to your husband and don't upset me in my grave." Tears streamed down the daughter's cheeks.

"I have no life here on earth," she wanted to cry out loud. "I have no life here, no life!"

At that moment Israel appeared in the doorway and asked how the sick woman was feeling. Miriam too, crept into the room quietly and leaned over the side of the bed.

"Come near, my darling," she murmured, "Let me touch you."

Miriam drew close to her grandmother and bowed her head down in reverence. The clock struck the hour of six. The day was declining to its rest and took with it a soul. There was weeping in the room. Israel ran out to call those who minister to the dead and the living.

5.

Prayers were held in Israel's house during the seven days of mourning. The shop was closed. The beggars came to solicit alms. The rabbi came with his beadle and offered the usual words of consolation to the mistress of the house. Although he was not the actual son of the deceased, Israel took the ancient book of Job out of his bookcase and began to read it, without really comprehending it properly. It had lofty and awesome expressions from a world which was strange to the Hebrews, and the time was not suited to absorbing them. By contrast the mourner's *kaddish* was a kind of praise. A man begins to read his prayer book in the morning and in the evening he repeats prayers which he says together with all the congregation.

Miriam went from room to room, looking for she knew not what. The heavens are low and the earth is deep. She had not accompanied her grandmother to the cemetery and had not yet seen *she'ol*, the grave of man who is made of flesh and skin, who moves about, talks, and afterward is silent...The old well-worn armchair, and the bed still stood in her grandmother's room; her clothes still hung on the peg, and death hid its face. The threads of life were broken and an old rope just lay there in the corner of the kitchen.

People were going about outside; smoke spiraled up from the chimneys. If she were asked anything she would not know what to answer. She began looking at Lermontov's poems and her disheartened spirit forged a way for her. The words gave her soul a prospect. She conversed and prayed in poetic language and in her soul she crossed the abyss. Man has ears and he hears, laments and sings.

Now come and see. When the thirty days of mourning were over, the city's matchmaker bethought himself—what the connection was I do not know—of visiting Israel and proposing a worthy match from a nearby town for his lovely daughter. He had in stock a young man of excellent family. He was enlightened, intelligent and could speak the vernacular.

6.

Miriam had four friends of her age; Hemda, Gittel, Malka and Milka. They were the daughters of the most prominent men of the city whose names we have mentioned. Hemda was the daughter of Simon the moneylender, Gittel of Menashe the leaseholder, while Malka and Milka were twins born to Mordecai the ironmonger by his second wife, who was an unsullied maiden when he married her.

The lovely twins also learned Russian from "Sheventy," but they had not developed a taste for literature. The world is alive only when the sun comes out, and at its setting everything is hidden. Jealousy reigned between them. Malka was already betrothed to a young man with a keen command of the Torah while Milka's match was still being negotiated. On the one hand a real bridegroom and on the other a bridegroom not yet in sight.

Gittel was a tall girl, whose personality always sparkled. Not a day passed when she did not visit her girlfriends. She was dissatisfied but were she given a husband, she would not love him. For her men were of two kinds, the old and the immature. Once she sat alone in her room staring out of the window and saw a dog running after a bitch.—She got up and stood in the doorway as two young men of the neighborhood passed by and stared at her. She went into the kitchen and bowed her head on the shoulder of the pale, gentile servant girl and cried, "Yarina, Yarina, you are not a daughter of my people and I am not a daughter of yours, and the land is a paradise…" I don't know how the matter arose but from that time on they talked strangely about her…

Hemda was a redheaded girl with a somewhat pointed nose, but her eyes were out of this world. She understood nothing of the Jewish people. Her father's ways were strange to her. She railed at Providence at times for having given her a moneylender for a father. The Lord is a God of knowledge and he distinguishes between him who gives and him who takes. The evening meant more to her than the day. A voice called in her ear at times and she did not know whence it came.

She happened to go on a journey once to her mother's family in a city in Bessarabia. There she saw different people and different ways. She remained with her relatives long after the time planned for her return to her father's home had passed…They pressed her to say why she did not want to go back and she burst into tears. At that time she was about fifteen. The reason for her refusal to return became known in Ladyna and they were astounded. Simon too was very upset and said, "That I have come to this!" For several Sabbaths in succession he did not go to synagogue.

7.

It was Sunday. Men were standing in small groups around the house of Yossi the Hasid, Israel's competitor, and talking to one another. The doors of the shop were closed that day, and according to the report, government officials had gone in there. Some rumored that Yossi had gone bankrupt; that his creditors claimed more than his stocks were worth and were trying to have his assets distrained. One skinny bystander opined that the shopkeeper had been dealing in stolen or contraband goods that had been smuggled over the border without payment of customs duty. The Jew goes through fire and water to win his livelihood and imperils his life to sustain his household with dignity. Yossi was an affluent man but his expenses were heavy. He was the first to outbid others when synagogue honors were auctioned. He supported the Hasidim. When he went to visit the rebbe he was accompanied by a whole train of toadies who went along at his expense. God's is the victory. Whosoever does not get drunk at every religious feasting and does not imbibe in full measure at the conclusion of the Sabbath, is not a God-fearing man and does not love Him. Jesse, the father of David, cast his glance upon his servant girl. The lass told her mistress who proceeded to adorn herself so that her husband came in unto her. Thus the sweet singer in Israel was born with strange premeditation and because of this his eye was dark with anger all his life. Now this is what happened to our Yossi. His wife bore him a male child and they hired a young woman to wet-nurse him. She was attractive and went with her neck bare all day. Yossi, who was a man of forty, talkative among his circle, at times envied his month-old infant. There is no known bound to man's lust. Once the nurse bared her full breast in his presence. There was no one else in the room. He drew near to her and pressed her breasts together. His lust burned in him and no living form appeared at the window to protest.—What did the nurse do? Shortly afterward she took some of her mistress' jewelry and hid it among her own things. When her theft was discovered she revealed the whole matter and there was a scandal in the house. That day the shop did not open and two officials came to investigate and take evidence. The chest was open in front of them in which had laid the pearls, earrings and rings. One official was writing notes in a pad and perspiring. The other was whispering to the maidservant. The mistress of the house was silent. Yossi was standing by the window, his fringes fluttering, and he was looking around as though seeking a cave in which to hide himself from utter shame.

At that time Israel stood in his shop which was bare of customers and thought about his competitor's wife. He hated Yossi in his heart and openly, but at the same time he recognized that Yossi's wife was pure of heart and different from his own. With the other he might have lived a tranquil life free from nagging. Why had Sar'l become his wife and why had Yossi deserved his fate? The God of knowledge plans His works for His own purposes.

8.

There was a man in Ladyna called Nathan Ben Abba. He was one of the conceited fops of the city. He always dressed in fine fashion and habitually made fun of devout, Orthodox Jews. During the Divine Service he would stand in the yard speaking light-heartedly even during the most solemn prayers. On *Simhat Torah** when women came inside the synagogue proper to see the processions with the scrolls of the Torah, he would deliberately stand near them and jest with them in front of everyone. Man has eyes, and his heart lusts. Nathan had a wife whom he did not love, who had borne him two daughters named Chava and Pnina. Chava, the elder, helped in the house. She was known outside only to her female neighbors. Her sister Pnina was much more attractive and a redhead. She was to be seen sometimes in this street and sometimes in that, and used to carry on with the boys. At night she could be seen whispering with the local officials.

* The Rejoicing of the Law, the concluding day of the Feast of Tabernacles.

Nathan was very strict about this and beat her with a strap whenever she came home too late.

A generation ago there lived in the city a man learned in the Torah who began having doubts about matters of faith and finished up by breaking all bounds. Usually one does not have to look far for those who commit petty offenses and even serious ones furtively. There is no community without blemish and in the heavenly book of sins are written at times deeds and happenings which the plain reader could never even imagine. But that a Jewish girl should run wild, leave her father's house, to dwell among gentiles, disgracing her people and family was unheard of in that town. When a woman abjures her faith they force her to go far away and there she can return to the bosom of Judaism. But what can you do with one who has sullied her honor and then sought the protection of officialdom?

In Ladyna there was a cantor whose voice had dried up and who had vacated his post for another. The retired cantor had a son of over twenty. He was an enthusiastic, hot-blooded young man. He was betrothed to a young woman from another town, and was eagerly counting the days and months to his wedding day. Once the young man was walking aimlessly down that street when Pnina saw him and decided to take him to bed with her. O, how he was beguiled!...He returned to his father's house, upset and remorseful. He climbed up to the loft and hid himself in the heaps of straw. They searched for him for three days and three nights and on the fourth day they found him, choked to death.

9.

In those days Arcady Gavrilov stooped to an even lower level. He was dismissed from his post in the prison and became the scrivener in the Jewish section of the municipal offices. There he "resurrected" people inscribed as deceased in the registers and "gave birth" to twenty-year-old sons for men who had no children. On Sabbaths he came to the chairman of the Jewish representative council to eat fish and enjoy the pleasures of the Jewish table. Once his hat was blown away by the wind. He could not find it and he went for a number of weeks with his hair wildly disheveled. There were days when he did not earn a single kopeck and his stomach had nothing to do. On the contrary, if a ruble chanced his way, he ran quickly to the tavern and spent it on a bottle of brandy mixed with water. He would add pepper to every glassful to make it taste stronger. A man and his glass are always faithful companions. Why should you speak untruths about life and its tumults? If he slept, snatches of dreams rose up in his mind to confuse him.... He had a mother but never knew his father. The world revolves on its axis. You count, one, two, three, four and so on; you stop and shake your head. God is Satan's companion!

Sometimes at twilight his soul just shrank within him and the loneliness of life was just too much for him. Nature favors no individual and affords no special gifts to its selected friends. If you boast about your lot you are just talking lies.

Arcady sat for forty-eight hours on the doorstep of Pnina's lodging, begging in vain for admission to the Jewish prostitute. He rapped on the window, banged savagely on the door, and even entertained the idea of getting into her room by going down the chimney. He begged and pleaded, spread himself out on the curb and banged the stones with his shoes. He wanted to talk with the Jewess, to kiss her, to take hold of her red hair and leap with her into the air. There are no restraints or limits in the world. Desire is a serpent and knows nothing of hell or the fear of hell.

On the morning of the third day, the girl got up, opened the door and thought to arouse the sleeping man and give him some milk to drink. She drew near him, shook him violently, but there was no response. His heart had failed and he never got to lie with her.

10.

From the tragic to the trivial.

Naftali-Menahem, the proprietor of the general store whom

we reckoned as one of the seven most wealthy and powerful men of Ladyna, had a spoiled only son. His father had taught him Torah and worldly matters and educated him in the way of affluence. When he was eighteen, a match was arranged for him with an orphan girl from Kishinev. She had a legacy of a few thousand rubles from her father, and could speak Russian. She was not especially beautiful, but nature had endowed her with lovely blonde hair which was worth seeing.

It is the accepted custom that the bridegroom should travel to the bride's place of residence for the wedding.

But since the bride had neither father nor mother, Naftali decided to celebrate the nuptials in Ladyna and made the necessary preparations for the bride as well as the groom. A wealthy man in the town who is marrying off his only son and who is also duty-bound to gladden the heart of an orphan girl, must certainly be lavish in his spending and make a wedding on a royal scale. He also must show his peers that he is able and willing to keep up with them. Everyone must know that Naftali-Menahem is Naftali-Menahem, who did not just know how to garner kopeck to kopeck, but also to spend hundreds and thousands grandly. I am not exaggerating. The town was happy and agog; there was dancing, feasting, itinerant musicians played. Gifts were given to the poor. They went out to meet the bride in carriages harnessed to spirited horses, giving her a royal welcome. The daughter of Kishinev would know that in Ladyna too they knew how to live on a grand scale. People hurried from all directions to witness her arrival. They made accommodation available for her with Mordecai, the ironmonger. There was a fence around his house on which the youngsters climbed to peep through the windows. They were unavoidably absent from *heder* that day.

And now just imagine. The bride would not agree under any inducement to cut off her hair when they came to cover her face for the wedding. Her mother-in-law was utterly dumbfounded.

"You are a Jewish girl, are you not? How can you have no pity for us and spoil our joy?"

The bride did not relent. She just would not cut off her crowning glory.

I shall not relate the end of the story.

II.

I have already mentioned Jonathan the miller as one of the seven mainstays of Ladyna. When he was advanced in years and had no heir, he was ousted from his tenancy of the mill by a new lessee who offered to pay a higher rent and so came to dwell in his neighbor's property.—The new lessee was called Isaac Lippowitz. He was tall, sallow and bearded. Aaron-Jonah, his brother-in-law, was his second-in-command. He was a faithful, reticent type, and one could detect a kind of shadow brooding over his face. Two sisters, not equally attractive in appearance, were the wives of the lessee and his aide. Each had been married to the sister of his choice, but the lessee came and interchanged the beds.—The brother in-law knew about it but kept it deep down within him for a long, long time.

The strange union was not hidden from the people of Ladyna, who passed the information on from one to the other. Isaac Lippowitz tried to gain a foothold in his new place of residence. He contributed generously to the needs of the community and knew well how to achieve dignity and respect in the sight of the congregation. He stood by the town's millers much more than had his predecessor. He was not a hard taskmaster, but neither did he play favorites and no one lingered long in his room. In the synagogue he used to pray with his face to the wall, while his brother-in-law occupied the adjoining seat. He was not an intimate of the town rabbi. He gave him his due of flour as fixed by the terms of his lease. He observed the custom and followed the manners of the town.

It happened that the wife of his brother-in-law became ill with a mortal sickness and now all the townsfolk could see clearly for themselves how devoted he was to her. Every day carriages brought doctors from afar. At his command they clamored to God in the synagogue. He gave charity for her sake and he was glued to the sick woman's room all the time, watching every slightest movement as she lay there. When heart is so attached to heart it knows no rest and he resisted anyone who came and tried to separate him from her. At that time Aaron-Jonah was distraught. He had made numerous errors in his accounts and at times was seized with an overpowering urge to take the thick ledger bound in rough leather and bring it down on the crown of his brother-in-law's head. Here is someone who is your own, and along comes the devil and takes her to himself in your very presence, in life and in death. The disgrace of the sick woman's sister I shall not try to tell. She was not well-favored and her thin frame became increasingly emaciated from year to year. But the soul is not something made of lime and stone. When the doctor said there was no hope, the lessee was unable to restrain himself and burst into tears in front of everybody. His wife stood at a distance like one utterly stunned.

12.

It was a dark night. The people of Ladyna slept in their beds, with big pillows under their heads and thick eiderdowns to cover them over. In the valley of sleep worries cease, there is no religious observance, and the God of Canaan, too, slumbers for there is nothing to do or see. And then choking smoke roused one of the sleepers from his bed of slumber. A strange cry was heard outside, "Fire! Fire is burning down the houses! Hurry! Get out of your beds!"

Doors burst open, men sprang out of their rooms with only their night-shirts covering their bodies. Raging flames in all corners of the town. The conflagration began in the house of the lessee of the mill, and a hot wind bore the sparks into the city so that a general blaze broke out. The water stored in barrels and jugs was quickly used up. Men and women ran around like mad carrying vessels, candlesticks and bumping into one another. The flames reached the piles of vessels and pillows and consumed what had been saved only moments previously. They cry and shout, sobbing over the destruction, but He does not hear, He speaks His utterance through fire. What men toiled to achieve through a whole generation is burned in a brief hour. In vain did the carpenter work diligently, the tailor toil in sewing a garment, the cobbler make shoes; every single thing went up in the fiery flames. The Sabbath candles were melted, the parchment scrolls in the synagogue were destroyed and God's own hand was on His Torah. Morning came to reveal only rack and ruin wherever one turned. Had the fire not occurred everything would have been as it was the day before. Now the eye sees only flickering flames and black snakes. Who decreed this and who carried out the cruel mandate? The man who was rich and has a full house is poor today. He who through the years amassed a fortune now stands under the open sky with empty hands. They say there is order and regulation in the world. It is not so.

Some say the fire broke out by accident. Some say the miller provoked one of his employees who went and set fire to his granaries. Among the strictly religious in Ladyna it was believed that the thing had happened because of the iniquity of the "two sisters."

Among the shops which were burned on the night of disaster was that of Israel, Miriam's father. It was almost completely consumed by the flames. He became impoverished in a brief moment and was left without any idea of what to do with his life. Miriam saw that from then on things would be very difficult in her father's house and that he would be unable to provide for her. She made a small pack of her belongings and began making her way to Honyrad. Her hopes were fixed on a relative of her grandmother's father.

Part II

Chapter five

The name of the kinsman in Honyrad to whom Miriam, the heroine of our story, set out after her father's house was burned down, was Yehiel Eichenstein. He was a son of that family I have mentioned, which had come down in the world. However, the wheel of fortune turned for him again. From his lowly estate he suddenly rose high, had a severe reverse, recovered and won a place for himself in life once again.

I will now relate it to you at length.

Yehiel was not a man of downcast mind, despite the hardship he had experienced in his life. He had married when he was twenty, when he owned nothing. His wife was a good woman and patiently adjusted herself to her difficult lot. For a time he was a kind of broker in the market place, working hard to support his household, but earning very little. But he saw that the world was big. We stand before full treasure houses, but the gates are closed. Only the lock needs to be opened. He cared about nothing beyond his family. He did not believe that it was a matter of luck: We are hard-pressed, and may have little in our hands today, but on the morrow…the sun shines.

One day toward evening, he was standing in a main street in

the city of Honyrad which leads to the public park. The rich people of the place were taking the air in their carriages, the horses prancing along. There is nothing more proud than a horse, and nothing which expresses power more clearly than to sit in a carriage. His eyes almost started out of their sockets with envy. A tremendous desire sprung up in his heart at that time, that one day he, too, would be counted among those so well endowed. Is man's hand too short to reach that far? He put together a number of bank notes and decided to go to Kiev when the great merchants assemble there from all districts in the province. His neighbors were surprised at him that he should have the audacity to do this, but he was resolved. In a few days he came to Kiev and plunged like Nahshon into the sea and brought up a large fish on his hook. He was an intermediary in a big sugar transaction and miraculously made a profit of thirty thousand rubles in one day. The regular brokers who knew the thronging streets and commercial alleyways of the city like the back of their hands could scarcely believe what had happened.

To these thirty thousand, another twenty thousand were added—then a further twenty thousand and ten thousand and so on. When he had made his first hundred thousand rubles, Eichenstein considered himself free from his narrow straits and continued to accumulate capital. He no longer made an anxious daily reckoning. He dressed like a rich man, stayed in a big hotel and was already acknowledged as the head of the small brokers and of the Jews in general. The latter were not actually allowed to dwell in the city, but they wandered in and out of hotels and market places every day, "licking at bones" and hotly pursuing any chance of profit.

Richly endowed with capital, Yehiel returned after a year to his home at Honyrad and began to live extravagantly. He purchased a two-storey house, filling the rooms with beautiful furniture and lived the life of a gentleman. Food was served at his table from silver dishes; there were numerous servants in the house. His wife conducted herself with dignity at home and when she went out, her jewels sparkled. Yehiel spent money lavishly and gave generously. He gave freely, and people knocked at his door from morning to night. People went into partnership with him, deposited things in trust with him and made loans to him. I hardly need mention that by this time he was among those who drive in the park, with their own carriages and horses. He had two swift black stallions, who could rival those of the governor of the province. The doors of life were opening before him! Eichenstein continued to do business. He was one of the aldermen of the city, gave to charity and was very generous. He found positions for all the members of his family and set them up in life. He was a real patriarch. Even government officials crowded eagerly round his door and he contracted with the Polish nobility. His house was open to rich and poor alike, to the devout and the ordinary folk. No one spoke scandal of him: on the contrary, his praises and the talk of his wealth were in everyone's mouth. A new star had arisen in the city of Honyrad.

Then came a cloud and covered the sun. The machine which had run so smoothly for so long ground to a standstill. Yehiel Eichenstein's extravagance exceeded all bounds. He had never kept proper accounts. If today found him hard-pressed, he believed that on the morrow things would be right again. He never changed his way of life and thus it came about that one day he stood before a tottering treasury…

Suddenly, failure came from all directions. Outcries and bewilderment. In the city many merchants lost all they possessed through the new magnate, but nobody accused him saying, "Have you killed and also taken possession?" A tragedy had occurred: a tragedy involving the one and the many.

Negotiations began for a settlement and compromise. The *dayan** of the congregation, a diligent man, but not specially learned, labored with all his might to make a compromise between Yehiel and the mass of creditors. Yehiel surrendered his real estate and his personal property. His mansion was sold, as were his horses and carriages. So were the jewels and silver plate. The assets realized met about a third or fourth of the creditors' claims. After a few months some arrangement of debts was reached with the creditors and the storm subsided into silence…

* Judge of the rabbinical court.

2.

During the last year of this period of crisis, Yehiel leased from a certain gentleman a large water-powered mill which had stood at the river falls in the upper city, for a period of thirty consecutive years. The premises included granaries and storehouses. Close-by were the living quarters for the foremen and a series of small cottages for the workers and laborers. The whole estate looked like a separate township nestling in the valley. As one went up from the valley toward the city, a castle could be seen, built of hewn stones. The windows were barred with iron and it was set in a park, walled in on all sides. The gate of the park was of wrought iron. The rulers of the city had formerly ruled from this castle in the days before the Russians conquered the Ukraine and annexed it to their many dominions. The castle had for many years been a residence for high-ranking officers of the army. Later it was inhabited by the governors of the province, and after that it became a courthouse. Now it was left deserted, without any occupant. This castle was also part of the mill estate and thus fell unto Yehiel's tenure for the period of the lease.

Yehiel had leased the mill, farming it out to another man because he had no experience in that business. It was agreed between himself and all those who still had claims against him that the business of the mill would be excluded from the assets to which his general creditors had recourse. This would enable him to stay on his feet, seeing that he had surrendered all other property in his possession. In concluding this arrangement he was greatly assisted by the diligent rabbi whom we have mentioned and whose name deserves an honorable mention. Yehiel now had net income of four thousand rubles per year from the lease of the mill, after he had given the gentleman his share. Certain of the castle rooms had recently been repaired and Yehiel wanted them as his residence now that he had descended from his seat of wealth.

At that time he was fifty years old. His wife had died during the critical days and he remained faithful to her memory and did not remarry. He had an older sister, a widow, and from that time onward she efficiently took care of his household and saw that he lacked for nothing. His eldest son had also died and he had become the father and guardian of his grandchildren. These were a boy of about fifteen and two girls, one of twelve and one of ten. The girls attended the municipal school, which was something of an innovation in the Jewish community. The grandson was privately tutored by an excellent teacher, Shlomo-Ozer, about whom more will be written. He learned a little Talmud and Bible. In general, Yehiel was an observant Jew keeping to the traditions, but he wanted his grandchildren to be more genteelly educated. At first, that is to say after Yehiel had moved into the castle, he was often visited by friends who tried to persuade him to engage in business again. However, he had seriously considered the kind of life he wanted to lead and so he sent them away. He had now become accustomed to a quiet existence, eating regular meals, sleeping at regular hours and praying alone for the most part. He still retained a position of honor and respect in the community.

He had a fair understanding of the Pentateuch and knew the weekly portion well. Now and again he thumbed through the pages of a Russian newspaper from Kiev. He had adopted this habit when the light of good fortune was shining upon his head during his business career and he was not entirely unacquainted with what was happening in the world and in the country. When he felt depressed, he used to walk in the park talking to his granddaughters or his grandson.

When time hung heavy on his hands, he would go down to the valley and watch the workings of the mill. The water, forcing its way through its channels propelled the paddles and this in turn worked the wheels. Here was a pent-up force building up power. The whole operation was interdependent. One compartment received the whole wheat and then transferred the ground meal to another. Flour dust covered everything. Standing in a small pathway between the great perforated baulks of timber where everything was roaring and thundering, one could gain some concept of the birth pangs of creation. When the rains diminished and the river abated its flood, then the driving, energizing force also subsided. Yehiel learned in those days of quietude to think deeply and to reflect…The city is a tumultuous arena in which business goes on all day long. Men make profits and losses, ascending and descending. The desire to gain a firm foothold in life and consolidate one's position never ceases. Everybody needs his neighbor, but never considers him at all. Men are hungry for money, eager to amass a fortune, but up in heaven matters are written down and sealed on an entirely different basis. Men were weaving their lives all the time with diligence, with complete dedication, with absolute commitment of mind and body, weaving without respite. But the ends of the threads had no knots; just a little tug was necessary and the whole fabric fell apart and nothing at all of the web remained...I could well understand Yehiel's thinking.

3.

I have mentioned the city of Honyrad twice. Now it became the destination of our heroine, Miriam. I ought to mention that it was also the place in which I, the author, grew up and obtained my first education. I remained in the city for a long time, and had a great affection for it, so the reader will not consider me tedious if I spend a few moments in its description.

Honyrad, the district capital, is composed of two adjacent townships, forming an upper city and a lower one, both of which have their own focal point. Stone steps lead from one section to the other. The central streets are straight. In the upper city the shops are wooden, in the lower they are of stone. Many Jewish prayer houses are found here and there, but there was only one synagogue which stood at the bottom of the lower city. One could see many fine houses. Some were of two stories with walls around them. Many were roofed with corrugated iron, colored green, some had red tiles and a few had wooden boards. In the suburbs of the city could be found houses with thatched roofs. In general, the streets were paved. Beyond the lower city was the river I have already mentioned, which encircled the city. On the far side was a great park which formerly one of the Polish noblemen had planted, but which was now a public place.

The street leading to the park was where the wealthy lived. There dwelt the leading lights of Honyrad and the members of the famous Shneursohn family. The palace of the provincial governor was there and this was without doubt the most splendid building in the city. Facing it stood the courthouse. In the upper city the most prominent building was the big Christian Brothers Training College. It was a long building, with at least thirty windows on the street front and visible in its whiteness from a great distance. The synagogue we mentioned was a new building made of red brick, built on the ruins of the old building which had burnt down. I ought to mention the magnificent residence of the renowned Jacob Karlin. This was a building set on solid hewn rock. It was not a conventional square building, but had many edges and was red in color. All those who passed by stopped to stare in wonder. Rivaling this building was an edifice erected by Nathan Shapiro. He had been a servant in his youth, and now counted his wealth in hundreds of thousands. This building was finished in green paint and the fence in front of the house was of wrought iron. One of the wonders of Honyrad was the Greek Palace, built as a square fortress, with a large courtyard in the middle. It resembled a city within a city. It had been built a century and a half previously by a certain Greek who, at that time, owned the whole city. His family line petered out, for he had had no children. For many years the palace was abandoned, uninhabited, with only goats to dance there. Later, it became a barracks for the army unit which was stationed there. The Christians dwelt in special suburbs beyond the center of the city, and to a stranger it appeared like the sundered members of the general body. Even Abraham, the Hebrew, had sent the children of Keturah far off to the East, away from his son Isaac.

Alongside the Jewish cemetery extended the Christian burial place. I also ought to mention the old cemetery situated in a particular valley where were buried those slain in the pogroms of 1648. In Honyrad, a special fast is added to the penitential days and commemorated on the twentieth of *Sivan*. The happenings and legends of those days of slaughter are written down in the chronicles of the Jewish people, and are still commemorated till the present day.

4.

The members of the Shneursohn family I have mentioned were very wealthy and were the "eyes of the community." Their name was known in many provinces throughout the country, and they had married into families as far away as Galicia. Their sons and daughters, their sons-in-law, their daughters-in-law, their stewards, their bursars and their agents, formed a complete tribe. Were I only to write about them, I would have to compose a complete volume.

The head of the family was Kalman-Joshua. He had been a servant in his youth, but arose to the highest levels of prosperity to which a human being could attain. By the time of his death, he left after him mansions, summer residences, mills, forests, and stores of gold and silver which his heirs and descendants divided among themselves. His first-born son, Lazar-Simon, was a harsh man, ruling with a whip. He found Honyrad too constricting a place of residence. He sometimes lived in the capital, Kiev, sometimes in the nearby Belaya Tserkov, and from time to time he came to visit his residence in the town of his birth. His house was built on a high hill with a castellated roof made of beaten copper which shone in the sunlight. He was not a member of this generation but a virtual descendant of Hiram, king of Tyre, who said, "I shall rise up on the high places of the clouds." His brother-in-law, Pinhas-Elijah, was completely different, a handsome man, but small of stature. He was God-fearing, observant of the commandments, devout in prayer, and a devoted follower of the *tzaddik* of Loton, whose whole household he supported for two months of the year. This rich man had no children. The wife of his youth, Kalman's daughter, had died and he had a second wife, taller than the first, of a beauty beyond compare, to whom he remained utterly devoted. However, there was one occasion on which this wife "sinned." She was once closeted alone with one of her male relatives in a room contrary to the law and the custom of Israel. The husband's relatives, who were very jealous of her, strongly urged him to give her a divorce, and the rabbi of Loton approved of this course of action. Accordingly, one of the *dayanim* of the city was summoned; witnesses and a scribe were brought to the magnate's mansion. They immediately listened to the testimony and drew up a bill of divorcement in the proper order. After the wealthy Pinhas had pronounced the verse, "Behold thou art permitted to any man," he burst into tears in the sight of all there assembled. He then took his bunch of keys, opened all his coffers and cupboards and said to the woman who had now become alien to him, "Take anything you want from my possessions." All the menservants and maidservants burst into tears, because they were much attached to the woman, and the whole mansion was filled with heavy gloom. The rabbi and the scribe received generous payment for their work...

5.

The second most important family in Honyrad was the house of Horowitz, who traced their ancestry back to the ancient priests. They were descended from the opulent and eminent Ish-Horowitz, who had once dwelt in a magnificent estate near Prague, the capital. Legend relates that this peer who was of priestly stock, that is a *cohen,** had twelve sons who were *cohanim*, and twelve daughters who were married to *cohanim*. Thus on festival days, when the priests were enjoined to fulfill the commandment, "Thus shall ye bless the children of Israel," with its allusion to the number twenty-five,† no less than twenty-five of them ascended the dais to do so.

The priests of the house of Horowitz were very strong minded and carried on a controversy for many years with Shmaya-Hillel, the presiding judge of the local rabbinical court. He was a distinguished scholar of noble descent who wore silken garments even on week days and was very meticulous about his dignity and position. Shmaya-Hillel was not subordinate to any *tzaddik*. He used to say that everything depends on the Law as revealed and only those who guard its keys are fit to pass judgment in Israel, and lead the people according to

* The plural of cohen is cohanim.

† The Hebrew letters have the numerical value of 25.

the law of Moses and the scribes. On the other hand, the priests of the house of Horowitz inclined to the rebbe of Sadigora, saying that his was the dominion and honor, the glory and the majesty. Menahem Horowitz set up a new house of prayer in Honyrad at his own expense. He built it of baked bricks, and with its long windows it could be seen from a distance standing on a small hillock, with stone steps leading up to it.

Menahem really wanted to divide the community into two factions by setting up for the hasidic congregation a new presiding judge of the rabbinical court who would displace the rabbi. He found a candidate of this sort in the keen-minded Nathan-Neta who took this office upon his shoulders. Shmaya-Hillel pronounced a strong curse on him and his only daughter died during the year of this controversy. Nor did his rival complete that year, but was taken to his grave when he was forty years old. Honyrad trembled to its very foundations.

6.

Also distinguished in the city were the brothers and partners, Benjamin and Joseph of the house of Nahman. They owned a brandy distilling factory. Brandy was a kind of liquor, of which nine-tenths of the value was paid as excise to the government after it had matured. The owner only benefited by one tenth. Nevertheless, they made great profits, both by lawful means and in contraband, from this business. These brothers spent a great deal of money on themselves and gave away much to their relatives. They furnished their houses with beautiful furniture and most of all with silverware. Indeed, this was their lifelong addiction. Wherever they saw a specimen of silver, they immediately bought it. Each of them had a cabinet made of glass, in which could be seen row after row of lovely silver pieces. Sabbath candlesticks, candelabra for *Hanukkah,** artistic *etrog*† cases, spice

* Festival of Lights.

† A citron used for ritual purposes on the Feast of Tabernacles.

boxes, spoons, forks, goblets and plates: all of pure silver, shining and displayed like objects in a museum.

Here I insert a note also about Shimele, "the well-born." Shimele inherited from his father a large and handsome legacy when he attained the age of thirty, and never passed a moment of his life in the shadow of anxiety. He built himself a beautiful house which contained a large salon with numerous windows. The floor in the hall was painted a dark, shining red. Sometimes, he would close the window shades by day, and sit by candlelight studying a volume of the Talmud bound in red leather. His longing for beauty and his visional qualities were to be discerned also in the pallor of his face.

To be esteemed likewise was Mottele Gad, a man who loved hospitality. He was the principal agent for the sugar industry. He was childless, and his house was open day and night to every wayfarer who passed by. Every poor and indigent man who traversed the city would turn to him and stay in the house for several nights, eating and drinking there until it was time to leave for some other place. On weekdays, Mottele was very busy, but on the Sabbath he sat at the head of his long table around which scores of guests, whose names he did not even know, were seated. He must have earned thousands every year, but when he died at the age of sixty, at the close of one Sabbath, it was found that he had left nothing behind…

7.

The Jews of Honyrad were mainly Hasidim, with a strong admixture of traditionalists. In Honyrad there were some very erudite scholars. One man knew something of the commentaries of Ibn Ezra, another the book *Duties of the Heart*, and the *Principia of Albo*. There was a third who looked into the *Guide for the Perplexed* and lost his faith. The rabbi who preceded the present incumbent was an expert in the *Sanctification of the New Moon* and popular among the townspeople. In the bookcase of the hasidic house of learning you will still find *Richness of Dew*, and nestling beside the folios of the Talmud, the *Shulchan Aruch* and the *Turim*, as well as books like *Kol Bo*, the *Book of Instruction*, and the *Sermons* of Rabbi Nissim. In the synagogue of the opponents of Hasidism, who were also called Litvaks, they used to study the Bible with the help of the commentary of the Malbim. In the upper city there was one well-to-do-man—I shall tell more of him later—who had the Book of Isaiah with Mendelssohn's commentary, although he did not actually subscribe to the tenets of Enlightenment. A broad spectrum: but even among the Hasidim there were a number of sects and among the householders there were several factions. However, the city was not torn asunder and its unity was not affected. The Sabbath, a common prayer book, the festivals, were not those given to all alike? Some kept more, some kept less, but all were Jews born of Jews.

I am not suggesting that there were not the ordinary passions among the inhabitants of Honyrad; and that they were not immersed in worldly things; that they did not deceive their neighbor, nor speak scandal, nor convert deposit monies to their own use, nor tell lies whether for profit or not. One had only to visit the Jewish law-court, presided over by the rabbi and the *av-beth-din** and listen to a few of the matters which came up for adjudication, in order to see the numerous disputes about buying and selling, about loans and inheritances, quarrels between relatives and brothers, between fathers and sons, personal disputes between man and wife. It is easy to see then how many serve the children of Satan here below, and how evil and full of jealousy is the heart of man. You enter a shop to buy two yards of linen or wool, and the shopkeeper swears by his righteousness, by the life of his wife and children, that it cost him so much a yard. But in the end he takes as the price of the goods less than he paid according to his own word. You go out into the market place and ask a man about his neighbor and he speaks only evil about him. The list of sins, iniquities, transgressions which our sages enumerated in the prayer books were definitely not confessed in vain by the inhabitants of this city. However, they all worshipped the same God of Forgiveness, and the same God of the Covenant. Together with the czar of the Russian empire, a monarchy mighty and terrible with none like

* President of the Jewish law-court.

it on earth, there rules here too an ancient king. Him they serve all their lives. The people of this place pay their taxes to the emissaries of the czar, through great hardship, or evade them by the seven types of deception. However, they also willingly give tribute without being forced to do so to the king from days of yore, the mighty sovereign who is called the Father of Mercy and who is a jealous God.

However, I have already said more than I should have done.

8.

In the street which leads to the large municipal park dwelt two more wealthy men, the brothers Nehemia and Jacob Trachtman. These men were engaged in lending money on interest to the nobility, an occupation they had inherited from their father. Nehemia was a religious man who observed the commandments, and was somewhat taciturn; he was very perceptive but whenever he was faced with a difficult problem, he followed the advice of his wife Pearl. She was much taller than he, and was well known in the city for her common sense. By contrast, Jacob, his brother, was inclined to take his religious duties lightly. He ran his house in rather a more modern style and was unfaithful to his skinny wife. Each brother went his own way, but prosperity shone brightly on both of them. Jacob had two sons and one daughter, whom he educated at home where they were taught Russian in addition to their regular subjects. Nehemia had an only son who did not wish to study and grew up in idleness. His mother, who loved him like her own soul, struggled vainly to make him into a decent man and to teach him good manners, but he listened neither to her nor to his father. Here was an only son whose pockets were always full, clad in the height of fashion, whose moustache was trimmed by the barber, who had his hair set every day and knew no responsibility. What did he have to do all day, except play cards, caress the necks of the maidservants and girls and kiss them at every opportunity. In this way he passed his twentieth year, twenty-second year and his twenty-fifth year. He never became engaged although he had honorable matches proffered him from all sides. He would have a marriage portion of at least twenty-five thousand rubles and all his father's wealth would ultimately come to him.

On the other hand, Nehemia's son found himself a mate whom everyone imagined to be far above him, though on more mature consideration she was recognized to be quite suitable for him. He married the very beautiful daughter of a certain rabbi. She had been ripe for marriage for some time now, but had never wanted to confer her hand on anybody who was worthy of her from the point of view of family status. She had, in a sense, alienated herself from the narrow environment in which she grew up and was looking much further afield. In this way, she reached her twenty-fifth year and was still single, which was a source of great annoyance to her deeply religious parents. The marriage brokers with their usual perspicacity came and delivered "Tamar" into the snare of "Amnon." The city of Honyrad was agog.

Chapter six

And now to the intelligentsia of Honyrad. First to my friend and companion, Yeruham. He was the son of a poor widow. If I am not mistaken, she washed clothes in the little brook which ran through the lower part of the city. She dwelled there in a small house which had almost sunk into the ground. The door of the narrow entrance was hardly eighteen inches wide and was broken. Through it one entered the main room which had two windows in front and one at the side. There stood the widow's bed and there she cooked on a small range; there was no stove in the house. This room led to a smaller one which had one square window, and was furnished with a small table, an overturned box which served as a chair and a tattered couch pushed up against a wall on which Yeruham slept in discomfort.

Yeruham had a sister who was married to a porter. She came occasionally to clean up the house and to cook when his mother, who was sixty years old, was out trying to make a living. Yeruham himself earned very little. He was intermittently a Hebrew teacher. He considered his time very precious and used the daylight hours given by nature for self-enlightenment. Yeruham loved "the Hebraic language" with all his being. He spent two whole years reading and rereading the novels of Mapu. In his small room he was pasturing his flocks on the hills of Judah and Israel. Then he became devoted to Smolenskin's *The Wanderer Along the Roads of Life* and its author was to him a prophet of the times. Then there fell into his hands a copy of *Hashahar* with J.L. Gordon's poem *Kotzo Shel Yod* which created a volcanic turmoil within him. Two or three friends were in the habit of gathering in his room, and he would read long passages of this poem to them in a powerful voice. In them his soul found greater expression than had even the author himself. When he opened with the line, "Hebrew woman, who can know thy life?" it was as though the foundations of the house were shaking.

In conversation, Yeruham never spoke about "Jews," but of the "people of Israel," or the "nation of the Prophets" and, in contrast, about the "guardians of the Law." He despised the Talmud, held the *Shulchan Aruch** in contempt, but was very careful indeed of the respect due to his mother. If he was walking bare-headed and saw her coming, he immediately put his hat back on his head. He read Russian without difficulty, learned mathematics and geography, but to him all these things were only ways and means leading to the language of the visionaries and the finest writers. He also read some of Brandstaedter's stories and liked them. In another issue of *Hashahar* he found the humoristic poem *Eldad and Medad* which sapped his melancholy when a cloud hung over his brow.

Yeruham was already acquainted with the term "literature," and it became the light of his soul from the moment it touched his lips. The incisive pamphlets of Kovner and Frischmann created a complete revolution within him and the entire structure of the world seemed to be in upheaval. But after this, he adopted their truth for his own, building his whole being on three pillars—true enlightenment, literature, and criticism. His mother, the washerwoman, could not understand her son's ideology, but she did perceive that his books ignored religion. But what can a mother do about her sons today?

* A codex of Jewish law as developed throughout the centuries.

She believed in Yeruham's sincerity and his desire to do good. Deep down she was secretly very proud to see how many companions came eagerly to visit him.

Of these, I shall mention Zechariah, a youth taller than Yeruham, whose father was a secretary in a certain moneylender's house. After reading Levinsohn, all his thoughts and ambition were aimed at enlightening his people to lift up its mind to "study and purpose" and to implant in them feelings of a "pure faith" combined with a love of wisdom. He also believed in the enlightenment of the ordinary people and in the triumph of light over darkness, in all the places where they dwelt. Another companion was Dan, the son of Naftali, the shopkeeper. In contrast to his friends, Dan still dressed according to the custom of the older generation and had not cut off his side locks. He was shaken to his depths when it became known to him from reading Mendele Mocher Sefarim and Bernstein that everything in the world was in a state of combination and dissolution and that the phenomena of nature had laws. A kind of patron and protector of these people was the teacher, Shlomo-Ozer, whom we have already mentioned. He was a man of small stature with a blond beard, already past his fiftieth year. He was a grammarian, knew the Bible, and loved philosophy generally. He had an irate wife. His time was filched away from him and he could not read many of the books he wanted to. He had to support a daughter who was a young widow, and who had two small children. It is true that his pupils were the children of the wealthy, but most of them were ignoramuses and brought him no satisfaction. What he lacked, he sought to see in others. Accordingly, he supported everybody who craved for enlightenment. Shlomo-Ozer used to visit from time to time one who had married into a rich family, a character whose name was Asher Yaffe. He was a scion of illustrious rabbinic stock and himself a talmudic prodigy but he had abandoned the Talmud and was now engaged in financial pursuits. When he had time, he dipped into books on logic. He had a clear, direct mind, and was inclined to rationalism. I shall have more to say of what happened to Yaffe eventually and of the sadness that befell his household.

2.

When I list the cavalcade of the "enlightened" of Honyrad, I cannot omit the family of Jacob, the cantor of the Great Synagogue. Jacob did not have a pleasant voice, but he could read music well and supervised the choristers who sang in the House of God. He was a man of not particularly strong character, slept a lot during the day, and was forever slipping away from home and going his own way.

His wife was a good-natured woman, diligent in her work. They had three daughters and two sons. The second son was a failure at everything and just helped around the house. The first-born was a bit too clever. He had a talent for study, but he did not work at anything, being of the opinion that all man's effort was for no purpose. He loafed around the street all day, at times not even returning home to sleep. His father and mother never rebuked him. On the contrary, they loved him and took great pride in him, praising his intellect. It was impossible to argue with him because he lashed anybody who opposed him with a sharp tongue, and he could demolish the strongest argument with one sharp, satirical barb.

We are here concerned only with the daughters of the cantor, in particular with the two youngest. The eldest did not amount to much. She had a past. In her youth, she had married a young man who appeared like a star in the skies of Honyrad and captivated people's hearts with his excellent sermons. I ought to mention that this region of the Ukraine is different from Lithuania, for here the business of preaching is an unusual phenomenon. At first, she enjoyed a good life with him and the other women of the city pronounced her fortunate. Later on, however, her husband began to drink to excess and treated her badly. Eventually, he left the city for good and nothing was seen or heard of him for twenty years. She remained a deserted wife in her father's house and had two children who trailed after her. Her two sisters were quite well-known in the circle of the town's *maskilim.* Their names were Ida and Leah.

Ida was the younger, but she was bigger, fuller and taller. She had a dark, attractive complexion, her hair was short and her eyes shone with intelligence. She welcomed visitors, listened to what was said, never interrupted a person who was speaking, and only afterward would she pronounce a decisive opinion of her own, which made a permanent impression on the minds of those who heard her. By contrast, Leah was a talkative girl with fair hair arranged in long plaits. Her eyes were blue and her skin was white. Her neck was a little short and when she sat down, it sank into her body like that of a yeshiva student. She was popular, but there were some who denied that she was beautiful. Both girls knew Hebrew, but Ida was better versed in it than Leah. Leah used to read poetry by Adam (A.D. Lebensohn) and Michal (M.J. Lebensohn) and even knew some of their poems by heart. In comparison, Ida was down to earth. In those days the monthly *Haboker Or* came to light and excerpts from Braudes' novel *Religion and Life* made a striking impression.

At this house, most of the group of *maskilim* whom we have mentioned above, came together. An exception was Asher Yaffe, the son-in-law of the great magnate. Yeruham was always arguing with Ida. If she criticized a certain article or new story, he would demonstrate at great length that it was not so. On the other hand, when she praised anything, then he would criticize it. Yeruham was the leading talker. In the depths of his heart, he was bound to Ida with bonds of love. There was another regular visitor at the cantor's house, called Nehemia, the son of Eisenstein whose business was printing dockets and account books. He was also something of a *maskil.* He had a quarterly subscription for *Hazefirah* and at every opportunity tried to prove that H.S. Slonimsky was better than any other living writer. He showed his love for Ida openly and she, even if he were not a superior being in her eyes, encouraged him more than she did Yeruham. So he concluded that Ida was superficial and somewhat insincere. I would be misleading were I to say that because of this he stopped loving her. Man does not function that way.

The elderly teacher, Shlomo-Ozer, found himself faced with a rival from outside the circle. This was a new Hebrew teacher, Ben-Moshe, who began to give Hebrew lessons. He thought a good deal of himself, was always twirling his moustache and speaking about Ben-Ze'ev or about Steinberg. The first time he stepped into the cantor's house, he desired that Leah should become his wife, and he carried out his intention. Ben-Moshe was hostile to Yeruham, because the latter was the better man.

Now the author once mentioned that his own enlightenment had its beginnings in this same town. He will keep his secret to himself. Now, on the boundary of the upper city, a Catholic church stood in a field. The few Polish nobles had established it. It was a circular, elegant building, surmounted by a dome of copper. The strips of wall between the long narrow windows looked like columns and pillars. A certain quiet surrounded the place, discouraging a stranger's approach.

Every Sunday, the Christian day of rest, numerous believers would gather there in the morning in order to pour out their supplication. The priest clad in his sacerdotal robes stood in the pulpit before the wall of the sanctuary and chanted with the congregation. The organ would be playing in the loft above. According to popular legend, every organ contains within it one strand of the fabled musical instrument which the Levites used to play in the Temple when it was still in existence. When any Jew heard this melody his soul would depart. I might not have known how to express my muse today, if I had not secretly stolen there time after time in the days of my youth, and had not inclined my ear from outside to hear the moving music which accompanied in a minor key the songs of praise. They said these were chapters of the psalms of David.

But I have again digressed from my path.

3.

Far removed from this group of enlightened Hebraists was the group of *maskilim* who read Russian. Among them there stood out three teachers of Russian, namely, Batlon, Babushkin and Barski. One of them will feature in my story so I shall therefore devote a complete chapter to them.

The teacher Barski was the son of a state-appointed rabbi. He attended a municipal school and afterward entered the first class of the horticultural school in Nemirov, the capital, and did well in his studies. Once he was walking in a park with a textbook in his hand, revising his studies—he was then about fifteen—when he encountered the daughter of his teacher, whose house happened to be in that park. The girl, a sweet girl, was very good-looking. He went up to her and kissed her on the mouth. The embarrassed girl ran and complained to her mother. He was expelled from the school. He did not regret what he had done and carried the image of this girl in his heart for a long time. He went back to his father's house, and inscribed the entries in the register of births and deaths. He would enter them, but his father sometimes changed or deleted them. His father was very keen on money, but he himself had not as yet realized its value. He abandoned this ignoble work and began to think what he should do with his life. He wanted to learn the secrets of chemistry, but he did not possess the elementary basic knowledge. He began to study afresh and applied himself diligently for several months. However, he fell into bad company. His new companions forcibly took his textbooks away from him and compelled him to go around with them day and night. Two years passed in this way—the world of desire is also a world. By this time he was nearing twenty. One day he adopted a new outlook and decided to escape from this evil environment. But he was already too exhausted to begin anything new. Occasionally he would read some article in a Russian monthly which he had borrowed, but nothing seemed to capture his interest. There was only one thing in which he believed, namely psychology. But this study, according to its exponents, had many different schools and he was looking for a clear-cut imperative. He wandered in this way from one city to another, until he came to Honyrad where he set up as a teacher of Russian. He earned ten rubles a week and sometimes more.

Babushkin was so different from him.

He was a young man of about twenty-two, with long, quite attractive hair. Whenever he removed his round hat, he would touch his hair with both hands, making a graceful movement with his head. He was facile in speech and action. When anyone met him in the street, he was always busy with something. He ran from lesson to lesson, sometimes forgetting the name of his pupil. He ate meals at irregular times, never washed properly and changed his lodgings almost every month. He used to smoke in bed and by this habit often caused damage to the pillows or eiderdowns. The word he used most frequently was *harasho,** with which he began and ended every sentence. He read every book which came to hand. When he was nineteen, he studied day and night for a considerable period of time. He acquired his real education at that time, and, by pure chance, read some essays of Michailovsky who became the spiritual fount from which he drew inspiration, although he did not do so systematically. He learned sociology from his teacher, but at the same time he despised the masses. If intellectuals were to disappear from the world, the sun would no longer shine. He did not believe in God, but he did believe in the power of Nature. Here is your proof. You are sitting on a chair and if you want to, you can get up quickly, you can put something on a table quietly, or you can bang it down so forcibly that the vessel is broken to pieces. He thus mistook one concept for another, one matter for another. His friends called him "the sophist." In fact, he was like an empty platter which a starving man licks. I do not know Babushkin's background.

4.

The first and foremost among the three teachers was undoubtedly Batlon, a fact that his two friends would have been forced to admit, despite themselves.

Batlon was a very tall young man, and made an impression even at a distance. In his walk, movements and speech, he possessed a certain nobility and was like a lawyer or doctor. He was meticulous about his dress. When he went for an evening stroll, he wore gloves and twirled his stick from side to side. He was an excellent teacher and knew the fundamentals of pedagogy. His Russian pronunciation was good and he emphasized every accent and nuance. He was not very sociable and was very deliberate in the things he did. He possessed a certain hidden melancholy. His nose was not merely ill-formed by

* Russian for "good."

nature, but was ugly and very thick at the nostrils. This changed the whole appearance of his face. His brow, cheeks and ears were regular. His eyes were bright. Ask a craftsman, why do you make certain parts just right and this one in the middle all wrong?

Batlon had the habit, when thinking, of putting his hand not on his brow, but off his nose. He disliked looking in a mirror when dressing. He did not read the monthly magazines, but preferred books. He really did study Buckle and Draeper. The development of civilization and culture were matters on which he thought constantly. He was not concerned with details, but with principles and basic structure. When he came to an important matter, he would read aloud, meditating and repeating every sentence to himself. He did not understand contradictions and did not seek proof. He could not comprehend that it might be possible to understand something in a manner different from the way he had been taught by his teachers. While he was still at the university city of Kharkov before he came to Honyrad he had met a certain student who read Schopenhauer. When this man tried to explain to him that thought could be a scientific process, Batlon thought he was feeble-minded. How was it possible for the mind to conceive of itself as something outside of itself?

Batlon regarded religious matters as being on a lower level of human achievement. The gentiles had religion before their legislators trod the earth with the rod of government in their hands. The Jews of today were just obstinate. He did not mix in politics. It was a tragedy that Russia stood at such a low ebb in the progress of civilization. He respected Alexander II and looked upon his emancipation of the serfs and his initial establishment of some equality of rights as a beacon of light.

Batlon's father was a fire insurance agent, a man who loved knowledge, not particularly observant in religious matters and considered one of the enlightened men in Tchernigov where he dwelt. Once he was led astray to enter into a conspiracy with a certain merchant who was in a hurry to get rich. The latter burned down his place of business, by his own hand in order to obtain a sum of money three times its value from the insurance company. The matter came to light, was brought to court, and the arsonist was sent into exile. The father of our hero fled abroad, wandering from place to place and living a precarious existence. His wife remained faithful to him in his disgrace. She left the children with her mother and after a year went to join her husband and stand by him. However, his homesickness being too strong—for he loved Russia with all his heart—he decided to go back to his country and stand trial, which he did. He was sentenced to only two and one-half years in prison, having received a lenient sentence because he voluntarily gave himself up and confessed. Later, he managed by hard work to establish some position for himself. However, he parted from his former social circle, and they say he even returned to God. Every morning he used to pray in private to the forgiver of sin and iniquity. At the same time he took great care over the education of his children, giving them a thorough knowledge of the Russian language. His eldest, that is Batlon, went to high school. Meanwhile, the father fell ill with a hidden heart complaint and passed away.

A day before his death, he called his son to him and bade him take care of his mother. She, however, did not survive him long and for the second time followed her husband into exile.

To describe what happened to Batlon thereafter, how as an orphan he applied himself to study and to self-perfection, how he went through all kinds of tribulations until he reached the city of Kharkov, the goal of all young Jews in that region, and how he came from thence to Honyrad like a ship's captain whose vessel has foundered in the ocean, would take too long.

5.

In order to complete the picture, I shall add a few notes on the leading lights of the intelligentsia.

There was in Honyrad an attorney named Shalita who was well known for many years. He was an excellent speaker, adept at capturing the hearts of the most inveterate judges. He knew how to get a man off a criminal charge and could make every crime and misdemeanor appear white as snow. It was he who secured an acquittal for the wife of the mayor of Ladyna when she killed the district commissioner who tried to seduce her. When he was defending an accused, he would speak in the high court for hours at a stretch without a pause. First, he would argue with reason and logic, but if he saw that was producing no noticeable effect on the jury he would appeal to their hearts. At one moment he would plead, at the next warn them solemnly of the great responsibility of condemning a man who may have only offended once by mistake, when such condemnation might ruin him. Extracts from his orations in the courts were bandied from mouth to mouth. People mentioned the name of Shalita with awe. Was this a small thing that within the city limits of Honyrad dwelt an attorney who in the course of time would without doubt rival Kiev's Kopernic! Abraham Kopernic was a converted Jew who had abandoned his faith in order more easily to devote his talents to the general good. He was the greatest genius of all the attorneys of Greater Russia.

There was no one on earth like him, as everybody knew. Well, most of Shalita's activity was in connection with criminal law. He had very little practice in the field of civil law. Once his wife fell seriously ill, and at one stage her condition was so grave that they spread straw on the pavement in front of his fine house to reduce the noise of horses' hooves and the rattle of passing carts and thus guarantee quiet for the patient. During this time, a certain Jew came to him, requesting him to honor a certain certificate of deposit for money which he had deposited with him. In his distraction, Shalita said "I don't know you!" What did the claimant do? He laid a complaint against him. The matter was investigated and it was discovered that the attorney had indeed disavowed the deposit. He was at once ordered to pay the sum—it was not very large—and his license to practice as a defense counsel before the high court was revoked. He thus fell from eminence in one day. His wife, still a young woman, died, and the inordinate grief he felt drove him to liquor. All that he possessed and all that he had accumulated with so much toil was swiftly dissipated. His winter overcoat was his sole possession and he wore it in summer too. He let his hair grow long. Occasionally, one of his friends of former times quietly slipped him some money. People who saw him wandering aimlessly in the streets or tottering along drunkenly, would say pityingly: "Those that were brought up in scarlet have embraced dunghills."

Zellin, the other attorney, was something entirely different. By contrast, he worked only in the field of civil law. In his youth, he had attended the *bet hamidrash** and had studied Jewish civil law, excelling in his understanding of the most complex treatises. One day, a thought, stinging as the venom of a snake, entered his mind and he asked himself "Why do you waste your time on vain absurdity? Come complete your studies and make a career in worldly matters." Finally, he threw off the yoke of the Talmud, went to Kherson and began with great assiduity to study basic subjects and languages. They said of him that he sat for two years in his room and did not for a moment interrupt his secular studies until he fell gravely ill. When he recovered, he took his examinations and was found to have successfully grasped all the subjects which a bright student would only pass after eight years of study. One of the teachers, amazed at his ability, interceded on his behalf in the capital, in order to obtain entry for him into one of the science faculties which were closed to young Jews. In the university, he studied jurisprudence, worked for a while on a comparative study of Roman and Jewish law, but soon abandoned theoretical studies, and emerged after a few years as a fully qualified attorney. He married a woman from a wealthy family, settled in Honyrad and worked diligently at his profession. On his table, there always reposed that section of the *Shulchan Aruch* which dealt with civil law. He was singled out by pious Jews who came to seek counsel from him.

6.

I shall only mention two of the doctors. Malter and Koch.

Malter was a slim well-groomed man, almost clean shaven, but

* Hebrew for "house of study."

with a thin wisp of a beard. His eyes were small and black, his hands white as a woman's. He would receive his patients standing, while playing with his gold watch chain. He did not ask many questions. In general, he rarely felt one's pulse and it was said of him that he could diagnose a patient's complaint from his face. His medical fees were very high and in this he blazed a trail for himself. He used to operate on injured people, cure eye diseases and give few prescriptions. He was accepted as being one of the intelligentsia. He could play a good game of cards and was known for the casualness with which he lost money. What he earned in a whole week—and it was by no means little—he might easily lose in one night's game. He did not live peaceably with his wife, but carried on an affair both openly and secretly with the beautiful wife of Tobazchik, the apothecary. The latter was a bald man, poorly skilled in his profession. When it comes to a doctor and an apothecary, it is the former who matters; the apothecary is of no account.

The second doctor, named Koch, was an unusual character. He was small in stature, corpulent, physically powerful and already advanced in years. He was one of those Jewish children who had been forcibly conscripted into the army through the edict of Czar Nicholas I, the father of Alexander II. They tore these children away from their parents' homes and dragged them off to distant provinces. There they worked as swineherds for the village serfs until they forgot the ordinances of Judaism and their mother-tongue. When they reached the age of fifteen, they began harsh military training, served in the infantry in border regiments, and fought dangerous battles with the savage tribes in the Caucasian mountains. For them, one year was reckoned as a day; ten years as a single year. They knew no rest and their lives were hard. When they were well on in age they gradually returned to Central Russia to a world which was strange to them.

Koch was trained to be a medical orderly in the army, became an expert in practical medicine and made tremendous progress. After he had passed his fiftieth year, he was released from the army and traveled through all the cities of the province of Kiev, until he came to Honyrad and settled there. In the course of the years, he achieved a reputation throughout the whole locality and people streamed to him from the neighboring villages. He was indeed an expert doctor and helped many people who were seriously ill to recover.

He had no wife and lived in a house in a large courtyard, wedged in between the upper and lower cities. At dawn, the courtyard was full of ailing men and women, waiting for him. When the door was opened, they came in, jostling each other. There were sick people who would bribe the gatekeeper with three rubles to let them in to the miracle man ahead of the others. The doctor himself received only one ruble. He himself paid no attention to the fees and just as readily treated people without fee as for payment. He often gave poor people money out of his own pocket. Although his labors were physically exhausting, he received patients without interruption from morning to night. He would go off in the middle of the night to visit a patient suddenly taken ill and neither rain nor frost held him back.

He had been stolen out of the arms of his parents when he was a boy of seven. He herded for a villager and was baptized by a Russian Orthodox priest when he was twelve. He was completely sundered from Judaism, not even knowing the name of his parents. One thing remained impressed on him from his tender childhood. On the morning before the day of a great fast, they used to take a cock, bind its legs, twirl it round their heads several times and recite certain words. After that they threw it on the ground and read verses from a book. Sometimes he longed for this ceremony. It once happened that the wife of the state-appointed rabbi of Honyrad was sick and this doctor came to the house to visit the patient. He asked the rabbi about the custom of the cock and he told him what he knew about it. From that time onward, the rabbi had to come to him secretly every year on the eve of *Yom Kippur**. In this way he believed he was following the custom of the Jews in the villages. The rabbi would translate the words into Russian for him: "This instead of me, this in place of me."

I, too, have seen this doctor.

* Day of Atonement.

7.

Tamar, the daughter-in-law of the wealthy Nehemia Trachtman, was wasting away from loneliness. Her husband, Amnon, was once again running wild after his fancies and often did not return to her for several days each week. Wealth may seem to declare itself, but may cast a shadow of dreadful silence. There can be anxiety in prosperous surroundings. Two people may meet in a guesthouse, become acquainted and yet there can be a distance between them. You can plant a tree, but it may not take root, you may make a compact and all it comes to is a document bearing witness to human bondage. She had gone astray in the house of her father, the rabbi, and no longer believed in sacred things. The ancestral customs were to her simply an artificial clinging to the past. She had no feeling for her people and no family attachment. When she woke in the morning her physical existence dragged her back from a long dream. Daylight was a bitter jest, days had no measure or meaning. What was she doing, who existed for her here? Her father-in-law and mother-in-law were not her keepers. Who had asked her to come here? Who would bother to go after her if she got up and went away? Who can explain what the heart is planning?

You stand looking in a mirror, face to face with yourself; movement imitates movement. You close your eyes and it is pitch dark, a silent unrest fills the room, you take the silver knife with which you cut the white Sabbath loaf and it slips from your hands, piercing your breast so that the blood flows in a curved stream on to the slippery floor. The speckled dog licks up the blood as it flows, drinking its fill. She would stand on the balcony and call to the people passing below, "Come up to me and I shall be yours and give you my body." There are iron bars round about. Men have no ears. They have lost their sense of hearing. Here is a garden ready planted but there is a gate within a gate.

During that time Dr. Malter became the favorite of her male confidants, and subjected her beauty to his will.

8.

It was midday. The sun shone fiercely, scorching the earth with a warmth which brought healing to everybody. Tamar tossed restlessly in her stifling room and longed to feel at one with a world which was both broad and narrow, possessed rivers and streams without number and yet man could not slake his thirst. She embraced the red bolster in her strong arms, closed her eyes and saw thousands, myriads of bright points of light with iridescent colors and her soul bathed in a sea of radiant blue.

She woke suddenly, descended from her couch and tore the curtains away from the window. She stood in front of the mirror and combed her hair, put on a loose yellow dress, and ordered the horseman to harness the carriage. She went to see the doctor.

A dark-haired girl received her and led her into the waiting room. She was alone. "There's another young woman in the doctor's room," the girl said. A quarter of a hour passed, half an hour. The clock chimes each quarter of the hour. She sat a whole hour on her chair consumed with jealousy. She could barely prevent herself from getting up and knocking on Malter's door. She must know. She opened the door quietly and saw a tall veiled woman leaving the doctor's surgery. She had an inner impulse to block the way and say, "Confess your sin with him, admit what you have done." She seized the door handle and leaned on it with all her strength. Her rival left the house. She composed herself and went in. Malter was standing looking out of the window and paid no attention to her. Tamar cried out, "I am here in the room; you have betrayed me as you always do." The doctor turned to her and said, "What do you want?" She burst into sobs. He drew near and took her by the arm.

"Take me to your house and I shall play my part. The idea that I am not the only one tears at my entrails. Let us both leave this place and go to a distant city! I don't want you to practice medicine any more! What have you to do with other people! Who cares whether the sun is shining? Close out the sky and bring me into a fortress, I am mad with burning passion for you and only fire can quench fire!"

She fell on his neck and embraced him, kissing him and crying out aloud, "You owe me something. My husband is no longer a husband to me. My parents are strangers to me. You have made me yours, and I live as part of your blood."

At that very hour Amnon returned home. When his servant told him that his wife had gone to Malter, the doctor, he also became consumed with jealousy and rushed over there. He hurried up the steps, came to the corridor, tore open the door in a fury and began screaming at both of them. The maids rushed in at the sound of the screaming. By evening the report had spread throughout the city. I shall not relate the subsequent course of events.

9.

A new district commissioner came to Honyrad. When he had settled in his office, he instituted a new custom. On every Jewish Sabbath and on the eve of the Christian Sunday, he sent officials to conscript some of the gentile maidservants in the houses of those observing the day of rest and forced them to work for nothing in his household and in his courtyard. This was purely an ad hoc regulation and was only known in that city. The residents grumbled inside their own homes, but who can contend with the authorities? There are a lot of things which are not signed and sealed in the highest quarters at St. Petersburg which are imposed upon the people throughout the broad reaches of the empire. And what can Jews do, who are inferior subjects?

But an even greater affliction fell upon Honyrad. After some time a new deputy commissioner was appointed to the district. He was a strange person. To everyone's stupefaction, he simply refused to accept bribes from anybody.

The land of Russia without bribery is like a land without air to breathe. It was as though every person were struck dumb and the power of speech had ceased in the world. How can a city continue to exist, which up till now had been accustomed to slipping something to an official for anything, great or small? In vain did Honyrad attempt to persuade this strange official to receive gifts. They tried to cajole him, even to force gifts on him—but he maintained his position. "If the man who gives the gift is right, then I am taking a gift for no purpose. If he is at fault, then let him bear the responsibility for his crime." This deputy commissioner was a bachelor and lived in a single narrow room. However, he had a mistress who cooked his meals and repaired his clothes. Even the notables and important people in the city besieged the doorway of this gentile woman and begged and entreated her to open her hand and receive something in cash or in kind from them. If this would not help to soften the heart of this hater of bribes—something like this had happened in another city and the leaders of the community had decided to hold a public fast. In Honyrad, it became a great affliction which was talked about everywhere.

But even this was forgotten when a young man of the royal family, who had disgraced himself, was forced to go into exile from the imperial city, the glittering capital of the empire. He was sentenced to spend several months in Honyrad. This brought great delight to the inhabitants.

All those connected with the local authorities took great pains to beautify the city and make it look new. A bylaw was passed forcing every man to repair his house and whitewash the outside walls. All the streets were newly paved with stones. The yards had to be cleaned and fine sand spread in front of every door. The poor were forbidden to appear in the center of the city in their rags and tatters. It was prohibited to litter the ground with seeds and fruit. Ordinary wagons were not allowed to pass through the beautiful streets. In the big shops, the most expensive items were purchased to adorn the dwellings of the czar's kinsman. Every day bullocks, lambs, and poultry were slaughtered without end to supply his table. They brought up the best of the wine from the wine cellars. There was a feast like that of King Solomon at the house of the czar's relative every day. Most of the guests were the rural aristocracy and they came whether they liked it or not to eat with the great prince. Every week there was a ball and celebration at his palace. Gaudily dressed prostitutes mingled with the wives of the local nobility. Fiddles, drums, and cymbals made constant music. Night after night, the city was illumined by lanterns and beacons. Fun and games, mirth and merrymaking! Nobody stayed home: streets and squares round about the tumultuous palace were filled with throngs of people. It was a great festive season even more gay than had occurred in the days when the nobleman of Zarkov had held his celebration.

On one tumultuous night such as this, Miriam, our heroine, reached the city of Honyrad.

Chapter seven

Strange events and unprecedented happenings took place at this time especially among the Jews of Honyrad. I shall relate them one by one, even though they are not all relevant to my central story.

A man learned in the Torah, who prayed in a small hasidic *kloiz** in the remote part of the city, peered closely into the books of scholarship and nature, and gave vent to a view that he believed only in a general Divine providence, but not in Divine providence for the individual. A great storm arose among the Hasidim, who began to persecute him and attempted to destroy the source of his livelihood. The man was in serious trouble. He was about thirty years of age and the father of three children. He submitted to public pressure and accepted chastisement for having suggested a diminution in the power of the Most High. This was the eve of the new moon, which is a small Day of Atonement for the God-fearing. The unfortunate wretch took off his shoes in the chapel, sat on the ground and began to make confession according to the ritual set forth in the prayer book.

* Hasidic prayer house.

Meanwhile, the crowd surrounded him and cried out, "You are our brother." While he was praying and confessing, one strict observer poked him with his foot. The eyes of the man seated on the ground filled with tears from the humiliation which he felt so deeply—and the man who poked him did not complete his year. In Honyrad, the district capital, such excessive fanaticism had not previously been known. This was something new.

Just near the edge of the upper city a certain man had established residence. He was already more than fifty years of age and associated with thieves. A whole gang of such thieves was at his beck and call, and obeyed his every command. He behaved as a wealthy burgher and most of the townsmen lived in fear of him. Many of the rich paid him annual protection money to keep their interests from harm. They treated him with respect because of their fear. No one dared say anything against him and he amassed wealth. Once when a famous *tzaddik* passed by Honyrad, it occurred to this head of thieves to visit the rebbe. The *tzaddik* gave orders that he was not to be disturbed and conferred with him for about an hour. The man returned to his house, divided all his property into three parts and gave one third to the rebbe, one third to the poor and one third to the state, in order that the local officials should free him from the taxes which he paid each year. Thereafter, he sat in the *bet hamidrash* like a poor man, eating from the soup kitchen and reciting psalms every day. No one who saw him could believe that this was "Moishele the Thief" as he used to be called.

2.

Not far from the big municipal park lived a man of just over forty. This was Manoah, the leaseholder. He was not a native of Honyrad, but had come to live there a few years previously. He only visited the city occasionally, spending most of his time on the leasehold estate a few miles from Honyrad, where he had a house. His wife was an embittered invalid and a hidden enmity prevailed between them all the time. They had an only daughter who had been married, but had got rid of her husband because she could not stand him. She was a tall woman, not without education. There was a certain dignity about the way she walked and, in general, she resembled her father, but there was one strange thing about her: since childhood she was forever terrified of thunder and lightning. It is impossible to describe the extent of this fear, it was so abnormal. Whenever her father visited his estate, she came to stay with him. As I said, she inclined more toward her father than toward her mother. It was a summer night and she had already gone to bed, when the whole room was illuminated by great flashes of lightning and peals of thunder. One thunder clap followed another, until it looked as if the world were falling apart and the house was being shaken to its foundations. Mortal terror overcame the young woman and she fled from her room to her father's and lay in his bed. Floods of incessant rain began to pour down into the earth. It seemed that cursed Satan had come back once again to confuse the world. Even before the morning dawned, the man got up, hid his face, and went on foot to the city where the rebbe resided. He had hardly set his foot over the threshold of this holy man's house when he heard a voice crying from inside "Go away from here: you are unclean!"

On the outskirts of the lower city lived a man who worked in leather, what the Talmud calls a tanner. He was redheaded, lively and well-to-do. His wife was barren and had ceased to menstruate, so that the man, who had longed for a son all his life, lost all hope. In his neighborhood he had noticed a strapping and good-looking young girl to whom he made advances and whom he tried to seduce. He pressed himself upon her so strongly that eventually she submitted. The man was elated by the outcome; nevertheless he continually exhorted her to cleanse herself ritually from her impurity and immerse herself in water as religion requires. That evening the girl went down to the river to immerse herself in the water while he watched out for her from a distance and made the blessing for her. She came out from the river furtively. The man had intercourse with her. Only the moon and the stars were witnesses. The girl became pregnant and at the end of nine months gave birth to a male child. The rumor spread through the city: so and so, the daughter of so and so, had borne a child through immoral intercourse. The Jews were unwilling to have the child circumcised. Then the tanner felt compelled to enter the *bet hamidrash* when the people were gathered there, and he cried out: "She is in the right against me!"

I have already mentioned the prosperous man who lived in the upper city and who possessed a portion of the Prophets with Mendelssohn's commentary. This man was a *cohen* of high repute among his brethren. A *cohen* may only take a virgin in marriage and a divorced woman is forbidden him by priestly law. He had married a divorced woman, he himself being a widower, his wife having died before she was fifty. In the lower city was a certain broker to whom the *cohen* used to go on business. He had a very beautiful wife, who was not faithful to him. Shalita was her lover in the days of his greatness. The *cohen* persuaded the broker to divorce his wife and advanced him the money to pay off her dowry. He duly divorced her and the *cohen* duly married her. A *shochet* who had been disqualified from office because of some irregularity, was persuaded for a fee to celebrate the marriage—to the dismay of the whole city. Sabbath after Sabbath, a crowd including many students of the law, gathered around the house of the *cohen.* If he or his wife dared to go out of the house they would assail them with curses and imprecations: One New Year's day, which is in truth the Day of Judgment in heaven for those who dwell on earth, the mob attacked the wife of the *cohen* as she was going to synagogue, in all her finery. They kicked her, injured her and stripped her clothes off her. It was only with the greatest difficulty that the local police saved her from those who were abusing her and cursing her. They took her home to her house clothed only in a shift.

For a long time the entire city was in turmoil over the dreadful event that had occurred in their midst when a *cohen* married a woman forbidden to him.

3.

Now here are two more incidents. A well-known man in the city of Honyrad was Absalom the miller. He was forty years old and sold flour in a large shop at the top of a flight of stairs. In the *bet hami-*

drash where he prayed, he was considered a respectable householder and quite learned. He had a wife and three children. From time to time Absalom used to travel to Belaya Tserkov. In that town lived two Christian missionaries who would give passersby books printed in Hebrew characters resembling the Bible. They contained chapters and verses, with vowels and sometimes even cantillation notes. They contained words of exhortation and parables: not statutes and regulations. In the place of Moses, the son of Amram, a prophet spoke who was called the Messiah and the son of God. Instead of Joshua, the son of Nun, there were twelve disciples corresponding to the number of the tribes of Israel.

Suddenly, the news spread in Honyrad that Absalom and his household had converted. The matter became known on a Sabbath, the day which has been the sign of the covenant between the Almighty and His people Israel from the very beginning. They were praying and offering thanks to God who weighs all deeds, to the holy God, whose day is holy and whose tribe is holy. The angels of peace stand on the threshold of every Jewish house as emissaries to the Chosen People from their Father who is in heaven. And now a member of the congregation had gone and abandoned his religion. One who had hitherto been Jewish now overnight had become a non-Jew. There was sadness and deep distress, but no heavenly voice burst forth, the Divine Presence did not burst into lament. But it was discovered after investigation that in the Great Synagogue the perpetual light before the ark had gone out by itself…

On the morning after the Sabbath day a great mob gathered in front of the flour shop to see the wicked profaner of the covenant. Many could not believe that Absalom had done as had been reported. He had arrived early at his shop and when he saw the mob gathered there, he went out bareheaded, stood arrogantly on the top step, both hands in his trouser pockets and called to the people, "Take a good look at a converted Jew!"

I am relating things as they occurred and I know of another event which took place at this time when another man was also caught in the net of subversion at Belaya Tserkov. It happened this way. He was a goodhearted person who had not yet reached thirty. All his life he had loved the depictions of sacrificial services in the prayer book. Avidly he devoured the first chapters of the Book of Leviticus, which is the Book of the Levites, the chapters about sacrifices in the Book of Exodus, and in the Book of Numbers. All his life he was grieved that the Jews no longer had a temple, sacrificial offerings, or a priest to preside over the sacrifices. True, Jewish sources state that prayer has taken the place of sacrifice. It is said that the blood and the fat which are reduced in the body on the fast days are considered in God's eyes like the bringing of sacrifices and sin offerings. But what are these in comparison with the burnt offerings which go straight up to God in smoke? Any such prayers and sacrifices, even if they are offered in place of burnt offerings to the Most High, did not reveal, to the eyes of man, the King or His throne. On the other hand, in days of yore, when the Temple was still in existence, a man stood up and offered his sacrifice and fire came down from heaven to consume the offering upon the altar. Now, one of these two missionaries in the city gave him a book of the Gospel, known as the *Epistle to the Hebrews.* In this book the atmosphere of the city where David dwelt prevailed. The earthly temple flourished as did that of heaven and the blood of the sacrifices shone with the strength of the sun. There were not many priests standing on duty, but the high priest savior, Melchizedek, ministered to the creation and offered his fat and his blood literally to make atonement for the world for the burden of sin. With the utmost reverence this young man read every chapter and deeply pondered every verse and thought. When he had finished reading the book, he was trembling. He fell on his face and wanted to cry out, "The Lord He is God and Melchizedek is His servant and His messiah." They say that at that time he saw the very image of his dead father standing before him.

But by now I have surely gone far astray.

4.

Yehiel Eichenstein welcomed his kinswoman Miriam very warmly. They brought her water to wash her hands and face from the dust of the journey. Afterward she sat down at the table to eat the evening meal together with the members of the household, but she scarcely touched anything. The sound of the drum and the fiddle could be heard as far as the house and her heart was faint. She was also weary from the burden of the journey. The master of the house did not press her to eat. He understood how she felt and had a deep compassion for her tender youth. After the meal was over, he asked his sister to arrange a place for her to sleep and left the room with a conventional "good night!" They cleared the dining-room for her and made her a bed on the wide sofa, placing a candle on the table for her. In the quiet room she sat on a chair, as though in a cloud. Spheres were spinning afar and the world had hidden its face. She wanted to cry, but had no resources to put against the emptiness she felt. Who does not recall the mysterious hopefulness one feels when one is young and is put up for the night in strange surroundings for the very first time.

Miriam rose in the morning, washed her face and hands, dressed, and went out and stood in front of the house. Yehiel's grandson, Gedaliah, also went out and said "good morning!" to Miriam, but nothing else. The master of the house had already solemnly recited his morning prayer and while doing so had reminded himself of the young guest who had arrived the previous day. He inwardly determined that he would protect her. God has compassion on his creatures: He is the Father and we are His sons. Arise, son of man, and speak with the God of the universe.

For the midday meal, the members of the household again sat around the table as on the previous day, but this time there was some conversation. Eichenstein, the head of the house, begged Miriam to feel at home. The grandchildren, Deborah and Pessie stared at her. Gedaliah looked down at his plate. It was a fine day. Yehiel was in the habit of taking a nap after lunch, but Miriam and Deborah went out for a little walk, in the course of which Deborah showed her relative the mill beside the river. A little later, Gedaliah joined them and stayed with them a while for company.

Gedaliah was a fair-haired youth, very eager to acquire knowledge, but what he learned he kept pent up inside himself and did not speak about it. He was accustomed to loneliness and kept recalling his father who had passed away. His mother had married again, and she saw him only on rare occasions. His sister, Deborah, a plain girl but sincere, was closer to him than the white-skinned Pessie. She was redheaded, freckled, and talkative, often humming a song as she went about from room to room. I have already mentioned Yehiel's sister, the widow, who kept house. Her name was Chava. She performed her duties faithfully and was free of envy toward other people. There was also a Jewish maidservant working in the kitchen and a gentile servant helping her to clean the rooms, light the fires, and milk the cows. She also fed the geese and hens in the yard. The Jewish servant wore shoes, but the gentile went barefoot.

Gedaliah's friend at that time was Yehezkel, the son of Solomon, who held on lease the post house for supplying horses to government officials en route. This lessee was one of the Hasidim. He had bouts of religious enthusiasm and was known for his hearty appetite. His son went to a religious school to learn Talmud and its commentaries. He was an imaginative person and liked Pessie but she persistently and deliberately avoided him. Pessie also had a friend, a lively, jolly girl called Esther. The oldest girl, Deborah, was friendly with two sisters, Rebecca and Mahla, a pair of beautiful twins. When they went out it was difficult to tell one from the other. Rebecca liked Miriam the moment she saw her, which made Mahla jealous.

5.

On the eve of the first Sabbath after Miriam came to the city of Honyrad, preparations began in the house for the holy day. They cleaned the windows, washed the doors and the floors, and spread white cloths over the tables. At Eichenstein's house on Sabbaths and festivals, they used to have their meals in the great salon which was closed the rest of the week. A chandelier of shining crystal hung from the painted ceiling and two wall fixtures for tallow candles of burnished bright copper were fixed between the windows. At one end of the large table stood a silver candelabrum with three stems on each of which were two branches. Every chair was covered with a white cover. Everything was spic and span. Eichenstein and his grandson had already returned from the synagogue. He was dressed in a closefitting robe of black silk, tailored in excellent taste. Gedaliah was wearing a woolen garment, also well made. Their hats were of silk. Deborah and Pessie wore dresses of expensive polka-dot fabric, and Eichenstein's sister, the housekeeper, wore a rich woolen kerchief of blue and gold on her head. It was she who blessed the Sabbath lights as was her well-established prerogative.

Yehiel greeted the ministering Sabbath angels, reciting the praises wholeheartedly, but with a certain longing in his heart. Who was finer than a woman of valor, he sang, and he gave thanks to the one who lived in his house and also to the one who had passed away. The God of the Sabbath now hovered in His high heavens listening to the songs of the Children of Israel wherever they might be. The master of the house poured the wine into a golden goblet and, after he had drunk from it, held it out to the women. After that, Gedaliah also recited the *kiddush.** They washed their hands for the meal and sat down to enjoy the Sabbath meal and then sing the Sabbath hymns. Miriam had never seen a Sabbath eve quite like that in her father's house.

After grace, the table was swept clean of the crumbs left over from the feast. Deborah and Pessie got up and sat in a corner, talking together, but they soon left the room. For a little while the mistress of the house looked into her *Korban Minha* prayer book, but she was weary from the toil of the day and went to sleep. Gedaliah took up the novel *Love of Zion* and began to read. Miriam was reading a Russian book. Yehiel was leafing through the pages of a Pentateuch containing the traditional commentaries. The weekly portion was that of Korah.

At this point the Children of Israel were in the wilderness, every tribe encamped by its standard. The craftsmen had built the

* Sanctification. A prayer recited over wine to sanctify the Sabbath.

tabernacle according to the plan which the prophet had seen on the mountain and it rose splendidly in the midst of the camp. The God of the Covenant dwelt within it, above the cherubim. Outside it, members of Levite families kept watch. This was a holy nation, the Chosen People whom God had bore on eagles' wings from the land of the sons of Ham. He had caused them to inherit His Torah, His eternal delight. Now He intended to give them possession of the land which He had sworn to their fathers would be theirs. Moses the son of Amram, the skin of whose face shone, used to speak with God face to face. He presided over the laws and statutes and also over the journeys from place to place. Aaron, his brother, the dedicated one of the Almighty, served as priest in the Tabernacle, and he and his sons offered sacrifices upon the altar and burning incense in the sanctuary. The incense was sweet of savor, pleasant to the Lord. There was no Satan and no trouble. The people's clothing did not wear out and their feet did not swell. A pillar of cloud and a pillar of fire made straight the path before the children of Abraham.

And now Korah, the son of Izhar, came out, joined by Datan and Abiram and they incited the blessed people against their leaders Moses and Aaron. Moses had not taken a single ass, he had not received any gift, he was not overbearing to the community—and now there was an outcry of murmuring in camp. "You take too much on yourself, ye sons of Levi!" Moses and Aaron tried to justify themselves before the murmurers, attempting to pacify the raging people, but the people determined to stone them. The same men, who in the recent days of Sinai, had heard the utterance, "thou shalt not revile God, nor curse the ruler of thy people," were now lifting up stones to throw them at God's emissaries. Yehiel's heart fainted when he read these verses in the Pentateuch. Even the commentator Rashi could not solve the riddle. Yehiel lifted up his eyes and saw that the candles on the table had already gone out, but there was a new star in the house. It was not the women of Israel who had taken off their earrings to make the golden calf; they had not rebelled against the word of Moses.

Feeling tenderness and compassion, he rose from the table.

6.

The next day, on the Sabbath afternoon, Yehiel went with his grandson and his kinswoman to see the sights of Honyrad. At that time Miriam was fifteen. She was taller than Gedaliah, who had already passed his sixteenth birthday. She walked gracefully and her features expressed a certain sweetness. All those who saw them walking together thought that the girl was Gedaliah's fiancée, although in Yehiel's circle it was not customary for the bridegroom to go walking with the bride. On the Sabbath, Honyrad was like a clock whose wheels have stopped moving. There was no hubbub in the streets. No business was transacted, no worry about livelihood or money. The fact that the doors of the many shops were shut increased the atmosphere of Sabbath tranquility.

On the next Sabbath, Miriam went walking with the sisters Deborah and Pessie in the great park. She wondered at its incomparable beauty. Gradually, she responded to the spaciousness of the new city. Here was a different horizon and a different kind of life from that in Ladyna. Fashionably dressed men were to be seen everywhere she went. The desire to stand and observe was very strong in her. Now that she had found in the place where she dwelt a feeling of greater intimacy, she was looked upon as a daughter and older sister. Gedaliah had lost his heart to her and was deeply attached. The father, Yehiel, appreciated her charm and would speak to her whenever he felt depressed. When they had prepared Miriam's bed in the room which we have mentioned, he would sometimes bring her her candle, sit down with her, and ask about the sort of book she was reading. Men who write down their thoughts in books are the teachers of knowledge. And those who read them are also stimulated to think. Yehiel felt that Miriam would in the course of time complete her studies and make a name for herself.

Miriam, however, was still far from tranquil. She began to read Gontcharov, but found that there was no magic in his descriptions. Everything was meticulously related but there was no warmth in his commonplaces. He did not take wing and offered no solace to the downcast. If she had had the opportunity of meeting a man familiar with literature, she would have expressed her thoughts on the subject.

Through his teacher, Shlomo-Ozer, Gedaliah had made the acquaintance of the *maskil*, Yeruham, and the latter brought him to the cantor's house where he spoke about his educated kinswoman who had come to his grandfather's house. They were delighted at this fresh blood, and invited him to bring her with him next time. Miriam was persuaded by Gedaliah to accompany him to this house of the enlightened and there she met all the group. Those who were gathered there were seeking something; they were cultured and knowledgeable. She had never before experienced a session like this, but she could not fully understand this sort of conversation and the things they talked about. She felt a warmth around her, but no light shone for her. When they left, Yeruham accompanied them. He was very anxious to explain to her what was going on in the development of modern Hebrew. Yeruham spoke to her with great conviction. He felt very eloquent but Miriam did not know how to answer him. Everything he said was so new to her. Until now, she had understood the Jews to be a dispersed ethnic group with an old religion and the books of the Prophets. She had no knowledge of the Jews as a people with its Hebrew heritage and contemporary literature.

7.

When Yeruham had to turn off for his mother's house, he stretched out his hand to say goodbye to Miriam and felt a certain inner heaviness. He wanted to say some thing more to her; he wanted to meet her again and debate with her. But he left her and went his way with a feeling of despair. Girls like her are necessary to the House of Israel, but they are not for us…You see flowers giving off fragrance—but the garden is closed. The Hebrew reader possessed a Jewish mother, pouring out her soul in supplication through the prayer book, but he had no Hebrew sister. Were the poet to sing songs of love, his beloved would not understand his language. There is no bond between equal souls. There is strength in Hebrew literature and a desire to enlighten, but it lacks tenderness and disregards the relation between the sexes. There is no ear to listen to the mouth.

Both Leah and Ida only had a passing interest in literature. He had long been aware of his inclination toward Ida and, if he was not deceiving himself, he was in love with her, but he did not really know how she felt. She wanted either inner illumination or some overwhelming sensation. He knew how to get at the inner meaning of a book better than she did. He had original thoughts of which she was not capable. However, he did not have sufficient power of expression to convey his feelings. He could either conquer her by a storm of feeling or by proving his superior ability. If only he had the skill to write a story or an article of merit, he would rise in her estimation. He had already begun to outline and put down his thoughts in writing. He had power of language, but he himself considered all he had done not good enough to print. He was very critical of his own work…

Ida was certainly aware of the thoughts which were troubling Yeruham. A girl who has matured has both strength and a self-protective power. She may make somebody happy, elevate him and give his spirit wings, but before this can happen, the man must give her own spirit encouragement. Expression is one thing and the will to love and be loved is another. Two people may sit down and talk, their subject may be basic principles or superficialities and one may rise to go and the other may go after him and embrace him. A sense of physical compatibility between the two sexes is a lofty matter. Poets speak about desires, longing, and romantic dreams which ignite the first sparks in the heart. Yeruham was not to be reckoned among those whom fire and passion intoxicate. In his view, pure love was only a matter of communion and compatibility.

He would wait a year or two until the relationship between him and Ida became clearer and stronger. They would marry and open a school for boys and girls. There had developed within him a determination to educate, to develop the intellect, to raise up a Hebrew-speaking generation which would be admired among the nations, and at the same time would come to know and value itself. There was no doubt that all the words of Peretz Smolenskin which had aroused enthusiasm in him for some time were quite correct. Up till the present time only part of that writer's ideals had been achieved. Yeruham did not have the power, nor did he expect to move the whole of the people, but he wanted to arouse their spirit and to pass on the light received from his own teachers.

After a few days he visited the house of the cantor but did not see Ida. She had a headache and kept to her room. This upset him very much because on that particular day he really wanted to talk to her and to see her. He felt as if he had just returned from a distant journey. As he talked to Leah the elder sister, he was somewhat wild and distracted, but she remained expressionless, talking to him exactly as usual. It was difficult for Yeruham to get up and go. On the table was lying the book *Zerubabel* by I.B. Levinsohn. He opened it and began to read the introduction. Secretly he was hoping for a small miracle, that the door would open quickly and Ida would appear, stretch out her hand to him and ask his forgiveness for having kept him waiting so long. He also thought he would let down his guard and write a letter to her for whom his soul longed, and reveal everything in this heart.

Love knows no appointed times. He walked back and forth in the room as was his habit when absorbed in furious thinking. Suddenly, Leah said that she had something important to do in the upper city and asked him to accompany her. Without a word, Yeruham put on his coat and accompanied her down the few steps which led to the street. The poor fellow did not know that he would never again return to that house...

8.

Ida had very lofty ambitions, and in her eyes the peak of happiness would be to marry a writer. At times, she thought of visiting one of her mother's family in Odessa, where she imagined she could become acquainted with the great writers of whom she had heard. She valued

Yeruham and his aspirations. She was not oblivious to the fact that she had a place in his heart. But he was shorter than she in stature and a rung lower in class! If he had only once squeezed her hand or casually run his hand through her hair, there might have been some inward change in her. You do not know women and the way they feel. On the other hand, if Nehemia, who, as we know, also used to visit her father's house, were to do this, she would immediately recoil, despite the fact that she had been friendly to him. She was not just an inert mass or a mere tool; she was longing for a redeemer or companion to captivate her and win her heart. She was looking for support and real fellowship. She had not known passionate love, but there were stirrings in her soul and these troubled her spirit...So the days of her youth had passed and the sun had not shone upon her. The garden was fenced around and hope was sleeping. The autumn of a young girl! Ben-Moshe, the teacher, was of little account in her eyes nor did she feel any envy for her sister. The teacher belittled Yeruham in her presence. While she paid no attention, it would have been better if his attack had not aroused in her the strange desire to take revenge on the man who idolized her. A person may be sitting by a table and lift a vessel standing on it, throw it to the ground and shatter it into fragments...There can be deliberate murder, without malice. She dismissed Yeruham without a word and Leah her sister, Ben-Moshe's fiancée, had set the seal on the separation. It would be too much to enumerate the details.

9.

When Yeruham realized what had happened to him in the cantor's house, he was like a wagon deprived of its wheels. However, he did not bemoan his fate, nor try to mend the breach, but took it as a sentence which could not be altered. He looked around, and saw that the world was going on just as usual, that the people he met in the street were carrying on with their work as they had done yesterday and the day before. "Night borrows from the day and the day from the night." There was no loss of proportion and no solace.

Nevertheless, when you sit in your room the walls seem to run together as though they are strangling you to death. A man leaves this life, they dig him a grave and fill it in. The living weep for the dead, but he who sleeps in the dust slumbers until eternity. Here on earth, one living thing is consumed by another.

Yeruham gave his lessons as he had done in the past, continued his conversations with his companions. He summoned the strength to endure everything in silence, but he was depressed. His mother noticed that something had happened to him, but she did not ask him what was grieving him and said nothing about it. She just took greater care of him than she had in the past, complained to him that he was not eating as much as usual. A mother's compassion is renowned.

10.

It happened during the month of *Ellul.* Yeruham had ceased to take note of the passing days, but now he did notice the way the Jews were running to worship God. He could see the difference between the penitential days and the rest of the festivals. On *Rosh Hashana** and *Yom Kippur,* he even entered the courtyard of the synagogue, and sat among those who were praying. Through the doorway he was aware of men pouring out their supplications to the hidden God and these men were his brethren and members of his people. On *Succot,*† the autumn festival, he ran about in the streets every day, going backward and forward to the lower city. Some nights, he did not even go home to sleep, but wandered aimlessly around the silent city. A secret grief was consuming his body and his mind.

His hopes that he would teach and impart wisdom were crushed. Life is treacherous and individuals can remain barren. What could he teach and impart any more? He read some chapters of Lilienblum's *Sin of Youth* and he was beside himself. He had not

* New Year.

† Feast of Tabernacles.

wept since his childhood, his heart had not failed him and he had not been angry at others. Man was born to work and reflect. Men are hungry to know and to understand. One becomes wealthy, another is burdened by suffering. It is our business to find a bridge between the several parts of the world. But he, Yeruham, was powerless. He might visualize the victory of the spirit from afar, but now he was like a prisoner of war. Despair lamented the downfall of hope.

A curtain was drawn over Ida's window, too. Yeruham spoke more than anyone else at their gatherings; he had enlivened the circle which met in their house and had lifted up his soul to her. It is like water to a plant for a woman to know that there is somebody who waits for her and that she is surrounded by a certain fondness. Now the rays of the sun no longer reached her. The vision and the daydream were ended...

II.

A breeze was blowing. It was evening. Yeruham was strolling in the park, immersed in a multitude of thoughts when he saw Shalita, the advocate who had come down in the world, sprawling on a white bench, clad in the uniform of the days of his greatness. He motioned to Yeruham to sit down beside him and the latter was a little disturbed. There was little in common between the Hebrew *maskilim* and the Russian intelligentsia.

Yeruham's eyes told Shalita that his heart had been broken by disappointed love. The latter placed his hand on the Hebrew teacher's shoulder and said "Come with me, brother."

They went together through the alleys and narrow streets until they came to the red light district on the outskirts of the city. Yeruham wanted to turn back and retrace his steps, but his guide pulled him by the coat and would not let him get away from him. They climbed a flight of stone steps to a fashionable looking house. A plump, heavily rouged woman wearing long bright earrings welcomed them. Shalita put his hand in his pocket, took out something and put it into the hands of the madam. The gay voices of girls could be heard from the open salon; the walls were covered with bright mirrors. Yeruham was confused by the dazzling light. Tender hands drew him to a room with a curtain over the window. The languishing soul plunged down through an infinity of caverns where every door was bolted with iron bars and flesh seized upon flesh. His youth was sullied with the unchaste kiss. Later, he rose and slipped out stealthily, deeply ashamed of what he had done.

Part III

Chapter eight

The whole week long Yeruham was unable to look his mother in the face and when she spoke to him, he turned his head away. On the Sabbath eve as the sun went down and Jews were hurrying to the synagogue, he was drawn as though by a hidden hand to the street of love though he knew full well how distressed his mother was whenever he failed to return home on the Sabbath eve. Boy goes after girl for a year or two singing to her the song which is in his soul. Today she seems to draw near him and on the morrow it is as though her heart were closed. This mating is an insoluble riddle. You traverse roads full of pitfalls and when you arrive at the fair land it turns out to be thorns and thistles.—Yet with a few rubles you are the lord of a body. The beloved object is obedient to him that chooses her and does not resist. Those who were distant draw close; one soul embraces an alien soul. Nature knows no father and no friend.

She was a redhead of about twenty-one, with blue eyes and almost invisible eyebrows. She had a pouting mouth which expressed wonder and warmth. Every visitor was a new man to her. When she dropped her soft dress to the ground and removed her slip, the visitor was confounded by a skin as white as the moon and two breasts undulating like the heads of paradisiacal fishes. Yeruham was bewildered at the sight of this divinity and he in turn began to shed his garments. He saw an eagle in full flight with wings outstretched. Sparks of green and red fire flared. Fire consumed fire and fire drank deep of fire. Flame seized the flesh, devoured it and crucified it. Later when he arose and went his way, it all seemed like a fleeting dream.

2.

The next day Yeruham came across Ida in a suburb of the city and turned his back to her. He walked away very slowly, marveling at his own self-control. He would be revenged on the female sex. Poets cannot be trusted—in vain did they project visions, in vain did they plunge into ecstasies of word and utterance. He had a rod of chastisement in his mouth; plague in place of praise. He would blaze a new trail. He would summon the youth to study and high purpose. He would be a national writer raising his voice for every lofty cause. The day was stealing away. Yeruham felt a weakness at the knees. He sat down alone on a bench to rest. There were very few passersby. If he had not felt ashamed, he would have burst into tears.

Ida too went home to her father's house ashamed and angry. Men are such cowards. Had Yeruham at that moment stood up in front of her and stretched out his hand, she would not have drawn back. He had not faded out of her heart and she often thought about him. Those days when he used to come eagerly to see her and talk at length about literature and life had been very pleasant for her too. Now it was all ended.—Why had she driven him off? Why had he slipped away from her? She had held everything in her hands and now she had nothing. Man is endowed with numerous talents yet the soul is unsatisfied.... The sun rises, everything is bathed in the divine streams of light. The heart burns and entreats for refreshment and compassion. You close your eyes and a network of golden rays fills the air and irradiates the darkness. Yet it can also happen that, for no good cause, day can be transformed into night and one cannot discern between left and right; one does not know oneself. Yes, she would write to Yeruham, drop him a note saying: "Come and see me and we will talk over matters between us." She would wipe out the last few days from her memory. He would be as devoted and loving to her as he had been in the past. He was hers; and she? It was in the balance. In her hands was the power of life or death—to draw him near or repel him; to make the soul of a man happy or to inject bitterness into it. She was full of power. She could make her voice sing or raise a wail of lamentation.

She could not sleep that night and saw her life clear and unveiled. She lay on her bed, her feet pressed tightly together and her soul as impressionable as sealing wax.

3.

Three days passed. It was the afternoon of a short winter's day. Nehemia Eisenstein was visiting the two daughters of the cantor and found only Ida alone in the room. She was delighted to meet him. She tapped him on the hand, chiding him because he had neglected them for so long. He sat down opposite her and she looked straight at him.—Now she was talking volubly and vehemently and he could not take his eyes off her. What was the matter with her now? A vital force was welling up in her and she was very desirable. He rose from the table for a moment and gazed outside. She, too, arose and placed her hand on his shoulder. He trembled inwardly...He turned his head toward her and mouth clung to mouth...

"Nehemia!"

"Ida!"

She took his head in her two strong arms and he kissed her with redoubled passion. The door opened. Leah came into the room and exclaimed with a laugh, "I saw nothing. I heard nothing. Congratulations!"

Nehemia and Ida reddened with embarrassment but said nothing. A quarter of an hour later Ben-Moshe also entered the room.

His friend drew near him and whispered into his ear to say nothing further but he ignored her and said, "I must congratulate the bride and groom."

Ida reproved him. Nehemia did not linger in the house any longer but took his departure. It was not a dream—he was wide awake. He had never imagined *yesterday* or the day before that Ida would be his. He was happy, but his heart was clouded…He had to think things out. He met a few friends but none of them knew what was the matter with him. What should he tell his parents? They would certainly not approve of the match.

4.

When the news of Nehemia Eisenstein's engagement to Ida, the cantor's daughter, reached Yeruham, his heart seemed to burst and he cried, "The rumor just can't be true." But he knew that it was so; that his former heart's delight now belonged to another. He had been in full spiritual communion with her and she had always been radiantly at one with him. Two people achieve togetherness, establish contact and then a third comes along and takes by force or guile that which is rightly yours. Now his mouth and not yours kisses the one you loved so dearly. It is not your hand which strokes her hair nor your arms which embrace her. You have hold of a cord and are drawing something toward you and suddenly there is nothing, only stupefaction.—Your passions nearly drown you, your soul is overwhelmed, and now you stand like a beggar at the door and are denied even a crust of bread. No! He is not a beggar, but one robbed and plundered. They have turned him into an empty vessel in the wide world, they have brought him down and utterly overthrown him…

For a moment he decided to seek out Nehemia and contend with him for taking what did not belong to him. Then he thought of writing a long letter to Ida in which he would pour out his heart to her. Once he had dwelt in Paradise; he had left it and wanted to return there but the gate was barred. He would stand in the main street and cry out: "How unfortunate I am, my life is ruined!" He would go down to the valley near the city and there dig himself a grave. He had no mother and no nation. He was a severed limb. His ultimate fate was darkness.

For seven whole days Yeruham lay on the broken couch in his narrow room, covered with a blanket and his eyes shut tight, without looking at that minute part of the world outside that was visible through the window pane. Man's thoughts may range far a-field and soar into the empyrean, but the body shrinks into insignificance. There is no compassion in the world; no refuge. Why struggle or strive for any goal since it, too, must come to nothing? A man is only half a person.…If there is no soul seeking out another, no spirit finding solace in another, what is life all about? There are laws which rule in nature and yet what happens to man is utterly accidental. Logically speaking Ida is the one destined for him and she and she only belongs to him. Is it not he who understands her happiness, and in the generosity of his heart is it not he who can make her happy? And yet she scorned him and chose a lesser man…He, the powerful one, had failed.…He, the first to be enlightened—nothing had fallen to him, just nothing. He tossed from side to side. He sank his head into the pillow and abandoned himself to grief…

His mother would keep coming into his room and asking, "What is the matter with you, my son?"

He did not know what to answer her. He was afraid to get up and go out—his feet might not support him. If only he would contract a mortal illness. If only he might shake off this mortal coil, he would feel some relief. There is long sleep and there is death which stalks in the recesses of the heart. The will has disintegrated and it is something of a wonder that it continues to exist…

Autumn came as it had before. A few days after *Succoth* was over the rains began to fall incessantly. The cisterns and brooks filled up and the sluices of water in the mill were angrily flooded with a violence which could be heard as far as Eichenstein's house up on the hill. Miriam was now reading the works of one of the great Russian novelists. He gave her a feeling of warm elation. It was Feodor Dostoievsky.

Misery ruled the natural world and all living things are crushed by the weight of their burden. Man crawls out of his closed cavern, dragging a rope behind him…The sun may have shone but it was not day. No shelter nor protection; if one stumbled, no helping hand. Blind of soul and lame of limb and body were those whom God had created to inherit the earth. The heritage given to us is nothing but a series of terrors. You encounter a fellow man and he is a stranger to you. You seek something all your days and are only rejected. Burn upon burn, bruise upon bruise, buffers to the right and the left; only failure rules. There is no escape, but the heart of man is sorely distressed. Speech is given only to obscure that which is within us. To cry out is of no avail. Ideals and opinions, ambitions, taking and giving, serve no other purpose than to break down the will, undermining the will which has long disintegrated. Creation is a living species consuming itself…

Many fragments of the dust of primeval chaos cling to the garments of the Creator and this debris fills everything He has made. He created Man to burnish the rust off creation, to purify and uplift it but Man has only become confused. Yet through guilt he is raised up and through degradation we break down the fence. If you fall, kiss the ground beneath you. Man is crucified more than once. Since the days of Abel blood has been shed. The whole wide world is only the horns of the altar of sin…

It so happened that Miriam met the daughter of that Manoah, the leaseholder, whom I mentioned previously. Autumn had completed its lament and winter reigned over the world. A gleaming white shroud covered the face of the town and footsteps echoed on the frozen pavements. At a square in the town a military band stood and played. It was an anniversary: the czar's birthday. Crowds gathered. Miriam, too, went out with Eichenstein's granddaughters. Behold, a tall young woman, clad in a long fur coat, stood not far from her. An inward trembling seized her. The music pressed on her soul. A kind of invisible thread went out from the shrouded woman and swathed her heart. It was a feeling as though someone unknown were crying secretly, the sound reaching only her ear…She felt too embarrassed to lift up her eyes and gaze at the strange woman. A mystery has a thousand mouths and only a few echoes may be heard to explain it. A hidden hand seized Miriam. She leaned on one of the girls who was with her to stop herself from slipping. Suddenly the daughter of Manoah stepped backward a few paces. The crowd pressed in from all sides. She trod on Miriam's foot and made her apologies in Russian. Her face was sad. Eichenstein's granddaughters whispered to each other…

5.

The daughter of Manoah, the leaseholder, lay on her couch in her spacious room at her father's house situated in the center of the upper city. Her hair was visible outside her kerchief. A chemisette covered her breast, and her feet were bare. Boredom and infinite depression possessed her. The heart twists and turns, barely sustaining the soul and the body, and everything is befogged as in a cloud.—There is no world at all, no life at all. There are just swirls of fog which mingle endlessly. Deep calls to deep, the hooves of the primeval calf are cloven.—

A young woman weeps alone amid an alien tribe. There is no one to whom she can open her heart. In the whole neighborhood there is no one to accept or to give. If the heavenly palaces had not been destroyed she would have summoned the hounds of the chase to accompany her there. Here on earth there is neither plain nor hillock, no refuge by night and no escape by day. The streets are empty, although men pass along them. You go out into the marketplace and all bodies are crooked; all those who see are blind. When you sit down to a meal, a crooked serpent eats together with you and drinks from your cup. You glance at a cask of water and it suddenly seems to want to swallow you up.

Manoah's daughter got up, put on her slippers, removed the kerchief from her head and began to do her hair with style and great care. She was a woman and a betrothed maiden. She had made a covenant with the hidden God and had broken every covenant and every law.

How what happened next came about is a mystery and must

remain one. On the Sabbath afternoon, a beautiful winter's day in a world at rest, the door of Eichenstein's courtyard opened and a young woman, Manoah's daughter, appeared on the threshold wrapped in her mantle. She asked for the young girl who was a guest there. When they brought her to the room where Miriam was staying, she hurried over to her, embraced her with both arms, kissed her incessantly and cried, "Be my companion. Be a daughter to me. Return my love and friendship! If not, I shall die."

Miriam trembled and did not know what to answer.

6.

Snow! When rain falls to irrigate the ground, we are reminded that there is a connection between heaven and earth and that there is a reawakening. God may open His reservoirs of water and ordain blessing for us or He may open them to engulf creation. Of a different category are the storehouses of snow, frost and hail. The world is stormbound. Nature is in a tumult, the angels of wrath are raging abroad or disintegrating, with innumerable drifts of whiteness filling the atmosphere between firmament and earth being deposited thereafter in layers as low as a handbreadth or as high as a cubit. The whole earth and the fullness thereof, from man to beast, is clothed in whiteness. There is no distinction and no escape. It faces us like an inevitable rendezvous and our days and nights are consumed.

The leaseholder's daughter got out of bed and put on her clothes. She wrapped her fur coat about her, covered her head with a kerchief and went out to wander in the squares and streets amidst the snowdrifts. Had she encountered Satan she would have seized him and become his slave. Snow was her food and snow was her garment. The world of infinite variety was no more; the soul consumes the body. When she sat down to rest on the steps of the mansion, her eyes were shut tight against the outside world, and the twilight of death came and kissed her limb by limb, and was absorbed by them.

In the morning those who were first out of doors found the

young woman frozen, stretched out in front of the mansion not far from the Eichenstein place. The sound of their cries drew all the neighbors who gathered round, amazed at the sight. Someone suggested taking her at once to Dr. Koch. They rushed her into a room and the doctor ordered them to strip off her clothes and rub her naked body vigorously with snow and icy water. After two hours of hard, incessant effort, miraculously she began to breathe again.

7.

Talking about the leaseholder's daughter reminds me of that very beautiful divorcee who was once the wife of the wealthy Pinhas-Elijah, reckoned among the magnates of the city. I shall tell you what happened to her.

For a whole year after her divorce, she stayed at the house of her younger sister who was married to the owner of a large estate in the vicinity of the city of Balta. The Jewish marriage brokers scurried to and fro, and one of the noted citizens of Yarmelinetz, a red-haired fellow from a large family, had his eye on her. He came from a great distance merely on the strength of reports he had heard, intending to take her back to his mansion at any price. As a result of the pressure exerted on her, she traveled to Loton, the seat of the rebbe, to seek advice from her former friend, the daughter-in-law of the *tzaddik*. She certainly had no idea that the day was approaching when she too would become a member of the hasidic court. Reb Yaakov, a cousin of the "king" (…who are the kings? The rabbis!), a portly man with all his wits about him, directed all the administrative affairs of the rebbe's court and was obeyed by everybody. He was the advisor of Reb David and his familiar friend if not his patron. This Reb Yaakov had become widowed at that time, his wife dying of an illness. He desired this wealthy woman and sent some of his confidants to approach her. The woman of rare beauty was inclined to accept the crown. The rebbe himself, as was his wont, wavered over the decision, but when the lady appeared in the inner sanctum of his room and stood before him like Abigail in her day, he understood again the mystery of divine beauty and could not withhold his blessing. The same mouth which had forbidden her previously to her husband because she had been found in compromising circumstances with another, now permitted her to his kinsman. There was a furor in hasidic circles. Hitherto, members of the rabbinic family had married only into families of similar status, and now a profane vessel was being used for holy purposes.

Two weeks after the wedding night a banquet took place in the *tzaddik*'s courtyard in honor of the local nobleman, the distinguished Prince Shubalov. He visited Loton, his ancestral city, only infrequently. Most of his time was spent in St. Petersburg where he had an established position among the great men of the empire. When the prince saw the rebbe's new wife, he was bewitched by her beauty. He was a man of sixty at that time. Afraid of his burning desire for her and being also a man who deeply respected his fellow men, he rose up precipitately from the table, gave orders for his horse to be saddled and sped through the city gate never again to return to his estates.

Some time later the lioness of the court was again found in compromising circumstances; this time with the local apothecary, and was held to be no longer fit for her position.

Reb Yaakov, the well-born patron of the rebbe's court, looked up the chapter concerning the woman suspected of adultery in the Book of Numbers and sought to penetrate the mysterious meaning of the texts. The letters in the Torah are souls, transcendental stairs, by which man may make his way from earth to heaven. This lady of consequence, who dwelt in the inner sanctum and whose splendid beauty had endowed him with a measure of great exaltation, must now be sent away from him and he dared not touch her, nor even see her again. She existed for him no longer. The world continued turning as before, but in fact things were not as they had been. Even the rebbe felt a certain emptiness in his heart since his court was deprived of her presence. King Solomon, also called Yedidya, was beloved of the Omnipresent, but his wives had offered incense to Chemosh. There is union and oneness but the eyes go a-whoring away from the higher light to degradation, and the Divine Presence is withdrawn…

8.

Now Ida, the cantor's daughter, was also at times indifferent to Nehemia, her intended. The hand which she extended to him was cold, as was her heart. What was there in common between them? His spirit had no wings and did not soar. Mouth might touch mouth and body embrace body, but there can be no bond without affinity and no affinity without reciprocation. What could he give her? What could she hope for from him? Many thoughts passed through her mind, yet whenever she was together with him she felt only emptiness. Yeruham had given her seven times as much as her fiancé. She had rejected him who was close to her and drawn near one who was distant. God alone knows the answer to the riddle of pairing and separation. If you take the wrong path, you will find contentment neither by day nor by night.

Nehemia never failed in his duty to her. Every afternoon he would come to visit, chat and stroll with her. He did not worry one bit about the future. He would earn money, build his house, and have an intellectual wife not one whit inferior to that of the doctor or the attorney. But he, too, knew nothing of that exciting love described in books. Young girls who have not fully matured possess a certain pleasing warmth but Ida had the advantage of him by two years or more. Stolen water is sweet, but it is different when a full cup is set in front of you and you are free to drink or not.

The power of attraction grows side by side with the power of rejection. Ida knew that it was entirely in her hands whether to be cool or kind. She also knew her destiny.—One morning she rose from her bed, washed her face, did her hair and looked out through the window on to an empty world. Nothing was left in her heart. She went into the next room, sat down at the table and wrote a parting letter to Nehemia in Hebrew. She was not suitable for him. She had come to this conclusion after careful thought. Let him not think it wicked on her part. She wrote and erased, altering the wording again and again. She put the missive in an envelope and sealed it. Her mind was a welter of conflicting thoughts. With restless glances, she paced the room from door to door. Afterward she went into the kitchen, threw the letter into the stove where it went up in flames. She went back to her room and sat on her bed, put her hand to her brow and wept silently.

That same morning Yeruham in his narrow room was more excited than he had been yesterday or the day before and did not know what was the matter with him…

Chapter nine

A number of other incidents took place in Honyrad. Some came entirely afresh while others evolved from and were intertwined with things that had gone before. I shall describe them for the reader one by one just as I have done until now.

Satan rose up against the wealthy priestly family of Horowitz in the form of a steward working in their business, who had been dismissed from his post because of some misfeasance. He went to the provincial capital and informed on them to the authorities accusing them of dealing in forged bank notes which he maintained was the source of all their wealth. One day a team of investigators swooped down on the residence of Menahem Horowitz, searched all his cabinets and confirmed that the steward's charges were well-founded. Immediately they sealed up his counting-house. They put the magnate, his sons and sons-in-law in shackles and incarcerated them in dungeons in the prison. They set guards at the gate so that no communication of any kind could reach them from outside. The town was shaken to its foundations by the news. Every prayer house buzzed with discussion whenever people came to services. The honor and good name of Jewry had been profaned among the gentiles. If the cedars of Lebanon bow their tops like reeds, what should happen to the lowly hyssop by the wall?

The brothers Benjamin and Joseph of the Nahman family who were partners to the brandy distillery, were also apprehended by the authorities, when they went too far by completely reversing the correct proportions. They gave one-tenth of the turnover from their brandy to the government treasury and took nine-tenths for themselves. Now in Russia this was an offense which could not be overlooked and one who committed this crime was never acquitted. The community felt as though its eyes had been put out when a house of magnates was ruined. The silver display cabinets of these wealthy men were removed from their mansions and transported in one fell swoop to the provincial capital. Some say the silver subsequently graced the house of the presiding judge; others say the halls of the local governor. Men rise and fall, wax rich and become poor. Even the luck of the wealthy has its limits. I mourn the sight of any great house which falls into ruin.

2.

A well-known character in the lower city of Honyrad was the wealthy Chaim-Yona Michlin. He was one of Loton's ardent Hasidim, and owned a well-stocked shop for expensive fabrics and wool, which brought him great prosperity. He was generous in his own circle and held very strong opinions. He had an only daughter, a tall, beautiful girl. When she was sixteen a match was made for her with a young man of fine family from Drashna in the district of Podolia. The bridegroom was learned in the Talmud and its commentaries, but was all skin and bone. They had not consulted the bride and she did not see the groom until after the ceremony. They celebrated the wedding with great pomp and splendor. It is reported that when the bride's parents went out to the gate of the city to meet the groom with carriages and prancing horses, those in the know began whispering to each other when they saw this skinny fellow taking pride of place that day. Certainly the bride's heart quailed when she saw her spouse standing before her. When she realized she was head and shoulders taller than he, she grimaced. She found no cause for rejoicing at all. Indeed she sat in her room and wept secretly. Her mother entreated with her vainly not to ruin the happy occasion. In vain her father threatened to disinherit her if she defied him and refused to give her hand to the one chosen for her. She had only one answer: "I don't want him. I hate him."

It was unheard of that a daughter of one of the most eminent Hasidim should even dare to speak thus to her parents at a time when the bridegroom's family were already sitting around the table in the great salon of the house with the bridegroom at their head. At this crisis Chaim-Yona, who had lavished his wealth generously on the nuptials, arrived. His brothers and members of his family also came from a great distance to participate in the happy occasion. Things seemed at a complete impasse. Just then the bridegroom's mother entered. She was a simple, unassuming person, and she pleaded with the bride, "Please, my daughter, do not humiliate us. My darling son is right for you. Take no notice of his looks. His heart is good. He will cherish you. We shall always treat you with dignity and you will be a daughter to us."

The girl relented and she went in to the guests. However, after the seven days of rejoicing were over and the in-laws had gone back home, she openly withdrew herself from her husband and refused to go near him, much to her mother's dismay.

After two months had passed they began to gossip in the town that something was going on between the Hasid's daughter and Amnon the son of Nehemia. Indeed the reports were well-founded.

I have previously told of the beautiful woman, divorced from her husband, who had later married a wealthy and illustrious *cohen* in Honyrad. She loved luxuries and, despite the fact that the community pointed a finger at her, she persisted in beautifying and adorning herself. Her chamber was full of display and splendor, with woven carpets on the floor. The effect on anyone who entered was overwhelming. She had no children. Her darling was a tabby cat which slept with her, ate from her dish and drank from her cup. When her passions were vaguely aroused she would fondle it and kiss it until her husband was jealous. Once when she was reclining on a couch in the middle of the day, this spoiled creature jumped on her face, and one of his paws inadvertently scratched her eyes, piercing one of them. Despite the efforts of the doctors it became clear that she would be disfigured. She said to herself, "Better to die than live like this!"

She climbed up into the loft and hanged herself. Her husband took her death and burial very badly. He wept for her and mourned her the rest of his life.

Now the third beautiful woman, who was from a rabbinic family, needs to be mentioned. At this time the decree of banishment had been lifted from that young sprig of the royal house who had been forced to find his pleasure in Honyrad. He and his whole retinue accordingly returned to the imperial capital. On this occasion, the bustling district capital was emptied out. Then it was that Tamar, the daughter-in-law of the wealthy Nehemia Trachtman, also disappeared. She abandoned both her reprobate husband, Amnon, and Malter, her lover, who had betrayed her. According to rumor, she became the mistress of that sprig of the royal stock.

I shall relate more about the life and adventures of this woman in the imperial capital.

3.

There was a rich woman in Honyrad called Chaya-Sara, who was well-known and who had been widowed before she reached the age of thirty. She was a vigorous fair and buxom woman who took excellent care of her hardware shop and brought up her two unattractive daughters Razia and Zir'l. When the elder Razia reached marriageable age she wed her to a handsome, pleasant young man, named Joseph, who was supported by her. From time to time he frequented the hasidic *kloiz* to talk with the scholars and occasionally he would open a book. At night he would do the books for his mother-in-law, for he knew accounting. His wife loved him dearly and doted on him. Even the heart of the mistress of the house was at times furtively invaded by strange thoughts. It can happen for a mother to be jealous of her daughter and sometimes this strange emotion is even felt by the matrons of Israel.

Once the young wife and her sister traveled to a nearby town to be present at their cousin's wedding. The widow, left alone in the house with her son-in-law, cornered him. The sages have legislated against such compromising privacy. The next day the young gentleman Joseph came to the rabbi of the town, wept copious tears before him and confessed his sin. Walls have ears and Honyrad was in a furor.

Asher Yaffe, the wealthy young *maskil* of rabbinical stock with considerable financial investments, had long had dealings with a well-known Polish noblewoman. She had a large estate and a great forest but was deep in debt due to her deceased husband. She labored hard to straighten things out. Asher, who could speak Polish, was her adviser and mainstay. She would converse eagerly with this enlightened Jew and his handsome face and black round beard captured her heart. Once he had stayed on till late in the evening in the village where the noblewoman had her home and torrential rain prevented him from returning to town. By some machination of the devil they found him a place to lodge in her courtyard. In the middle of the night the noblewoman summoned him to her bedroom which was redolent with heavy perfume. He fell a captive to her seductions and made passionate love to her.

That night was the one on which Asher's pure and innocent wife, who loved him dearly, had gone to the ritual bath to be cleansed according to religious custom. She came back home as pure as a fresh young bride. Her husband evaded her and ignored her. She sat on the bed with tears streaming from her eyes.

The world was in turmoil over the twofold sin.

4.

What I shall now relate seldom happens in the Jewish quarter.

The name of the man involved was Bunem. He was about fifty and his beard was sprinkled with white. He was meticulous about his attire, and was well known and respected in his circle as an intelligent man versed in the ways of the world. He was among those who revered the Malbim and knew how to answer heretics even in matters of philosophy and theology. He was counted among the richer classes although he did not deal in anything in particular. If a man had a dispute with another over a financial matter or two brothers quarreled over their father's inheritance they would choose him as an arbitrator. He knew how to bring both sides together and be remunerated therefore. By nature he was not easygoing and he took good care of what was his. However, he would not barter his integrity for any pecuniary gain. In synagogue, he was usually the last to be called up to the reading of the Torah and he intoned the benedictions in a pleasing voice. Bunem had an ugly wife of a sour disposition and she made his whole life miserable. He never answered her when she quarreled with him, but he inwardly harbored a secret hatred for her. He had married her when he was sixteen and she had borne him no children. Although by rabbinical rule he could have divorced her, he had not parted from her and had not haled her before the rabbinical court.

It happened one Sabbath morning that Bunem rose early, washed his hands and face, put on his Sabbath garb and was reading his Pentateuch before the service began. His wife was in the next room and she also was about to don her best finery in order to go to synagogue. She stood on the threshold of the wardrobe to take out her fine silk coat, when the wardrobe fell on her. She could not cry out because of the weight pressing on her mouth. Bunem heard the noise of the fall in the next room and hurried to the scene. He stood there stunned and terrified and did not lift the weight in time. Then he ran outside and called in some neighbors to help. When they lifted the wardrobe she was lifeless. She had suffocated. The efforts of the doctors to revive her were of no avail. When the Sabbath was over they quickly washed her body and bore her to her grave. During the week of mourning itself they began to talk about Bunem and suggested that he was not guiltless of the crime of murder. The matter came to the ear of the authorities and he was charged with murder. The procurator tormented him daily with numerous questions about his past and the nature of his life with the deceased woman. He did not waver. He was not guilty. He denied the charges. After some months he was put on trial and a famous advocate cleared him.

At that moment the accused stood up and said, "I am certainly guilty. The death of my wife was what I wanted and in such matters the thought is like the deed. I deliberately did not hurry to save her."

Another subject of conversation at that time was the man of great substance Yehiel-Ber. He was over sixty years old, elderly and respected in his community. His wife died and he grieved over her for three months, after which he decided to marry an eighteen-year-old girl, the daughter of a certain distinguished scholar. His married sons and sons-in-law were united in their opposition and protested violently. They were afraid he might sire a son who would share in their inheritance. The whole street shook with the reverberations of the dispute.

5.

To Miriam's mind, there were two kinds of people in the world, the good and the bad. There are some who have a clear goal and purpose and others who are just aimless. The former are up early in the morning seeking the right path at all times; the latter have neither will nor strength. There are great guides and momentous thoughts but everything is clouded by crudeness and ignorance. She had not read Job, nor had she heard the voice speaking out of the whirlwind, but doubts were already beginning to torment her. A man might lie down, cover himself with a garment, hold his feet close to his body and close his eyes when inner clouds would come and cut him off from all light. But when he rose up, shook himself and lifted up his head he would renew his strength and assert, "I have still not lost my hope." A young girl of pure soul cannot find the answer without any allies. She herself had no sense of power but she did know that purpose, prerogative and sovereignty do exist.

A certain Menashe Margalit, an acquaintance of Eichenstein who lived in the district of Heysin, came to Honyrad on business and lodged at his friend's house. They had previously been closely connected in the capital Kiev in the days of his prosperity and phenomenal success, and the period in between had not estranged them from each other. Menashe was a man of about forty, "short above and long below." Outwardly he observed the Jewish ceremonies but inwardly he was easy-going, and had little respect for religious principles. What was above was above and what was below was below. He who doesn't enjoy life doesn't live, and whoever lives, enjoys life. He who is diverted from his way does not know what is ahead of him.

Every mealtime Menashe saw this beautiful young girl sitting at the table and eating the same dishes that were set before him. He wondered at this rose growing in the garden in the sight of everyone with no one approaching. He had his eye on her and secretly determined to lie in wait for her but at the same time was uncertain of himself. Miriam was afraid of him and did not know why.—One day she refused to come to lunch and said she had a headache. She sat alone in her room and sad thoughts filled her heart. Outside the day was drawing to a close and her heart was empty. She did not understand men's conduct and how they behaved in life. Each went his own way. She was confused. She had sat pondering in this way for about two hours when the door opened quietly. The guest had decided to come in and make his advances to her; but when he saw this image of youth and her appearance like the moon in daylight, his determination failed and he withdrew. He went into the next room and leaned his head against the wall.

The next day he left Honyrad on foot although his friend Eichenstein pressed him to stay.

He walked night and day from village to village until he reached his hometown. When he came to his house he did not speak to his wife or children. They did not know what was the matter with him.

6.

The little boy whom that girl had borne to the redheaded tanner without benefit of wedlock was now five years old. In fear and trembling his mother brought him to the religious school. She slaved at making underwear to gain a precarious livelihood. She lived in a rented room and was rejected by her father, mother and all her relatives. Some evenings the tanner would call on her furtively, at a time when he could be quite unobserved, and bring her some gift. He never touched her again. She was forbidden to him from every aspect, but there were times when a part of his soul remembered her, even when he was praying with deep piety. God in heaven! Does not sin come from You also? There is no free will; but there is retribution; there are precepts, laws, and admonitions.

Itzik was the name of the thin child. He had an abnormally large forehead for his years, and green eyes, but no self-confidence at all. On the contrary, he was timid and fearful. He was upset by the appearance of the straight-backed teacher with a wart on his left cheek. He was simply terrified of the monitor. The pupils in the school, of all classes, from the youngest to the oldest would single him out. A bastard was sitting and learning the alphabet trying with his inadequate mind to grasp the fact that five letters of the Hebrew alphabet change their form when they appear at the end of a word.

At four in the afternoon the bonds of school were loosened. The door was opened and the boys and girls hurried to leave the enclosure. Itzik too hurried after them. Suddenly within the little compound a voice was heard shouting "Bastard! Bastard!" The boys and girls hemmed him in on all sides. One tweaked his ear, another pulled his nose. They grabbed at him from all sides. One snatched his cap off his head. Had not the monitor rushed up to drive them off with a rebuke, they would have severely beaten him. Weeping bitterly the child made his way to his mother's house. All who saw him pointed at him. I shall not describe the heartbreak of the young woman when she saw her poor child coming home with tears streaming down his cheeks. I do not want to pronounce judgment on my own people.

A week passed and the teacher Yeruham, the one who knew the Prophets and read the periodical *Hashachar,* volunteered to teach this rejected child the Hebrew alphabet. Even the father of the child came openly that day and proposed to the mother that he, too, would instruct his son. They spoke about this for a long time in the lower city.

7.

That young yeshiva student who had been confused by the *Epistle to the Hebrews* in the New Testament and wanted to subject himself to the sovereignty of King Melchizedek, also known as Shem, King of Salem, began to delve even more deeply into the Kabbala and also found there Metatron, the ruler of all the angels on high. His crown outshone the orb of the sun. He was beloved by the Divine Presence and Metatron was her son. God had a throne and so did he. God was the God of light and he too was all light. God was holy and to be hallowed and he too was holy and pure. The first cause, God, partook of duality and was not a unity.

The name of this student was Naftali the son of Samuel. His father had died when he was ten and his mother when he was twenty. He was an only child with neither brother nor sister. He married when he was twenty-one and his wife died three months after their marriage, leaving him alone to seek the path to God's nature. He had his fill of mankind, and now he was engaged in a battle with Satan. Now one must increase one's strength, one must be cleansed of the pangs of the exile and rend asunder the sovereignty of Edom. The Divine service must be restored to the sanctuary and the way must be found from the earthly to the heavenly Jerusalem.

At that time Naftali joined up with a kabbalist novice like himself. They went knocking on the doors of the wealthy to collect funds to repair the tomb of Rachel, which was what a rabbinical emissary, one of the men of Sadigore, had told them to do. It so happened that when they came to the Eichenstein house they saw Miriam. They were both awe-inspired by her pure beauty and stood stock-still on the threshold like pillars of marble, utterly speechless. I shall not relate here what happened to these two.

8.

At that time, Shimele the Well-Born, whom I have mentioned previously, became mentally ill. This is how it came about.

Not only did Shimele love the Talmud, edited by Rav Ashi and the Saboraitic rabbis, but also the Five Books of the Pentateuch which were printed on superfine paper in rectangular format and handsomely bound in elegant green leather. With avid interest every Sabbath eve he would go over the weekly portion, reading the Hebrew text twice and the Aramaic version once. He would chant every word distinctly and take pleasure in the sound of his own singing. That Sabbath the *sedrah** was *Ki Tissa* dealing with *shekels* and the spices in the sanctuary. It also dealt with the eternal covenant of the Sabbath of solemn rest and the affair of the golden calf. The Children of Israel strip off their ornaments. Moses pitches his tent outside the camp. Now he stands in the cleft of the rock and God speaks to him. "You shall not see my face. My back shall you see, but my face you shall not behold."

Shimele was terrified. There can be no thought which perceives God. He has no face nor likeness; there can be no bodily description. He has no neck nor face, and how could He speak to the faithful one of His house.—His heart reproached him because he had felt doubts about the Divine Presence. The finer spirituality which used to burgeon within him at the approach of the Sabbath, disappeared. He spoke to no one. During the next week he fasted on the Monday and Thursday. He dissolved in tears crying aloud, "Answer me, Oh God, answer me!"

At night he dreamed that he was passing through a forest with a load of wood on his shoulders. Suddenly he heard a roaring noise behind him. He turned his head to discover the source of the sound. His neck became twisted and he could not straighten it again. He understood full well why he was being punished. When he awoke in the morning it seemed to him that his face was indeed turned

* The weekly portion read from the Bible.

backward. In terror he roused the people in the house and cried, "Surely because of my sin, my face has been turned around?" They all wondered at his words because they found no change in him. He kept saying, "God has surely chastised me in this world." Shimele lost his mind and from morning to evening bewailed his fate.

Eichenstein came to visit him. The afflicted man complained, "As God lives I am not demented. I have been burned by a coal of strange thought and God's hand is against me."

Two years later Shimele died and found no solace for his soul.

Chapter ten

The snow dissolved, the frost and ice melted away, the floors dried out and became clean. Buds appeared in the parks and gardens of the city, harbingers of spring. Passover, the festival of freedom, was on the way. There is no freedom from continuing slavery. There was bustle and preparation in the upper and lower city, all undertaken with excitement and delight. Had not Moses spoken, and had not the sages elaborated his law, and generation after generation conducted themselves accordingly? Israel is the first-born son of God and is bound to serve Him by baking unleavened bread and removing all traces of leaven. The Great *Hallel** is recited and the Passover sacrifices recalled in the prayers. Even the poor duly celebrate the *seder*†. God's hand does not fall short in all the places where His great name is mentioned.

In Yehiel Eichenstein's house they celebrated the Passover with all the trimmings. The large salon was illumined sevenfold. The head of the house, clothed in white, reclined on a couch specially prepared

* A series of psalms recited on festivals and holidays.
† The service held at the evening meal on Passover Eve.

for the occasion. The table was laid as in a royal palace. Soft singing filled the air. The children of freedom were sitting down at feast and hearing the tale of how the yoke was thrown off in days of yore.

Suddenly a bone stuck in the throat of the master at the head of the table and he began to choke. His eyes bulged and those sitting around were terrified. The widow jumped up from her seat and tried without avail to give her brother some relief. Gedaliah rushed out to fetch Dr. Koch, who was a friend of his grandfather, and hurried him to the house. In the meantime, Yehiel coughed up the bone but was exhausted and sank back supinely on the cushions. Everyone arose in honor of the guest, and eventually a place was set for him. It must have been nearly fifty years since Koch had seen a Jewish Passover. He had come from a far off wilderness to an oasis of fragrant ease. He knew the girls Pessie and Deborah from previous acquaintance, but who was the lovely maiden sitting between them? She wore a white dress and a band of black silk around her hair, and was gazing directly at him.

Every soul has a body and every body, a soul. Elijah the Tishbite once journeyed into the desert for a long, long time. There was no brook from which to drink and no bird flew in the sky. He lifted up his eyes and saw a fine-looking juniper tree. His soul was awakened and he said, "I too have had a dream." But I shall not talk in riddles…

2.

The vaults of heaven were opened and the rain came pouring down without pause. The regular seasons were confounded, spring had turned into autumn.

Manoah the leaseholder was sitting with his daughter in the manor on the estate he had leased. She no longer allowed him to go out alone and a secret fear whispered in her ears. The end had come! The floodwaters were accompanied by an inner disquiet. Nature was opening wide her mouth and revealing her hidden secrets.

Manoah's head ached. He lay on his bed and had a feeling that he was being led to the scaffold. A silent terror pervaded the whole room. Hot vapor covered the windows. A sound of knocking. What have you to do here and who do you want here, you who carry the sword of death? The angel of death has descended here below from the heights. Suddenly a black dog bursts in and starts licking around the legs of the bed with his tongue. Trembling seizes the whole body of the leaseholder and he emits a high-pitched scream. His daughter stands aghast at the door of the room. Manoah screams, "Go away! Be gone! Don't come near me!"

The stalking pestilence fills the room. The daughter, consumed with terror and fright, cannot utter a word. Now the toll was at last being levied from the height of heaven and the earth dissolved in fear.

The report of the appearance of the black dog in the house of Manoah ran through the city. Men of deep piety and ordinary people came to visit the sick man and found him in the throes of his struggle with the angel of destruction.

"Woe is me! Alas for my soul!" muttered Manoah. "I have sinned. I have done wickedness. I have transgressed. I am befouled by my incest. Now I am come to judgment. They are tearing my flesh!"

Those present were moved to penitence, and looked meaningfully at each other. In the time of the great kabbalist, Isaac Luria, and the first Hasidim, manifestations like this were seen and heard every day. But whoever dreamed that such a thing could happen in their own time, in a city as large and as enlightened as theirs? Now one could say to all these enlightened rationalists, "I told you so!" Now let them deny the evidence of their senses; now let them dare continue to poke their noses into the mysteries of life.

Manoah lingered for three weeks on his bed of suffering. His daughter was ashamed to go out. Many said she had taken leave of her senses. On Thursday at noon the sinner gave up the ghost and was buried that evening. Only a few people attended the funeral.

That same day a wedding was celebrated in the city. Of this I shall speak in the next chapter.

3.

On a slope, at the outskirts of Honyrad, stands the wee house of prayer where the few Lithuanians in the city pray to their Maker according to their custom. Among this group was one Meshullam the Cohen, a man of dignity, and a kabbalist. He was a respectable householder, learned in the Torah and an observant Jew. He was well-versed in the Bible and even possessed the Book of Isaiah with Luzzatto's commentary. He had an only daughter, Yocheved, who, when a young girl of sixteen, had been pledged in marriage. Her betrothed was a *maskil*, a man of talent, well known in his home town Heysin. He became stricken with tuberculosis and traveled each year to a vine-growing district seeking a cure. It proved of no avail and the date of the marriage was constantly postponed in the hope of his regaining his health. The bride reached the age of twenty, then twenty-two and then twenty-five. For over ten years she had sat in her father's house waiting to be claimed. Among the Jews one does not set aside a prenuptial contract even if there be good reason to do so. Perhaps God would have mercy. However when there was clearly no hope that the groom would recover his health and Yocheved was nearing thirty, the in-laws decided that the marriage should take place. It was not right that the man should go to his grave unmarried or that the woman, a girl of mature years, should remain without a matron's kerchief in her father's house.

They were married quietly with few guests on the Sabbath night after *Shavuot*.* Nahum Sharoni, that was the bridegroom's name, took the virgin Yocheved, daughter of Meshullam, in marriage according to the religious rites. A room was provided for the couple in the house of the bride's father. He coughed every morning, drank his medicines and kept away from damp air. The young wife, Yocheved, occupied herself with the care of her husband's health and cherished him dearly. The Hebrew-speaking *maskilim* of Honyrad, in particular

* Pentecost.

Yeruham, were constant visitors. Word had spread that Nahum's ideas were profound—he was a new bright star.

Nahum Sharoni had already read Krochmal, knew the writings of S.Y. Rabinovitz and was so well-versed in the works of Isaac Ber Levinsohn that he could almost recite them by heart. But he had also struck out on his own.—He was far from extolling the wisdom of the rabbis or praising Jewish scholarship. He did not believe in the need to perpetuate the Jewish people. Once he was sitting alone with Yeruham and said explicitly that the Law of Israel is not a law of loving-kindness, but one of censure and verbal castigation. The Jewish lawgiver knew of nothing except to curse His people. He did it once in Leviticus, and again in Deuteronomy.... These powerful curses have troubled us to this very day... Yeruham's mind reeled at these views and he was occupied with his friend's ideas all that day and night....

4.

It happened between the New Year and the Day of Atonement. Yeruham was again sitting in his ailing friend's room. Nahum, who was coughing blood from time to time, began to speak.

"There are those among us who dream of the revival of the people, but they are nothing but God's wrath to us... Israel is a slave in body and mind. Those who nourished our spirits were slaves and not free men. The narrow framework of the Talmud is stifling... Hillel, the Elder, Akiva, even Judah the *Nassi*, spent their whole existence trying to weave ropes of sand and filled the storehouses of Judaism with emptiness and frustration. Even Maimonides, Yehuda Halevy the author of the *Cuzari*, and the other thinkers were wide of the mark and erroneous in their premises. Not one flicker of light breaks through from what has been said and handed down. When we dwelt in our own land we dominated our enemies and now in the exile they are getting their revenge. The world is not plotting evil against us without cause. The eternal hatred for the eternal people has its basis in religion. The prophets created a breach between people and people and between tribe and tribe. While they rebuked with words they tore out everything by the roots. They proclaimed enmity and brought a heritage of perdition...."

Yeruham cried out excitedly, "Were there not sublime utterances in the mouths of the seers, incomparable on this earth? Is not our preeminence over the gentiles inherent in this fact?"

Nahum was silent, gazing at his friend with eyes of despair and shaking his head. There was an interval of silence in the room. Yeruham found himself powerless to continue. Suddenly everything was choked up within him. The sick man seized the table with a hand shaking with a deathly palsy and continued. "I shall depart hence and never see the sun again. To me the whole thing is a dreadful joke. You may still find the answer...Terrible times are ahead of us. I have had premonitions of them every night. What is there for us here or there? Better for us not to learn our language any more, not to read books any more, and to repudiate our heritage of learning through all the generations. In days of persecution our enemies used to burn the Talmud, and other books in public bonfires. Still there was much left over." Yeruham did not know what to reply to his friend.

A few days after this conversation, the morning after the Day of Atonement, Nahum Sharoni succumbed to his illness, aged thirty-one. He was buried that evening. The city's *maskilim*, including the teachers of Russian, who had heard something of his gifts, paid him their last respects and gathered around his bier. Even Gedaliah and his kinswoman came to the cemetery. This was somewhat unusual in the Honyrad community. While this small group was mourning, the teacher, Batlon, met the provincial Miriam, and was deeply moved by her beauty and charm.

5.

Withdrawn from his fellows, Batlon went home. When he tried his key in the door, he found that he was in the wrong street. He was in a mood of complete distraction and despondency. He retraced his steps, biting at his moustache. Now he was mulling over a new idea, unlike any he had entertained previously. He would go off to India, prostrate himself there to the god of the sun and make entreaty to him for grace and loving-kindness. There is naked light and shrouded light, spirit from within and spirit from without. From one side flow streams of boredom and infinite dejection and from another fragrant tranquility. Soul seizes upon soul and flesh grasps at flesh. You climb up into a tall tree and the earth lies beneath you in broad panorama. The world has many gifts but you will only be granted what is yours. But take heed, you are only one step removed from dreadful emptiness. What is there for you, and whom indeed have you in the world here? You will never know love for you have never laid your hand on a girl who is dear to you and never poured out your heart to a sympathetic ear. You get into bed and the walls seem to contract, the ceiling presses down and the room becomes a tomb. You wake up in the morning and there is no one to say a word to you, no one is waiting for you. You have a debt to pay but no one knocks at the door to collect it...

Who has apportioned the multitude and their lives? Who takes and who gives? Who rejects and who draws near?

Who pierces the heart and who sows a seed of hope?

Batlon found himself drawn to the spacious city park. He would pitch a tent for himself on a lofty mountain. On his way, he chanced upon a bubbling spring. Who was this strange girl whom he had seen in the courtyard of death? Never before in all his life had he beheld such wondrous charm. His soul was awakened. He seemed to be soaring upward and upward. He wanted to ask every man his name and pour out his heart to him. He would seek a new direction in life and plot a fresh course for his spirit. The broad avenues of science were open before him. He would achieve sublime creations. He was no longer Batlon, the teacher, but a man of genius and wide fame. He would press the hand of this young girl and weep tears of happiness. Happiness everywhere, a world suffused with happiness. He had never imagined that what he had longed for a whole lifetime could be. Look at the blessing in the world, the joy of fellowship that it contained. Even night was conscious of the bright emanations of the day. He was a poet and could compose verse. Give me a sheet of paper and a scribe's pen; give me trumpets and cymbals. Toward evening he went back to his narrow room, stretched out on his couch, closed his eyes and was bathed in a hidden light.

6.

The order of life is not a sealed book. Eye to eye we can see the intricacies of fortune and the weaving of chance. There are not just two ways in life but an infinity of directions. One man's soul is consumed by fire, but the body survives, while another collapses under the burden of his imaginings and the concepts of his mind. The elder serves the younger and he who holds the birthright is regularly disinherited. No one dwells in the highest heaven. When the days of creation were concluded God submerged Himself in the ocean of chaos from whence He spake to prophet and priest. He who searches for truth will find it in dark deception.

Since the death of Nahum Sharoni, his mystical friend, Yeruham had gone about in black dejection. Nothing any longer had purpose and who could know his people's paths? The divine prophets had wandered far away and the nation's heritage was nothing more than sterile customs and superstitions.

Nahum had given utterance to views which were not written down in the books of the chronicles. Anyone who spoke or thought in that vein was denying the mission of his people. Perhaps the Jewish people no longer possessed a mission? Perhaps even Krochmal, Smolenskin and Lilienblum were in error. There can be those who justify and those who impugn the Law of Israel. There is a clear line traceable from Hosea and Amos to Hillel and Akiva and through these to the *geonim** and on to the rabbis. Then Abraham Ibn Ezra, Gersonides and Maimonides created new theoretical teachings whose swaddling

* Heads of learned academies, mostly in medieval Babylonia.

bands were dark obscurity. Were Nahum alive now he would have pestered him with questions and sought clarification from him. He knew of the views of the Karaites through A.B. Gottlober. There was a possibility of negating the whole Talmud and still remaining within the Jewish people. It was similarly possible to undermine the Mosaic law. Did not God also ordain the animal sacrifices? Yet these were considered by the prophets to be sacrifices of the dead. That self-same Torah contained the rules about not mixing wool and linen, and about the fringes. The Jews were slaves to statutes and commandments.

One night Yeruham went to the quarter of the city where the house of prayer was situated in which that Torah scholar who had denied divine providence used to study. He had been excommunicated by his brethren. A light shone through the windows of that synagogue. Yeruham turned in there and found the student sitting on a bench with the volume *Gate of Heaven* open before him on a reading desk. The scholar was deeply moved. Hitherto no *maskil* or devotee of modern Hebrew literature had ever greeted him. Yeruham wanted to lead him into a theoretical conversation. The man refused, saying, "Our fates have nothing in common. You investigate history and literature, I seek for God in the hidden secrets of nature."

That month the Torah scholar died suddenly and left a manuscript behind him. His wife burned it on the advice of the warden of the synagogue. But the manuscript which Nahum Sharoni had left behind was not committed to the flames but passed from hand to hand until in the course of time it fell into this writer's possession. I readily and freely admit that many of my own views emanate from this source. Through him I have wandered still further. I am not the source of inspiration, I am no more than an armor bearer. But Yeruham—Yeruham remained confused, unable to find his way....

7.

They ultimately broke up. The tenuous bond between Ida, the cantor's daughter and her fiancé, Nehemia Eisenstein, just dissolved by itself.

She closed her heart to him completely and he too ceased visiting her and made it obvious to everyone that he had serious intentions toward another girl. In matters of union and dissolution the will may prevail but chance too can play its part. Whoever affirms that everything in this universe is determined by God is simply mistaken.

Ida sat desolate in her father's house recalling those former days before the group of *maskilim* had disintegrated, when Yeruham had her in his thoughts in everything he said and gave expression to. He had not betrayed her—she knew this although she was estranged from him.—If she but called him saying, "Come and visit me and let us have a talk," he would again come to her eagerly.—Yeruham too, knew how things were with her. On more than one occasion he had thought of approaching her again and often pictured to himself the sweet poetry of their meeting. But he never carried out his intention. Happiness may be only one step away from you and yet the distance is great. Yeruham sat thinking of her sadly while she waited for him. But he never followed the dictates of his heart by hastening to her. One imagines something is in one's own volition but it is not. There is no freedom of choice.

Ida scorned the sincerity of men and at times mocked at their failings. She was mature, eager for embrace, but there was no one to take her in hand. The spirit is lauded for its attributes, all the cells of the soul are the focus of attention, but there is no one to sing the praises of the body and no one to heed its cry.

At that time her father engaged an assistant chorister, a well-set young man of twenty-three, broad-chested and of powerful voice. He saw Ida every day and she often glanced at him. One Sabbath afternoon, after lunch, when her parents had gone to rest in their room, the chorister was sitting on one side of the table and Ida sat opposite. He looked around warily and saw there was no one in the room. What did he do? He bent his head toward the girl, placed his mouth on hers and kissed her fiercely. Although she felt some trepidation, Ida did not evade him or protest. The fellow stood up boldly, took her to him with both arms around her neck and rained incessant kisses upon her. She closed her eyes and emotion overcame her. A man was standing close to her and she was at his disposal.

8.

A girl grows up before our eyes and reaches maturity. Her flesh grows delicate, the flower becomes a fruit, the vague imaginings of adolescence become dreams of day and night. The poetry of longing is the poem of the future. But the body has a soul and a spirit, and the spirit has a body. They grow up together on the same stalk and struggle together. Only when one hand presses another can it know the pulse that beats in it. Love is the height of passion but is only the daughter of passion. The joining of body with body is no more than a sign and a symbol. An eternity can be a fleeting moment and there can be something which never comes again. We enquire desperately but the answer remains behind the locked door.

After a time of passionate intoxication, Ida's lover withdrew himself, and was gone.—She knew exactly how things were with her. Her diadem was gone and a quiet sadness overcame her and entered her heart. She walked aimlessly, she was low-spirited. When she bared her arms and looked at them they seemed to be alive.

Once when she was sitting alone a terrible thought struck her. People will discern what has happened and you and your father's house will be disgraced. The daughter of the prayer leader of a great congregation has strayed from the path of virtue. She was filled with a terrible fear and apprehension. In whom could she confide? Who would protect her? She tossed upon her bed at night and saw her malignant fate. There is no refuge from sin and no recalling what has been done.

When she woke in the morning she dressed hurriedly, walked to the upper city and wandered through the nethermost streets which were strange to her. People were going their several ways, children were sitting and playing on the ground, a wagon loaded with merchandise passed by. A water carrier went by with his dripping cask and a lad selling pretzels loudly proclaimed his wares. The sun was dull as the sky was overcast. If she did not return to her father's house they would come looking anxiously for her. She was a lost lamb with no shepherd and no pasture. A few hours passed and she came to the city's river.

She stood on the bank and gazed fixedly at the waves. She could not summon up the courage to leap into the water.

9.

It was a cloudless morning. Yeruham awoke from sleep and lay on his bed in the narrow room into which only a faint light penetrated through the window. He had neither the strength nor the will to get up. His hopes had been dissipated one by one. Every day man was crucified and they brought him vinegar and not wine to drink.

The picture of two girls rose up before his mind's eye and he thought about them. He could understand what went on in the mind of the visitor at the mill but he could not comprehend Ida to whom he had spoken so much and who was even now intertwined with his heart. What you have experienced cannot be rooted out and what has newly happened is evident to all. If you have strayed from the way, you cannot cross over to the other side.

His mother entered the room and placed her hand on the brow of her eldest son. She had borne him in her womb, had delivered him in travail. She had reared him and he was her portion. There were many things she wanted to ask him, but he refused to talk to her saying, "Leave me alone now!" He woke for the midday meal, ate without appetite. Chaotic, half-formed thoughts filled his mind and conflicting ideas troubled him. The days journey on, men's lives go their monotonous round, no one can foretell even the immediate future or what is hidden in the enigma of the next hour. Who knows what is on the other side of the door?

Toward evening the cantor's daughter had reached the end of her endurance. She dressed, veiled her face and made her way down to the poorer quarter of the city where the widow and her son lived. She rapped on the window and Yeruham came out, astonished, to meet her. She begged him to accompany her to the park. A whole hour they walked together without exchanging a single word. When they sat down for a while on a bench to rest, speech suddenly burst forth from Ida.

"I am guilty."

Teardrops suffused her eyes. Yeruham was stirred to the depths of his being.

Speaking with great difficulty and in incoherent phrases she revealed her plight. He listened with great perturbation and could scarcely believe that it had all happened. Neither could he believe that he was sitting there with her so close to him. He roused himself, took her hand and said, "Calm yourself. I am with you."

Ida broke into unrestrained sobbing.

10.

Yeruham lay on his bed that night and revived all that had happened to him in his life. He did not know where his road began or ended. We are all wayfarers with a burden on our shoulders and where we lie down we do not always awake. You think you are climbing, but you are standing on level ground. You feel manacles on your feet and they are only branches of wood. You seek, and find a stone on your heart. Whoever thinks there is an imperative in life or free will is lying about both.

On the third day the widow's son became betrothed to the cantor's daughter. His mother was torn between joy and anxiety. She knew that it was all God's doing, but she had not really expected that things would happen so quickly and that she would with her own eyes behold her son's bride, and her new-found daughter. Before a month had passed they had celebrated the wedding, with no elaborate preparations and with rather few guests, not as one would have expected for the daughter of the cantor of the congregation. Those who stood near the poles of the bridal canopy saw neither clouds of morning nor of evening. Both bride and groom felt perplexed and bewildered. Six months later the young woman bore a son, but the delivery was difficult and she died.

Now there was a man of good birth, who was of unblemished reputation and a model of integrity. He had a sweet, adorable wife who was loved by all. The couple lived happily and harmoniously giving bread to the poor and whoever came to their door could not but bless them. It chanced one day that the wife climbed on a chair to knock a nail into the wall in order to hang a picture. Her foot slipped and she fell, knocking her head on an object on the floor, and injuring herself. The wound festered. A doctor came to attend to the wound and treated it badly. She developed a high fever which consumed her body and within three days she was dead. The man took a tiny bone, like a barley seed from her body, placed it in his knapsack and traveled with it from town to town and district to district crying out; "There is no justice and no judge. If a God does dwell in heaven, then His work is iniquity and He is not just. See how He slays for no transgression and separates those who cleave together. He casts them down and humiliates the decent and blinds the eye of the sun. Why should you praise Him, why laud Him and ascribe sovereignty to Him? He has no clear purpose and no method. His right hand gives and His left takes away again. He cuts down the beloved of your soul in your very arms. He shatters the life of the son or daughter to whom you have given birth. You plant a garden and He uproots it. You till your land and He withholds the rain. On high there is nothing but falsehood, violence instead of justice. And yet we are expected to worship the God of Truth!"...

Thus he railed against heaven and whenever he recalled what divine providence had stolen from him, he would beat his head against the wall, weep and wail and refuse utterly to be comforted. Our Yeruham too, mourned a long time and could not solve this mystery.

Chapter eleven

It once happened in a far off land that recluses of one of the Israelite tribes swore vows to the House of God, on the Temple Mount. They traveled for a long time through desert lands hoping to reach the city of priests and offer sacrifices on the altar of the Almighty. They reached Mount Scopus and saw a pillar of smoke in the distance and thought it was smoke rising from the wood on the altar. Then came a messenger who said, "The sanctuary has been burnt, all the sons of the Levites have been slain, the city of the scribes is destroyed and its foundations utterly razed." They rent their garments and began to roll in the dust.

Something of this kind happened to me. I am engaged in the birth pangs of creating a memorial for the people of my generation, to give a pen-picture of life in the towns in which I was reared. Many thoughts were mine, emotions of my youth surged up in me, my mind was thronged with different faces and events, transient personalities, shadows of the warp of life and the woof of former things. Son am I of the men of the exile and from this time-old goblet I have drunk my fill. And behold, the destroyer came to all these towns, swooping down upon that life and those books. A period of total destruction fell upon all those places where my hopes and my muse have revealed their tender buds. My native town was laid waste, the enemy's hand ruined all that was dear to me. The God of righteousness relentlessly swallowed up all the habitations of my people, He had even desolated the souls of His instructors.—My harp sounds an obsequy, my spirit moans, mourning consumes soul and flesh. Lamentation is all I know now. How shall I tell the tale of a young girl, of everyday incidents, snatches of the song of everyday life. Only a few brief pages are left to me and I shall set them before the reader in turn and they will be all that remains.

In the lower city, at the time I really left it, never to see it again, lived a certain man called Reb Shlomo, the Elder. He was a descendant by direct lineage of one of the martyrs of Nemirov, who had died to sanctify God's name in the year 1648. This venerable Jew used to fast each year on the 20th of the month of Sivan from sunset to sunset. He would read the sad records of those evil days, which have still not passed, and would dissolve into tears because the Mighty One of Jacob has no pity on the remnant of His people, and constantly abandons them to the hand of the enemy eager to annihilate them. Where is the Guardian of Israel? He asked this question over and over again. The promises of the prophets and seers have not been fulfilled, God gives the lie to His Book. This saintly man, too, fell into a reverie and thus saw the smoke from the altar pyre rising up and soaring high, and looking here and there saw that there was no altar and no burnt offering. He sought to leap into the midst of a cloud and found a yawning abyss at his feet.

I, too, as I busy myself with my work, find my spirit storm-tossed. God has turned His sword against the children of my tribe and none can deliver them from His hand. The throne is toppling. "The Divine Presence is confused and ashamed."—There are stones on my shoulder, my heart is bursting as I copy down events of long ago.

2.

I shall relate the story of a whale which I read in an old book.

In the ocean lived a great whale who had only one eye in his forehead. He used to swim six months from the East to the remote boundaries of the West and would return in six months from the West to the East. The whale had no female spouse and no near kin. Whatever he met on his way he devoured. A scarlet fluid streamed from his nostrils and caused the waters to seethe. Billows as high as mountains were raised up when he threshed about with his tail. Once, between summer and winter, he fell asleep and reached dry land where his head became wedged between two rocks. He awoke after his months of hibernation and behold, the whole of existence was nothing but darkness. Little pebbles kept falling into his mouth and cutting his tongue. A fish came out of his back and another from his belly and they began to leap about and spread out over him and surround him on all sides. He shook his tail and it became a thousand times its original length. It surrounded all the limits of the sea and coiled out without measure or end. The whale tried to release his head and found that his teeth too had grown large and had extended to become entangled with all the terrifying mountains and trees of the forest. The elements above and below mingled together, root with branch. Every fin bludgeoned at nature, every scale covered a star. Creation moaned with fearful desire and there was no light to this day.

I will tell you yet another story about a flower and a seed that I read in another old book.

There was a flower growing in a field, shining amid the grass. Its appearance was ruddy from the light of the sun and it begged compassion from the god of the sun. Grasshoppers leaped around it; mosquitoes and ants marshaled in regular formations and battled around it. The world was holding converse with the Creator and sporting with the Creator. Night came and brought its offering from beyond the sacred veil. Morning succeeded and trumpets sounded for the morning prayers. Now beside the flower lay a seed, moist within and dusty on the outside, which at times was jealous of the flower. It happened one day that the burning hot sun, its rays flaring across the firmament, scorched and dried up the flower even as the seed ripened, burst and cast its shell. It took root and there grew a lofty tree with green foliage. The tree was false from within.—It was hollow from the bark inward. A long human hand could grope inside it digging out its skeleton with its fingernail. The tree sang with a raucous voice. On flat ground there rose a hill. The ants have their hill, the mosquitoes their wings. There is no strife, only fellowship. There are no different languages, but one common speech.—And this too is the kingdom of darkness. There is no God, but Satan, half male and half female. He consumes and vomits forth flowers. To him everything is a game. He is as cruel as an ostrich in the wilderness.

All these things I read in an old book by candlelight. I dozed off into slumber and awoke.

3.

Miriam's spirit soared aloft on wings of imagination but it was also hemmed in against the wall. Long are the nights and days but they all have a beginning and an end. There are many thoughts and opinions; there are motivating forces, Nature has its ways, and morality its paths. You are not alone. You may not have absorbed in learning even one drop of the vast ocean of what is to be comprehended and known. You have not grasped the ways of society and no door has opened for you into the chambers of the soul. Jews and Christians live in a common environment. The former have a God in writing and the latter a God in image. These pray by uttering words and those worship by making the sign of the cross.

The Russian people are a people with a dogmatic faith, the Jewish people live by their customs. To which should one give allegiance? To which should she dedicate her life; to which did she belong? One question immediately provokes another, a thought draws yet another in its train. Nothing is clear, she feels no inner certainty. She seems to have no place in the universal scheme and nothing to hold on to.

Where should she go? Where can she find enlightenment? The longings of Miriam's soul to know and comprehend completely immersed her. A small shadow seemed permanently to haunt her brow and it enhanced her charm. The purity of her beauty was incomparable.

She stood at the courtyard gate of her abode and gazed at the large empty square. An army officer rode by on his thoroughbred horse with two soldiers riding behind him like shadows stretching behind a tree.

The one that gives the orders has a powerful personality, and those who obey him are insignificant in comparison. The eagle soars into the sky and the creatures that crawl upon the ground are there only to be trodden down by its feet. Miriam's mind was agog with ideas and emotions. There are day dreams, too. You lift the veil and things are engraved there which you do not know how to read. The will is summoned up and recedes but it is in fact just a tool of one's desires. Never before have you been so attentive or sensitive of hearing as now? There is no one to talk to. You turn to go backward and the world is a blank wall. Hens peck in the yard, a white goose stands at the side. Miriam is weary and downcast in spirit.

She goes back into the house. In the corridor she meets Gedaliah who is surprised by her appearance. He had been sitting with her twice a day at mealtime but she is a new riddle to him every time he sees her. Her hands have an eerie transparency, which at table is like a flame in daylight.

4.

It was a bright morning. The sun had wiped out all traces of mourning in the world and suffused every place with its full splendor. The heavenly bodies take care of what belongs to them day by day and sustain their orbits. There are those who continually call upon the treasures of the Almighty, who is continually bestowing and giving while we are just bodily finite creatures, even though we may be made in God's image. I shall not talk in riddles.

Miriam found it constricting to stay in her room. She tied a fine white kerchief about her head and went out. There was nothing special she needed or thought about. The road stretched out to the right and left. The houses stood in a row and she could see no purpose in anything. She had an urgent desire to talk and converse with some knowledgeable person about the why and wherefore of life and the hidden things of the soul.

Have not all men a destiny and is there not an answer to every question? Who was there to reveal the meaning of life? Where could she find the key to philosophies and definitions? She felt the insignificance of her way; nevertheless the secret place of her soul was continually exalted. A tabby cat jumped in front of her as she walked and she felt a great pity for all living things. She would learn natural history and would examine the Almighty's creatures. There is one principle but differing structures, there are pressure and relaxation, desire and will. She reminded herself of her father, of her mother also, but they were not there. What would she say to them if she met them? And what could she say to her relative when she was again seized by the desire to go wandering far away? She had wants but no way of fulfilling them. She had no cohesive energy to marshal her faculties. An entrance opened before her, and when she went in, there was yet another entrance.

She still retained a faint recollection of the *maskil*, Yeruham. If she met him now she would ask him to go for a walk with her and she would talk with him. The Jewish people was disintegrating and the Russians were in the vanguard. She went down into the valley, stepped on to the bridge and looked at the waterfalls. Wave met wave in forceful flood. Nature has a mouth and a pent up strength. Who is the servant of whom? Who gives the orders, who decides and who dominates? A servant girl was standing barefoot in the water washing white clothes and repeatedly beating the shirts on the rock. She does not think at all, yet she has a soul, a spirit and expressive eyes. There is an affinity between man and nature. She must have concepts and thoughts. She also does not know where she is going even though the world had something to give; there are reward and recompenses. Miriam wanted to weep but had not the strength to do so.

5.

It was a summer evening. Yehiel Eichenstein sat on the steps in front of his house immersed in his thoughts. A man sundered from the world of business with nothing to do, living away from the rest of the community and almost forgotten by them...If a man is not taken up with material things then his spirit awakens. When the tumult of day is still, the evening speaks. The voice of the majestic stream is heard from afar. The frogs croak and open up the heart of man with their sadness. Eichenstein remembers his wife, gone to her eternal rest. He recalls how the hand of God raises up and casts down. He thinks of many things he has experienced in his lifetime and probes and looks into his past. What is left seems stable at first sight but the present always becomes empty and what tomorrow will bring will also perish. Here you stand among the many and are intertwined with them, you leave them and they abandon you. Evil is powerful; it consumes but is not consumed, while good is feeble. There is no measure for measure, there is no weighing up and evaluation. But despite all there is providence and reward and punishment. You begin by sinning and then you repent. You dwell in the shadow of the Most High, and seek Him, find Him and again turn aside from the way. A poor man is of no more account than a dead man, and a rich man has cause for concern; the righteous man founders and the wicked flourishes. Had Yehiel been a cantor he would have raised his voice in prayer, cleansing himself before the Omnipresent, and would have cried out and wept before the God of hidden mystery.

He went into the dining room which also served as Miriam's bedroom, in order to place a lamp on the table. He saw her sitting there desolate, a circlet of spun silk binding her hair, her face like the moon. He stepped a trembling pace back from her loveliness with tottering knees. He was like a priest who enters the sanctuary and suddenly the cherub above the veil has the likeness of a young girl...Yehiel had never been a merchant, never served Mammon, never labored in his life and never sought to come near his God. A new soul sprang from his plain soul. There was a special soul within it and that soul had spirit, which opened the heart, quickened all the senses and confused them at the same time.

He retreated without saying a word, because he was shaken to the core…

6.

Honyrad had three days of rain the like of which it had never experienced since it was first founded. The sky was dark with black clouds. The horizon had contracted and was suffused with the smell of brimstone. Lightning flashes rent the black bowl and shed an eerie light while thunderclap after thunderclap was heard from all sides making a deafening assault on the ears. The skies opened up and sheets of rain began to fall, streaming down from on high and piercing like needles. These were not beneficial rains but a downpouring of wrath and cosmic hatred.

The world could not be tranquil but was warring with itself and venting its wrath on all who dwelt in it from man to beast.

Isaac Batlon, the teacher, lay on an old rug and covered himself with his winter overcoat because he felt cold. His mind was emptied of all ideas and thoughts except for one obsession. Who knew whether he would again see in his lifetime that wonderful young girl he had looked upon at the cemetery? Would not she too be destroyed by the flood of water? The dry land is only like an island in the sea and above it are reservoirs which have opened up.

God has no sense of touch. He is like a long pipe which gulps up nothingness and brings it forth in crude masses. Batlon had once read a theory like that in a book which came from mighty Germany. He was afraid of such theories.…There is a big difference if you are clothed or standing stark naked. He roused himself and got up from the rug, ran his hand through his hair and said to himself, "All things have an end and a finality, the sun will shine again." He felt stronger when he was standing on his feet. He had the feeling that he was carrying the whole world on his shoulders without feeling the weight at all. He would find what he was seeking! Something new had become clear to him....

Isaac Batlon found an escape in science. In the four corners of the world dwell people and tribes, some of whom are uneducated and some of whom are enlightened. Education and knowledge are the inheritance only of the enlightened. On the other hand there were once enlightened nations that now no longer exist. He was afraid that there was a limit to development. Sometimes the intellect progressively increased and at times it seems to become quite inbred, like a wheel revolving on its axis. Are the laws of the mind like the laws of nature or have they a quite different character? It seemed likely to him that there were filaments extending from the brain case to the ventricles of the intelligence. A human being lives and feels and other living things have feelings and instincts. The ox knoweth its stall. The dog recognizes its master. The cat may be a wild animal but it also feels affection for the house in which it lives.

Now you read a book which a man has written and he becomes your instructor, teaching you understanding. You close it and open it again and you draw idea after idea from it. Some things you forget and some you retain. You press the hand of your neighbor but you are unimportant to him. Batlon did not believe in mankind but he did believe in the tenderness of women. That was another phenomenon. Happy is the one who has found requited love and woe unto him who remains alone in life. He would go upward. As God lives, it was in his own hand to achieve higher education. All he needed was a helpmate and spiritual support. Two who are one are more than just double. He would not rest or relax until he had attained his goal. Honyrad and all its masses were in one pan of the scales but he would outweigh them all....

Batlon sat in his narrow room looking out at the empty street and his heart was like a stone. He rose from his chair, closed the book which was lying open on the table, straightened the tablecloth and began to count the days of the month. A dreadful loneliness seized him. He wanted to put on his hat and go out, but had not the energy to move his body. He did not know where he was in time. His mind was rent in two. He had a feeling as though he were holding something in his hand, like a panting dove from the roof for whom they had set a trap. If he had some matches in his pocket he knew that if he struck one there would be light and perhaps a shred of hope in his heart. But he also knew this, that from fire, blood emanates and this adds wound to wound.

Suddenly his spirits revived. He began to walk round the table and beat it with his hand. The glass of water which stood there danced. So did the bottle.

7.

Batlon achieved his heart's desire. He began to teach Russian to Eichenstein's grandson Gedaliah, and so crossed the threshold of the house where the hidden light was shining. The world is half-clad and half-naked. With a vessel you draw up living water from a well; but turn your face around and you have a desolate wilderness. You have held your heart's desire in your arms, breast presses close to breast and heart cleaves to heart—when suddenly you are bereaved, maimed, and to your right and left, above and below, is empty air. God has removed His Divine Presence from nature and suddenly light shines again. Light irradiates out of the crevices of the universe, engulfs you, brings your soul exhilaration and moves your spirit deeply. You are walking by the way, all is silent, the sky is tranquil, the earth is still, when an abyss opens at your feet and you fall to perdition. There is no one who remembers you, no one asks after you by name, no one knows that you have been blotted out from the muster of the living and that from the infinite number, one digit is missing. Then lo! a voice calls to you and just to you. You are on an infinite plain. You are saved from the abyss.

Batlon met Miriam on many occasions when he came and went from the house to give his lesson. He spoke to her, chatted with her; she asked questions and he answered. Sometimes he would ask and she would not answer, but would look with startled, wondering eyes on this discerning man who knew the underlying explanation of things and could clarify ideas. Notions which one derives from a book are not as decisive as those transmitted verbally. This teacher expounded everything according to its own terms. He would begin an explanation indirectly, then adduce a particular consideration, or some historical event, and proceed immediately to adumbrate a system or establish principles. The vessel of his reasoning never capsized. After he had gone, Miriam would continue to think about him.

The heart is uplifted and is bewildered. There is no searching out human beings nor any limit to what does or does not happen. The world becomes illumined and near but the blessing does not come from yourself but from another. Isaac Batlon loved Miriam. It was quite clear to him and he firmly believed it to be so. His soul responded to her superlative grace and yet he experienced tension. She was right for him, was created for him. He adored the flutter of her eyes, the shape of her face, her every movement. Every crease in her clothes was poetry to him. When she set down her foot, the very ground came alive. But he was not and could not be hers. She shared his thoughts, he was a man of learning in Honyrad, but there was a distance between them. If he were to go and prostrate himself before her she would not want him. If he wandered far away and she saw him no more, it would be complete desolation.

You may not understand the soul of a young girl, but Batlon did, knew it so well that his soul was completely maudlin and depressed.

8.

A disquiet such as she had never previously experienced took hold of Miriam. She could discern a path through the enigma of life but at the same time it remained blocked. It had all been woven into a pattern but had disintegrated again. She was drawn intellectually by the conversation of the teacher and his words of scholarship, but she continually retreated from him. She was afraid of him, yet went to meet him or waited for him. There are stars in the universe and windows in the world. Man has a mouth and his fellow has an ear to listen to him. One heart takes hold of another, then it slips away or becomes closed. In all things there is conjunction and separation. There are tribes and peoples, camps and fellowships, families and homes; and behold there is also loneliness. The day goes on and is swallowed up by the night which, too, slips away before morning. There is no stability in the universe, only change.

Miriam struggled vainly to make herself sympathetic to the teacher, to be a companion to him. What and who did she have in the world? The memory of her parents had almost faded from her mind and she would not stay with her relative in Honyrad forever. How would she earn her living? What purpose could she establish for herself in life? She had already conceived some notions about property, labor, economics and liberty. Tyrants rule to the detriment of other men. The rich man oppresses the poor and even the day laborer is deprived of his wage. She had already heard of Lassalle and Proudhon. She had also read in a book about St. Simon and Rousseau. Their complete denial of the value of culture seemed terrible to her.—On the other hand she did understand the worth of nature. Was not the life of the rustic superior to that of the city dweller? On the one side was innocence and simplicity and on the other man's artifice.

No! She would not strip herself of the diadem of logic and knowledge and cast it behind her. She would not deny recognition and contemplation. She made up her mind to argue with Batlon and force him to reveal the ultimate mystery to her and lay bare the universal secrets. What she could not grasp—he had the power to show her. Were not his statements clear? Nevertheless when she had parted from him and thought them over, they were no longer so clear.

On one occasion when he was talking to her, he took hold of her hand and she trembled and did not know what was the matter with her. He was explaining the ways of the universe and wanted at the same time a personal relationship. She had read about that sort of thing in books, and now here was a man standing before her whose appearance was distasteful but who possessed a tongue.

That same evening she went walking far from the mill house and searched her mind for an explanation of all these things. She sat on the stump of a tree to rest awhile and stared down at the caps of her shoes.

9.

Miriam lifted her head and there was Batlon standing in front of her. The girl shivered and stood up. He stretched out his hand to her, his eyes fixed upon her. Life and death were now in her hands and he was driven out of the world, a passerby now seeking grace and compassion from her. From east and west, north and south, the ways were tortuous with treacherous rocks. Woe to the man whose soul is consumed with famine and anguish while before him is a delicate rose, a soul breathing in the body of a goddess. By the living God! There is no other girl like this in the whole wide world, and here she is near him and in his power.

She has no desire for his company and he pours out his heart to her. He had prayed for someone like her all his life; she was the dream of his soul. He would completely rearrange his life. He had his bearings in the field of knowledge. He would complete his studies in ancient languages; in sociology and psychology. If she would go with him, he would go abroad where there was a freer, broader and more intellectual atmosphere. It would be a terrible crime if she rejected him and refused to be his partner in life. He spoke in an excited ceaseless torrent, joining his arm to that of the terrified girl who begged him to let go of her. Any moment he would embrace her and join his mouth to hers. However, something stopped him from doing that. He felt completely at a loss. He had been born a generation too soon or too late. He took hold of both her hands and tried to penetrate her soul.

He pleaded and entreated her with a flood of words and passionate supplication and she remained silent without uttering a single word. Around them was stillness. If he had had a knife in his hand he would have plunged it into his heart. If he attacked her and strangled her, who could call him to account? The world extends in all directions, yet he was alone, and she was alone facing an abyss over which there was no bridge.

No! He would not let go of her. Either they both went back to the city together or they would not return at all. Miriam begged him to accompany her to her relative's house so she would not be late. In his heart he entreated her but she did not hear.

"Miriam!" he passionately implored, "I beg of you. Do not leave me alone. I came here only to see you and let you know what was seething in my heart. Let us join our lives together or just blow them up. Without you there is nowhere in the world to turn. And you too will be destroyed, destroyed, destroyed…"

10.

Miriam did not answer him one word. She was trembling all over. Every word he uttered hit her like a blow. She was helpless to aid either herself or him. What did he want of her? He had waylaid her far from her home in a place where she had come to find a refuge and she only wanted one thing of him: "Leave me alone. It is too much for me!" She walked along slowly and he paced beside her. He had been overhasty in approaching her, revealing what was in his heart. He should have waited a few months, a few weeks until he had won a niche in her heart and she had really begun to understand him. Would she only forgive him? Could she not forget everything he had said and let things be just as though they had never occurred? He would talk to her again about science and the ways of society after his lesson with his pupil and he would again be content to look at her beauty and cherish her in his heart. He would go on doing this for years and years until he was old and gray.—As for the girl, she would be an eternal symbol. Who drove him to this pass? Who took him by the hair of his head and flung him into the raging sea? Who was it who first destroyed all the restraints of his world? His heart was broken, his mind was deranged, every member of his body was trembling and driven mad. He would not let her go back. When they got to the bridge he would throw her into the water and jump in after her. The pangs of death might be icy; there was a dreadful desolation in loneliness. There was no freedom anymore, only uncontrollable impulse, impulse and perdition. "Go away from me," Miriam implored him almost demented with terror. "Leave me to go back alone."

The overwrought teacher blocked her way with his arm. He was remorseful about everything he had said and done. He would have been happier if only he had stayed in his room and had not encountered his heart's desire at this time and opened up his soul to her. But what he had done he had done, and now he would have no forgiveness. He had lost absolutely everything that he had ever had. He had made one slip and no one could help him retrieve it. He would be happy if the depths covered him, and everything ended in dark destruction. For a moment he stood motionless completely at a loss. He tried to bring out just one more word but he had lost his tongue. Batlon had not lost his reason but his soul was gripped with iron pincers. He continued to walk back with Miriam to her abode. They were both silent. Not a word was spoken. They came to the bridge which led to the mill. Night had fallen on the world. Suddenly Miriam slipped and fell into the water. And he—some say he had pushed her—did not hasten after her to rescue her. Indeed he fled away as though in peril of his life. He had never shown cowardice in all his life. What had happened to him?

As evening had come, he had gone insane over a lovely girl and the radiance of a body had destroyed him. He was overcome by a black, utter depression the like of which had never been known. His teeth chattered and his voice changed. His landlady, with whom he had lodged for a year and a half, hardly recognized him. She cried out as she met him, "Oh God and his son!"

Miriam screamed. The mill workers rushed to pull her out of the water. She fainted with terror as her wet garments pulled her down. They carried her to the house. When Yehiel heard from a distance what had happened, he had a heart attack and succumbed without regaining consciousness. His house was plunged into bitter mourning.

The next day he was buried amid a great throng of mourners. The grave was closed over a man, respected in the community who had not left his like behind. The house where this throbbing soul had dwelt was left empty. Its occupants were once again bereaved and desolate.

II.

Three days and nights Batlon ran along footpaths and roads. He crossed through wheat fields, slept in thick forests and neither ate nor drank. His hair was matted with dust, his eyes were red from stress, misery and grief. His soul had disintegrated, shattered by mental and emotional stress while his outside world had fallen apart. Where are the ravening wolves? Where are the young lions to eat him alive? But he had neither flesh nor bones.

What had happened? What had he done? He fled and everything seemed to pursue him. He turned right and bruised himself; left and was thrust aside. He was one of the sons of Cain. He read again the beginning of the Bible and the Books of Kings in Russian. The covers of the books opened and a voice cried, "Thou hast murdered but not taken possession. Cursed is the ground because of you, cursed are the waters of the stream, cursed are the living and the dead."

Clouds darkened the sky. Batlon crawled into a cave hewn out in a stone quarry which had long been left without a watchman. He stretched out on dry grass and blood flowed from his nose. The bleeding would not stop. He did not try to wipe it with a handkerchief. He did not staunch it. He said, "Let me die and lie rotting here like a neglected corpse."

He turned himself over and buried his face in the grass. The world went black from one end to the other. He fell into a deep torpor and slept for hours in the pool of blood. Stones dropped down, lightning flashed from time to time and illumined the darkness for a moment until it, too, was lost in eternal blackness.

In the morning he rose early, his hair in wild disorder. The world was hiding its face. He was more bewildered than during the past two days. He stumbled around in a narrow circle, his eyes staring at the ground. Silence bore in upon him from every side, something was tearing at his spirit, choking up his throat while his whole body trembled. Suddenly he started to weep and he burst into violent sobbing, his heart twisted with the crying anguish of his broken soul. No one answers or listens, not even an abyss opens up to swallow that worm, the son of man. The world is empty of its God. There is no purpose nor goal any more, just frustration and hopelessness. His tears flow unrestrainedly and the weeping has a rasping sound. Were he to get to the bank of a river he would throw himself into the water. If he had a rope he would hang himself from a tree. If he found some poison on the way he would swallow it at once. The fetters of his soul were loosened and misery and distress had returned to their source. The emptiness was not to be filled.

As Batlon was passing through a certain village, he was stopped by a policeman and placed under arrest because he had no identity papers. He refused to give his name and was taken in fetters together with two peasants who had committed some offense, to the prison at Balta. There he was thrown into a cell. He made no protest and accepted his guilt. The desire to live had disintegrated. He did not wish to persist any longer. Let Satan come and blind everyone's eyes and destroy every stretch of ground. Let the earth no longer bring forth grass or herb. Let the ox no longer know its master. Let the sun be confounded and shine no more.

In the depth of the night when all those sentenced and cast away in the prison could be seen, every man lying on the ground a prey to lice and fleas who with avid enjoyment sucked the blood from their emaciated flesh, the teacher, too, rubbed his head and his body. Despite the darkness his eyes saw what a man does not see when he is awake. There is a small place in the soul which only opens to a person on the verge of death. When it is opened then we descend into the depths, we sink into the deep and behold there is the great whale of the universe crawling on its belly, twisting eternally and horrendously. At that time man's consciousness is overthrown. The extortioner is finished. We are the children of a banished idol.

12.

Miriam tossed on her bed for a whole month. She was very ill. They put her bed in a room to which the sun penetrated every morning and it made her feel better. They brought her hot soup or warm milk. From time to time, Dr. Koch came to visit her, felt her pulse and spoke gently to her. When he went away, the room was empty. She was wandering in a wilderness bereft of speech or thought. Who was it that pushed her into the water, who had rescued her, who was it who was healing her? Her uncle used to care for her and was her patron and protector and now he had gone far away. If she called him now, he would not come from the next room to be near her. It is difficult to understand the question of death. One soul grows near and closely intertwined with another; who can know the beginning and end of it? Who is it that says to one man, 'Arise' and to another man, 'Lie down'? The grace of the young girl, covered with a white sheet and with eyes eloquent with innocence and compassion struck a chord in Koch's heart when he came to visit her in the afternoons. When he took hold of her hand, he also touched her spirit. The mystery of youth and old age is also a matter of poetry. We open doors in a wall and we close doors; there is a window in the room and over the window a curtain is drawn, the wind murmurs and is silent. God has left His dwelling place and spreads Himself throughout creation, seen neither by him who is near, nor by him who is far away.

At the end of the room a tall man clothed in a white robe appears. His eyes are closed, his shadow surrounds him and he himself resembles a shadow. Miriam was afraid to raise her head and was terrified of this apparition which manifested itself by day. She had spoken with this man; that she knew. She still had another question. Her speech disappeared into the lofty air. There were bright flecks of blue, the man moved and lowered his arm, his robe dragging along the ground. He was one of the sons of death; he was not dead, but neither was he alive. Deep sleep fell on the girl and she woke up emerging from the throes of anguish and wonder.

13.

It is sunset on the day of rest.

For Dr. Koch this is an hour of surcease from the toil of the week. He does whatever he can to be of service and is a barrier to extinction. All who live are the debtors of death and you, the doctor, confront the creditor. There is a remedy for sickness, alleviation for pain. You remove poison from the body and strengthen the heart. You return a mortally ill child to its mother. You give sustenance to the hungry. Whoever quarrels with his neighbor or oppresses him is not a man, but a worthless fellow. Nevertheless, you must take care even of him who piles wealth upon wealth and hastens to become rich.

The poor are like weakened lambs and you are the shepherd in the midst of the flock. You dwell between two tribes, the Jews and Christians; there is eternal rivalry between those who worship God and those who worship His son. The first is the living God and wanders with His people; the second was crucified and died and lived again and went up to heaven and his spirit remained on earth.

Old memories rise up in Koch's mind: One morning, he was riding his horse among the craggy Caucasian hills. He was then about thirty. He looked up and there was a vulture flying in the sky, its golden wings outspread and its long tail soaring upward. He too was exalted and said, "If only I had wings, I would fly." The horse stumbled on a stone and hurt its leg. He got down to bind it up when a wild boar came charging at him, foaming at the mouth. He shot at it with his rifle and killed it, piercing a hole in its belly through which the dung came out. The vulture came down from the sky, began to tear at the corpse and pierce out its eyes. The horse was suddenly immobile, stood there like a stone and he could not get it to budge from its place. The skies darkened with clouds and a heavy sleep fell upon him. He slept three days and three nights, and when he awoke, the whole vision had disappeared. He was lying weary and exhausted on his bed. A tall girl was standing beside him, offering him water from a flask. He thought she was his daughter. In fact she was the daughter of a peasant couple from that village. He did not press her to his heart. He arose that evening, went away and never saw her again.

Koch felt a profound melancholy. He no longer had any purpose and was completely desolate. He had healed hundreds and thousands of people. He had found his work in the world but was only a cog in a machine. There was no difference between right and left, but some things are wrapped in mystery while others are bared for all to see. We look for some expression for our soul and for some cover for our body. The chasm in the world becomes wider and wider, but at times it is closed up. The loneliness at night, when there is no one about and no one to speak to, is a heavy yoke.

Once again a memory arose in his mind.

He was on his way from the borderlands to Greater Russia. A world passes by and a world opens up. He was lodging in a village with its overseer, one of the Russian Orthodox faith, a man very set in his opinions and ways, and prone to talk a lot with his visitors. The master of the house had a long, flowing beard while he, Dr. Koch, was clean shaven. He had never before argued about religious matters. This time some hint of the divine messianic era and its rebirth of the world caught his ear. The life of all the generations is just a preparation for the Day of Redemption. Happy is the man who is purged of his sins, and woe to the man who dies in his iniquity. It was then that he heard an explanation for the murder of Abel by Cain and the reason why a flood came to destroy all flesh. He considered going to a priest and seeking pardon from him for his deeds. One morning he woke early and bowed down to the God of the sun. He felt an inner illumination for many days and longed for light.

14.

After Eichenstein's death his household began to crack up. It was as though everything was going downhill. Once in motion there was no stopping. Miriam was as one stunned and bereft of purpose. The thought of returning to her father's house appalled her. To serve as tutor at a nearby estate was unacceptable. She had no one to whom she could open her heart. She was an orphan with no kith nor kin, no brother nor redeemer.

She read one of the books about religion and morals by the novelist, Tolstoy, and a new world opened up for her. The mysterious God traces out a path in the universal scheme, while men who should be executing His loving-kindness profane Him. They have become corrupt and serve idols of their own fashioning. They yield themselves up to lust and social depravity. They worship beauty, hedonistically intoxicated with absorbing every kind of pleasure and delight, despite the fact that the earth is not just a garden and there are other things in the meadow besides flowers. Do not eat your own flesh and blood. The day of God begins to establish itself through His Son. Break through windows to the kingdom of heaven. Throw away the abominable idols you have fashioned. Let man become conscious of his neighbor's trouble; let him share his piece of bread with everyone who is unrelated to him and inferior. Let him forget family relationship and the indulgence of the flesh. Every rich man is poor. Even if you cram your treasure-house full, you will find nothing but treacherous disillusionment. The bright morning does nothing but dazzle. The sacrifice the poor man makes is what the gods feed upon.—If you are worthy—you are worthy; if not—you are a demon, companion to the Lord of Destruction. Happy is he who paves a way for himself, and bears the stones of creativity on his shoulder.

It happened toward evening. With a small bundle under her arm, Miriam departed from the house where she had stayed. She went to the courtyard of Dr. Koch, waited until the last patients had left and then entered the examination room, having left her bundle at the entrance. The old man stood up after his day's toil and stretched out his hand to her with feelings of compassion and affection. She, for her part, looked down bashfully and said, "I am your handmaid. Let me help you take care of the sick and I shall serve you truly."

He kissed her on the forehead and said, "You are my daughter. Great is your kindness to me."

Translated by A.S. Super

About the Editor

Avner Holtzman is a professor of Hebrew literature and head of the Katz Research Institute for Hebrew Literature at Tel Aviv University. He is also director of the Berdichevsky Archive, *Ginze Micha Yosef,* in Holon, and editor of the complete edition of Berdichevsky's writing. His recent books include: *Aesthetic and National Revival—Hebrew Literature against the Visual Arts* (1999); *An Image Before my Eyes* (2002); *Literature and Life—Essays on M.Y. Berdichevsky* (2003).

The fonts used in this book are from the Garamond family

The Toby Press publishes fine writing,
available at leading bookstores everywhere.
For more information, please contact
The Toby Press at www.tobypress.com